Paradoxes Of Life

James Wright III

ISBN: 978-1-7371589-2-9

Dedication

This novel is dedicated to the Dīn of al-Islam and all it stands for in every aspect of the Quran and Sunnah of the Prophet Muhammad - May the Ultimate peace and blessings of Allah be upon him and his family.... Amīn.

Acknowledgments

There isn't many people I care to acknowledge so this section will be brief.

Foremost, all praises are definitely due to Allah! Secondly, I'd like to acknowledge my lovely mommy (Sharon Wright) for being the best mom one could be in a really tough struggle! Mom's like you are amazing!

I'd like to acknowledge Danyell Brown (Drum-roll Lol)…. Allah knows that you're one of the most gracious personalities I've ever had the privilege of acquainting thus far! Wonder Woman indeed! Loving you for life! Y'all check her out at ImpactfulPerceptions.com, as well as Impactful Perceptions on all platforms: Facebook, Instagram, YouTube, Spotify, Apple Podcast, Google Podcast, etc.

A special shout out to Toinette Downs! You better know I'm always praying for you. You are a dear friend. Family for life! And shout out to the boys Tyler and Jr! You guys take care of your mommy! She's awesome!

A dear shout out to Rajib Miah and Muhammad Sabbir Bhuiyan over in Bangladesh at WebExpertTeam.com and Grow On Line! You two brothers are phenomenal in not only your expertise, but in your Islam! You bros are the true embodiment of what it is to be of the mu'minun! I have the slightest idea as to how I truly even met you brothers on a completely different continent – but it can't be attributed to none other but Allah! Allahu'Akbar! I love you bros! I'm so greatful for the love you brothers have shown me! Some of the things you brothers said to me made my heart cry and softened it beyond comprehension. Shakrun jazakallah, ikhwan! You bros are true Muslims! May Allah elevate you brothers in both worlds! Amīn.

Without question I want to acknowledge the big bro Leroy (Luqman) Smalls! Sorry Master P, but this is the real Kernel! Lol Big shouts out to you akhi! May Allah grant you freedom and success! And great peace upon your little brother – my friend – Antonio "Baby" Smalls.

Shouts out to the bro Sulayman! I will never forget the support you brothers gave me when it mattered the most! Likewise with you Robert "Iceberg" Isom!

Shouts out to all the stone-cold Muslims in the system, and the Ummah abroad! As salamu alaykum warahmatullahi wabarakahtuhu, ya ikhwan!

And finally, a fervent shout out to all my inarcerated comrades fighting for their lives that get up everyday with the set objective to GET FREE OR DIE TRYING!

- Part One -

In The Name of God, Most Gracious, Most Merciful.

"And remember when Ibrahim (A.S.) said: 'O Allah! Bless me with a child amongst the righteous!' –So We gave him glad tidings of a boy ready (to be born), to suffer, and be patient." – Surah As-Saffat: 100-101

Prologue

Charleston, South Carolina
January 3, 2014 – Thursday

As salamu alaykum warahmatullahi wabarakahtuhu. How are you?" Al-Salam answered his phone inside the plush confines of his study after the call had been transferred by his servant.

Caesar returned the greeting."I'm fine, akhi. All praises are due to Allah," he sighed. "Things aren't looking any better over here in America for Don. I'm beginning to think that there's nothing we can do at this stage."

They were Muslims. Not Taliban, terrorists, nor any of the extreme factions that western society had so hatefully rendered all Muslims. They were of the Quran and Sunnah. They did not deviate into innovations and the extreme things that many other sects incorporated into the religion. Neither of them were amongst the pious because they still fell short in areas that was unpleasing to Allah but they were true to their faith and strove to become better Muslims daily.

"So what's the word with the infidels, and how did the

meeting go?" Al-Salam inquired fervently as he strummed his fingers through the soft, white beard that hung from his chin to the middle of his chest.

"Brody isn't talking about shit, akhi. He keeps going on and on about the political underpinnings of the case because the girls grandfather and his prestige has no one wanting to interfere.... We're on our own."

"Listen, akhi," Al-Salam said with forbearing patience. "Allah is the best of planners so don't fret. One way or the other Don will be fine, Insha'Allah. It's no doubt a tough situation and we are all angered and enraged by the alleged accusations against him but trust in Allah,akhi. Keep me posted, and at the conclusion of things, contact me and we'll move from there."

"Insha'Allah," Caesar replied.

"Well, I don't mean to run, but I have some pertinent issues to attend to. Tell Don and the other brothers I send my salutations and be cool. Talk to you soon, akhi."

Salutations were exchanged and Caesar disconnected the call. He sat inside the driver's seat of his powder blue Bentley Coupe about a block away from where Senator Brody's yacht was docked. After a long moment of cogitation he started the car and headed back to his office. He was already late for his evening prayers.

After Caesar had performed his prayers, he sat inside the cool confines of his office in the comforts of a worn, but comfortable, leather chair introspectively. The top of his enormous mahogany desk was cluttered with documents and contracts that he had neglected for the past couple of weeks. He knew that his associates were angry but he didn't care. He was the head-negro-in-charge!

Around the office was partly bare. The walls were adorned

with Islamic calligraphy. Plain, but elegant. Beautiful carpeting with embroidered masjids from around the Middle East covered the floor from wall to wall. Other prayer rugs that he used to pray were neatly hung from a solid gold rack at the back of the office. He had a beautiful panoramic view of the Cooper River and the splendid bridge that crossed it in all it's glory from where his office was located on King Street in downtown Charleston on the 13th floor of his building. But at the moment, he had the plush, Arabian drapes pulled shut. His mind was on his son.

He massaged his temples for a moment and reclined in his chair. He took his feet out the Ferragamos he wore and relaxed them on top of his desk as he pondered his son and the only confidant he had in the world.

He had met Al-Salam Abdullah Muhammad during deployment in 1992 when he was in the U.S. Marines on an unclassified mission to take out a band of Islamic extremist. During their mission their convoy was hit by a tank in Saudi Arabia. Everyone on board was killed save him. The band that ambushed them continued on, thinking that they were all dead from the strike. The only thing he remembered was waking up inside something that resembled a palace.

Al-Salam had been returning home from a business trip in Afghanistan and had noticed the destroyed vehicle and burnt body slithering on the other side of the road near death. He had his driver pull over and had his orderlies gather Caesar and they took him home and aided him with the finest medical attention. As he gradually regrouped, Al-Salam took a great liking to him. As always, there was a method to Al-Salam's madness. After all, Caesar was an American soldier – the enemy. But he knew that there lie greater possibilities in having an American on his side. He hated attributing negative things to the decree of Allah, but his wisdom allowed him to see past the surface of complex things. The catastrophe that the Saudi tank had caused, Caesar should not have survived. Then, he came along to discover him. To him, this was nothing coincidental. This was why he had brought Caesar to his home instead of letting him die on the soil he had come to stain with the blood of his kith and Kin. And, when he had stepped from the back seat of his Range Rover to observe Caesar, there was something that struck him to his soul in the gray eyes of the American.

Caesar reflected upon Al-Salam's account of how he discovered him. After he had come around full-circle and was well enough to depart, he decided to take Al-Salam up on his offer to stay as long as he liked.

Throughout the few months he dwelled in the grandeur of Al-Salam's palace, he was taught a great deal about the true religion of Al-Islam and began to see it from a different perspective that had ultimately changed his life forever.

Al-Salam was of Arab descent. He was a very large man with deep set black eyes. It would be discovered over the decades of their companionship how treacherous the man could be; his dark eyes were soft and filled with compassion and did not possess one hint of treachery. He was the most kind, gentle man Caesar had ever had the privilege of meeting in his life. But there also lie another side to the man in how he obtained his wealth.

Al-Salam was one of the most dominant forces inside the heroin trade in the Middle East. As time progressed he spent a lot of time with Caesar. He entrusted in him his position, his capabilities and what he had in mind of him becoming a foreign affiliate in the heroin business while in the United States of America.

To Caesar, he had struck gold. His luck couldn't have been any better. He was giving up his career in the Marines anyway. He was done executing Uncle Sam's injustice. But, the Marine Corps had saved him from the savage streets of North

Charleston's Macon in South Carolina where he'd been a low level pimp.

After 4 months in Saudi Arabia, Caesar had returned to the States, notified the military of his return and went through the necessary procedures of resigning. He was given a purple heart, an honorable discharge, and returned to the dilapidated streets of his neighborhood where he had a modest 3 bedroom house off Chicora Avenue where his bottom whore awaited him along with the 3 other whores he pimped. Although the Marines had listed him "Killed In Action",Sterling, Caesar's bottom whore, had been sent a postcard informing her that he was still alive and well and would return home soon.

He had confided in Al-Salam of his struggle back home in the states and told him his aspirations. Just as Caesar felt he had struck gold with Al-Salam, Al-Salam felt he had struck gold with him. He even sent 10 thousand dollars to Sterling for him. Although Sterling had worked the strip for him, he was in love with her. If life had dealt him a better hand before he went into the military he would have never subjected her to the streets as a whore. But hey, it was what it was.

When he returned home he inseminated the love of his soul inside of her womb and had planted quadruplets. During her birth, she succumbed from complications along with 3 of her boys. Don had been the only survivor.

After coming into wealth, he had his name changed to Sulayman Azeez Mustafah and incorporated all of his businesses under the umbrella of his birth name. His savvy in business, along with the long arm of Al-Salam, made everything he touched a success. Al-Salam had made sure that fluent shipments of pure heroin reached him through underground channels. The drug was so potent, it took not only the City of Charleston and the state of South Carolina by storm, but the entire eastern coast.

Eventually he had to diversify and before he knew it, he was responsible for a major fraction of the heroin in the entire country.

Al-salam had plugged him into all the political connects he had around America; so with this, along with the electrifying charisma he possessed, he became a hit in various industries. He was domineering at 6 feet 3 inches, 230 pounds. His physique was muscular and solid. He wore his head bald at all times with a full beard that was always properly groomed. He had dashing white teeth, dark skin like milk chocolate, thick eyebrows, long eyelashes; his eyes were steel gray.

Now a multi-millionaire and with all his money, influence and political clout, he couldn't help his son. His meeting with senator Brody was futile and it troubled his soul because they'd established a bond over the years. At least that's what he thought. Although how he felt wasn't apparent on his façade, inwardly, senator Brody had him infuriated because if he really wanted to assist Don he had the power to do so.South Carolina was his state.

But while they sat on the upper deck of the 70 foot yacht the Senator owned, all he kept reiterating was the media hype surrounding the case and the importance of the victim because of who her grandfather was.

"Fuck the media, Brody!" Caesar had spat. "And you're talking about the importance of the victim because of Elfane, which is understandable. But what about the importance of Don because of who I am?" Elfane was the grandfather of the girl his son had been accused of slaying.

Senator Brody, composed, just went on to explain that there was nothing he could do; Don's fate was out of his hands.

Caesar knew that they had a difference of opinion in the

decision he and Al-Salam had made in shutting down the lucrative heroin operation due to their strive for righteousness in their religion as the poison they manufactured and distributed went against all Islam stood for. They had shut down the operation before the month of Ramadan last year in which severed a serious flow of cash for the senator and his affiliates so he knew that Brody's standoffishness in the matter of Don was personal. The amicable relationship he thought they shared, and the times his son had spent with Don growing up, had all proved itself to be worth nothing. Money and the drug had been the motivation. He was nothing amongst their ranks. He was nothing but a hoodlum that had lucked up and made it big.

The media had relentlessly publicized the fact that Don was the son of Muslim tycoon Sulayman Azeez Mustafah.

The victim was some little spoiled white girl named Fedora Armanti-Teressa Sanstrom. She was the granddaughter of a very wealthy aristocratic retired judge by the name of Elfane Alexander Sanstrom III. She had been raped and murdered after returning home from a party on the Isles of Palms in Mount Pleasant, South Carolina.Witnesses stated that she had left the party with Don and that they had headed to her condo in his Lamborghini. Though this had been true, somehow someone killed her soon after Don's departure and he was being accused of it.

The media was propagating the case so raw and viciously and so many people were lobbying around the country through talk shows, radio and social media about the case stating ugly things about Muslims and their associates, he knew that Don didn't stand a chance. The state was ready to try the case after 8 months of chaos and confusion. They had Don's DNA. There was no doubt that he had been with the girl, but how she died, Caesar was unsure. But what he did know was his son and he knew that he was above such a thing in moral.

He just couldn't grasp Brody leaving them out to dry when he knew Don was incapable of such an horrendous act. He had watched Brody as he threw the untouched shot of scotch down his throat and sat the crystal glass back on the table, and without uttering another word to the Senator, got up and departed, leaving his apologies suspended in thin air.

He had hired Don a prestigious attorney but was told that what the state would present was going to seal his son's conviction. There was really nothing anyone could do. So, as he sat inside his office, he left it all in the mighty hands of Allah. If it was what He decreed then there was no one that could frustrate it. Life was full of paradoxes. Good things weren't always good, and bad things weren't always bad. Allah was, indeed, the best of planners.

But in all of this, he would not allow his son to rot in the hands of South Carolina's corrupted penal system as a prisoner of war. One day, he would be free. Fuck Brody!

Chapter One

Orangeburg, South Carolina
January 19, 2014 - Saturday

Her living room was a mess. It looked as if a gang of impish 3 year olds had stormed through it, tossing everything to and fro in their wake. Clothing articles she'd neglected to put in order and fold were strewn about; stale popcorn that she'd picked over the previous night had somehow found its way on the beautiful burgundy carpeting of her floor after spilling from the bowl it had been in atop her living-room table; a tall cup of strawberry Kool-Aid had also found its way spilled on the floor but had long dried leaving a darkened stain.

The kitchen was in disarray; her bedroom was in disarray – she screamed out in frustration as she laid sprawled on the living-room floor in a pair of short pants spandex and tank-top. She had just completed a 45 minute workout of aerobics. Lazily, she reached for the remote control and switched the channel to the news. As it was for the past 8 months the media had been bashing the striking features of a 19 year old young man that they were now showing being escorted from an unmarked squad car in handcuffs into the towering courthouse in downtown, Charleston. Photographers, cameramen and reporters bombarded him with questions regarding his innocence or guilt for the alleged crime he was being charged; neither he, nor his attorney said a word.

As she watched him enter the courthouse gracefully, she couldn't help but notice how strikingly attractive he was. Today was the first day of his trial. She didn't know what it was about him that stirred things deep within the wells of all she thought she had lost 6 years ago with the death of her fiancé, but God, it was as if the mere sight of him touched her.

Feeling ridiculous as always, she sighed incredulously, powered off the TV and stared into the ceiling as her heart rate decreased from the intensity of her exercise.

She thought about all that she'd been neglecting in her duties. Her life was a mess. Even after 6 years she still couldn't let go of the man she so wanted to spend the rest of her life with. Her psychologist had told her that time would heal her scars and that it would all result to beautiful memories but this prophecy had yet to come into fruition. It seemed as the further time came in between them the closer they became. The visits of his spirit hadn't stop and neither had the vivid dreams that she often had of them living the most beautiful life and having the greatest sex. Since his demise, she had yet to sleep with, or even think, about another man. She never even masturbated. The only time she ever had the experience of feeling her love flow was through the erotic dreams she so compassionately shared with her deceased fiancé. Her counselor had told her that she should start dating and doing things that could help in her recovery of the loss but there was no use – at least it seemed. She had tried several times over the past 3 years of her therapy to no avail.

Every day since her fiancé's death presented a test of

perseverance for her. The things that she did do was because it was mandatory and essential to her survival. She had no family, she had no friends. Every once in a while she would call her late fiancé's mother to see how she was getting along, other than that, she was a loner. The only reason she began exercising 3 years ago was because her mental health counselor had recommended it for therapeutic purposes. She didn't need to workout to maintain her shape. Sex appeal and beauty was not an issue of hers. She was – for the lack of a better choice of word – a very fine bitch. She stood 5 feet 9 inches, 150 pounds. Her weight fluctuated between 144-151 pounds regardless of what she did and how she ate. She counted this a blessing. Her hair was of spun gold and hung to the middle of her back, but the only thing she ever did was keep it in a ponytail – with the exception of her job where she worked in corrections so she wore it in a bun because her hair wasn't allowed to touch her uniform. She had a beautiful golden complexion that almost matched the color of her hair. Her lips were luscious and full like ripe grapes. Her eyes were dark and questioning. She had beautiful feet and hands, beautiful white teeth, and extraordinary panache. She was a diva. Though listless, she exuded an enthralling aura; she was very quiet and poised. Intelligent. But in all honesty, she had come to hate life once again.

Growing up, she hated life. She'd been an orphan. What really happened to her at birth – ambiguous. All she'd been told growing up in group homes was that her mother had never returned. This had weighed on her enormously, causing societal detachment from the world and it's treachery. This was why she didn't have any friends growing up and didn't have any now.

She grew up in Orangeburg, South Carolina. After completing high school, she went to South Carolina State where she obtained a bachelor's degree in Criminal Justice with aspirations of becoming a prominent attorney, but those dreams were quickly shattered. This was where she had met the man that somehow swept her off her feet, then it all changed.

Justin Rose. He was majoring in political science. They saw one another around campus from time to time and then he approached her one day and said the most ludicrous thing to her but it made her smile. She could've tell that he was nervous and somewhat unsure of himself and it intrigued her because, basically, he admitted his short-comings about 30 seconds of standing before her at a loss for words: "Listen," he commenced, "I don't know what to say to you because I'm not good at this part and, I'm somewhat shy, but I really do like you. Would you help me talk to you? After you help me get past this part I got it from there."

She thought he was cute. She beamed at the memory. His honesty won her instantly. She took control of the situation and asked him to have lunch with her and from that day forth they became inseparable. In the 2 years they courted they shared so much with one another they felt as if one couldn't live without the other. He was the first person in the world that she had ever loved. She had never believed in God until she met him. In fact, he became her god and she his goddess. They had their entire lives planned out in all that they aspired. Everything was magnificent in her life until the day he went home to Columbia, South Carolina to never return to her. He'd been killed the same night in the state's Capitol by a stray bullet from an assault rifle. He rode directly into a gang war in the neighborhood where his mother resided. He was pronounced dead on the scene.

Tears slipped from her eyes and she sat up and looked around her junky home. She wasn't nasty and filthy. In fact, she was very scrupulous. Her apartment was clean, she just had neglected to keep everything in order.

She lived in a handsome apartment complex called Angel

Estates. They were all flats. Hers consisted of 2 bedrooms, one and a half baths, a mediocre size kitchen, a living room and den. It was small but yet spacious and cute. The ceiling was high and laid horizontally. A beautiful long arm ceiling fan hung from the living room ceiling. All the walls of the apartment was peach. Peach and burgundy was her favorite colors – well peach was her favorite color and burgundy was Justin's, but what the heck, if it was his favorite color it was hers as well.

There also existed a washer and dryer that sat between the two bedrooms. All the furniture in the living room was burgundy leather and the tables were cherry oak wood; she had neglected to dust them so a few layers of dust coated them. Her lamps were also burgundy porcelain with peach shades.

She got to her feet and looked around her home. Damn, she hated how listless she felt. She was far from a lazy woman, she just didn't have any energy. She had long refrain from taking the medication that her counselor had prescribed her because it made her feel like a patient in a psychiatric ward. The energy drinks was better. And as it was, cans of them littered her apartment from her bedroom to the kitchen counter. Coffee had also become a must have over the years. They were the only things that made her wheels turn.

But today, she would clean up the mess that surrounded her. She had turned 29 a few days ago and had done nothing but work, come home and watched TV until she fell asleep,then got up to go to work again. This process had repeated itself year after year. She hated life and wanted to die but she didn't have what it took to accomplish such feat as suicide.

She walked into the half-bath and peered into the mirror at her reflection. Actually, she was surprised at her appearance. There was no exhausting bags under her eyes, she still looked youthful and pretty. She looked into her eyes as if asking herself if Canary Rose still existed in not the physical, but in soul. Although she and Justin had never married, after his death, she changed her last name to his in commemoration.

"Canary Rose," she uttered softly as she continued to look into the soul of her own eyes. For a fleeting moment something seemed to manifest itself, but just as quick as it came, the light went back to the stark darkness of her soul.

God, she so desperately wanted to experience that fire she once had that Justin introduced her to. But who would ignite it? Better yet, who could ignite? She pondered as she switched off the lights, left the bathroom and headed to the kitchen to put on a pot of coffee. It was almost 12 o'clock in the afternoon. Today she was off and would be for the next 2 days. As always, when she had her days off, she told herself that she would do a thousand-and-one things that she would never do; but one thing was for certain this time; she would clean up her sanctuary.

She started the coffee and headed to the living room, turned on her stereo, and allowed her iPod to do its magic. The sounds of Ushers "Climax" filled the air. As his croons drifted from the speakers of her entertainment system she began her chores and, introspectively, thought about where she was at in life.

As always, as it was for the past 4 years, her job at Palmetto Correctional Institution seemed to be on her mind half of the time. Even when she didn't want to think about the sickening environment where she worked as a correctional official, it was hard not to in light of all the things she witnessed on a daily basis while back there. After she had lost interest in pursuing the life of an attorney after Justin's death, a professor at the college had told her about the institution and encouraged her towards internship there so she would have the experience and field hours under her belt for whatever decision she may make in the future. At first she was appalled by the suggestion because all she could conjure was the many murderers, child molesters and rapists that pervaded the facility. And, it was a level 3 maximum security facility. The worst of the worst.

Over the years she had heard many stories of its corruption along with all the illegal activities that transpired between the officers and inmates but she had thought that it was all hype and legend. But after touring the institution she didn't think it so bad after all. All the inmates seemed to praise and admire her. She had even seen some of them masturbating in distant rooms and shower stalls but paid them no mind. After all, they were destitute of women; what did one expect? But in the same rhyme this unnerved her and alerted her to the potential threat of being raped. She didn't know what compelled her to go through with taking on employment, but she did.

Now, here she was 4 years later, a year and a half after the professors suggestion with really no regret in the decision. She wasn't content with her choice of employment because she was far above the moral conditions of a woman working inside a prison as a low level correctional officer who was expendable in the event the inmates decided to take over. Her life would not be considered in saving to gain control of the facility. The state would use all of its resources to maintain control even if she was killed in the process. Staff members could not be used as bargaining tools. And even in this, she still accepted the conditions. Life really didn't matter to her anyway. She conceded that this made the decision all the more easier.

But between the inmates and her colleagues, she didn't know who was the worst in character and conduct. They all made her sick but she maintained her fortitude because the job made ends meet, although barely.

She had threatened many of her colleagues with sexual harassment and had reported them to the warden. Everyone seemed to have an undying thirst for her attention and panties but she wasn't interested in any of them. She had even seen desire swimming in the eyes of the warden, but he knew that she was one of the female officers he would never have the pleasure of possessing in any way. She was only social on a need-to-know basis. She was the most talked about amongst her colleagues, and inmates. The inmates flocked her and attempted to shower her with money and gifts; she declined them. Most of them were very attractive men but she kindly requested to be left alone. But some of them were very persistent; with those ones, she had to threaten with solicitation charges. After charging a great many of them around the compound for this, along with the ones that expected her to watch them ejaculate as they openly masturbated, she quickly became known as one that didn't tolerate the bullshit. She didn't care about the drugs and cell phones they smuggled, used and distributed, she only wanted to do her 8-12 hours and go home and relax. She wasn't there to oppress them anymore than they already were. During her shifts in the beginning, she sat and read magazines and books on business, or spent most of her time off the wing's in the lobby of the dorm conversing with whomever officer she worked with until she began moving up in rank.

Although amongst it, she still found it hard to believe that some of the inmates lived the life they lived. Financially, some of them were doing better than people in the free world. She now understood why some of the officers succumbed to illegally dealing with some of the inmates. The fruits of the inmates was in comparison to the apple in the Garden of Eden: very tempting and alluring.

Palmetto Correctional Institution was by far the most corrupted in the state. It was a world of its own. The warden didn't even care. Female officers sold sex. Inmates laid up on cell phones like they were sitting in the living room of houses at home. The air in the dorms wreaked of wine, cocaine and marijuana. Officers were being assaulted left and right. Inmates were being brutally stabbed and murdered. Punks walked around like Cover Girl models. It was insane but yet there lie an inexplicable excitement to it all!

In the parking lot of the facility sat expensive cars and SUV's and it made one wonder how such people could afford such extravagance on the mediocre salaries they made. But once the life of the prison was discovered, all the answers lie inside the confines of the concrete and steel structure. The underworld of the facility was a multi-million dollar industry in itself. Everything went on from drug smuggling to white collar schemes. It also housed some of the most talented and intelligent people in the world. This intrigued her more than anything. Intelligence always attracted her. Her experience at the prison made her realize that the penal system in America was a university in itself with people mastering and majoring in various sciences of life from crime, politics, religious studies and beyond. And although she had come to the realization that everybody incarcerated wasn't bad people at all, but individuals that had made mistakes, she still couldn't find it in herself to indulge in any forms of relations with them. But although she held this position, she understood why some of the people she worked with did.

But in all of this, she knew who she was and always had. She was beautiful and sexy without even trying to be. She would run circles around the prison if she chose to but she didn't have the slightest desire.

The coffee pot beeped, alerting that it was ready. She made a strong cup of coffee, hot chocolate – something she'd seen various inmates do at the microwave while she sat at the officer's desk at work years ago, tried it and hadn't turned back since – oh, she almost forgot to add sugar and cream! The things you learned back there, she thought inwardly as she stirred the thick mixture that never failed to give her the RPM of a Mustang!

She sat at a small table in her kitchen and read the newspaper as she sipped the drink. After she consumed all of it, which was about 30 minutes later, she stored away the paper and began cleaning her domicile, starting with her kitchen.

Chapter Two

Charleston, South Carolina
February 5, 2014 - Thursday/ 2 Weeks Later

It had been a very short trial. Exactly 2 weeks. There was no need prolonging it because there was nothing in his favor that would help him whatsoever. For this matter, he didn't select a trial by jury; he selected a bench trial. There would only be a judge to hear, and rule on his case, which was already done. The verdict hadn't been shocking to him, nor anyone in the nation. He had been framed and railroaded. Why? He didn't know and didn't possess a mustard seed of an idea. All he knew was that he had not so viciously murdered the girl he had rendezvoused with. As usual, their friends had thrown a wild party. After it was over, he departed with her in arm. They got in his Lamborghini and went to her condo and had hours of raunchy sex; he went home thereafter. It was as simple as that. Nothing more, nothing less. Fedora Armanti-Teressa Sanstrom had been a brat but she didn't deserve to die the way she had, and for the past 8 months of the horrifying reality that he found himself inside of, he could not think of a single reason why someone would kill such a sweet, free-spirited girl and accuse him of it. This wasn't one of those freak incidents where the killer had partied, got wasted out of his mind and didn't remember that he had killed someone the night before. He didn't use drugs, alcohol, nor tobacco products; never had in his life.

"Donatello Furqān McFadden, I sentence you to the remainder of your natural life…" The verdict of the presiding judge careened through his head. Twenty-four hours ago, his life had been taken for something he really did not do. He sat in the dull confines of a one-man unit waiting to be transferred to the institution where he would begin serving his new life.

He sat on the edge of a concrete slab a thin mattress laid on top of with his head cupped in his hands. He hadn't cried once. He was strong. He'd been raised thoroughly. Though raised under the banner of Islam, he had never taken its Testimony of Faith, but knew in his heart that Al-Islam was the truth. He just hadn't reach that point in his life where he stood on its principles and lived by its moral codes of conduct. But his father saw to it that he was well versed in the religion. And even after enduring the calamity that had befallen him, not understanding why, he did not question Allah because he understood that no one could confuse, nor frustrate whatever He willed. He knew that this misfortune was a trial. He also knew that in misfortunes lie seeds of greater benefit. Allah was putting him through the ultimate test.

His father had come by the jail to visit him yesterday, and even under the harsh conditions of what they were both going through, father and son, they still laughed, talked about their future, and so forth.

"Son, I want you to know that I love you. You said that you didn't kill that girl, you didn't kill her. And even if you did, it wouldn't change how I perceive you. You are my lil' man. Don't ever second guess what I think of you. I just wanted to tell you that so you'll be assured," his father had told him. "But you won't be caged up like an animal forever, son."

"I know abu," Don had returned earnestly.

"Just allow Allah to have His way and in due time we'll overcome this obstacle even if we have to break you out of here ourselves." His father had been calm and collect but very serious. "Just roll with the punches while Al-Salam and I try getting to the bottom of what's going on. I prefer to get you out of here legally so it may take some time. How much? I don't know, Allahu' alim. But just rest assured that in the event things don't go as plan the brothers will come and get you, Insha'Allah.

"But for the meantime, stay up and trust in Allah and remember the crocodile and the lion. I know you can handle yourself amongst the toughest of men because you were taught well. Just be cool son."

"I got you, abu."

"I love you for the sake of Allah, son."

"I love you too, abu."

Don sat in the cell reflecting on the visit with his father. He always made him feel as if nothing in the world could stop him. He gave him strength of profound measures. If his father said he would be free one way or the other, he would be free – one way or the other. He was sure.

He got up from where he sat and removed the gray uniform shirt and T-shirt he wore, tossed them on his bed and began stretching in preparation to workout. He had a very fine physique. At 19 years old he was – physically – in the glory of his youth. Growing up he had been trained by his father and two of his most entrusted men: Jabbar and Ali. They had taught him various forms of fighting arts and self-defense. Surely, as his father had said, defending himself would not be an issue. For his age, he was very mature and grounded. No one would have any problems with him unless they brought it on themselves.

Life had been an adventure for him as he grew up in the luxuries of his father's many homes around the country. His father had never left him alone while he was out on business. He went everywhere his father went. He had a personal tutor that traveled the world with them. He had obtained his high school diploma at the age of 15 and had been studying business extensively. He was following in his father's footsteps as an entrepreneur. Though every bit of his father in ways, actions and thought, they looked nothing alike. He had all the features of his deceased mother. Although he never had the privilege of meeting her, his father had many pictures of her. Her name was Sterling Silver and she possessed every bit of the shine in her smooth, dark skin that the precious metal possessed. So much his father had told him about her he felt as if he had known her all his life. She was an amazing woman.

He dropped to the floor and began to do push-ups at one-hundred a set. He was 5 feet, 11 inches, 190 pounds. He had a burnt bronze complexion. Where it came from, between the dark skin complexions of his mother and father, he wasn't sure. He was handsome and stylish and had been schooled in mannerism and proper etiquette. He had the very same poised calmness that his father possessed and the free-spirit of his mother. Although he had been safeguarded from the ills of growing up in the ghetto streets, his father was treacherous and had taught him to be as well. His father had the mentality of mafia dons and Roman emperors. These characteristics were evident in not only his father, but he had long seen that his mother had possessed them also and he had inherited it. Their eyes burned of fire and ambition.

As he began a set of squats the words of his godfather swam through his head. He began to perspire; droplets of sweat slipped from the smooth features of his face: "Paradoxes, akhi. Always remember the paradoxes of life because it may well be that you dislike a thing that may be good for you, and it may well be that you like a thing that is bad for you. Allah knows and you do not." The words of Al-Salam echoed through the depths of his mind.

Al-Salam had given him the attribute of Furqān and had played an essential role in mentorship throughout his life. The name was one of the attributes of their Holy Prophet and, it was also a chapter in the Noble Quran. It was the criterion to distinguish between truth and falsehood, right and wrong; a deeper level of sagacity.

He stood in the middle of the floor rotating his head, loosening the tension in his neck. His body glistened from sweat. Although the perpetual repetitions of push-ups, squats and sit-ups didn't change his circumstances, it did relieve his mind, body and soul of the tension and stress that attempted to consume him.

The officers announced that it was time for recreation and the electronic locks on the steel doors disengaged. Expeditiously, he fetched his soap, towel and wash cloth, and headed to the shower stalls. He didn't have an extra pair of briefs so he would have to wash the one he wore while inside the shower. He had about an hour before it was time for dinner. He needed to make several phone calls because after they ate, rec would be over and they would be herded back to their cells for the remainder of the day. The unit he occupied only got rec one hour a day: Twenty-Three and One. It didn't matter though, because after tonight, he would be transferred to what supposed to be his final destination.

###

Orangeburg, South Carolina

February 6, 2014 - Wednesday

The last time she had slept in her bed she wasn't sure. Lazily, she laid in the comforts of her living room sofa wrapped up like a cocoon in a yellow and white comforter that Justin had bought her while they were in college. She was trying to muster the strength to get up and start her day, but the coldness of the apartment had her subdued to the coziness of the blanket and sofa. She had a 10:30 A.M. appointment today to see her counselor; it was already after 8 o'clock.

She groaned in complaint then inhaled deeply as if summoning a force only known to her for strength. Finding it, she threw off the comforter, sat up and looked around the living room of the apartment as if something had somehow changed since she last saw it.

She got up and the bottom part of the T-shirt she wore slushed its way below her voluptuous hips and buttocks then stopped mid-thigh. She ambled over to her entertainment system, powered it on FM where Steve aired, and headed to her bathroom to brush her teeth and shower.

She stepped out of the shower 30 minutes later. Steve had just broke for commercial. She walked over to one of the 3 dressers inside her bedroom and pulled open the top drawer. A variety of different bra and panties were piled atop one another. Some matched, some didn't so she just grabbed whatever her hands touched first and slipped them on.

It was the end of Spring. The weather was warm so she retrieved a pair of beige, cotton slacks from her walk-in closet by Ralph Lauren, pulled a white button down shirt from a hanger to go along with it, and slipped her pedicured toes into a pair of cute white sandals that she had picked up at a Payless shoe store some time ago.

As she headed to her bathroom to comb out her hair from the wrap she had placed it in the night before, Steve continued, but she couldn't hear what the topic of discussion pertained to.

After combing her hair out, she pulled it into a tight ponytail, applied a light coat of Mac lip gloss to her sensuous lips, licked them, and looked at her reflection inside the mirror. And as always, she thought of Beyoncé.

Everywhere she went people told her that she resembled the star. She denied it at first, but when she really thought about it, she accepted the fact that they did resemble one another. But to her, she looked better than Beyoncé. So, if anything, Beyoncé looked like her. Besides, she didn't wear make-up. It had never been her style. And, the golden texture of her hair wasn't due to cosmetics.

She replaced the cosmetics she used back in their respective locations, flipped off the lights in her bedroom and headed to the kitchen to put on a pot of coffee and make a light breakfast of toast, lemon jelly and scrambled eggs. She fetched an energy drink and drained it while she did this.

Steve and his cast were in a deep discussion about someone receiving a natural life sentence and quickly, she realized that they were talking about the young man that had been accused of murdering some prominent judge's granddaughter. She listened intently and thought about the young man as she scrambled a couple of eggs. From what the media had been broadcasting about the case over the past months, she knew that he didn't stand a chance. But, as Steve said, it wasn't fair that America had already tried and hung him long before he was granted the opportunity to argue his case. She couldn't believe that he was sentenced to life a few days ago. The time, nor the crime fit his description. She knew that a book couldn't be judged by its cover, but there was something about him that just screamed innocence.

Steve's cast went on discussing the case as they took calls from the public.

As the eggs finished cooking she toasted several slices of honey wheat bread then turned off the burner and moved the pan to a cool burner at the back of the stove. She retrieved an almost empty bottle of lemon jelly from the refrigerator and fixed a cup of strong coffee with extra cream, stood at the counter and began devouring her meal while sipping the hot liquid from a green ceramic mug.

The voices of Steve's cast drifted away from her as her thoughts drifted towards the celebrity murderer. She wondered if he would be shipped to the prison where she worked. There was 7 level 3 maximum security prisons in the state and he could go to anyone of them. But more than likely, he'd be shipped closer to home. It would be several weeks before she could check the data-base at work to see where he would be classified because he had to go through the Evaluation Center in Columbia first.

She sucked her teeth at the absurdity in the interest she had in him because she knew that she would never see him. He was too high profile and his lawyer would see to it that he stayed as close to Charleston as possible. And even if she did see him, so what? He was in prison and had a natural life sentence without parole for crying out loud!

She discarded the thought and ate the remnants of her meal, left everything where it was after downing the remainder of the coffee in her mug – dreading to clean up the mess when she returned -- and went to fetch her pocketbook and keys. The apartment was meticulous outside of the minute mess she was leaving behind. After she tackled it two weeks prior she decided to clean as she went along to alleviate unnecessary work from piling up on her.

As she headed through the living room she pressed the power button on her entertainment system and headed out of her apartment into the coolness of the morning air. It was 10 o'clock on the head. She would have to push the gas. Her counselors office was about 45 minutes away. She didn't like being late for appointments.

She deactivated the alarm as she walked towards her Chrysler 300. She loved her car, and as it stood, it was the only thing that she really loved and gave any of her time aside the horror/action/comedy flicks she watched and books she read. The car was white; white leather seats, peach carpeting with white Asanti rims wrapped in Pirelli tires. She had a nice JVC sound system. It was all she needed. She didn't crave the other accessories.

She waved to a couple of Caucasian females that exited an all black Avalanche. She looked at her car in defeat as she approached it. It was way over due for a wash. She'd stop by a car wash on her way back home. She stepped in, cranked it, and pulled out of the parking lot.

###

She made it downtown earlier than expected. She hadn't been inside her counselors office no more than 15 minutes before the receptionist told her she'd been summoned.

The office was small, but comfortable and homey. It was connected to a row of other office establishments. Downtown, Orangeburg was small. It had what it needed. Nothing more, nothing less.

Inside, there was a reception area; a waiting room sat off to the side with several comfortable chairs along with a play area for children. In the back, there was 3 offices other counselors occupied.

Doctor Brown, her counselor, was the sole proprietor of the practice; the other two counselors was under her. As far as she could tell they were all doing well because her counselor drove a 750i series BMW and the other counselor's drove an Infinity and an Audi. They were all 2013 editions.

She saw her counselor twice a month. The bill was something she preferred not to think of. Besides, her counselor had become more than a counselor, she had become a friend of some sort. Hell, she was the only person she spoke to intimately.

Soft jazz wafted through the cool air of the practice at a discreet volume. The receptionist was a 30-ish Afro-American woman. She wore her hair cut short with very tiny curls. It fit her small, pretty face nicely. She wore a pair of non-descripted blue framed glasses. She had on a dark blue business suit that snugly complimented her petite frame; no stockings, blue pumps.

The walls was a soft pastel blue with flowery borders of colorful roses. The floors were beige towels that were buffed to maximum shine.

The receptionist poked her head inside the waiting room. "Ms. Rose, you can go on back; Doctor Brown is ready to see you," she smiled warmly. Her eyes sparkled through the glass of her glasses.

"Ok," Canary replied as she grabbed the handle of the pocketbook that sat on her lap as she stood up.

###

"Hey girl," Canary greeted as she entered the spacious office.

"How are you, Ms. Rose?" Doctor Brown returned. "You

look great!"

"I'm making it. How about yourself?"

"I'm blessed, I'm blessed." Doctor Brown smiled.

Canary seated herself where she sat every time she came. Doctor Brown's desk sat in the middle of her office. Two beautifully crafted wooden chairs with cushioned back and seat sat in front of her desk. The room was shaped like an irregular polygon. One of the large windows gave a panoramic view of the bustling shops and brick buildings that lined the main street. Several file cabinets lined another wall; pictures of her accomplishment's and degree's lined another wall. The pictures was of family from where she was originally from in Charleston, along with pictures of her with other doctor's in her field. Her desk was neat and orderly.

"So," Doctor Brown began as she browsed through Canary's file. "How has things been going with the dating; any luck?"

Canary sputtered through her lips, "I haven't even tried."

"You're really not up to it, are you?"

Canary pursed her lips and shook her head.

"Well, how has your energy been coming along?"

"Still dependent upon coffee and energy drinks," she quipped.

The questioning went on officially for about 15 more minutes then Doctor Brown sat back in her chair. Canary wasn't like any of her other clients who had severe psychological problems, she was just finding it hard to let go of her deceased fiancé. And really, there wasn't anything anyone could do. The only antidote for her recovery was time.

"You know, I've been thinking lately; I'm not suppose to get personal with any of my clients but I've grown to like you as a friend over the past three years. I truly think that you are a magnificent person with beautiful ethics and morals. I would like to solidify our friendship," she spoke articulately.

Canary blushed. The compliment was flattering. It warmed her.

"Friends?" Doctor Brown smiled. She was a pecan complexion, plus-size woman. She wore her natural hair short above her neck line, but more than often she kept it braided in different presentable styles. She had full lips, a cute nose; her brown eyes were always smiling and bright. She was very attractive. "I can't keep taking your money. You don't need me as a doctor; you need a friend."

"Ok," Canary accepted.

"Well then, it's no more 'Ms. Rose' and 'Doctor Brown'. Call me Danyell," Dr. Brown said girlishly.

"Call me Canary."

They both giggled.

"How about we go out some time if you like?" Dr. Brown offered as she closed Canary's file.

"Terrific. When?"

"How about I give you a call later this evening and we'll go from there?"

"That's fine," Canary stood to leave.

Dr. Brown stood, rubbed her hands down her voluptuous thighs to smoothen out the white linen skirt she wore, and maneuvered from behind the desk towards Canary with extended hands. They shook hands casually and together they walked out of the office. "I'll talk to you later, girl."

"Ok," Canary said as they entered the reception area. She twiddled her fingers at the receptionist and headed out the door.

"Bye-bye, Ms. Rose," the receptionist returned.

Canary walked out of the office. The sun had already reached its zenith in the sky and it radiated a soothing warmness. People moved about the busy street. She headed towards her car with a gratifying sense of relief washing over her. She wanted it to end long ago but kept deciding against it because Danyell had been the only person she had to talk to. She thought about how ridiculous this was as she got in her car. She needed a friend so goddamn bad she used her counselor as a means to satisfy this end and been paying for it handsomely!

My God, she thought. Well, it was over, and she still gained a great friend out of the deal. So, in a sense, it was all worth it.

She waited for an opportunity to join the train of traffic.

Chapter Three

Great Falls, Montana
February 7, 2014 - Thursday

"Don't worry Sulayman, I'll handle everything with precision."

"I trust that you will Khalil, Insha'Allah. Just call me if you need me."

"Insha'Allah," Khalil replied from the main office of McFadden & McFadden Enterprises in Charleston, South Carolina.

"As salamu alaykum, akhi."

"Wa alaykum as salam."

Caesar terminated the call. Khalil was Caesar's most trusted CO; he was Muslim. In fact, all of his top executives were Muslims. There were others he employed that were non-Muslims, but he didn't entrust them to hold executive positions in his empire and it was stipulated in his contracts.

He had met Khalil during an Islamic convention in Charlotte, North Carolina and had taken a liking to him and his intelligence instantly. He had offered him the position and Khalil had gratefully accepted; this was over 15 years ago.

Caesar sat in one of the exquisite Lear jets he owned on the airstrip in Billings, Montana awaiting his car that was late due to a flat tire it had caught.

He sat on the soft leather seat, eyelids myopic, cogitating all that lay ahead of not just him, but the fate of his son. The sentence he'd been given was staggering! He couldn't think with a clear head so he decided to surrender his reign of command to Khalil until he got a grip on things.

He owned a ranch house in Great Falls, and would rendezvous there in worship of Allah for the proper guidance. He had hired a team of thorough investigators in the Charleston area with connections in urban, and upper-class areas. He doubted that it would turn up anything but he had to exhaust all of his options. He also had the murdered girls family, friends, and associates under investigation. There were no strings left untied.

"As salamu alaykum akhi, your car has arrived."

Caesar opened his eyes and nodded to his on-board attendant. "Wa alaykum as salam; shakrun jazakallah," he replied kindly.

Caesar's Caucasian flight attendant was also Muslim. He was around 5 feet, 7 inches, 190 pounds. He had stunning male features with sparkling blue eyes. His name was Husayn.

"Take care Husayn," Caesar said as he gathered his bearings and departed the aircraft.

"You too, Sulayman. I'll make du'a for you and Don." Husayn replied earnestly.

Caesar smiled at him and journeyed down the steps of the jet and walked over to the black Range Rover with tinted windows that awaited him.

"As salamu alaykum wa rahmahtullah, akhi," Ali smiled at his boss as he stood next to the open back door of the Rover.

Caesar returned the greeting and climbed inside the vehicle. He greeted his driver Jabbar, and the greeting had been reciprocated.

Ali got in the front passenger seat, closed the door, and they raced across the black tarmac headed toward the exit road of the airport. The roars of the great 747's could be heard as they landed and took off from the runways.

Ali was Caesar's man. He was born Bobby Jenkins, originally from Myrtle Beach, South Carolina. Ali had become Muslim while incarcerated for murder, doing a 30 year stint that had been overturned 15 years later. Caesar had met him at one of the mosques in Myrtle Beach during the time he'd been scouting for potential bosses to hold down particular cities in the heroin trade. Through official sources it had been conveyed that Ali was a true Muslim to the heart and a stone-cold-killer. After spending a great deal of time with him, Caesar gave him the key to his city and made him an under-boss. Ali had never let him down. Through money, murder, and Islam, Ali had been loyal. So, when he and Al-Salam decided that the game was over before the month of Ramadan 2013, he decided that he would pull Ali with him and make him head of security over McFadden & McFadden Enterprises; he handled it superbly.

Jabbar was also Caesar's man. He was born Tony Lee, originally from Augusta, Georgia. The same way Caesar became acquainted with Ali was the same way he became acquainted with Jabbar.

But Jabbar and Ali were like night and day. Ali was cold, relentless and vicious; very impulsive. Jabbar was warm, compassionate; he had enthralling fortitude. But beneath the surface of it all lie dark perils. He and Ali balanced one another perfectly. They both were well kept. Both dressed down in tailored suits, Ferragamos and Stacy Adams. But when lounging leisurely, Ali preferred urban sporting wear. Ali was the gangster; Jabbar the gentlemen. Both of them were workout fanatics. Jabbar was taller at 6 feet, 3 inches, approximately 200 pounds, very sculpted physique. Ali stood around 5 feet, 8 inches, 180 pounds, very muscular and toned. Both wore bald heads with neatly trimmed mustaches and beards; Ali wore glasses. Caesar had depicted them "The Executioners." Although they were now living a different life trying to be the best Muslims they could be, they still emanated quiet danger. Together, they were a formidable trio.

Inside the Rover was cool. The weather was nasty; the sky gloomy with dark, ominous, gray clouds waiting for the command from God to release its nature upon the earth. Caesar didn't know if the weather was the same in Great Falls where they were headed, as it was in Billings, but it didn't matter, he didn't have any immediate plans other than relaxation.

"So, how's my lil' bro, Azeez?" Jabbar asked Caesar by middle name. He didn't take his eyes off the road as he piloted the vehicle along the mountainous roads.

Caesar sighed, "He's hanging in there, akhi. He's built like us. He told me to tell you two what's up and hold it down. You know he's crazy about you two cats," he laughed.

Jabbar and Ali were like big brothers to Don.

"Yeah, I know. I miss my lil' bro already," Jabbar said sympathetically.

They ended up lost in their own thoughts. The loss had affected them all a great deal.

Caesar dozed. When he woke, they were on the 1,500 acres of land he owned, meandering up the dirt road to his ranch house. By the grace of Allah, it appeared as if the rain had already passed them by; remnants of its existence prevalent. The grass was wet, the dirt was soggy along with all the foliage that surrounded it. The moisture intensified the smell of the forestry. He never got enough of the scenery of this place with its sprawling fields of green pastures, grazing livestock, other forms of wild life and beautiful mountains that made up the horizon in every direction. Allah's Majesty was so enthralling! He thanked Him daily for allowing him to possess such fortune and be able to enjoy the splendidness of it all while praising His name.

"You brother's want to offer congregational salat together or y'all need to handle some other things?" Ali inquired as they ambled away from the Rover towards the beautiful house that was made of log wood and glass.

The house was two-and-a-half stories with tall ceilings and windows. Windows were everywhere. The house was 50 percent log wood and 50 percent glass.

"Nah, we'll catch Maghrib together, Insha'Allah. I need to do some personal things first," Jabbar replied. He needed to use the restroom and shower because he wasn't too pure at the moment from an earlier escapade with a promiscuous white chick that lived about 45 minutes away from the ranch. He shook his head dismayingly. He'd have to repent and ask Allah to forgive him. But man, did he love sluttish white women, he thought with a bemusing grin plastered on his face as he headed to the shower.

###

It had been over 2 years since Caesar had last been out to the ranch. The reason he chose the ranch for a place of solitude out of all the property he owned around the country was because it was where he and Don had spent a major part of life together. Don loved this ranch. It was the second piece of property that he purchased outside of South Carolina after his home in Charleston.

The ranch wasn't extravagant inside. It possessed a large living room with no chairs nor couches, just green, plush carpeting with several larger prayer rugs laying about. Colorful wall rugs with surah's from the Quran inscribed on them hung on the walls. A 63 inch plasma TV hung on one wall. There was a kitchen, a den, a game room, a personal study where he conducted a lot of business from that consisted of a computer, printer, scanner and fax machine that sat on top of an expensive titanium table; a soft cushioned swivel chair sat in front of it. Two file cabinets sat at the back of the study along with a bookshelf with books on business by Napoleon Hill, Robert Kiyosaki and many others.

There were also Islamic books, and books on black nationalist's and activist's throughout history, such as: Harriett Tubman, Rosa Parks, Asatta Shakur, Angela Davis, William Edward Burghardt DuBois, Marcus Garvey, Carter G. Wilson, Huey P. Newton – the collection went on. But most of all he was in love with Harriett Tubman; the truest African American that ever existed! So monumental she was, and still was to this day, she was depicted the "female Moses" because she led her people out of bondage just as Moses led the Jews out of servitude of Pharaoh.

The entire ranch was carpeted in green, which was the favorite color of the Prophet Muhammed. The ranch also possessed a prayer room that possessed a large window that gave a panoramic view of acre's upon acres of grazing field and meadows that ran in to mountains where the sun set. It was beautiful. Other than that, the house had 2 full baths, 3 half baths. It had 3 bedrooms along with other minute features that was really useless to Caesar. A lot of it was for show and tell.

He headed to one of the half baths, made ablution and headed to his prayer room to make up the prayers he had missed along with the one that was in.

###

After Caesar had offered his prayers, he changed the suit he wore into more comfortable attire. He had informed Ali and Jabbar that he was going out to a part of the ranch he depicted "Sabr". Itmeant "Patience" in Arabic.

There were many things around the ranch. There was a stable of thorough-bred horses; there was a shooting range; there was a go-cart/four-wheeler and dirt bike trail, a hiking trail, an in-door gym and pool; there were canoes and kayaks for the river, and the ranch possessed all the necessary accessories to enjoy all of its activities.

With his hands stuffed inside the gray, Jordan sweat pants he wore, he headed outside the house through the front door. His feet was cladded in a pair of orange, black, and gray Mountain Gear boots. He headed away from the house towards the wood line where a neatly trimmed path ran through the forestry.

A woodpecker banged its beak into a tree rapturously while other unidentified birds chirped jovially and could be heard as their bodies fluttered through the wet trees. The shrill cry of a hawk pierced the skies.

After about a 15-minute hike the path ended and opened into an acre gap cut into a rectangular shape in the middle of the forest. The rectangle was divided into 2 sections. Each section

30 feet deep. Over the middle between the 2 boxed in environments was a sleek, steel and titanium bridge for the sole purpose of watching the man-made habitat below it on both sides. One side contained a family of 6 lions; one male, 2 female adults, and 3 cubs. There was a field of tall grass, trees were sporadically spread around the ground, a pond, and large boulders of mountain rock were sporadically sprawled across acres of the habitat. The lions laid about lazily. The 3 cubs laid in apparent exhaustion, from playing, on top of a large boulder. They looked up at Caesar uninterestingly and plopped their head back on the boulder simultaneously.

On the right side of the bridge was a pit that housed Nigerian crocodiles. Half of the pit was grass and muddy dirt and the back half of the pit was a body of dark, murky, salt water.

Aware of his presence, the crocs slithered into the water instinctively as if he was prey. Surreptitiously they stalked him, waiting for him to slip so they could tear his ass apart! He loved these animals because of the wide range of wisdom in their nature. The lion and the crocodile was the most treacherous killers. They weren't untamed, murderous renegades; they killed without any forms of malice. The act was for one purpose and that purpose was survival. Other than their beloved Prophet, these 2 creatures was the only things in existence he strove to emulate. Profound wisdom was in these creatures treachery and patience.

At the very beginning of the bridge was a black marble sign that read: Sabr (Patience); it was engraved in gold. Below this was a verse out of a surah in the Quran called Al-Imran: 3:200; it was engraved in Arabic. It read: "O you who believe! Be patient (persevere through what befalls you in this world in Allah's cause); encourage each other to patience vying in it with one another and outdoing all others in it; and observe your duties to Allah in solidarity, and keep from disobedience to Allah in due reverence for Him and piety, so that you may prosper in both worlds."

Among the creatures of this world, human beings was the only creatures besides the jinn that were given free-will to choose between right and wrong. All other creatures were instinctive and totally submissive to the decree of which they had been created. But man was rebellious, egotistical and arrogant, and due to this nature and his desire for wickedness, he was tried by Allah in his patience. Patience was steadfastness in carrying out the obligations and refraining from prohibitions, resisting the temptations to sin of the evil commanding, carnal soul and Satan; enduring disaster, and showing no haste in pursuing those of one's hopes or plans that required a stretch of time to achieve. This was what made the attributes of the lion and the crocodile so amazing and rich in wisdom. Totally submissive to what they were created for and patient throughout the calamities they were faced with. They hunted to survive; after hours of stalking prey that only escaped them in the end, they didn't grunt, groan or thrash about in frustration. They simply waited for the next opportunity to hunt again as if what they experienced hadn't happened at all. And even if they were subjected to famine in the land that led to starvation they still didn't complain and curse Allah or the day they were born. After trying to find sustenance to no avail they readily accepted their fate and welcomed death with forbearance and fortitude. They weren't rambunctious. These creatures were true Muslims.

It also unnerved him how people had misconstrued what a Muslim was. The word Muslim was a two-pronged Arabic term that translated, "the one that submitted to the Decree of God." So, technically, the tree's and everything else in the universe that submitted to God's decree was Muslims. Plain and simple.

When Don was a kid growing up he would sit with him for hours on this very same bridge explaining the nature of these very same creatures in how he should learn from them and heed the wisdom in their nature. This had been the sole purpose of him obtaining these animals in particular. They had never owned any other animals pet wise. Caesar had been infatuated with these two creatures ever since he was a young boy. Their viciousness and deathly silence when executing a kill intrigued him. There used to be times when he'd watch the discovery channel, he'd root in anticipation for the lion to strike a zebra when he thought it should have and would call it all sorts of derogatory names and then – BAM! – it would strike and he'd be breathless at how it killed. He had always been attentive, and as he grew older he began to understand the animals and the importance of patience.

Caesar's father had died in prison when he was 9 years old; he had robbed an inmate and was killed in retaliation. His mother had died of ovarian cancer several years later and his grandmother on his mother's side had raised him; his mother had ben her only child. His family on his father's side had never shown him any concerns so he grew up oblivious of their existence. The house he had on the Macon in North Charleston had belong to his grandmother. She had left it to him when she died at the age of 73 from heart failure a week after he graduated high school. Soon after, to make ends meet, he began distributing cocaine, met Sterling at a local club, told her his plans and ideas – she was opposed to him becoming her pimp – but after falling in love with him, she allowed him to be just that and this was how they survived up until his decision to join the U.S. Marine Corps.

He enjoyed the solitude and tranquility that the environment always seemed to envelope him in as he reminisced.

After realizing that he wasn't going to be something to eat, the crocs began leaving the water and laid on the bank continuing to watch him predatorily. The lions were asleep. The animals were fed from his livestock. Someone was paid from the

Department of Wildlife to ensure that they were fed accordingly. They ate buffalo, deer, wild hogs, wild turkeys and other wild game.

A streak of lightning flashed across the sky above; he could tell that it was about to rain once again. The sun couldn't be seen because of the weather but he could tell that it was beginning to set. it was almost time for Maghrib, which was the fourth prayer of the day. It was offered right after the setting of the sun.

"Be patient son," he muttered as he turned towards the way he came and started toward the path that would lead him back to the ranch house.

Chapter Four

Ogeechee Correctional Institution

Red Top, South Carolina

February 7, 2014

The ride from the Evaluation Center in Columbia, South Carolina to Ogeechee Correctional Institution had been one of excruciating dimension for Don. Along with 33 other inmates that had been classified to the prison with him, they rode in silence for two-and-a-half hours on a brown in color prison bus with leg restraints; their hands were shackled to a chain wrapped tightly around their waist.

The bus had rumbled on annoyingly; the many cages, gates and padlocks on the bus clattered from the power of its engine and the cracks and bumps along the dilapidated highways. The bus had been silent the entire trip as they all thought about what lie ahead as all but a few of them were first time felons.

The prison system in South Carolina had been over crowded for 2 decades and the state had been trying to get the government to give them funding to build more prisons but the government was against it because the state was already flooded with institutions that it could barely run adequately as it was. But the demand for space had become too much of a necessity because of the rapturous rate of men being locked up and sentenced to serve outrageous sentences for petty crimes. Inmates around the state had filed so many lawsuits against the state for housing them in unfit living conditions, cruel and unusual punishment and had sent so many pictures to news stations from the phones they smuggled, the state nor the government could no longer hide and prolong the poverty they'd subjected the prisoners to without doing something about it so the government had finally gave in about 8 years ago giving them the funds to build a state-of-the-art facility which was the largest in the state. The prison housed men and women. It comprised of 2 separate yards with 10 dorms that housed 600 inmates each. The yard for the women had 4 of the 10 dorms and the yard for the men had the remaining 6. it was huge!

But unlike the other prisons in the state, nothing could be thrown over the fence by the friends of ambitious inmates attempting to smuggle contraband. The concrete walls around the prison were enormous and towered towards the sky. There were 8 gun towers and armed guards inside them 24/7 around the prison. Although security was tight it did not negate the fact that there were many other ways of smuggling contraband for the inmates. Ogeechee Correctional Institution had its fair share of corruption; it was just on a more mediocre level than the many other prisons around the state.

The prison got its name from the Ogeechee river that started in Florida and ran all the way up to Georgetown, South Carolina. it was about 10-15 minutes outside Charleston's city limits in the middle of an area in a country called Red Top.

The bus lurched as it halted at the entrance gate of the prison and a 50-ish, caucasian brunette came out of the guard shack and fetched one of the roll-aroundground mirrors that leaned up against the shack. The mirror was designed to give the guard a view of the bottom of the bus to ensure that no one, nor anything, was entering or existing the institution that wasn't supposed to.

The woman started towards the bus and began circling it as the two officers that drove the bus grabbed the two shotguns and pistols they carried along with a crate containing the files of the new arrivals. They went inside the shack to hand it all over for processing; the guns would be returned to them upon departure because they weren't allowed beyond the gate.

After about 20 minutes of waiting in the bus that was becoming irritably hot, the officer's returned and started the engine; it rumbled to life as the gate slid open.

Don looked at the enormity of the prison in awe as the bus traversed the paved road around the many concrete buildings. He couldn't see anything save buildings, and from where the bus had moved so far, none of the buildings had any windows. As he had scrutinized his surroundings he came to the realization that he was only seeing the outside of this particular part of the institution. This area was more of an intake and out-take area; not the main part of the facility.

The bus pulled up and stopped on the side of the paved road in front of a windowless building that had a set of grey, steel doors with no door knob or handle. The building was connected to an array of other buildings that went beyond his line of sight.

"Alright, gentleman..." One of the transportation guards stood at the gate of the bus that separated the passengers from the cockpit. He wore rainbow tinted glasses. He had an up-tempo gait and wasn't big in size at all. "When I call your name, come on and lets get this show on the road so y'all can get situated. I know you're hungry so we're going to get you inside as quick as possible," he stated as he unlocked the gate. He whimsically chewed a wad of gum, flipping it about in his mouth as he began calling names from the pad he held.

It was about time, Don thought. the restraints were killing him and had already made deep impressions in the flesh of his wrists as it pressed against the bone. His stomach was turning upside down, rumbling more than the bus had. He was famished.

The driver had departed the bus and was unshackling prisoner's as they stepped from the can. Guys stretched in apparent relief of being relieved of the discomfort of the iron chains.

"Donatello McFadden..."

Phew! It was about friggin time, he thought! He got up, ignored the ache in his body, and penguin walked towards the front of the bus.

After they all had been unshackled they stood in an uneven line. Two officers wearing dark brown army fatigue pants, boots and tan uniform shirts materialized from the back of the building through the steel, gray door to intercept them and escort them to a holding cell where they would be for a couple of hours.

There were benches inside the holding cell but after long hours of sitting on them they became tiresome and uncomfortable. The officers were aware of this and used it at times as a tool for disciplining. Since it was so many of them, they had been divided and placed in 3 different cells.

"Y'all boys be easy. We're going to get y'all situated and bring y'all something to eat." The officer that spoke was one of the two that had escorted them. He was a young black male around 29 years old.

"Alright," some of the inmates responded listlessly. The rest of them just looked at him like a foreign object that didn't interest them.

The young black guard rolled a cart back through about 30 minutes later. It carried several stacks of styrofoam trays; he began passing them out.

Don grabbed his tray and reseated himself where he sat in a corner at the back of the cell. He lifted the lid off the tray and was somewhat surprised that the food didn't resemble slop as he'd seen in prison movies. The trays contained macaroni and cheese, one ground beef patty, a side of corn mixed with green lima beans, 2 yeast rolls and a bland piece of cake. Although the food wasn't as great as it looked it got the job done. And, it was better than the food he ate inside the county jail for the past 8 months. They were all given an orange Juice Train that came in pint cartons. Out of the entire set-up, the juice had been the most refreshing!

As they sat inside the holding cell, inmate workers and other officers and case workers moved about purposefully; they could be seen through the large barred window of the holding tank. Some of the inmates stood to the window and watched on as they ate and others began to complain in anxiety and stress of wanting to get where they were headed so they could shower and rest.

Don had outstanding stamina so he wasn't too bothered. He waited patiently as he watched several attractive women, black and white, walk past the holding cell through Operations. He really couldn't believe that such beautiful women would work inside such a hardcore environment. They couldn't possibly have boyfriends or husbands. What man in his right mind would allow his lady to work under such extreme conditions? The answer was beyond him. But what he did know was that no woman of his would dare!

Laughter and loud voices could be heard echoing throughout the cells and walkie-talkies clattered with coded jargon of requests and orders.

It was getting late in the afternoon and was almost time for the workers of the main administration to clock out: 4 o'clock.

The young black officer reappeared with a stack of small slips of paper. "Listen up, fellas. When I start calling your names come on up and grab one of these slips. On them is the dorm and shit that y'all are classified to. As soon as y'all walk out the door," he pointed towards a steel door with a little square window that led to the main yard, "it's a window to the right. Stop by there and show this slip along with your ID and you'll be issued cosmetics. All the other extra shit y'all may want that the prison don't supply would be purchased from the canteen with your personal funds. Other than that you're assed out," he stated in an "it's not my fault" manner and began calling off the names handing out the slips.

So far, no one had seemed to recognize him as he had loss a considerable amount of weight in the county jail from a bit of stress and not being able to eat how he was used to. He looked ahead at the enormous compound and couldn't believe the size of the dorms and everything else around it. To say that it was a penitentiary the architectural design of it was flattering with it's many tree's, flower beds that sprung gorgeous roses and flowers; and the walkways were perfectly manicured as it meandered and stretched for what seemed like miles. Very few people could be seen walking around the compound. It was around 5 o'clock in the evening and all the major activity of the rush hours had been long over with. Several guards stood around the compound at different posts as it was dinner time. The dorms were released one at a time for the chow hall; inmates were already inside eating. There weren't any windows on the huge cube structure of the cafeteria. Only traces of activity and life that came from the building was the steam that billowed from the exhaust shafts on top of the roof.

The dorm Don was assigned to was located at the far end of the compound; he had another 5 minute walk before he reached it. The dorms were named after different areas in Charleston. The one he'd been assigned to was called Summerville. The others were: James Island, Goose Creek, Mount Pleasant, West Ashley and Hollywood; he looked at the names on the signs as he passed the buildings. Several of the inmates he came with trailed behind him as they were assigned to the same dorm and the others branched off towards the dorms they passed.

The uniforms that all of the prisoners wore state-wide were powder blue, two-piece sets with buttonless slip-over shirts and pants with elastic waist bands. The canteen sold a variety of shoes in solid white from Nikes, New Balance, Converse, boots and other soft sole shoes for people with bad feet. But at the moment, Don wore the white, state issued bobo's that he'd been given at the Evaluation Center.

He neared Summerville with his white mesh bag containing a blanket, 2 sets of sheets, 2 more sets of uniforms, shower shoes, 2 extra pairs of boxers and socks, 2 wash cloths and towels, several razors, and state issued cosmetics. He pulled the door open at the dorms entrance and entered the lobby. It smelled of fresh floor wax and bleach.

An inmate clerk approached Don and the other 7 inmates that came along with him that stood inside the lobby. "What's good, fellas?" The clerk greeted. "Y'all follow me."

The clerk led them to an office with a sign on the window of the door that read: Dorm Lieutenant. Don peered through the window of the door before the clerk had opened it and noticed a huge, burly black man with a bald head sitting behind the desk dozing in and out of sleep. He looked at them as they entered. His name tag read: Lieutenant Bell. He scratched his head and the side of his face as if he was under the influence of morphine.

His belt was unbuckled and the tail of his uniform shirt hung from his pants unprofessionally.

"These are our new arrivals, Bell," the clerk stated. He went to the back of the office to a file cabinet and retrieved a manila folder.

Bell nodded affirmation and his eyes closed as he dozed back in his stupor. Right then, Don realized that the lieutenant suffered from narcolepsy. He was amazed that he'd been allowed employment! The clerk looked at them and laughed.

"Y'all boy's that's just Bell. He's good people. One of the best lieutenants we got around this place. As long as you ain't doing nothing outrageous he don't care, just be discreet about your business," the clerk stated while he filled out the paper work on the clip board he now held.

Bell began snoring.

Some of the new-comers snickered. Don just looked on incredulously. And what did the clerk mean by "just be discreet about your business?" What business could they possibly have that was private in prison? He guess he would soon find out because this was all new to him. He didn't have the slightest idea of prison life or what went on besides tattooing and homosexuality and none of those things would be going down with him at all!

Very faint noises could be heard drifting from the 4 wings of the dorm. The building was very clean and well kept. The floors were polished and the walls were freshly painted.

After the clerk had finished recording their names and information to the dorms roster, he handed them back the slips and told them that they were free to go to their wings to do what they wanted.

“Keep y’all ass out of trouble!” Bell barked before they departed his office. His eyes had opened briefly.

Don shook his head in amazement! He was assigned to C-Wing. He ambled towards the door. Several inmates stood in front of the door on the opposite side yelling for the officer that worked the wing to come open the door. Moments later a light skin complexion female appeared and the first thing came to Don’s mind as she unlocked the door was “another attractive woman?”

she looked at him as he walked on the wing and he handed her the slip of paper. She took it and looked at it. “You’re on the third tier in room Four-O-Seven-C, Mr. McFadden.”

“Alright,” he responded and ambled towards the nearest stairway; there were 3 different flights of stairs. The wings had 3 different tiers.

Inmates watched him as he headed up the steps. He was a new-comer and inmates wanted to see if they knew him or recognized him. Some of them had beef from the past and needed to know who were amongst them. Some of them wore short pants and T-shirts. Some of them were shirtless, showing off muscular physiques and tattoo’s.

The wings also had a phone room with 8 phones for collect calls that was located on the first floor. Another room possessed 6 TV’s. There was a dayroom for games on each tier along with a prayer room for the Muslims and another room was reserved for multi purposes. The barber shop was in the lobby of the dorm and was large enough for 8 barbers to cut at once.

As he ascended the steps he noticed that he was being eyed by inmates that leaned up against the railing of the top tier balcony and some stood in the threshold of their doors. Surprisingly, none of the stares that he had seen had been hardened or threatening.

"What's up, player?" An inmate greeted that leaned up against the wall listening to his walkman.

"Maintaining," Don replied in stride and continued to look up at the room numbers above the doors. As he rounded the tier headed to his room he was greeted by some of the inmates and ignored by others.

He finally reached 407-C. He peered through the small window on the door and then pulled it open. By the property inside the cell on the bottom bunk he knew he had a cell mate but he wasn't inside the room. He entered the neatly kept cell and closed the door behind him. Momentarily he looked around the room. There was 2, steel, double door lockers that was bolted to the wall side by side about 3 feet above the floor. There was a porcelain toilet and sink; above the sink was a large mirror. A wooden table and chair with a red back and seat sat at the back of the room on the far wall. Above the table was a nice size window that gave a decent view of the yard. Several issues of various magazines were neatly stacked on top of the table along with a clear plastic cup. His roommate's bed was neatly made military style with the corners of the sheet tucked at 45 degree angles. Other than this there was nothing else inside the room. Other rooms that he had passed, that he briefly glanced inside of, were filled with other accessories like TV's and food items. He concluded that his cellmate was less fortunate.

He sat his bag under the table, slipped off his shoes and neatly placed them under the bed, jumped up on the top bunk and laid back and relaxed on the bare mattress. He wanted to shower but he would rest first. He quickly slipped into oblivion.

###

Don woke up disoriented. The room was dark. Faint light swam into the room through the room windows. He had to piss and his bladder strained from the fact. Beneath him he could hear a light breathing that sounded like soft whistles of breath. He laid on his back looking into the dark shadows of the ceiling as his mind slowly registered where he was. He realized that he had slept the remainder of the day away and it was now lock down time. The doors wouldn't open again until morning.

He sat up quietly and got out of bed, careful not to disturb his sleeping roommate. He must have really been tired or his roommate had taken special precaution not to disturb him because he hadn't heard when he came in. He wondered what time it was.

He fetched his flip flops out his mesh bag, slipped them on and walked to the door and peered out the window into the quietude of the wing scanning the walls for a clock. He spotted one high above and it read: 12:03 am.He yawned and headed to the toilet, pulled out his penis, that had hardened due to his dire need to urinate, and began flushing the toilet as he relieved himself. His roommate stirred in the bed, grunted, but did not wake. He didn't know who his roommate was. He didn't even know what color he was as he slept with the covers over his head.

After he finished relieving himself he cleaned up behind himself; wet his hands at the sink and swiped them over the front area of his pants to cleanse any impurities that may've come in contact with him from the urine. The Prophet had legislated this for all Muslims. And after defecation one had to properly clean themselves. Cleanliness was godliness and the true Muslim had the best etiquette in hygiene amongst mankind.

He headed back to his bed. He still slept coverless on the bare mattress. The room was cool but it didn't bother him. He was immune to climatic changes from the different places he lived.

He would shower in the morning when he woke and get himself and his things in order. He had about 5 grand in his institutional trust fund so he would stock up on food and purchase any and everything he was allowed to buy. He would most definitely make his stay as comfortable as possible. He'd find a canteen list later on in the day.

As he laid on his back with his eyes closed, hands clasped across his abdomen, he thought about his father, Ali and Jabbar, and as always, he thought about Fedora, the girl he'd been accused of killing. He had really liked her and, she was fun to be with. Although he would have never wedded her because of herpromiscuity, they were still cool. He wondered who had killed her. All of his friends in this particular circle had abandoned him and he had received many ridiculing and hateful mail correspondence's from them and it had hurt him because the only friends he had outside of Ali, Jabbar, Al-Salam and his father, had forsaken him for what they believed he had so savagely done. But all in all, even though it struck him painfully, he understood. There were many female companions that he had scattered around the country from his travels with his father and they wrote from time to time, he even called from time to time but none of them really meant anything to him.

He drifted off in the darkness of his thoughts and slipped into a dream. Inside the dream he was at his father's ranch in Montana sitting inside the habitat of lions they had. The sky was dark; it was a crescent moon and a star twinkled beside it. He sat with a wool blanket wrapped around him covering his nakedness as the 3 cubs slept at his feet. The male lion and the two female lion's perched next to him proactively, ever so watchful as their eyes glowed in the night. Fear was something that did not seize him. Actually, he felt safe and comfortable in the den of lions just as Daniel had when he'd been thrown inside the den to be torn to smithereens in the Bible but his forbearing trust in God had made the lions submit to him as if he was one of them.

Soundly, he slept.

###

The door to the room was unlocked. The sound of the steel lock turning over caused Don to open his eyes and look towards the door. The door opened and a dark skin complexion woman stood in the doorway. Another woman! He couldn't believe it. He thought he was still dreaming until she yammered rambunctiously with no regard for the quietude of the dorm.

"Get your bad ass up and get ready for work Cedric before I pull your skinny ass out that bunk," she laughed and pushed the door close.

"Crazy ass bitch," Don heard his roommate drawl annoyed. He looked out the room window and saw that it was still dark outside and realized that he hadn't been asleep no more than a couple of hours. He could hear the noisy broad as she opened other doors around the tier as she woke other inmates. He didn't know where his roommate was heading for work so early but since it wasn't any of his business he closed his eyes as his roommate got up and silently moved around the dimly lit cell preparing to head out to work. He didn't even glance at him; he turned over on his side facing the wall and went back to sleep.

Chapter Five

Ogeechee Correctional Institution

Red Top, South Carolina

February 7, 2014 – Friday Morning

Don stepped from the phone room on the bottom floor and overheard a very vehement argument transpiring further down from where he was. He looked in the direction of the argument and saw a bunch of inmates aggressively approaching the room where about 20 guys were already gathered. So many of them were talking at once he couldn't decipher what was being said. He'd seen situations like this in county jail and knew that a fight would most likely ensue, but what he didn't know was, where he now reside, was beyond anything he'd ever witnessed on TV nor the little 8 month stint inside the county jail. Unbeknownst to him, Ogeechee Correctional Institution was one of the top three most vicious prisons in the state.

As hard as he tried to mind his own business and head back up to his room to gather his things for a shower, the altercation kept drawing his attention. The entire wing of the dorm was on the brink of eruption right before his eyes! Other inmates from the top and middle tiers came pouncing from their rooms and skipped down the stairs towards the commotion like baboons and apes and before he could properly get his footing in perspective to ascend the stairs, almost everyone that had their hands stuffed in their pants pulled out various sharpened steel, and other blunt objects, and he realized right as everyone started assaulting one another that they had been clutching weapons the entire time!

Amazed by the ferociousness of the melee, he stopped on the stairs and watched the bestiality of the fight as they all bashed and stabbed one another relentlessly! Some of the guys fought one-on-one; some ganged up on others with savage hostility, and others ran while being chased around the wing in attempt to escape the vicious onslaught of their pursuers. Some of them were caught and Don watched as one of them fell while trying to run up the stairs. The inmate that chased him jumped on top of him, sat on him, and began plunging the huge knife he possessed into him! There was no officer on the wing.

It seemed as if they'd been butchering one another forever before the guard finally appeared on the wing. Shift had changed earlier so this was another one of the many women that worked at the facility. She was a red bone amazon. She stood about 6 feet, 2 inches; very curvaceous. She wasn't gorgeous but she wasn't ugly either. A look of disbelief washed over her face as she canvased the wing. Unbeknownst to Don, all the bloodshed and commotion wasn't the cause of the dread that plastered her face, but one that was from the guilt of being the reason behind it all. He watched as she grabbed the walkie-talkie from her hip and radioed for help.

Don didn't know where all the guards had appeared from so quickly but he could have sworn that their response time had been under a minute flat which made him wonder for a fleeting moment if they were already on stand-by and prepared for this incident.

When the guards ran on the wing some of the inmates scattered and began throwing weapons while others continued to pound and assault their victims.

"TO YOUR ROOMS FELLAS! NOW!" The dorm lieutenant yelled, shirt still untucked haphazardly, belt still unbuckled. Don wondered if it was just his style. But what he wasn't, was affected by his syndrome; he was very much alert!

Don headed to his room promptly along with other by-standing inmates as he watched more officers storm on the wing and began breaking up the scuffles that continued. The inmates that resisted in violent rebellion were gassed and tased. Slowly, the guards began to gain control of the wing.

A team of nurses had arrived with wheel chairs and gurneys; a helicopter could be heard landing outside the dorm on the yard. Some of the inmates was severely wounded and would need immediate medical assistance.

Don got to his room and closed the door behind himself as guards were aggressively shoving inmates in cells locking the doors. From his room window he could see where he'd witnessed one of the inmates brutally stabbed: he was dead. He looked over to the room on the second tier where he had seen the killer escape to and for a brief moment they locked eyes. Don looked away. He didn't care. It wasn't any of his business anyway. But he did think that it was smart of the killer to be calm and act as if he didn't have anything to do with the altercation instead of acting like an intractable ass and get caught up. He didn't know if the killer would successfully get away with the murder, but what he did know was that, if it depended on him revealing this fact it would never be solved. He began coughing and sneezing. The fumes form the gas irritated his sinus.

About 16 inmates had been escorted out of the dorm in handcuffs, drenched in blood soaked uniforms. 5 were carried out on stretchers and rushed to the medical infirmary or the helicopter, and the one lifeless corpse remained of the slain inmate.

Don had had enough of the hysterics and needed to allow his brain to compute all that had transpired in the last 20 minutes or so.

"THE YARD IS CLOSED! THE YARD IS CLOSED!" A female voiced boomed over the institutions loud speaker. "ALL INMATES REPORT TO YOUR LIVING QUARTERS! THE YARD IS CLOSED UNTIL FURTHER NOTICE!" She reported thrice. With this order all movement would cease for precautionary purposes and every inmate worker and school attendant would report back to their dorms.

Don looked at all the knives and other steel weaponry scattered about the wing. Blood puddles was everywhere along with innumerable, bloody footprints. Inmates that came off the yard gagged when they entered the wing from the potent gas. They were ushered towards their rooms and told to stand by their doors until an officer came and let them inside. He still had yet to meet his roommate. All he knew was that it was someone named Cedric. At least it was what that broad had called him when she woke him for work.

He walked away from the door and sat down in the chair at the table and introspectively looked out the window as officers and inmates moved about towards dorms. The helicopter had already departed.

Outside looked beautiful; the sky was clear and bright and it made the ugliness below it unreal. It wasn't even lunch time. It was around 10 am. He had missed breakfast, which was around 5 o'clock, so he was starving. He had got out of bed as soon as the doors were opened at 8 o'clock and had planned on calling his father to let him know where he'd been located, which he had done, then he was going to take a shower, get cleaned up, and go talk to the female guard about what he needed to do to order accessories and canteen. But all of this had been sabotaged. Momentarily, he pondered the types of beef that could have warrant such brutal retaliation.

The sound of the door being unlocked broke his reverie just as he situated the chair to lean his head against the wall. It was his roommate.

"Peace," Don greeted him hospitably as he entered the cell.

"What it is, town?" He replied with his back facing Don. He looked out the window at the lifeless corpse of his homeboy's body. It laid sprawled on the steps of the second tier. "Damn town, what happened in this bitch?" HIs voice hinted solicitude.

"I don't really know," Don answered from where he sat. "I came out the phone room after talking to my father and all hell broke loose."

"Man, that's my homie laying dead on thosesteps, town," Cedric said ruefully.

"Yeah?" Don returned.

"Word. I told him not to get involved in that shit with those niggas behind that bitch!" Cedric spat.

Don wasn't one to pry anyone for information. He didn't know what "bitch" his roommate was referring to and really didn't care so he didn't inquire. He remained quiet and cool.

"What's your name, town?" Cedric asked, his back still facing Don.

"Don."

"'You from Charleston?" Cedric asked distastefully.

Don caught the insidious retort in the question. He'd heard how people from other geographical locations in the state disliked dudes from Charleston. Why? No one had really given him a plausible explanation other than the way they talked, which was preposterous to him. If there was any other reasons he wasn't aware of them. But what he did know was that Charlestonians were a people of sui generis with a dialect comparable to tropical islanders. "Yeah," he replied proudly but not arrogantly. He couldn't see his roommate's face because his back was still turned to him but he was sure, for some reason, that his expression wasn't pleasant. He didn't care.

Don watched him from where he sat and instantly disliked the energy that his spirit emanated. He was trouble. He didn't bother to tell Don where he was from or who he was, but Don could tell that he was probably from Columbia by the way he talked because he spent a lot of time up there also. He had also been informed while in county jail that Columbia was Charleston's arch nemesis along with other counties. As he saw it, he was in the room with the enemy. But as long as Cedric remained cool and respected him, he'd respect him also. He wasn't judgmental and would not partake in such simple mindedness. But he didn't like the capricious air that permeated from him. The devil and his army of diabolical jinn were formidable creatures. Don knew all too well that the devil would surely take advantage of the access he would have through his roommate to create chaos and confusion so he would beware until he could better his living arrangements.

About 20 minutes later don watched as Cedric pulled the white uniform shirt and T-shirt over his head and tossed them across his bed rail. Cedric's body was covered with tattoo's ranging from portraits of children to various types of writing and graffiti. He was sculpted and toned but Don could tell that his tone wasn't due to exercise but because of his 160 pound slenderness and youthfulness. He stood about 5 feet, 11 inches. He figured Cedric to be around his age. He had a walnut complexion and sported a low cut Caesar.

Cedric plopped down on his bed and laid back after kicking off his boots. "We're going to be locked down for a second so you might as well grab a snickers, town."

"It's all good." Don looked at him with dull interest as he – Cedric – plucked his fingernails.

"How much time do you have, town?"

"Life."

"Damn, town." Cedric looked over at Don momentarily and returned his attention back to his nails. "Look like you' handling it like a soldier, though. That's what's up..."

"Those magazines on the table are old but you can check them out if you want to. I don't have much shit around this bitch but the tables always turn. You hear me, town?"

"Yeah. You're right about that, babe." For a moment Don wondered if he had misjudged his roommate but he trusted his intuition; the devil was indeed crafty and cunning.

"You play cards, town?" Cedric looked over at Don again.

"What kind?" Don asked.

"Casino."

"Yeah."

"What's up, want to do a lil' something? Cause shit, we're not coming back out these rooms for a week or two. We got a new Warden. This one isn't as power struck as the last one. As long as they get the people who was involved he won't drag us with lock down too long." Cedric got up and went inside his locker to retrieve the cards and tossed them to Don. He needed to do something to get his mind off the fact that his homeboy was laying dead on the other side of the door with his eyes open. "I wonder which one of those bitch ass niggas killed him. You saw that shit, town?"

"No. Not that part," Don lied. "I was still standing in front of the phone room and couldn't see through the crowd when it happened." Don took the cards from the box and began shuffling them. Although this was his first timein prison he wasn't stupid enough to get caught up in any you-say-I-say drama. He thought that his first day in prison was one hellafied way to start his ride!

Don dealt the cards and they conversed leisurely, mainly Cedric. Idle conversation did not interest him so he listened and answered when asked something. He could tell that Cedric was loquacious, which was another ungodly trait he learned his roommate had. A person that talked too much spoke measures about their character; for a person that talked more than they listened and think, minds were advocates of the devil. He also knew that Cedric could sense his novice in prison life and it gave him a false sense of superiority. Don quickly realized that his roommate was a follower; one that hadn't been exposed to anything other than strife and ignorance. He was easy to influence and as he continued to ramble on, Don realized that Cedric had took on the position of teacher and he was the student. He also had discovered that Cedric worked inside the cafeteria.

"So what are you down for, town?" Cedric asked in the same breath, not even putting a period at the end of his last sentence before starting anew.

"Murder," Don replied coolly as he picked up a pair of sevens he built.

"You did that shit, town?"

"No. And I prefer not to talk about it," Don stated flatly.

"Yeah, that's what they all say. And you don't got to be all uptight, town. I just asked you a question." Cedric responded defensively.

"Listen man, you don't know me and I don't know you. I don't deal with egotism. I just told you straight up. There was no pun intended but there was no other way to put it. I'm a man." Cedric looked up at him and Don could tell that he was being sized up. He laughed inwardly but remained aloof.

"You' cool town, you cool," Cedric stated after briefly assessing his new roommate.

Don knew that Cedric couldn't figure him out and it would stay that way. After several minutes of silence had passed they continued to play.

For the past 2 hours or so, the wing had been deathly quiet and now it echoed from walkie-talkies, nurses, guards and coroners. They were finally taking the body that had laid on the steps until the South Carolina Department of Law Enforcement Division had cleared it to be moved.

Cedric got up and went to the door. Don watched him as he crossed his chest and uttered: "Rest in peace, town," to his comrade.

Chapter Six

Ogeechee Correctional Institution

Red Top, South Carolina

February 24, 2014 – Monday/ 2 Weeks Later

Don sat on the rec field outside the dorm on a wooden bench drinking a can of cold, grape soda. Although the soda was not his brand of choice it was refreshing. He enjoyed the sweet taste and the light burn from the acid as the liquid cascaded down his throat. The weather was getting warm. They had been locked down for two and a half weeks. The state-wide shake down crew had come through and thoroughly shook down their dorm.

The rec field was very large and a major fraction of all 4 wings occupied it. It was mid-afternoon. It had been two days since they'd been off lockdown. The rec field consisted of two handball courts, two basketball courts, and a paved track circled the perimeter for inmates to walk and jog. Inmates worked out and some sat, and stood in groups chatting about past lives on the streets, ambitions and aspirations.

The dorm lieutenant had made a call and had gotten them

inside the canteen earlier so he had been able to get the necessary things he needed. He also ordered a TV, walkman, shoes, boots, electric shaver, hot pot, and a type writer. Including the $125 he spent on hygiene, food and snacks, he had spent around $700. The property he ordered would take between 2 weeks to a month to arrive at the facility. At least it was out of the way, he thought introspectively as he watched a familiar face approach. It was the same guy that killed his cellmate's comrade during the riot. He'd gotten away scot-free! He knew that this moment was inevitable, because ever since they had been off lockdown, the dude had been watching him quizzically. Oblivious of his intentions, and although his demeanor wasn't agonistic or threatening, Don knew his capability. He sat his soda on the bench and stoodto face him.

"Nah bruh, be easy babe; everything's peace," the dude that approached stated. "They call me 'Scramble Egg'," He extended his hands.

Don looked at the extended hand and quickly assessed the situation as he looked from the hand to the eyes that bore into him. The eyes were dark and strong, even intelligent. He didn't pick up any negative vibes so he reached out and shook hands with the dude with the absurd name. His grip was firm. "I'm Don."

"Cool, cool, that's what's up; but check it," Scramble Egg released the grip of the hand shake and sat down on the bench.

Don followed and picked up his grape soda, cradling it in both hands as he listened.

"Dawg," Scramble Egg commenced. "I know you just got here and shit and probably don't know too many people. I don't know if this is your first bid but from my perspective you kind of seem new to all of this. But to get straight to the point," he stared Don in the eyes. "I know you witnessed what happened that day –"

Don interjected: “Listen man, you’re right about me being new to all of this, but man, I am not a snitch. Your business is your business and it doesn’t concern me. I didn’t see anything so leave it at that. I don’t even want to talk about it.” he raised the can of soda to his lips.

“Say no more, babe.” For some reason Scramble believed him.

The both of them sat in silence on the bench watching the basketball game about 15 yards away from them until Scramble Egg broke the silence.

“Where are you from, bruh?” Scramble asked coolly.

“Charleston,” Don answered as he drained the remainder of the soda from the can and crinkled it and sat it beside him.

“Word!?” Scramble brightened. He could’ve tell that it was a good chance that Don was from Charleston because of his accent but was somewhat unsure because Don’s educated articulation diluted the thick, Gullah-Geechee dialect.

“Yeah,” Don looked at him and smiled. He already knew that Scramble Egg was from Charleston by the thickness of his accent. He was Gullah-Geechee to the core.

“I’m from Charleston, too.”

“I know.”

“What part of Charleston are you from?”

“Mount Pleasant. I grew up on the Isles of Palms.” Don looked at him and noticed the surprise in his eyes. “Yep, the little rich kids,” he added suavely. “My father is off the Macon in North Charleston, though. Serendipity changed his life forever so I was fortunate.”

"Seren -- what?" Scramble asked, perplexed by the word Don had used. "Man, I don't understand all those huge words and shit; what do that shit mean?"

"Serendipity is a sort of luck in continuously finding good fortune. But anyway, I'm not a lame ass dude so don't get it twisted." Don squinted his eyes against the brightness of the sun.

"Nah bruh, I know thoroughbreds when I see them. You' good..."

"So what do you have on the agenda for the rest of the day? I saw that you went to the canteen and tore that bitch down!"

"Hell yeah!" Don laughed in agreement. "I don't have anything planned, though. Hell, it isn't much to do.... Is there?" Don looked at him questioningly.

"You'd be surprise, lil' homie," Scramble answered hintingly.

Don caught it but didn't question into it.

"And on another note," Scramble started seriously. "You need to watch your roommate and keep your shit locked. That little motherfucker is a known thief. And, that little situation was a Columbia and Charleston thing so keep your guard up; you're guilty by association," he warned.

Don heeded the warning that only solidified what he had already concluded about his cellmate. He hoped that Cedric never attempted to violate him because he would surely break his face! "Thanks for the warning. But hey, man --" he smirked impishly, "how in the hell did you end up being called 'Scramble Egg'?"

Scramble snickered. "Drugs. When I was thirteen or so my big cousin was a king pin and he used to show me the ropes in how cocaine was properly cooked and the different things that could be done to it to stretch it as far as I could. I caught on quick and was good at it and he started calling me Scramble Egg and the name just stuck. Cat's around the hood picked up on it and it became who I am. Motherfucking name came up in all kind of niggas paper work with the Feds about seven years ago. I got lucky though, and escaped their fury but shit, I still ended up with a twenty-five year state bid for getting popped with a kilo. Pussy nigga set me up," Scramble reflected disdainfully.

"Damn," Don uttered. "How old are you?"

"Twenty-eight. How old are you?"

"Nineteen. I'll be twenty July twentieth."

"Damn, lil' homie, I thought you were a little older than that. You carry yourself on some grown man shit. That's what's up, lil' bruh. What the fuck got you cased up, though? Seems like you should be out in college doing some big shit."

"Murder," Don answered and, surprisingly to him, briefly summarized his situation.

"Damn, babe. So you're the one who's the son of the rich Muslim cat?" Scramble stated. He looked at Don as if seeing him for the first time and slowly began to recognize him as the dude he'd seen all over the news for the past year or so. "Damn bruh, it is you."

"Man, I didn't even do that shit." Don didn't know why he felt the need to justify this to Scramble but it just came out.

"I didn't say you did, bruh. I don't know why though, but I don't think that you did that shit unless you're a good ass actor at fronting."

"Nah, I really didn't do it, man."

"Just stay cool and fight that shit. I know you got some strong people's on your team so just hold your crown up and hold it in the road. Don't even stress that shit."

Don liked Scramble and could tell that they would have a promising relationship. Scramble stood around 6 feet, 2 inches; about 220 pounds solid. He was light skin complexioned with large lips and a wide nose. He sported a miniature afro. Don thought that he resembled Craig Mack.

"Are you fucking with that kitchen for dinner?" Scramble asked.

"Hell nah, man. I'm not eating that stuff if I don't have to," Don replied in opposition of the food the prison served.

"I can smell that," Scramble agreed. "We can get together and cook something together if you want. I don't fuck with that kitchen either."

The prisons canteen was stocked with a variety of foods: instant rice, can goods, pre-cooked meats and fish, et. al. It was like a miniature super market.

"I know you probably already ordered personal property and shit, but man I got an extra walkman that you can use until you get your shit; and I think I got a pair of boots that'll fit you. They're not new but they're not busted either. It'll hold you down until you get straight because those bobo's isn't nothing; especially when it rains. And those shit'll fuck up the arch in your foot. What size do you wear?" Scramble asked.

"A ten."

"Right on time. They're a ten and a half. Come on, let's go to my spot." Scramble got up and headed back inside the dorm to his room.

Don grabbed his shirt and the crinkled soda can and followed behind his new found comrade.

Don admired how Scramble had his room organized. It smelled like Somalian Rose, and it was cozy and laid back. The table was set up nicely with a large white towel covering it. Condiments were neatly placed: jalapeno peppers, mustard, mayonnaise, etc. A boom box played at a discreet volume. There were two TV's inside the room; one belonged to Scramble and the other belonged to his cellmate who laid under the covers on the top bunk comfortably as he watched Judge Joe Brown. He looked up at Don as they entered the cell and took one of the earbuds from his ear. The TV's were speakerless so the headphones was required. Don greeted him with peace.

"What's good, homie?" Scramble's roommate responded kindly.

"Cam, this is my lil' homie, Don; Don, this is my crazy cool ass roommate Cam, from Greenville. Both of y'all are good people so fuck with each other," Scramble introduced them.

Cam reached from the bed and gave Don a pound and turned his attention back to Judge Joe Brown.

"That nigga love that Judge shit," Scramble told Don about his roommate.

Don snickered and continued to look around the room at the beautiful greeting cards and pictures that Scramble and Cam had posted around the room. Under the table were stacks of hip hop urban novels. He had heard about them but had never read one before.

"Try them shit's on." Scramble handed Don the boots.

Don looked at them and thought they were brand new. He sat down, removed the bobo's from his feet and slid a foot in one of the boots. They fit perfectly. "I appreciate it. What do I owe you for these, man?" Don asked as he put his foot in the other boot and laced them up.

"Nothing lil' homie, you' straight. Good people do good things," Scramble answered as he fetched the walkman along with a set of batteries and earbuds. He handed the items to Don.

Don accepted them appreciatively and figured that he would find some kind of way to reciprocate the gratitude.

They sat inside Scramble's room and conversed as they listened to the radio. As they parlayed, Don noticed how different inmates kept stopping by the room and quickly figured that his new found comrade was "the man" in some form or fashion. "The man" of what, he didn't know but would find out soon enough. There were no secrets in prison – well, almost no secrets.

"But shed, lil' homie, I don't mean to interrupt our lil' vibe, but it'll be count time in about twenty minutes and I need to handle some business before they lock these doors. We'll get up later and chop it up."

"Alright, that's cool." Don gave him a pound and thanked him for all that he'd given him before he left and headed to his cell.

After the 15 minute warning had been announced for count, Scramble appeared at the window of Don's cell door.

Don sat on the top bunk with his legs leisurely dangling off the bed while he listened to a hip hop station on the radio thinking about life as usual. He looked towards the door and noticed that Scramble was there. He smiled and removed the earbuds from his ears, and with a hand, motioned for him to come in. "What's up, Scramble?"

Scramble entered the room with a stack of about 6 books. "I know you're probably bored in this bitch with that clown so I brought you some of these to read." He sat the books beside Don. "These shit will take you in my world, lil' bruh," he winked.

"World of the ballers."

"Appreciate it." Don picked up one of the books and looked at its cover. The name of the book was called "A Penitentiary Holy Book" and it was based on a true story. The publication company was familiar to him because it had been one of the first black owned lines to come out of Charleston. The others were by other popular urban novelist's. He sat them back down.

"When you finish those I got about a million more."

"Yeah, I know. I peeped your arsenal under the table."

"Some of them are good and some are whack. I don't even write books and I can write better stories than some of those shit. Some of them make authors look bad. I swear that urban book shit is a scam on some legal white collar shit. But those ones right there are hot!"

"I'll check them out for sure."

"I just came through to drop those on you, though. Later, bruh." Scramble threw up the peace sign and left.

Don leaned over and sat 5 of the books on the table along with the walkman. He kept the book "A Penitentiary Holy Book" and kicked back atop his bunk. He read the synopsis and could tell that the book would be interesting. A Bible and Quran graced the front cover with prison bars swarming with deadly poisonous snakes.

There was also a large picture of the author on the back of the book. Don observed him then read the About The Author inscription and saw that he was also from Charleston. He was also incarcerated, currently fighting an unlawful murder conviction. He was the founder of the brand, and he was Muslim.

Cedric was at work and wouldn't be in until later so he had the room to himself. After reading the synopsis, he cracked the book open and began reading.

###

The wings were shaped like awkward triangles; rooms lined two sides of the angle. The other wall of the angle consisted of offices and rooms for activities, services, and staff. The officers at Ogeechee worked 12 hour shifts and the shifts changed at 6 o'clock.

Shift had changed about 30 minutes ago. A very attractive caucasian female officer worked the wing. She was petite and small. Don gave her no more than 5 feet in height. She looked as if she could be in her late 30's, early 40's; blonde. He watched her as she walked around the tiers making her rounds, socializing, kindly smiling with the inmates as she moved along

He was leaning on the rail in front of his room listening to country music while his roommate relieved his bowels. Country music had been something that had grew on him due to the versatility and diversity of his up-bringing. At the moment, he listened to a song by Brantly Gilbert called "Kick It In The Sticks". It was like gangster country music; one of his favorites.

His stomach was full. He still had half of the food left in his bowl that Scramble had cooked after count. He couldn't believe how the food tasted! It tasted exotic. They ate sautéed onions, chopped up spicy beef sausages, chunks of roast beef, tomatoes, okra, and rice.

"I'm good, town," Cedric tapped Don on his shoulder alerting him that he was finished using the restroom. He pushed the door wide open to air out.

Don leaned up from the railing and looked back as he lowered the volume on the walkman. "Alright," he replied coolly as he watched Cedric amble down the tier towards one of his hangout spots eating the bag of Dorito's he'd given him.

Don allowed the room to air out for about 20 minutes and went inside; he closed the door behind him. He flicked the switch on the small lamp that he bought from the canteen and sat at the table and reopened the book he'd started earlier. He thought that it was good so far.

About 30 minutes had elapsed before Scramble materialized. When he entered the cell he pulled the door open on Don's locker to block the window on the door so no one could see what they were doing inside the room. He reached inside his pants, pulled out something and handed it to Don.

Don looked at the sleek device in astonishment. He thought he knew what it was, but due to where they were he second guessed what he already knew. "What is this?" He asked stupidly.

"Man, get the fuck out of here! You just came off the street so I know you know what that is," Scramble ejaculated sarcastically.

Don moved towards the lamp and raised the device for a better view. It was exactly what he knew it was! A Motorola Droid, 4G. He eyed the device incredulously and looked over to where Scramble stood with a grin on his face. "How did you get this?" He asked. Then: "Never mind. I don't even want to know," he added and then handed the device back to Scramble.

"I brought it for you to use," Scramble offered before he accepted the device back.

"I'm cool right now. Only person I holler at is my father and my two big bro's; I already spoke to all of them earlier."

"You don't have any bitches you want to get at?"

"Nah, not really. I was on some single shit out there just

having fun preparing to be a multi-billion dollar entrepreneur. I have female friends scattered around the country, but I'm not in the mood; maybe when I'm more settled."

"Word, that's what it is, lil' bruh." Scramble took the phone and placed it back inside his pants. "But you know you got to put me down with some of those rich bitches," Scramble said humorously.

"I got you, Insha'Allah." Don laughed.

Scramble closed the door on the locker. "Well check it; I got some mixing up to do so I'll get back at you before we go in for the night. I just wanted to make sure that you were good. When we sit down again I'll put you up on game and show you the ropes to this shit. I can see that you're lost like a motherfucker.

"But due to your financial position, all of this shit won't mean anything to you anyway, but it's still good to know."

"Man, I appreciate everything you've assisted me with for real," Don expressed his gratitude. "If there's anything I can do to help you, no matter the degree, just let me know and I got you , Insha'Allah." He meant this.

"It's all love, lil' bruh. It's some other homies around here that's good peeps. I already told some of them about you. I guess you'll be able to meet them later or whenever you feel like it. I can tell that you like staying to yourself pretty much so we'll move at your pace."

"Alright, bro."

They shook hands, embraced, and Scramble departed.

More and more Scramble intrigued Don. He thanked Allah for placing him along his path. He sat back down in the chair and looked off in space thinking about his new life. He was beginning to think that maybe his stay wouldn't be so boring and lonely as he thought it would be after all.

As the months progressed Scramble taught him the ropes of the underworld and essential etiquette in conduct that he needed to have amongst the many different personalities he now lived amongst because proper mannerism would alleviate a lot of unnecessary drama. As Scramble educated him in this area he educated him in business on how to become a successful entrepreneur. Because of him, Scramble had enrolled in school to obtain the GED he didn't have. Scramble had had the misconception that, just because he was going to be independent, he didn't need a GED, but Don had informed him of the importance of credentials in the business world. They broke barriers.

There were so many people from different walks of life with different up bringing's, more than often it caused clashes. Life in the penitentiary was a science in itself and if one didn't master it he would always find himself inside unwanted situations. Some inmates had extremely poor hygiene and manners; jealousy, envy, and hatred was prevalent. It was a world of snakes, crabs, hyena's, vulture's and sharks, so it was imperative that the required skills be acquired to deal with and repel these evils.

Scramble had also given him an 8 inch ice pick. He had refused accepting it but Scramble had been adamant about him taking it because one never knew when he may need it and that it was better to have it than not, and when he reflected back on the riot he witnessed, he concluded that Scramble was right so he accepted the deadly object.

The job board had place him inside education full-time as a teacher's assistant since he had finished school already. He liked the job, and he thought that the principal was cool. She was a feisty, older, brown skin complexioned woman with extremely long hair. Her name was Ms. Bratton. The other inmates hated her, but as he quickly discovered, attitude and seriousness was a defense mechanisms that were essential tools in such environment or people would take advantage of you, so he understood her. They got along perfectly.

He and Cedric had been getting along fine. He had actually begun to think that he was an alright dude. He was just lost and misguided. Whatever he had he welcomed him to it. Cedric wasn't a room person. He liked this because it gave him space. Cedric was gone as soon as the doors were unlocked, running around getting in whatever mischief he could find.

Don had met everyone in the dorm on all 4 wings from Charleston. He had also met a great many around the yard from other dorms. Some of them were cool but he still pretty much stayed to himself. Only person that he was really fond of was Scramble.

Scramble was very crafty and incalculable. He had all sorts of things going on. Don had discovered that the riot had been behind the red bone Amazon that had worked the morning it happened. One of the inmates from Columbia had been trying to extort her to no avail. They knew that she'd been having sex and bringing contraband in for Scramble's right hand man – someone named Chess. She told Chess; he told her to be cool, and then one morning, an inmate from Columbia spotted her placing the contraband she brought inside a desk in the multipurpose room; he stole the package when she left. Chess, along with Scramble and other guys from Charleston tried to handlethe situation diplomatically but it was taken as a sign of weakness; this initiated the war. Chess drew first blood but was also stabbed in the process.

Now, Scramble was handling all the business with the female officer for Chess because he'd been transferred to another institution because of the riot.

Only time Don had ever seen an abundance of exotic marijuana was at the parties he attended with his friends, but he had never seen crack. Scramble kept a lot of it all! This was why he was "the man". Don had seen him pull 20 thousand dollars in less than a week! He was enthralled. Scramble had offered him a position but he had declined.

"Yeah, I know that you're already rich, nigga!" Scramble had teased playfully.

Don had laughed. He wasn't avaricious. And besides, there were other less fortunate people that needed assistance and opportunity. But, he was contemplating getting his own personal phone. He missed the internet. For the meantime, he studied his Quran and books his father and Al-Salam constantly sent him on Islam and business, worked out religiously, and played basketball although he sucked at the sport.

He had began gaining his weight back. And the urban novels that Scramble had been giving him had quickly played themselves out. There were certain authors that he liked, but overall, he felt as if the books were dumbing him down in education, and with his aspirations, he couldn't afford to be dumbed-down. They promoted excessive ignorance and confusion and rarely sent positive messages. And, the intellectual literary structure of them were poor. Some of them had compelling story lines but he felt that the authors needed to be more vivid in scenery, structure, and etiquette and, the publishers needed to properly edit the material and its content before releasing such garbage wrapped in intriguing covers!

He was still waiting on his property to arrive. It had been a mix up with the orders that had to be worked out with the warehouse in Columbia where they kept most of the items stocked. It should arrive any day now.

It was the last Friday in May, and although while growing up he had never submitted wholly to the decree of Allah, he was Muslim at heart so he got up and got ready to participate in the Jummah service that was held every Friday at noon inside the prison's gym. He had already showered and was dressed, waiting on the noon movement, which was called every hour up until 3 o'clock for inmates to report to designated locations.

The prison had a large body of Muslims. Many of them were inside his dorm also. They also gravitated towards Don as they were all now familiar with who he was.

He stood by the wing door with a number of Muslims waiting on the movement to be called. While they waited he spoke with a very humble and soft spoken brother attributed Jamal.

Jamal was originally from New York. He wore rimless glasses and had soft wavy hair; a very dark prostration mark stood out in defiance on his forehead in witness of his faith in that he prayed faithfully. It was the mark of the believers. Don liked his energy. Jamal had also became a companion of his that he chose to spend a lot of his time with. He had even introduced him to his father.

Different fragrances of oils lingered in the air with a pleasantly thick aroma from the many Muslims gathered by the door. Jamal stood with a beautiful, burgundy prayer rug draped across his broad shoulders, as many of the other Muslims did.

"Movement! Movement!" A caucasian, male officer shouted gruffly as he walked through the throng of Muslims to unlock the door.

"Come on akhi, lets roll so we can get these blessings. Insha'Allah," Jamal told Don, and they departed with the crowd.

Chapter Seven

Great Falls, Montana
June 2014

Slowly, Caesar rose from his slumbering but did not open his eyes. He laid on his back with his hands clasped across his abdomen reflecting upon the dream he just had. He'd been sitting at the table with his deceased grandmother in the house she had left him in North Charleston, South Carolina. Although she had never been Muslim, in the dream she was dressed like one with herself properly covered. Tears continued to escape from the crevices of his closed eyes as he reflected upon all that she had told him. He had sat quietly at the end of the table across from her as she spoke of atonement and expiation of sins. A large glass bowl of sliced mango's, cantaloupe, honey dew melon, berries, peaches, cherries, and pineapples sat before her.

Fervently, she ate as she spoke. A brilliant light surrounded her. "Sugar," she had begun. "You've come a long way since I left you and I'm so proud of you.

"But sugar, what you're experiencing with your child is due

to the sins of your own hands. Have you ever thought about all the people you've hurt and families you've destroyed by the tons of poison you've pushed into society? You've oppressed millions of people indirectly for personal gain. We don't realize the severity of the decisions we make at times," she continued to speak through bites of the luscious fruits. "Allah has bestowed His mercy upon you because you were in a state of ignorance and weren't aware of the calamities you caused to befall so many people around the world. But still, you were in error because you knew right from wrong and profess to me Muslim.

"Donatello will be fine, sugar. You are just being tested and taken through this trial as a form of atonement and expiation for your sins. There are many fatherless and motherless children because of you. There are many people in prison because of you. Many people have been killed because of you. A quarter billion dollars came to you at the expense of other people's misery, so don't be selfish and weep as if you've been forsaken like you've done no wrong!" A bit of anger seemed to rise in her voice but quickly dissipated.

"Yes, you love your child, but didn't Allah say that He will test you with your wealth and offspring? This world is nothing, sugar. And yes, you've repented for many things but you have never repented solely for the destruction you have caused. Allah must favor you to show you such mercy to allow you to go through this to expiate all you have done, because if He didn't, you would surely burn in Hell forever," she said matter-of-factly.

"If you could see what I've been allowed to see by looking down over the world at all the discord you've sewn you'd be appalled! Repent, sugar. I love you for the sake of Allah."

The dream had went blank.

Caesar had saw his grandmother many times before, but never had she uttered a word. He would just catch quick glimpse's of her and nothing more. Never had he had such intimate interaction with her.

He opened his eyes and looked into his mirrored ceiling at his reflection. The windows inside his bedroom were high and bear. The room was exceptionally bright due to the strong rays of the morning sun. The day would no doubt be beautiful.

He looked out the window into the sky; it was so clear and crisp with beautiful, fluffy clouds, it resembled an animation in the likes of the sky in the Simpson's cartoon. Allah was surely the most magnificent creator of pulchritude!

He closed his eyes again and continued to ponder the dream. He reflected on the story of Joseph in the Quran and it made him reflect deeper upon his very own dream.

After coming to terms with what the dream implied, he said "Alhamdulillah", threw the covers off of him and sat up. He cracked his toes by flexing them and stood up, stretched, and headed to the bathroom to clean himself up to offer the repentance prayer that he was way overdue in performing. He had a long day ahead of him.

Over the past couple of months, he'd been advocating for his son. He was determine not to let the RPM subside surrounding his case. He figured that as long as he kept him in the hearts and mind's of the people something would surface in their favor. He'd been on talk radio programs and talk shows. In the next couple of weeks he was scheduled for a special appearance on Steve, and Ellen's talk show and radio program.

He spat the toothpaste into the toilet commode after brushing his teeth, flushed it and picked up the tube of toothpaste again. He stared at it. The name of the toothpaste was called Confident; it was one of the many items off a cosmetic and fragrance line he had started. He reflected on his past and a sense of angst washed over him as he thought about all he had acquired from the heroin he pushed.

He looked at the elegance of gold, silver and marble that surrounded him. All of the hygienic products that littered the bathroom was his products: shampoo, deodorant, lotion's, oil's, soap's, mouth wash, grease, et. al. His product's rivaled the best of them. He looked at all the blood red container's containing the product's and became dizzy. He dropped his toothbrush inside the sink and braced himself on the edge of the marble basin.

After regaining his bearings about 5 minutes later, he performed ablution and went to offer his repentance prayer for the blood, misery, and tears that brought him so much lavishness.

Caesar hung up the phone in his study. He'd just been informed by Jabbar that their flight had just landed. They were back in Montana; huge fans of the sporting world they'd been following the NBA finals.

Ali and Jabbar had parted a few weeks ago. Really, they were away more than often. They had their own lives. Besides, they weren't his bodyguards, they were security forhis enterprise. Their job was to make sure that things stayed in order within the organization. Really, they had the easiest jobs. Well, that was if violence didn't bother one. They were on call 24/7 in case a problem arose. It had been rumored that Caesar had used them to muscle his way in some industries but the rumors weren't true. But a time had yet to arise where Ali and Jabbar had to be hands on since their departure from the underworld.

Caesar had time to make a few calls before Ali and Jabbar arrived. They were all headed to South Carolina to see Don. Years ago, when all was peaches and cream with their friendship, Caesar had Senator Brody pull some strings to have Ali and Jabbar's record clean because they both had done time for felonies.

He had already dressed down in a pair of soft sole, brown, Polo dock shoes, linen Polo shorts and a linen, Polo button down shirt with a tank top beneath; cladded his face were a pair of lightly tinted titanium framed Ray Bans. It was almost mid afternoon. They would board the jet around 2 o'clock.

He picked up the cordless phone again and left the study headed to the kitchen to fix a cheese sandwich; he would eat on the jet. He dialed the number to Wilson's Intuitive Investigative Firm, which was the firm he had hired to investigate his son's case.

"Hello, Mr. McFadden," Cecelia Wilson answered.

Caesar had phoned her direct line. "Salam, sweetheart," he said smoothly as he dropped a few slices of white bread in the toaster.

She smiled at his charm. She liked him.

"How's things progressing? I know you said that you'd contact me as the investigation progress, but since I'm on my way back to the Carolina's, I just thought to check in on things."

"You're fine, Mr. McFa--"

"Sulayman," he offered kindly.

"Sulayman," she articulated as she leaned back in her leather recliner twiddling her pen through her fingers. "We haven't come across anything yet but we've pretty much combed the hairs thoroughly of all prospects. Only thing we can do is continue to network and see what pop's up. One thing's for certain, and that's if there was any foul play and your son had truly been framed, there's something to be found. It's just a matter of who, what, where, when, how and why?

"I also paid your son a visit recently to see if there was anything he forgot or left out about the night of the incident, but he said what he'd stated is all that he remembered...." She paused briefly. "What about you Sulayman; do you think that it's possible that your son could be collateral damage for something you may've done?

"Forgive my temerity to delve, it's just the investigator in me. And, I've seen the unthinkable in this business so nothing surprises me. I also looked into your background."

"That's cool. It's what I hired you to do. And yes, it's a possibility that Don caught a bullet from a past foe although I can't think of any enemies who would orchestrate such a thing to get back at me. Yes, I've distributed drugs in my past, but I've never wronged anyone to the magnitude of this type of retaliation." Even as he said this he wasn't so sure. "I think," he added meekly.

"We'll see. You've hired the best. If there's something waiting to be discovered beneath the surface we'll find it."

"Ok, I'll leave you to your field of expertise."

"So," she relaxed into a more sensuous tone and asked, "how long will you be in town?"

Caesar noticed the change. "I was just coming to see my son over the weekend and look in on my business before departing. Why?"

"Ahh, because I was wondering if you would have time for dinner," she was trembling.

He laughed.

"Wow, You're laughing at me?" she sat up. "I feel so stupid."

"No, I'm not laughing at you – well, yeah, I am but it's not how you think. You just caught me by surprise. I wasn't expecting that or the straight forwardness. That's a trait that's rare in women."

"Well, yes or no, Sulayman?" She asked, confidence restored.

"Yes, Ms. Wilson, I'll accompany you to dinner. So, we have a date?"

"Yes," she secretly expelled a breath.

"I'll call you."

"Ok," she responded, then added, "By the way, you looked marvelous on Ellen. Bye."

He looked at the phone as the line went dead and sat it on the counter top. He thought about her. She was in her late forties. A beautiful woman. Petite and tall. It seemed like eons had passed since he had been on a date and hadn't had a serious relationship since the death of his wife, though he'd had many flings. What this would be with Cecelia Wilson, Allah knew best, but he would give it a shot.

He looked at the unwrapped cheese and the golden toasted bread that had long ago popped up in the toaster. So caught in his conversation with Cecelia he had lost the taste for the toast and cheese.

Just as he replaced the cheese inside the refrigerator and threw the bread inside the trash bin a horn blew outsidethe ranch. It was his boy's, his brother's. It was time to roll. He thought about the comment Cecelia had made about seeing him on Ellen and laughed as he fetched his keys and headed out the door.

Chapter Eight

Ogeechee Correctional Institution
Red Top, South Carolina
June – 2014

"So, how are you fairing, Mr. McFadden?" Ms. Bratton asked Don as she accepted the stack of graded papers he handed her.

"I'm cool," he smiled. "I saw my father and two brothers this weekend. Other than being inside here I can't complain." He stood before her desk inside the small confines of her cramped office inside the education building. The desk in itself took up a major fraction of the room. On top of her desk sat a computer; folders and other paper work clustered her desk. Behind her on a bulletin board were an array of notes and memos. He looked at her and pondered why she always showed him so much concern. "Ms. Bratton, can I ask you a question?"

"Sure," her usual hardened gaze and tensed facial features softened and relaxed as she looked up at him from where she sat.

"Why do you favor me?"

She smiled. "Because of your mannerism and intelligence. And, I really think you're innocent. You may not be aware but you're quite often the topic of discussion amongst the staff as well as your peers. Your situation had calmed quite a bit but due to your father's recent television and radio interviews it kind of placed you back in the spotlight," she said. "You know people live for gossip. But personally, I see you as a son that I would have liked to have had given the opportunity."

"So you're telling me that you want to meet my father?" He humored impishly.

She laughed naughtily. "Child, you are too much. I'm just saying that you deserve to be treated kindly and don't forget that."

"Thank you, Ms. Bratton," he didn't know what else to say, her response had warmed him.

"Well, it's about time for me to get my butt up out of here so go ahead and get back to your dorm. I'll see you tomorrow."

"Drive safe," he replied with a smile and turned on his heel.

"Mr. McFadden," she called after him.

"Ma'am," he answered as he looked back over his shoulder.

"Keep up the good work and stay out of trouble."

"I will," he replied and headed out the building. He had been the only remaining inmate. He had taught his class the rules of dealing with Integers in mathematics and had stayed behind to grade papers.

He headed across the large expanse of the yard. It was Monday afternoon. The weather was steamy and humid, the mosquitoes and nat's were terrible. He hadn't even made it halfway across the yard and had already started to perspire; rivulets of sweat rolled down his back and soaked into the band of his boxers. He couldn't wait till he reached his dorm.

Inmates and staff milled about the yard. In the next 30 minutes or so it would be time for the 3 o'clock count.

Over the past couple of months things had progressed as smooth as could be expected. He had fallen perfectly into the groove of things around the prison as if he'd been doing time for years. He spent his time further educating himself, surfing the web, and getting to know some of the guys that surrounded him. He was learning more than he ever thought possible in such predicament!

"What's up, Don?" An inmate greeted in passing.

"Trying to get out this heat," Don replied in stride. He didn't know the inmate personally, but he knew that he was one of his homeboys from Charleston that stayed in one of the other dorms.

"I know that's right. It's hot as a motherfucker out this bitch!" The inmate spoke louder as the distance grew between them. "Hold your head, homie."

"You too," Don returned. He swatted at an aggravating mosquito that pursued him with invigorating determination. "Damn!" he yelped as he smacked his neck in irritation, squashing the delicate bloodsucker. He took a paper towel from his back pocket and removed the smashed body and gore from his neck and quickened his pace.

The month of June had been eventful. He'd received the personal property he ordered. He had also spent a considerable amount of time breaking in his typewriter putting together business plans he sent his father. Then, earlier in the month, the lady over the investigation firm his father had hired had paid him a visit. She had asked a slew of questions about the night of the incident. Something about suppressed memory and how the brain later recollected things, she had said. But he couldn't remember anything more than what he had already told them about the night of the party. Nothing distinctive stood out about that night. She had told him to give her a call if he remembered anything at all; even the smallest detail.

But the most eventful of all was when he saw his father on Ellen's talk show! He had been aware that his father would be appearing on several talk and radio shows advocating his case but to actually see him on the little 7 inch TV he owned inside the prison cell was – well – cool! He couldn't deny the fact that he enjoyed the attention his celebrity brought him, although he was famous behind a horrendous murder.

And last but not least, he was in possession of an iPhone 5. The phone was awesome!

As he neared the dorm, he reflected back to the visit with his father, Ali, and Jabbar. He beamed inwardly. It had beenhis first time seeing his brother's since his incarceration. They spoke about everything under the sun over games of Uno while he stuffed himself with food from the vending machines. A major fan of Lebron James, he got as much information as possible about the basketball star from Ali and Jabbar since they had followed the games in person. His father had told him that the investigation hadn't produced anything so far but was expected. Whomever had framed him had made sure to do a clean job and had left no stings untied. They had come to the realization that they needed to find a motive. It was the only thing that would give any indication as to where to start. Did he have any enemies? Not that he was aware of. He had never done anything wrong to anyone. But what about his father? They all pondered this. He knew that his father's past life was comprised of drugs, money, and murder. Growing up around his father's operation, too much of anything was concealed from him. His father had been ruthless. He remembered seeing a human skull on the bank of the crocodile's habitat when he'd been younger so he knew that the animals had been fed human bodies. Then again, maybe they were being too novel and Hollywood; maybe Fedora's murder had nothing to do with them at all. She could have brought it on herself due to her promiscuity, or her family could have been tied into some shady dealings. He could well be a victim of circumstances. Who knew?

The visit had been Saturday, his father had returned home the following day to spend some quality time with him. As usual, he gave him indelible wisdom and strength. He'd also told him that he had a date that night with the lady investigator. He was happy for his father. He deserved to have a good woman in his life. He didn't know if his father would take her panties momentarily before carrying on because he'd matured so much as a Muslim and was trying to abide by the laws of the Quran and Sunnah of the Prophet in dealing with them lawfully, not outside of wedlock, it was a good chance that the sexy investigator could be his step-mother. It was fine with him. He approved.

He finally made it to the dorm. He pulled the door, and as he stepped into the cool confines of the lobby, he thanked Allah for allowing man to conceive air conditioning!

The 15 minute warning to count was announced as soon as he got to his room and pulled open the door. As usual, his roommate was absent.

Don took off the white and blue Nike tennis shoes he wore, placed them beneath the table, then he took off his uniform shirt and pants, folded them and placed them on the seat of the chair. He slipped into a pair of short pants, which was a short version of the uniform pants, then slid his feet into his flip flops.

After fetching his washcloth he went to his locker an fetched his soap dish and went to the sink to wash his face and wipe the perspiration from his body where he'd perspired. It would have to due until he could shower later.

Only light that lit the room came through the window of the cell door and the little cheap lamp that he had turned on upon entering the room. The lamp had a homemade shade covering it so it only produced a faint, red glow. The back window had been covered with cardboard that was freshly painted the same color of the room. Some officers complained about it being up and some didn't. With his property and all of the extra things he had obtained and placed around the room, the ambiance of the room had changed. It was full and cuddly.

After cleaning the sink behind himself, he rehung his washcloth and returned the soap dish back to his locker. Before closing it, he grabbed a can of smoked oysters and a bag of jalapeno pretzel pieces, fetched a cold can of Minute Maid Lemonade from the ice chest he bought for 30 bucks from another inmate, and sat down to watch a bit of TV and cool out.

A wooden TV stand sat on top of the table. He had it crafted by one of the inmates that worked inside the hobby craft wood shop to hold the little 7 inch flat screen as all other inmates did that owned one. He looked at the stand in confusion – his TV was missing!

After the count cleared, Don headed to Scramble's room to inform him that his TV had been stolen. As he headed down the stairs to the second tier he casually looked around at the ambulanting inmates as if he would see something out of the ordinary that would give him an indication as to what had happened to his TV, but everything appeared as it always had. Inmates moved about and one never knew what the other was up to unless you were of the esoteric.

Nothing had ever been stolen from him so he never knew how it felt until now. He wasn't mad that the TV was missing but he was becoming infuriated because of the lingering suspense of not knowing the culprit.

He knocked on Scramble's door. Cam was at the sink rinsing a bowl, he pushed the door open in invitation for Don to enter.

Scramble sat on his bunk bagging ounces of mid-grade weed and 50 dollar grams of exotic weed. "What's up, lil' homie?" he greeted.

Don closed the door behind him. "What's good, fellas?" he returned.

"Cooling out; about to eat a bowl of Captain Crunch," Cam answered as he headed towards his locker, the many gold teeth in is mouth shimmered brilliantly. He was high and had the munchies!

"Man, I hate to rain on you guys party, but I have a little dilemma," Don hated being the cause to another man's grief.

Simultaneously, Cam and Scramble ceased what they were doing and looked at Don quizzically. They had never seen him unnerved.

Scramble stood. He'd been incarcerated long enough to know the signs of a problem; and, he'd become over protective of Don in the love he had for him. "What's wrong,lil' bruh?"

"Someone stole my TV while I was in school."

"What!?" Cam, and Scramble ejaculate simultaneously. They were expecting to hear anything but this.

Don continued: "When I came back from school I noticed that it was missing. This morning I kind of got up late so I was running behind and forgot to put it up and lock my locker."

“Anything else missing?” Cam asked as the bowl dangled from his hand.

“No. Just the TV. It's really not a big thing. I'll buy --”

“Whoa, whoa, whoa, lil’ homie,” Scramble interjected. “It is a big thing and it won’t go unpunished! We'll find out who did that shit. Trust me. Where's your roommate?”

“At work.”

“He probably orchestrated the whole thing knowing his grimy ass!” Scramble was furious. “That lil’ nigga think he got all the sense!

“But listen Don, shit like this ain’t tolerated! All violations get dealt with bruh, no matter what! You heard me?”

“Yeah, I hear you,” Don answered as he rubbed his hand over his face in aggravation.

“Just be cool and let me handle this shit,” Scramble stated. “Don’t even say anything to your roommate. Just continue to play like you don’t know what’s what because we can’t say for certain that he had anything to do with it or not. These niggas talk so it’s going to come out. I'm connected around this whole yard, someone will end up telling me what it is. When we find out we’ll handle it!”

“I’m going to get with my brother’s also and make sure nobody within my ranks had anything to do with that shit,” Cam announced as he sat the bowl on the table. He had lost his appetite. Scramble was like a brother. They had built a profound bond of love over the 2 years they’d been cellmates. Don was Scramble’s lil’ homie, so he was his lil’ homie also. He was also a high ranking affiliate in the Blood organization. “You’re Scramble’s people’ so you’re my people’ also. I'll be standing right there when it all goes down,” he said solemnly.

"Thanks for the support," Don told Cam.

"I'm going out here to get at my homies and Blood's to see what's popping. I'll get back at y'all in a few." Cam left the room.

Scramble had begun putting the marijuana and other paraphernalia away. A more pertinent issue was at hand. "Just go fall back lil' bruh, and let me go network real quick. I hate these stupid ass niggas! They act like they don't care rather they live or die! These motherfuckers got death wishes Don and don't even really be ready for the drama that comes behind this kind of shit.

"But see, motherfuckers take humbleness for a weakness and that's where shit get twisted!" Scramble said as he slipped into an old pair of boots and drew the laces tight. He was ready to engage whomever in combat! "When we find out lil' bruh, it's going down! Don't let me down; I got you," Scramble looked at Don seriously.

Don didn't flinch. "Not to be arrogant Scramble," he started, "but on some real shit big bro, the average dude can't fuck with me," he stated calmly.

Scramble had seen Don's agility along with subtle hints of a trained fighter during workout sessions with him but really didn't know the extent of his expertise. But as he had seen from day one, there was an inexplicable fire of sureness that swam in the eyes of Don that gave one an impression of superiority and strength.

Truth be told, don wasn't unnerved or scared of the potential violence that lie ahead. But as he witnessed Scramble do, he didn't want to end up with the death of his peers on his hands behind something so insignificant as a 7 inch TV! But even in this, he understood where he now was and knew that he had to handle his business if it came to it or he would continue to be victimized by the predators and vultures of the underworld. These trifling bastards was going to respect him! He was far from contentious but he wasn't passive either. "Well, I'm going to go kick back and touch bases with home. You know where to find me."

"Don't let this shit fuck with you, lil' bruh. It done happened, now it is what it is," Scramble stated as he embraced Don.

"It's whatever Allah wills so I'm cool, big bro. Besides, it's inextricable."

"There you go with those crazy ass words again. Inex—what?"

"It means something that cannot be undone. Like you said, it already happened so it is what it is. Inextricable," Don smiled.

Scramble went around and notified Charleston affiliates about what happened to Don, then he went to the head members of each gang and other organizational bodies: Folks, Crips, Rastafarians, Five Percenters, and the Muslims. Cam had the Bloods covered. He stood inside the cell of the leader of the Folk Nation. The room smelled of burnt marijuana and wine.

"What's up, black man?" Big Unc asked Scramble. He was inebriated but coherent. He stood shirtless, his arms folded across his broad chest.

"Check it. I'm not saying that your people is responsible but someone stole my TV today while he was in school. As I said, it could've come from anybody's group so I'm going to everybody telling them the same thing. We want the property returned in forty-eight hours. If it doesn't resurface in 72 hours who ever we feel responsible got action." His diplomacy was respectful but yet firm.

"Respect. Handle your business comrade." Big Unc offered

a fist and Scramble touched his fist against it and departed, headed to give each group and geographical denomination the very same message.

###

Don had gotten up, took a shower and returned to his room. He felt a little bit rejuvenated. Jamal had been the first to return. As always, his roommate was missing-in-action.

“Salam, little brother; how’s everything?” Jamal asked as he entered the room and closed the door.

Don sat inside the chair applying lotion to his legs and feet before slipping on a clean pair of socks. He shook his hand dismayingly. “Wondering what is it that I’ve done to deserve all that I'm going through.”

“I feel you little brother, but we’ll never be able to comprehend Allah’s infinite wisdom in why inexplicable things happen to us. As long as we stand firm in our fortitude and be patient, we’ll be successful. If not in this life, in the Hereafter.

“You should come on into the folds of the Deen akhi, so Allah can strengthen and broaden your insight. I know you study but it’s not enough without the obligatory acts of worship.”

“I know,” Don breathed deeply as he brushed his hair. Jamal never relented in attempt of getting him to officially become Muslim.

“I heard about what happened to your TV. That's some foul stuff. The brother’s are concerned. We got your back, though. Believe that, little brother.” Jamal jumped up on Don’s bunk and relaxed. Y'all don’t have any idea who done it?”

“No, not yet. I know Scramble spoke with a few people but I haven’t spoken with him since earlier. It kind of made me weary and I ended up falling asleep." The brush clattered as he placed it on the table.

Jamal and Don looked towards the door as it opened; Scramble entered without knocking along with a few of their homeboy's from Charleston. For now, formalities were out the window.

"What's up , Dictionary Don?" Scramble said and the room stirred with laughter. It was a little nickname he had given Don because of his broad vocabulary.

"I'm maintaining. Any good news?" Don inquired hopefully, as he gathered his cosmetics and handed them to one of his homeboys that stood near him. "Put that in my locker please."

Sinso placed the items inside the locker.

"Nah, same old two-step. Still waiting to hear something. Don't worry, something will surface," Scramble assured.

"What's up with your celly; he been acting funny?" Mario asked.

"I can't say because I haven't been up since he got off work."

"For some reason I think that him and those other two cat's he's always with got something to do with this shit because I remember earlier today before the twelve o'clock count those two niggas been moving real funny. I think after your roommate saw you leave your shit out and unlocked he told them to clip you," Mario rationalized. "It doesn't take a rocket scientist to figure this shit out. Shit back here ain't as complex as it seems."

Don liked Mario. He was off the Macon in North Charleston where his father was raised. The other 3 homies of his present was Hook; he was also from North Charleston. He was serving a 10 year stint for home invasion. Sinso was from the east side of downtown Charleston. And, a tall, dark skin complexioned dude they called Rumble, was from an area in North Charleston called Liberty Hill. They were all there to support.

"Yeah, most likely, that's exactly how it went down. Let's just wait and see what pops up in the next forty-eight hours. If nothing don't pop up, fuck 'em! We'll just serve them niggas for it since they're known thieves! Coward motherfuckers!" Scramble spat. "A bitch is going to pay for this violation rather they did it or not. Y'all know my motto: zero tolerance!"

"Those lame ass niggas ain't doing nothing but trying to support those drug habits. Stupid niggas ain't trying to come up." The red glow of the room bounced off the gold slugs inside Hook's mouth.

"Man, y'all boy," Rumble spoke gruffly, "just let me know when y'all ready to ride. I got some loose ends I need to tie up before shit get' real." He began giving everyone a pound in the room before departing.

"That's what it is Rumble," Scramble stated.

"How do our arsenal look?" Mario inquired.

"We strapped up like Al-Qaeda, babe," Hook informed.

"I'll be through to pick something up. My last banger got knocked the last time those pigs came through," Mario said. He sneezed and retrieved some tissue to blow his nose.

Jamal blessed him.

"Thanks, ahk," Mario told Jamal.

"Man," Don stood, "I appreciate you guys support. Word!"

"Dawg, this is how we mix! You' good babe, just lay," Sinso finally spoke. He had a few months left before it was his time to go home but it didn't matter, he was going to hold his comrades down. "I don't like those clown ass niggas anyway!"

"I thought that after that last situation with those niggas leaving their homie in distress when that shit went down with them Blood niggas behind that phone Roger stole they kicked them niggas out the fold," Hook stated.

"Yeah, you're right but you know some niggas will still hold each other down because of a bond or friendship, or some homeboy shit, then all that gang shit go out the window," Sinso said. "But fuck those clowns! I still owe one of them an ass whipping anyhow because one of the main motherfuckers that had their hands in that shit that happened with Chess is still running around like shit' all good. I'm going to push his shit back first chance I get!"

"Everybody just stay cool. Lets see what this forty-eight brings." Scramble said. "But shed, what are you about to do Don?"

All eyes were on him. "Call my father like I started to do before I fell asleep earlier and cool out afterwards. I'm cool man. I'm not even tripping. Trust me, I'm ready."

Scramble didn't know the cause for his sudden thought of Don as he looked at him, but as Don spoke, his body posture reminded him of a panther. "Well go ahead and do you. You know where the team will be if you need us," Scramble replied and gave him a pound.

"Hold it down, babe," Sinso and the rest of Don's supporters saluted as they departed.

All of the inmates that leisurely moved about the wing looked up at Don's room as the group from Charleston departed. Everyone was already aware of what had happened and they knew, by the individuals involved that left Don's room, that blood would inevitably be spilled behind the violation.

Jamal hopped down from Don's bunk. "Well little brother, I

see that y'all pretty much got things under control. Me and the brothers will make du'a for you and your homeboy's that y'all prevail, Insha'Allah.

"Like I told you earlier, akhi – this thing back here ain't no joke. I've been here for a long time, little bro. Allah has blessed me not to experience such a thing, but I have seen these situations time and time again.

"But listen, Don," Jamal rested his hands on both of Don's shoulder's and became very serious. "When this thing actually goes down, don't play no games, akhi. When you get your man make an example out of him! Me and the brother's got your back so don't worry about nothing. Just handle your business." Jamal looked in Don's eyes for a moment longer allowing his words to sink in before releasing his shoulder's. He pulled him into his bosom to let him know that he loved him unconditionally for the sake of Allah. He was the son of a Muslim!

"Go ahead and contact your father, little bro. Tell him I send my salam and gratitude for the money he sent me."

"Ok. And thanks man, for everything," Don almost choked up on his emotions. He was not a gangster. All the love and support overwhelmed him.

"Alhamdulillah!" Jamal smiled and departed.

Don sat by himself momentarily as he thought about the hand that had been dealt to him along with the strange, new people in his life.

After a deep breath or two, he got up, quickly retrieved his phone from the contrapment he had had built to secure it from search teams, and called his father.

"Ahhh, what's up, hot boy?" Caesar teased as he answered the familiar number.

"What's up, abu?" Don responded.

"What's wrong, son? I can hear the agony in your voice." Caesar became concerned. "Are you okay?"

"Yeah, I'm fine. I just stumbled across a little problem." He explained the situation in its entirety from beginning to end. "We're just waiting now," he said after he finished.

Caesar sighed, "Well, it sounds as if things are being handled accordingly. You have every right to defend your property and retaliate. Your property's sacred. I'm not going to tell you to do otherwise. Just be safe. I'm confident that you'll be fine so I'm not even worried. Allah will always see to it that the righteous prevails. As I always refer to the lion and crocodile, employ those same tactics of strategy when you prepare your attack and be relentless! Insha'Allah, you won't kill anyone, but don't allow anyone to kill you. You are my only child Furqān, I swear I'll blow that motherfucker up if anything happens to you!"

Don listened to his father and knew that he was troubled because it was seldom he swore. "Jamal sent his salutations and thanks for the money you sent him."

"Ok. Tell him I send my salam."

"Abu, I know that you're worried but I'll be okay," he assured his father in attempt to assuage his trepidation. "How's Al-Salam? I haven't spoken to him in a while, is he okay?"

"Yeah. You know the old man is as strong as iron. He's just caught up in the excitement of the new masjid he's having constructed over there. It's almost done. He haven't forgotten you." Caesar's stomach was knotted in guilt. Ever since he had that dream with his grandmother he'd been feeling guilty by the least little thing; now this. Contrition had him feeling as if he was going to explode, but he knew he had to maintain his fortitude for his son.

"I know. So how did things go with the sexy investigator?" Don attempted to lighten the mood.

The thought of Cecelia Wilson forced his lips into a weak smile and his eyes glinted at the thought of her. They had had a very nice time at a very exquisite restaurant on Charleston's historical Market Place downtown where slaves was once sold. "I like her. Things went exceptionally well – I think. There lies possibilities for future things, but right now my focal point is you and I kindly told her so. She understood. She has a very beautiful mind, understanding, and intelligence. If I'm not careful, the old man could be in trouble," he admitted.

"Don't let me hinder your happiness. I'm fine. Allah will take care of everything."

Caesar listened but didn't respond. Nothing would really be of any significance until his son was safely out the hands of the devil. Nothing mattered but him.

They spoke a bit longer and ended the conversation just as Cedric entered the room.

"what's up, room-dawg?" Don greeted his roommate with his usual zeal.

"Cooling," Cedric responded with apparent intoxication. Then: "Man, I just heard that your shit got stole! Word Don, I didn't even know or realized that shit! I thought you had it put up or had allowed one of your Muslim brothers to use it as you do at times," he said. "When I came in here from work you were knocked the fuck out and nothing seemed unusual."

Don looked at Cedric through the reddish ambience of their cell and thought that he was in the presence of the devil himself. He was trying to read Cedric but his antics was that of a concerned friend. But Don was very analytical; Cedric would not look him in the eyes as he normally did.

“Man, whoever did that shit got action, homie! “That’s a straight violation! Crossing that threshold and violating where I lay my head is enough! When we find out we’re going to set this bitch off like Jada Pinkett!” Cedric sat on his bunk; he looked infuriated.

Don watched him in amazement. Cedric hadn’t displayed a fraction of the viciousness he was now showing when his own homeboy was killed! Don took this as an act of guilty conscience. He remained cool. “Man, don’t even sweat it. It's a small thing. Just like I told my homeboys; I'm not getting all bent out of shape behind something so minute. I'll buy another one,” he feigned as if he wasn’t entertaining the situation. “Don’t sweat it. Whoever did it will get theirs one way or the other. God don’t like ugly. I'll let Him handle it. My mind is on bigger things.”

“Yeah, I feel that, homie. But that’s still some fucked up shit. Just know if you find out and want to ride, I'm riding with you.”

“That’s what’s up.... You want to use this phone before I put it up?”

“Nah, I'm cool. I just got through using one of my homies jump-off. I just came up here to see about this issue with you to make sure you’re straight. I know you’re from Charleston and I'm from Columbia but roommates are suppose to stick together.” Cedric stood. “I’m about to go back and finish smoking on that Kush my homie got. You know my M.O. You won’t see me till count time.”

“Alright, babe.” Don watched as Cedric left the room. For a moment he remained seated, reflecting on the past 15 minutes he spent with his roommate.

After concluding that Cedric was guilty in one way or another, he slipped the phone in his back pocket and headed to Scramble’s room to share his opinion.

But what if he was wrong? He thought as he headed down the steps to the second tier.

As he walked towards Scramble's room, he was oblivious of the culprit that surreptitiously watched him from a darkened room on the first floor.

Chapter Nine

Ogeechee Correctional Institution

Red Top, South Carolina

June – 2014/ The Following Morning

The following morning Scramble sat at a table in one of the classrooms inside the education building learning how to properly construct an essay. It was a very important part of the GED as it accounted for one-third of the final score.

The classroom wasn't full; it never was. Most of the inmates preferred to occupy their time lost in illusions of the drugs, cell phones, and other ignorant factors that would be the cause of them finding themselves one day forever stuck in prison regretting the fact that they hadn't taken advantage of the opportunity to educate and/or free themselves when they had the chance to.

There was 3 other classrooms besides the one Scramble was in; the others were for the inmates who scored low on their placement test. There were about 9 other inmates in attendance with him. He had dropped out of school in the 10th grade, but he wasn't illiterate. He scored on an 11th grade level.

As he read on, he looked up as the door to the classroom opened. It was Big Unc – the leader of the Folk Nation. He made way to the table and seated himself.

"What's good, black man?" Big Unc spoke at a whisper.

"Just chilling, bruh. I'm trying to get this GED shit under my belt. What's up with you?" Scramble inquired quizzically. He had never seen Big Unc inside the education building. He was an older guy – mid-forties maybe, Scramble wasn't sure. He may've had his GED already or maybe even a high school diploma.

Scramble didn't know Big Unc's reason for being in the building though, but knew it had to be for a reason. Guys frequently met up inside the building and other locations to conduct transactions or whatever it was they were up to unofficially.

"I looked into that situation and it wasn't any of my people, black man. But one of my people got a lil' inside scoop on the B.I.

"Usually, I don't get involved in shit like this but you came through for me when I was on my ass so it is what it is. Just keep where it came from between us," Big Unc stipulated.

"Respect," Scramble agreed.

They spoke at a discreet volume.

"One of my lil' G's said that nigga Roger and that nigga Kane did that shit."

"You talking about those Crip niggas who's roommates on the first floor who be fucking with Don's roommate?"

"Yeah. But the word is Cedric and those dudes had a lil' fall out last night becausethey went and did that shit behind his back. Roger and Kane on some fuck it type shit, and since their tight, Cedric just told them to leave him out of it.

"And, I don't know if you know because you're not affiliated, but the leader over those Crip cats boycotted those two idiots permanently. Cedric ain't even suppose to be fucking with them, but you know how that homeboy shit is back here.

"'Shit wasn't even planned. They just walked past and stumbled across opportunity."

"Appreciate the verdict babe. Word. Secret sworn!" Scramble gave him a pound.

"Hold it down black man, I'm out." Big Unc departed as Don entered the classroom.

Scramble watches as Don headed behind the desk to perform whatever teacher duties it was he was up to. Last night, Don had told him what he had concluded but his conclusion was inconclusive. They were all wrong in assuming Cedric's involvement. But it still didn't exclude him as a potential opponent when it went down because Roger and Kane was his homeboys and most people supported their own in right or wrong.

Don looked up from the desk at Scramble and smiled in acknowledgement.

"Look here for a minute, lil' bruh," Scramble told Don. He closed the text book he'd been reading.

"What's up?" Don approached.

"Sit down and let me holler at you real quick."

Don pulled out a chair and sat next to him.

"I got a solid confirmation on what's what. We were wrong

about your room dawg," Scramble explained the situation. "But it doesn't exclude him getting fucked up because he might roll with his clique. Go ahead and get what you got to get straightin here. You already know what it's hitting for. I'm out. I'll see you in the dorm. I'm going to get the team right."

"Alright, peace."

Scramble departed and the reality of the situation came tumbling down on Don like a ton of bricks. The moment of truth had arrived. All of his life he had never been in any altercations. Not even a vehement disagreement. The fighting skills he possessed had never been used in a real life situation although he had very intense spars with Ali and Jabbar. But the real thing was always different. His stomach tightened and he lost the appetite that had been burning his stomach. There was approximately 30 Crip members in their dorm – not including the homeboys of each member that may support. Things could very well turn into–

"Mr. McFadden?"

Don regained focus and looked up to where the feminine voice had come from that broke his reverie. It was Ms. Bratton. He cleared his throat, stood and headed back to his desk.

"Are you okay?" She asked.

Don looked her over before answering. "Yes, I'm cool,"

She didn't believe him. "You know you can talk to me, right?"

"Most definitely. I'm just beginning to realize that I'm really in prison with a life sentence. Too much think time," he lied, but she seemed to accept it because the tenseness around her eyes relaxed.

As usual, Ms. Bratton had her hair pulled into an extensively long ponytail. She wore a blue and yellow dress that flowed around her ankles and her toes were painted the same hue of blue; the yellow sandals she wore exposed them. She looked around the classroom with stern, watchful eyes, making sure that the other inmates were in compliance. She looked back at Don. "Well, if you need me, I'll be in my office."

"Okay." Don was really beginning to wonder if her interest in him was beyond the norm of motherly concern. He was beginning to think that she was attracted to him. He watched her as she left. And no sooner than the door had closed behind her his mind immediately went back to the problem that awaited him inside his dorm.

###

Charleston, South Carolina

With the new chain of events that was transpiring between Don and Cecelia, Caesar thought that it would be best if he stayed home.

The house was grand; 3 stories, but not as huge as one may think. It sat in a row along the road with others of its caliber just as houses in normal suburban areas. More than anything, he had paid for the grandeur and historical value the house and the land held. From his living room he could look straight across the river on the other side of the street and see the fort where the first shot was fired that started the Civil War in 1863. The Battery was a major tourist attraction. It was located on the outskirts of the city. Tourist's was sight-seeing, and students from near-by colleges jogged.

He sat on one of the expensively stiff, Burberry couches in his living room with his legs crossed, enjoying the view while sipping from a tall glass of iced tea. He was on the phone long distance with Al-Salam.

"That's a mighty deep dream you had there, akhi," Al-Salam said after listening to the dream Caesar had told him about that he had with his grandmother. "And it's true," he added.

"I know, akhi. It just really stresses me to actually see things from that perspective, because now, not only do I grieve Don's plight, I'm also at fault. And, the situation he has on his hands with those fools back there just adds fuel to the fire of guilt that's riding me.

"And what makes it even worst is the fact that if he was really framed, it was because of me." Caesar lowered his eyes ruefully and expelled a breath of pent up frustration.

"Easy now, akhi. Don't go beating yourself up. It's not like you planned for this to happen or knew this would happen. And, for it to have happened, it's only by Allah's leave."

Caesar leaned over and sat the half-empty glass of tea on a cup holster on the cherry red Chippendale table that sat near where he was seated. He scratched his face through the soft hairs of the plush beard he wore and sat back and continued to gaze out of the window. Cars drove by slowly; he could also see people leaning on the protective rails over-looking the broad expanse of the river.

"Let me ask you a question, sheikh," Caesar scratched his face through his beard again. "Do you think that Don could have possibly been set up for something I've done in the past?"

"It could very well be possible, Sulayman. It was a very dirty game we played. Lots of money was involved. We fed a lot of people, and we've hurt a lot of people as well. And don't forget that by us backing out and shutting down the operation, we left some very powerful people angry because the flow of money was clipped.

"So yes, it's possible that Don could have very well been set up because of something you've done," Al-Salam answered with a thick, Arabian tongue.

"But why Don and not me or one of the other brothers?" Perplexity exuded his façade.

"I don't know, Sulayman. Allah knows best."

"I've been wrecking my brain trying to see if I remember anything from the past that would provoke this but I keep drawing blanks. Strings were never left untied for anyone to retaliate that provoked our wrath. You know that. It's why we were so successful."

Al-Salam agreed.

"It's more to it than that unless he's actually guilty," Caesar concluded. "Do you think he's guilty, sheikh?"

"No," Al-Salam answered adamantly. "You know he's not guilty. It's good to play devils advocate in situations like this but I think Furqān would have came to us if he had. Allah knows all that's in between and we know not. It never crossed my mind that he killed that girl so obliterate that thought and seek refuge with Allah because it's nobody but the Shaytān that's sending those insidious suggestions."

Silence fell between them momentarily.

"Well I hope this investigator thing and advocating through these shows cause something to surface. As of now, the investigators have produced nothing."

"Be patient, Sulayman. Trust in Allah. If something is meant to surface it will. If not, we'll put something together and prepare an escape for him. Lets just wait a while and see what Allah has in store. Okay, akhi?"

"I got you, sheikh." Caesar stood from where he sat and

walked to the window, his hard bottom loafers clacked against the polished, mahogany floor. He stuck his free hand in his pocket and watched the activity outside his home. "But enough about me; how are you getting along?"

"Alhamdulillah! I'm fine," Al-Salam puffed up euphorically. "I don't have any complaints besides Fatimah. She's so caught up in all of that westernized propaganda it makes me sick! She doesn't even dress properly anymore, and she has abandoned the salat. I just leave it in the hands of our Rābb. She's grown and will have to answer for her own soul. I can only make du'a." Fatimah was his intractable daughter.

"I'll make du'a for her also, akhi."

"Other than that, retirement is wonderful." Al-Salam smiled through his words. "The new masjid will be completed in two more days. It's so enthralling Sulayman, I can't wait until you see it! The pictures I sent does nothing for the splendidness of it in person!"

"Alhamdulillah! Insha'Allah, I'll get over there soon after things settle a bit." Caesar knew that the masjid was amazing. The architectural design was nothing short of a miracle in itself. Al-Salam had kicked out a cool 33.7 million U.S. currency to have it constructed. "And, Ramadan is less than two weeks away. Don will be twenty years old on the twentieth. I have to get in tuned with myself."

"Yes, you're correct, akhi. Ramadan is here once again. And Furqān is getting older. Almost old enough to buy the alcohol I hope he never buys. Subhanallah!" Al-Salam confirmed.

Silence fell between them again.

Caesar spoke. "So when do you think you're going to make it back over here to the 'land of the free, home of the brave', sheikh? Don is dying to see you. He ask about you all the time."

Al-Salam snorted in derision about America being the "land of the free, home of the brave."

"You mean 'land of the beast, home of the slaves'!" He chuckled.

Caesar laughed.

"Tell him to call me, akhi. I don't want to see him in that place. It saddens me enough knowing that he's there." Al-Salam stood on the palisade of his place over-looking the city of Jeddah. The sun was beginning to set where he was and the orange glow casted an assortment of pastel colors off the beautiful surrounding structures of cathedrals and masjids. "But I don't know. I'm due for a trip. Who knows? Soon I suppose."

Caesar looked at the Cartier watch on his wrist and stepped away from the window. "Well sheikh, it's about time for you to pray so I'm going to let you get to your duties."

"Insha'Allah. Oh, I almost forgot – How's things with the new lady?"

Caesar brightened. "She's fantastic! We're getting together later this evening. You'll like her, sheikh."

"You need the comfort. Lighten up, Sulayman. It's not the end of the world."

"Yeah, you're right about that old man," Caesar said teasingly.

"That I am," Al-Salam shook with a bit of throaty laughter.

"But I'm not going to keep you. Tell everyone I send my salam."

"Insha'Allah. you do the same Sulayman and trust in Allah."

They exchanged salutations and Caesar cut the connection.

As soon as he headed to plug the phone up to its charger it rang. It was his son.

###

Myrtle Beach, South Carolina

“Salam lil’ bro, what’s up with you back there?” Ali asked Don as he left the gym where he worked out. He got to his Porsche truck that was parked in front of the gym in a space reserved for important members, opened the door and sat in the drivers seat with his legs outside the door.

“These stupid ass dudes back here stole my TV while I was in school. We found out who did it now we’re about to go to war,” Don stated.

“Listen D, your pops just called me and told me what was up a few minutes ago,that’s why I called you real quick.” Caesar had told him that he was going to let Don know he would be calling immediately. “I used to be back there going hard. Niggas respected my gangster!

“In the beginning of that prison shit, cats always misconstrue what they can’t decipher and it takes you to fuck some of them up to make understanding understood so it don’t need to be further explained.

“I've stabbed many of them; not only because of their stupidity but mine also. I was thugging.

“But man D, fuck all that fighting and shooting one-on-one's and shit. Yeah, use what you’ve been taught but push that fucking blade and do it relentlessly!” Ali was on the brink of rage. He hated the fact that Don was in the position he was and wasn’t able to help him.

“I got you, big bro.”

A swarm of seagulls flew over the parking lot and one of them defecated on the windshield of his truck. “Punk ass fucking bird!” Ali spat as he looked in the sky at the swarming birds.

“What are you talking about?” Don asked quizzically.

“Nah D, fucking bird just shit on my windshield!”

Don laughed. “Man big bro, you’re crazy!”

“Nah lil’ bro, but on some real shit, handle your business and be victorious! Point blank!”

“Insha’Allah. Listen akhi, the homies just came through. Everyone's ready to roll. Insha’Allah, I'll holler later.”

“Hold it down, Don!”

“Salam.”

Don's line went dead. Ali's blood was boiling! For a moment he looked in the sky at the fleeting birds and reflected back on the days in that hell hole and the many times his bellicosity had left many casualties. Don had Allah on his side so he knew that he’d surmount.

He slid his legs inside the truck and closed the door. He pressed the automatic start button on the steering wheel and the engine came to life. He looked at the milky looking feces of the bird that ran down the windshield, flicked a switch on the left of the steering column ejecting soap and water on the windshield, then activated the wipers.

As the wipers moved in synchronization removing all traces of the birds droppings, he began to dhikr in remembrance of Allah to suppress the truculence that had quickly came to a boil within him. His anger was his ultimate jihad. He’d been doing well in his strive to keep the perennial effects of it subdued but he hated for his family and fellow Muslims to be violated! And even though Don wasn't officially Muslim, he was not only like a little brother, he was the son of a Muslim!

Chapter Ten

Red Top, South Carolina

Ogeechee Correctional Institution

June – 2014

The element of surprise was a very crucial tactic and aspect of advantage in war. Scramble had been incarcerated long enough to have gained the sagacity in not moving so recklessly as so many inmates did. This was dangerous because it only alerted potential adversaries of your intent to strike. Tranquility in movement at all times was imperative to keep the enemy off balance and he instilled this in his comrades. He had read many books on war and strategy but it was nothing he hadn't learned firsthand from the hard-knock streets and the penitentiary. He underestimated no one: man nor woman, because the same way he plotted and strategized, others did as well – even on more profound levels. Arrogance in war was detrimental. The faction that out strategized the other would indeed be the victor.

Scramble and Rumble were the Senior O.G.'s in the dorm from Charleston that most of the Charlestonians respected.

Scramble, Rumble, and Don stood inside Rumble's cell on the bottom floor. They were a couple of rooms away from Roger and Kane's. The other members had been strategically placed around the wing for drama control and had been instructed to feign as if they were normally passing time. Mario was inside his cell with the lights out, his room engulfed in total darkness as he stood to the window of his door on the second tier surreptitiously over-looking the floor of the wing. The way his room was positioned he had a panoramic view of all angles of the wing. He was acting as an anchor and would spring into action if necessary at the sight of any insidious transgression towards his team. Hook and Sinso were beating on the window of the laundry room as they took turns rapping, something they did regularly, but this time they were armed, ready to burn whomever with the fury of fire that burned within. Jamal and the other Muslims were in their group sitting on prayer rugs near one of the far walls on the wing as other inmates milled about oblivious to the excruciatingly hot water that was about to boil over and spill. Cam and a few members of his organization laughed and joked with one another in the middle of the wing awaiting the display of fireworks.

Rumble discreetly looked out his cell door. "I don't see any of them walking around," he stated. "They're probably inside the day-room or their cell." They were trying to locate Roger and Kane.

"Is Cedric still inside him and Don's room?" Scramble asked.

"Yeah," Rumble answered as he looked up towards Don's room. Cedric had the door window covered; probably masturbating or using the restroom, Rumble conceded.

"Walk through and see if you see any of them," Scramble told Rumble.

Rumble departed the room.

"Are you ready, lil' bruh?" Scramble asked Don.

Don nodded affirmatively as he headed to the door where Rumble had stood. He was definitely ready! He rotated his shoulders and stretched his neck. The only concern he had in the matter was the innocent people involved. Even after everyone telling him that they were all one inside the struggle it still didn't sit well with him. He told them to let him handle his own business and only get involved if necessary. "Just watch for interference," he had told them. He couldn't wait until it was all over and done with.

The officer that worked the wing was a very cool, dark skin complexioned older broad that stood around 6 feet. Don thought that she was attractive in a quiet sort of way. She was built firmly and very well kept in hygiene. She stayed off the wing more than often, most of her time and energy was spent eating whatever goodies she brought to work with her.

Scramble left Don to his thoughts as they awaited Rumble's return. He had a 30 inch prison-made machete on his hip. Don had the same ice pick he'd given him when they first met. He tried giving him a more fierce weapon but Don had declined.

Scramble looked at Don as he looked out the window in the dimly lit room to see if he detected any signs of fear, but all he saw was an unspoken somberness, strength, and determination; his posture upright like a soldiers. He was alert like a cat stalking it's prey. Then, without a word, he watched as Don opened the door and simply left the cell.

Don had spotted Kane sauntering across the wing towards the row of rooms where they were. Kane was holding a honey bun by the corner of the wrapper it was inside of because it was hot. Apparently, he'd just come from the cook-room where the microwaves were located.

Just as Don left the room Rumble was returning. He uttered something to Don, but whatever it was, it fell on deaf ears because all of Don's senses were focused on Kane.

Kane and Don were approximately the same size in weight and stature. Kane had a very high yellow complexion; freckles dotted his cheeks. He was partially stoned from the exotic weed that he had bought with the proceeds from the TV he stole. Ready to demolish the soft, creamy bun he held, he anxiously headed back to his room.

As Don neared Kane reality seemed to come to a crawl; the noise from the many inmates a distant echo. As he closed in on Kane they locked eyes.

Aware of his infidelities, when Kane saw Don approaching with a vengeance, he discarded the honey bun and quickly reached beneath his T-shirt for the flat-blade that was tucked inside his waist band....

Scramble had departed the room behind Don and immediately saw the reason he'd left. He was going to handle his business. Scramble walked up to where Rumble had stopped and the both of them stood together at the ready for whatever ensued after Don struck.

When Kane drew his weapon everyone around the wing stopped what they were doing, total silence engulfed the wing as they watched. Don never drew his weapon; this caused his team to spring into action to assist but just as they did, Scramble, and everyone else, abruptly stopped in their tracks in stunned amazement at what took place next....

Kane recklessly swung the blade at Don and just before it struck Don in his face he side stepped it, and with profound ineptness, went from Steven Segal – to Wesley Snipes – to Michael Meyers in a fluent hail of blocks and strikes relieving Kane of his weapon, snapping his wrist and arm in one fluent motion; several lethal kicks flattened him on his back. Don sat on top of him and began stabbing him in his face and chest with the weapon he had relieved him of. Kane's blood splattered his face and uniform as he fought for his life with the one good arm he had left.

Don's ice pick was still tucked on his hip.

The popping and cracking of Kane's bones could be heard around the wing and some of the on-looker's cringed as he screamed out in agony. His scream had not only snapped everyone out of the hypnotic state they had fallen in from shock of what happened and how, but it also alerted the homies he had that were either oblivious to the fact that it was him, or they were in rooms unaware that he was in distress. Doors began to swing open around the wing as inmates came out their rooms.

Kane's partner-in-crime, and Cedric, each came out of their rooms along with other Crip members around the wing. When they saw that it was Kane that Don was malefically assaulting, they drew their weapons and charged towards where he was being slaughtered just as Sinso ran to Don and pulled him off of Kane to prevent him from killing him if he already hadn't; Hook in tow.

With Kane no longer a factor, Sinso, Hook, and Don stood canvassing the wing.

Sinso and hook snatched the stainless steel butcher knives from their hips simultaneously. Don threw the bloody knife that belonged to Kane next to where he laid. Finger prints weren't a factor because the handle was made from torn strips of bed sheets. He knew the gesture in itself was intimidating because Cedric and Roger stopped in their tracks as if second guessing the situation.

"What's up!" Sinso spat towards Roger and Cedric as he began to bounce towards them, his face scrunched murderously, teeth baring tenaciously in his lower lip like an animal. Don stopped him by grabbing him by the arm just as all involved drew weapons. Scramble snatched the machete from his hip just as Rumble drew the axe he carried.

"LET'S GET IT!" Scramble raged as he positioned himself in the middle of the floor with Sinso, Hook, and Don; Rumble followed.

Jamal and the Muslims positioned themselves around the perimeter of the wing. They did not draw weapons. They were militant and patient but they were armed and ready to strike if Don's enemies got the best of him and his supporters. But at the moment, they had everything under control.

Cam asseverated a war cry towards the Crips. "What do y'all want to do?" He sneered pugnaciously as he looked around, two lethal icepicks clenched inside his fists.

The chain of all these events happened instantaneously.

Mario, acting as a sniper, stayed behind the door and played it cool as he watched the hysterics below. His adrenaline was pumping appallingly after watching Don in action! For a moment he thought he was at a cinema watching a movie. Don was deadly! Majority of everyone below had their backs to him on the opposing side. When, and if, things became barbaric, he would simply slip from the room over the railing of the second tier and begin slicing and dicing their foes!

"Peace! Peace! Peace!" The ranking leader of the Crips bellowed over the chaos below after he came out of his room and saw the individuals involved. "Crips! Y'all fall back and stand down!" He ordered. "Fuck them!" The ruling had been passed from the head member that resided in the Mount Pleasant dorm on behalf of the permanent boycotting of Roger and Kane for other violations. "Anybody that doesn't obey this order got to see the committee and flags will be snatched!" He threatened at the members that continued to face-off the Charlestonians.

Approximately 9 Crip members had drew weapons ready to battle. Gradually they retreated and began tucking their weapons.

Cedric looked at Roger, then he looked down at Kane who he thought to be dead so shallow his breathing was. It hurt him deeply to leave them for dead but he had no choice. He retreated.

The ranking Crip member looked at Roger. "And matter-fact Roger, when those crackers come and get Kane, you better leave out here with him or you're next!" He threatened over the thick silence of the wing.

"FIRE IN THE HOLE!" Inmates alerted, signaling the officer's return on the wing.

Everyone dispersed the scene of the crime. They were scattered around the perimeter of the wing now or were standing in cell doors as if normal observers. Roger was the only remaining inmate standing in the middle of the floor, lost in direction.

"Come on, Don!" Scramble ushered him along back towards Rumble's room as the officer ran over to Kane's body, simultaneously radioing for assistance. She'd been eating in the lobby while everyone was on the brink of killing one another. Kane's broken and battered body did not disturb her at all. She was use to the carnage.

Don was drenched in Kane's blood. Inside Rumble's room, Rumble gave him one of his uniforms and Don quickly changed clothes and went to the sink to wash the blood away that had splattered his arms, hands and face.

"That's how you handle that shit, lil' bruh!" Scramble commended and gave him a pound.

After invigorating applauds from the group, expeditiously, they disassembled and headed to their respective locations.

Discreetly, Scramble tossed Don's bloody uniform in one of the shower stalls as he headed to his room.

"Alright, C-wing! To your rooms! NOW! Y'all know the drill!" The woman officer bellowed over Kane's body as every available officer stormed on the wing.

Casually, Don sauntered to his cell just as the First and Second Response teams rolled on the wing. He looked at Kane on the floor in the middle of the wing laying several feet away from his honeybun. An animalistic surge of elation permeated through him from his head to the top of his toes. His adrenaline was in conniption!

The wing officer, along with officers from the other wings in the dorm, kneeled beside Kane coaxing him to hold on until help arrived. Cedric was already inside the cell when Don got there.

"What's up!?" Don asked him acrimoniously as he closed the door behind him inviting Cedric to a duel if he wanted it.

Despite Cedric's fatuity his acumen was enough to discern that Don would hurt him. He'd been leaving their room headed back to Roger and Kane's room when Kane drew his weapon to strike Don. From childhood, he was always an aficionado of martial arts but had never acquired the skill. Don's skills fascinated and frightened him. He didn't want any problems. He sat on his bunk; a sign of peace. “Man Don, me and you are cool, town. You did what you had to do and I respect that.”

“No you don’t because just a minute ago you were ready to roll with your homie until your Crip brother ordered otherwise,” Don countered.

“Yeah, you’re right, but man, I didn’t have anything to do with your TV being clipped. Stealing is no longer my strive. Word, town.”

“I know you didn’t. I know what happened.” Don said as an officer locked the door to their cell. “I just wanted to make sure that you and I were cool. I don’t even like the fact that resulted to this.”

“It is what it is, town.” Cedric leaned over as he sat with his elbows on both of his knee’s looking at the floor adrift.

Don fetched his face cloth and ran hot water over it at the sink. He plastered the hot cloth over his face and allowed the steam to settle his nerves as he breathed in its warmth. After he was done he rehung the wash cloth, removed his shoes and jumped up on his bunk and laid back just as the chopping sound of a helicopter's propeller thundered as it landed outside.

Cedric got up and walked to the cell door and felt as if the past had repeated itself. Once again he was watching another one of his homies carried away on a stretcher. He didn’t know if Kane was going to die but by the looks of the situation with all the nurses hovering over him pumping away at the oxygen distributor they’d connected to him as they rushed him out the dorm to be medevac, only God knew.

“I know that was your partner Ced, and regardless of what he did, I know you’re going through some things. But for whatever it’s worth, I really do hope he be alright; for his sake and mine,” Don said fervently as he glanced at Cedric who was leaning against the door with his forehead braced on the window.

Cedric didn't respond. He continued to look out the window. Two officers were hand cuffing Roger. They escorted him out of the dorm. He checked in on protective custody as he'd been told.

Cedric sat back on his bunk, removed his shoes and laid back just as the roar of the helicopter's rotor became faint with increasing distance.

Don relaxed as the flow of adrenaline simmered that pervaded his soul. Silently, he asked Allah to let Kane stay alive, because if he died, it would only worsen his situation and land him on death row in light of the life sentence he currently had for murder.

His situation was antithetical to Scramble's incident because he had been the only person that witnessed Scramble slay his victim. In this instance, the entire wing had witnessed him take Kane down and surely, there were many snitches around the wing that would cash in on a sure ticket for their freedom or a time-cut to escape the misery of the penitentiary. This worried him. He was sure that someone would snitch him out just to get the dorm off lockdown or just to receive some type of incentive from the administration, which would be no more than a cheap, confiscated walk-man, some canteen, or a TV. The inmates often sold one another out for such ridiculous rewards for insignificant gain.

An hour had elapsed since the drama. Inmates could be heard yelling to one another through their doors. Someone bellowed "FIRE IN THE HOLE!" alerting everyone that the major and other ranking officials were entering the wing.

Scramble stood to the door of his cell watching as the major, along with the wing officer, and other officials ascended the stairs up to the third tier headed to Don's room. "Man, I think

Roger spilled his guts to those pigs," Scramble relayed to Cam who was sitting at the table eating a peanut butter and jelly sandwich.

"That shouldn't surprise you. Look how he went out. Like a straight coward!" Cam retorted.

Scramble watched the officers take out a set of hand cuffs and opened the door to Don's room. Don came out of his room with his hands on top of his head and faced the wall. He was then hand cuffed. Cedric was ordered to step out and a quick search was conducted by the officials while the major observed them. They were looking for weapons but found none. "Hold your head up, lil' bruh!" Scramble yelled and Don looked toward him and nodded his head.

The officials exited the cell, ushered Cedric back inside and descended the stairs with Don in hand cuffs. He was being taken to solitary confinement.

"He'll be alright," Cam stated and licked the oozing peanut butter and jelly from the side of the sandwich he prepared to bite into again. "The officer didn't witness it so he'll beat the charge." He bit into the sandwich.

"Yeah, you're right, but first he got to get past the part of Kane living or dying, because if he dies, the lil' homie is going to be fucked up." Scramble turned away from the door as Rumble and others yelled supportive words to Don as he was escorted off the wing and out of the building.

Cam agreed. He hadn't taken that factor into consideration.

"Well, it done happened now. We all know the possibilities in these things so it's in God's hands now." Although Scramble expressed this, the situation enraged him all over again. He had really grown to like Don as a little brother. It would shatter his heart and spirit if Kane died. "God please let his stupid ass live!"

He pled.

He switched on his boom box at a level volume. “Man Cam, roll up some of that Kush I gave you. Shit got me stressed the hell out,” he groaned as he slumped on his bed and laid back.

Cam looked at Scramble with befuddled astonishment because he didn’t smoke. He sipped a little wine every now and then but that was all he had ever seen him do.

After concluding that Scramble was serious, without question, he retrieved the necessary amenities, cracked the window to their room after placing a damp towel beneath the door, rolled the blunt, and passed it to Scramble along with a lighter and allowed him to do the honors.

“To Kane,” Scramble sat up and placed the perfectly rolled blunt to his lips and lit it. “To Kane,” he reiterated as he took a deep toke of the weed. Instantaneously overtaken by its potency, he collapsed in a fit of coughing. “To Kane,” he managed to cough out after regaining balance of his equilibrium.

###

“You did a pretty good number on that kid, Mr. McFadden,” the Major told Don as he escorted him up the walk-way towards operations accompanied by his administrative captain and lieutenant.

“I didn’t do a pretty good number on anyone. I didn’t have anything to do with that stuff at all,” Don denied the allegations knowing that it was a subtle remark designed to provoke a confession.

“Oh, that’s right, I forgot – you're the son of Mr. Sulayman Azeez Mustafah. Surely you’re innocent twice,” the major snorted in derision. He hated Muslims. He was a short, burly caucasion man with bad skin that had a yellowish tint as if he was infected with tuberculosis or some other disease.

House niggers, the captain and lieutenant snickered.

Don remained quiet. He knew that majority of the caucasian officers that worked in the system were racist. He also knew that a major fraction of Americans disliked Muslims and the religion of Islam because they didn't understand the true teachings of it. Everything they got from the media had been distorted by western bigots for reasons of ideal.

"So, what happened in there, Mr. McFadden?" The major continued to pry. "It's a good possibility that that inmate will die so you better speak now or forever hold your peace or you'll be wearing another murder rap that you supposed to be innocent of," he stated with emphasis on "suppose".

Don continued to look forward in silence as they approached the back door of operations.

"Alright, suit yourself tough guy. Lock his ass up!" The major told the captain and lieutenant as the electronic lock on the door disengaged allowing them entry.

When they entered the building, the major headed to his office and the lieutenant and captain, who were both black officers, escorted Don to the Security Max Unit where he would be held under investigation until further notice.

The lock up unit was a huge 6 story structure that housed men and women on different floors. Before Don's departure from operations, he'd been placed in leg restraints also. After leaving the Security Max building, two other security officers wearing tactical vests and head gear with face shields had intercepted him from the captain and lieutenant. He had boarded the elevator with the two officers and had got off on the 4th floor. As the door to the elevator opened to the wing a blast of loud screams and racket could be heard reverberating through the wing from the caged inmates. Each floor comprised of 3 separate wings. They entered B-wing and the stench of musk immediately assaulted Don's nose on the stuffy wing. The unit apparently had air conditioning problems or the officers were being spiteful. More than likely it was the latter.

Sporadically, along both row's of rooms on the wing, little glass objects shimmered as they protruded from different doors and Don immediately realized that they were mirrors that the inmates stuck through the crevices of the mesh windows of the door to see down the hall.

"What's up, play boy?"

"What dorm you came out of, town?"

"Who the hell are you, punk?"

The wing erupted with laughter at the last remark. Don ignored the questions and remarks. He was in no mood to talk.

"Boy Krayola, you're off the chain!"

The screams and racket continued and Don thought he had entered an insane asylum.

They stopped to a room in the middle of the corridor and one of the security officers unlocked the door and notified the inmate inside to come to the door. There was two doors. The outer door was a solid steel structure with a mesh window and flap for serving trays, and the inside door was bars with a slot also.

"You got a roommate," the officer told the inmate that laid on the bunk in a pair of dingy, white boxer shorts.

"Man fuck!" The inmate complained. He didn't want a

roommate.

Don locked inside the room at the white boy. He appeared to be in his early twenties. A pair of thick, state-issued bifocals made him appear dorky. The cell was dull and filthy. Dust mites covered the floor. Don hated this! It would have to change.

The white boy came to the door spurting obscenities towards the officers. They ignored him and began placing the hand cuffs and leg restraints on him so Don could enter the cell. They did this for security precautions because most of the officers had made enemies with the inmates and had been stabbed and cut by razors and doused with feces by unchained inmates in retaliation.

"What about my property?" Don asked after noticing the room was void of a mattress and other necessities for him.

"We'll get it to you," one of the officers stated flatly.

"Man, those bastards isn't going to bring your shit until after mid-night!" An inmate said from a room behind where Don stood.

"Step to the back of the cell, sir," one of the officers ordered Don's roommate.

The white boy ambled towards the back of the cell and Don was told to enter after the door was unlocked. The shackles was removed from him and his cellmate and the officers locked them inside.

"My name's Brandon, man," the white boy stated as he sat on his bunk.

"I'm Don," Don replied as he looked around the room disapprovingly. There was a back window but it was translucent.

"Man, these dudes around the wing will tell you that I'm cool. Easy to get along with. I just like to talk a lot but if it bothers you just let me know and I'll shut up. My psych meds have me geeked and makes me ramble."

"You're cool," Don said, "But I'm not a very talkative person. I pretty much stay to myself. I'm also very clean so we'll have to tighten this up. I can't live like this."

"Okay. I have a cleaning rag and an extra bar of soap. They only bring cleaning supplies around once a week so that dust backs up pretty fast. It comes from under the door. I'll move these things down here out the way so we can get the floor cleaned up."

Don thought that he should've been using the rag and soap he had!

"We won't be roommates no more than a day or two because I'm about to go on C.I. so I can beat this new charge I just caught. I can't afford it. I already got too much D.D. time."

"What's C.I., and what's D.D. time?" Don asked. "I'm new to all of this stuff."

"C.I. is Crisis Intervention. You tell the officers you're feeling homicidal or suicidal, they come and strip you of all your property, place you inside a one-man cell naked and monitor you. It's a little more to it but that's basically the jist of it and if it's done the right way it can be used to beat your charge because they can't serve you papers on C.I. or anything they think you could use as a tool to harm yourself or others. Therefore it causes the time to expire on the statute they have to serve you the charge papers and take you before the board," Brandon explained.

Clever, Don thought.

"And the D.D. time is Disciplinary Detention time or Day for Day time that you have from charges you catch. I have almost five years of backed up D.D. time. I have too much family issues to be sitting up here for five years. And my brother just died. I can't do it. Something has to shake. They have to put me on the yard or ship me."

Unbeknownst to Don, his roommates was a hell raiser and had brought all of his problems on himself because he couldn't control his temper when it came to the officers. His recent charge was for hoarding his pills and being caught with Threat Group material. He was an Arian. But just as most members of the Arian Nation concealed their identity when out numbered by blacks, Don never could tell that his roommate was even of their nation. This would only be discovered by over-hearing a conversation by Brandon and another individual up the hall that had sent him the material he was caught with. Don wasn't stupid, he read between the lines. His roommate was part of a hate group. He didn't care though, as long as he wasn't affected by it.

Later that night, after 10 o'clock in the morning, the outer door to the cell opened and Don was given his mattress, an extra pair of boxers, socks, state issued hygiene supplies, his sheets, blanket, and shower shoes. The door was closed.

"Yeah, it sucks how they play you up here. I heard that it's different at other prison's," Brandon yawned as he relaxed on his back.

Don had already cleaned the floor and sink and had wiped down the walls. "Yeah, well, I hope they hurry and ship me," he said as he tossed his mattress on the top bunk, made it, then jumped on top of the bunk and relaxed.

"Most likely they'll ship you regardless of what happens. They usually ship everybody that gets caught up in situations like yours."

Don had told Brandon what he'd been "accused" of–nothing more, nothing less.

Don laid back and tried to drown out the preposterous conversations that the other inmates around the wing held. The wing hadn't been quiet since he arrived. It was like being stuck on a play ground with grown men with childish minds. Whoever resided next door to them continued to bang on the wall as he had been doing to get his attention even after Brandon had told him that he was resting and not up for talking.

"BRANDON!"

"Man Krayola, fall back and get some rest!" Brandon yelled.

"Okay, okay, okay. I'm going to fall back but tell your roommate I'll be back first thing in the morning!" Krayola said comically and retreated.

Don laughed. Krayola must've been standing on top of the sink speaking through the vent both rooms shared because Don heard his feet hit the floor in a hard thump as if he jumped off the sink. "Man, that dude is crazy."

Other inmates around the wing laughed also. Apparently, whomever it was that they called Krayola, was the comedian of the wing because since Don had been up there all he had been doing was making people laugh.

"Dude next door is alright. He's funny as fuck," Brandon yawned again.

"Yeah, I can tell. But man, I'm about to see if I can get some rest. I'll holler at you later," Don said as he closed his eyes and tried to block out the conversations his new neighbors held openly about female employee's that liked to discreetly watch them masturbate. No wonder why ships tended to always sink back here, Don thought. These dudes just couldn't keep sensitive things to themselves.

"Yeah, I'm about to crash also."

Don had been fast asleep before Brandon finished the last word of his sentence.

Chapter Eleven

Red Top, South Carolina
Ogeechee Correctional Institution
July 2, 2014 – Tuesday

The very next morning, Krayola, true to his word, had woken Don and his roommate to the sound of pounding on their wall. It wasn't even 5 o'clock; breakfast hadn't even been served! Don opened his eyes incredulously and looked into the water-stained ceiling of the brightly lit room.

"Man, that dude is a retard!" Brandon pulled his sheet over his head as if it would block out the noise of the pounding. Krayola screamed his name.

"I wont stop until your roommate answer me, Brandon!" Krayola said.

Light laughter could be heard in the distance from the few inmates that were woke.

"Man, please answer that dude," Brandon pleaded.

Don didn't know if he should laugh or be mad, it was madness! “Man, I don't know that guy. If he wants to be an ass, let him. He's not bothering me,” Don lied. Krayola was driving him crazy.

After about 10 minutes of pounding it ceased, and thereafter, the officers came around with trays of cold yellow grits, two biscuits and slimy looking half cooked scrambled eggs. Don gave his tray to his roommate. He'd have to build a serious hunger to stomach the trash they served.

“Thanks, man,” Brandon said as he accepted the tray. ”Man, tonight I'm going on C.I. I can't take anymore of this; and I have to get away from Krayola's crazy ass.” He took a hefty scoop of the runny eggs and shoveled it into his greedy mouth.

“Man, who is that guy?” Don asked as he began washing his face at the sink. Good thing he was a morning person because if not he would've probably wanted to kill Krayola.

“They call him Krayola. He's from St. Louis but he lives in Charleston from my understanding. I guess y'all are homeboys if you look at it,” Brandon shrugged and continued to feed his face.

Don went to the cell door and listened to Krayola continue to antagonize other inmates on the wing. The odor of the eggs permeated through the air of the wing. Don couldn't see anything save three of the rooms on the row across from him. He saw why the inmates used the mirrors. He thought about an extensive stay on lock up and cringed inwardly. His roommate said he had 5 years D.D. time and saw why he was about to go on C.I. If he'd been in his shoes he'd probably do the same. He wasn't used to living this type of life at all. And all of a sudden, his situation begun to sadden him like it never had before.

“Man, do they ever out these lights?” Don squinted at the

brightness of the large fluorescent lights in the ceiling as he turned away from the door. The lights were extremely too big for the small confines of the room.

"Hell no," Brandon ejaculated. He downed his cup of milk, belched and didn't excuse himself. "They cut them on at four-thirty and out them at eleven-thirty. It sucks."

"How long do they have you under investigation?" Don asked as he jumped back on top of his bunk.

"It suppose to be twenty-one days but the Warden can have it extended if necessary. But sometimes these assholes do what they want so if you go outside assistance I suggest you contact them and have them call the Warden here, and Headquarters if need be." Brandon got up and sat the trays in theslot of the cell door for the officers to retrieve.

"How can I use the phone?"

"You have to fill out a request form and give it to the dorm lieutenant and they'll bring the phone on the weekend. You can't use it through the week days unless you're calling a lawyer. All you get is one call and that's if you're not on restriction. You're fine unless they charge you. If they do you'll have to settle for the letters man. And, to make matters worse, they only pass out two envelopes a month. It's bullshit!"

All of this made Don weary. He laid back and folded part of his sheet over his eyes to block out the light. Fedora ran across his mind just as Krayola banged on the wall.

"BRANDON!"

"What's up!?" Brandon answered irritably.

"Ask your roommate where he's from."

"He's from Charleston Krayola, and he's resting!"

"Take that base out your voice Brandon, you know you're not built like that!" Krayola laughed. "But that's what's up! Tell him since he's from down the way I'm going to allow him to get a little rest! You heard me? I said a little rest since he just came up here!" he emphasized "little". "But I'll be back! Do you hear me He-Who-Does-Not-Speak? I'll be back! Ask your roommate. I always come back!"

"What the fuck?" Don tried not to ever use profanity but Krayola was ridiculous! He shook his head dismayingly.

"You haven't seen anything yet! He's funny, he just don't know when to chill."

Don sighed and drifted back into his thoughts about his situation as the wing settled in calm quiet. A few toilets flushed around the wing. Anguish began to overtake him. Silently, he asked Allah to give him strength to stay strong.

###

A couple of days had passed. It was Thursday night, the 4th of July. Krayola had yet to relent in his hilarious antics but Don had continued to ignore him which only seemed to drive him! But tonight, Krayola had been rapping for the wing along with a few other inmates so the wing was in a rambunctious up roar.

He was surprised at the change of seriousness that Krayola took in his music and could tell that he was passionate about it. He was talented! He didn't know how Krayola looked because he had never seen him but his voice was strong and distinctively captivating. Don immediately thought that he could succeed inside the music industry.

Brandon had pulled his C.I. hoax so Don had the room to himself. He'd been washing at the sink in his room just as many of the other inmates did because the procedures that the officers wanted performed before leaving the cell was border line homosexuality and went against his morals. They wanted him to strip naked in front of 3 men, stand in the middle of his cell with his arms out-stretched – roommate present and all – like hey, look at me in all my glory; lift his testicles and move them from right to left, squat and cough – all to take a shower! He would never do this as long as there were other means of improvising!

The trusty that came around to clean the wing in the evenings had brought him a kite earlier from Scramble. He hadn't read it immediately because he'd been working out when it came, but now he took the time to read it before the lights went out. It read:

Peace, lil' bruh. I hope you're holding your head up. If you haven't heard, Kane survived! Thank God! I was praying that his bitch ass didn't kick the bucket because I couldn't stand to see you in more bullshit than you already are. I called your pops and told him what the deal was with you. He said call him if you can. Ali and Jabbar said stay cool and hold your head up. The other homies said the same. I got your info so we'll always keep in touch. They still got us locked down for that bullshit but fuck it! The Warden said he might let us off this coming Monday. But anyway, you shocked the hell out of me and everybody else!!! Me and Cam blazed a blunt to that shit and you know I don't even get high! I didn't know you had that Jet-Li shit in you! I guess it's a good thing I approached you the way I did when we first met because you would've whipped my ass! (LOL!) But anyway, get word to me through your pops when you call him or send me a kite through the individual that gave you this and let me know how you're holding up. And, if you're up there with a homie named Krayola, that's my lil' fam. Tell him I said what's up and find out if he got those food and hygiene items I sent him before those last trustee's got fired. He's good peoples if you meet him. I got something coming to you also. Cam also said what's up. Hold your head babe....

Scramble.

Don laughed throughout specific parts of the kite. He sure needed the upliftment it brought him. He knew that he had surprised everyone with his fighting skills. It even amazed him!

But Scramble knew Krayola! "Damn!" he uttered. Now he would have to talk to him to let him know what Scramble said. He'd tell him in the morning. But even after that he wasn't up for chatting or meeting any new friends.

The lights had been terminated about 5 minutes after he'd finished the kite. He crumpled the paper and flushed it down the toilet. There was no need in keeping Scramble's kite for the CO's to find.

After Brandon's departure, he wiped down his bunk area and moved his belongings to the bottom bunk. As his fellow inmates rapped in the background he thought about the birthday he had approaching. He would be 20 years old on the 20th. Ramadan was also a few days away. It began on the 10th. He got up and began pacing the room back and forth, back and forth. Eight steps concluded the length of the room to and fro. As he reflected upon his fate and destiny, Krayola began ad-libbing another song he prepared to start. He was screaming some record label. Don had never heard of he label but suspected it was an underground label he was apart of or one that he aspired to start.

The way Don's mind worked, along with his knack for business, he couldn't help but envisioning stardom for Krayola. He liked his music and energy.

But more than anything, it was reassuring to know that he hadn't killed Kane! He immediately thanked Allah for the blessing of mercy. Now he just had to see what else awaited him with the outcome of the investigation.

###

The next morning Don got up just as the officers came around with the trays. The milk was sour. He flushed the milk down the toilet. One of the circular slots on the tray contained about 5 table spoons of generic Frosted Flakes. The rest of the tray was the usual: grits, eggs, and two biscuits. The cereal was only served on Fridays unless you were on a special diet. Don sat down and began eating.

It was Friday morning. As always, Krayola woke up screaming and making all types of noises from music to animal sounds. He was really an unbelievable dude with a peculiar character.

Don finished his food, sat the tray in the slot of his cell door and called Krayola's name.

"What the HELL!" Krayola responded animatedly. "Is that a ghost I hear?"

Don wasn't up for the games nor jokes. "Man, I'm just passing a word to you for Scramble. He told me to ask you if you got that stuff he sent you? I got a kite from him yesterday."

Krayola became serious. "Nah, man. I didn't get anything. Those trustee's got knocked off with everything," he responded.

"Alright. I'll let him know. You might want to send a message back also."

"Alright, pimp."

"Peace." Don ended the conversation.

"Aye, man!" Krayola called out.

Don didn't answer so he began beating on the wall.

"Man, He-Who-Does-Not-Speak, don't do that shit!"

Don still didn't respond.

"Man pimp, you be acting like a ghost or something! Did you really just spoke to me a minute ago or am I hearing shit?"

The wing erupted with laughter! Laughter rolled inside

Don's stomach and chest.

"That's alright, man. I'm going to holler at Scramble and find out about you because you're spooky, pimp!" Krayola chuckled.

"But nah, I know if Scramble embrace you, you got to be good people. But I'm still going to bother you until you start speaking! I hope you're not stressing over there. If you are, just let me know and I'll sing you a few songs even though I'm only good at rapping!" Krayola added.

Don continued to laugh. He saw why Scramble could like this dude. Humor was indeed necessary in this environment!

"You're lucky I been up rapping all night! I'm about to catch some sleep but this will be continued, ghost man! Thanks for the message."

About 30 minutes after the trays had been collected, the cart that the nurses pushed around could be heard rolling on the concrete floor of the wing. For most of the inmates the arrival of the nurses and other female employee's high lighted their day. He listened to the many derogatory and sexually explicit remarks and statements that was blurted out to the nurse. What was baffling was that the nurse was a jolly, old caucasian woman old enough to be all their grandmother! And to make matters worse, she seemed to enjoy the attention!

What a place he had found himself inside of!

Chapter Twelve

Ogeechee Correctional Institution
Red Top, South Carolina
July 8, 2014

The weekend had went by slower than a sloth. It had been an exceptionally quiet two days in light of people like Krayola being present. Don guessed that there were times that the harsh, depressive conditions subdued everyone.

Saturday, he had spoke with his father letting him know he was fine. His father had also contacted the Warden. The Warden had told his father that he would be shipped more than likely. The little 15 minute call had seemed to end just as quick as it had began. But he was relieved and felt a little bit more at ease after hearing his father's voice along with the reassuring words that he was a master at delivering. He was proud of his father and thankful that he had a dad of such great caliber. He wouldn't trade him for anything in the world! He missed him dearly and hoped that Allah brought them back together again one day.

With such deep and intense thoughts about his father after

speaking with him, he had cried like a baby for the first time since the misfortune of Fedora's murder had been attributed to him. His chest had trembled with agonizing sobs. He had a life sentence in prison. Being on lock up along with all that had transpired, reality came crashing down on him. After crying his heart out he felt rejuvenated.

Now, it was Monday afternoon and Krayola was standing in front of his cell in hand cuffs and leg irons as the security officers secured him before opening the door to let him inside the room. Don didn't know who he was at first until he spoke. Don looked up at him, smiled, and shook his head in wonderment as he entered the cell. He was a towering figure. Don guesstimated him to be around six-feet-seven or eight.

"What's up, He-Who-Does-Not-Speak?" Krayola smiled wickedly at Don as the officers uncuffed him.

Don laughed.

"You can't hide from me."

"Whatever," Don said amusingly as he ambled to the door to be unchained.

"Nah, I'm just tripping. After I saw that you were in here solo I had them move me over here because my roommate been on some clown ass New York shit and I was about to whip his ass with a little mid-western and southern hospitality.

"And, I wanted to see who the hell it was that lived next door to me."

"Man, you're a crazy dude. Why aren't you on somebody's stage doing comedy or something?" Don stated as he headed back to sit on his bunk after the officers departed.

"I'm not with that shit. I'm on that music shit, pimp. Maybe if my music career pave the way for that in the future I'll do some movies on some Mike Epps, Chris Tucker type shit. But right now, I'm thuggin',” Krayola said as he straightened out his things on the top bunk.

Don didn't respond.

“But damn pimp, what's your name?”

“Don”

“Oh, oh, so you one of those mafia dudes?” Krayola asked humorously, then added, “I didn't know they made black Italians. You must be related to Master P?”

Don laughed. He caught the joke. He remembered Master P's movie The Last Don where he portrayed to be the heir of an Italian Crime family after the demise of his Italian father. The movie was ludicrous because Master P didn't have a grain of Italian in his African blood!

Don like Krayola's spirit. With all he was combating he needed the humor to balance him out before he slipped into a psychological abyss of chaos and confusion. Allah had bestowed another form of mercy upon him by placing Krayola along his path, because with the many deranged and troubled souls that surrounded him that pervaded the prison, he could've ended up with a wretched soul of corruptness. Allah was indeed the most gracious and most merciful to the one's that sincerely strove to do right. “Man, how tall are you?” He looked up at Krayola from where he sat.

“Six-seven on the head,” Krayola answered. He jumped up on his bunk.

Through conversing, Don discovered that he was a good fellow with a bright spirit.

Krayola was fit in his athletic physique of 200 pounds. His skin complexion was that of a brown crayon and the top and bottom rows of his teeth gleamed in 22 karat gold. He was born in St. Louis, Missouri. His nick-name had derived from his colorful personality and Don thought that it was the coolest nick-name ever. But after his mother died when he was younger, he and his brother, who's was decease, moved in with their father who was from Charleston, South Carolina. After getting caught up in the urban streets of his father's four-mile neighborhood in Mount Pleasant, he ended up in prison with a 10 year bid for robbery. With 6 years in, under the guide lines of serving 85 percent of his sentence, he was under two and a half years before it was all over and done with.

Being that both of them was from Mt. Pleasant they were familiar with the geography of the area. But due to the difference of their social status they didn't know the same people. Krayola was also older than him by a couple of years.

After being in the room with Don for a week or so, ,Krayola had calm a bit due to the profound discussions he and Don shared. Don had taught him a great deal about business, opportunity, and Islam as Krayola entertained him with ludicrous stories about past escapades. They laughed about movies and various other things as Krayola's memory was in the likes of ancient Arabs.

But more than anything, Don had discovered that his overall aspirations was to be a successful recording artist and he could tell that it burned him to accomplish this feat. Night after night they sat up discussing everything under the sun until breakfast was served. Krayola had fell back from screaming on the door so his audience around the wing felt as if he had left them hanging and teased him jokingly about being intimidated by "He-Who-Does-Not-Speak." Every once in a while he would converse with them and partake in rap sessions but he had begun to readjust his mind-state; conversations with Don was more interesting and meaningful. And, the female that he was dealing with in the free world was taking him through a lot of emotional distress due to her promiscuous infidelities so he was becoming more of a recluse.

###

Ramadan had commenced two days ago. He was fasting with the Muslims. He laid behind a sheet that was draped from the top of Krayola's bunk reading his Quran while Krayola washed up at the sink. As he read about paradoxes in Moses' journey with a very knowledgeable man by the name of Kadhir, he heard Krayola snicker. The snickering stopped and started again. He wondered what was going on with him. It wasn't unusual for Krayola and his comical mind to do something hilarious out of the ordinary, but due to the quietude of the wing it was strange. "Man, what do you have going on?" Don asked quizzically as he placed the Quran on his chest.

Krayola began laughing, "Man if I tell you what just happened you got to promise not tell nobody, Don – I mean nobody!" he emphasized comically, but seriously.

"Man, you're tripping," Don chuckled.

"NO!" Krayola snapped adamantly. "I'm serious!" he added with humorous drama.

"What do you mean?" Don was perplexed.

"Man, a fly just flew in the crack of my ass –"

Deep laughter erupted through Don's chest and exploded from his mouth like a bottle of shaken champagne! The laugh was so deep it tightened his chest and facial muscles. He felt muscles tighten in his face he didn't even know existed!

"Man, that shit isn't funny, Don! Stop laughing!" Krayola laughed himself as he stood on the other side of the sheet butt-naked with suds cascading down the length of his body. “Word, man. I was just washing up thinking about the plans we discussed last night for when I go home, washing my neck and chest and the little fly just landed in the crack of my ass. I got to kill him, Don! I can’t let him make it out this room alive. Because if he do, he’s going to tell all the other little flies, then all of them will think that they can violate me like that! I can’t go for that shit, pimp!”

Don was crying in laughter. He could barely breathe. “Man Krayola, stop it before you break my fast!” he pleaded as he tried to regain his composure from the laughter that continued to roll inside his chest. Don thought that he was beyond hilarious!

“Alright, alright, alright,” Krayola relented. “But man, just remember that you promised not to tell anybody!” he added.

“Man, I got you. Go ahead and finish washing up,” Don said as he wiped away the tears of laughter that had tumbled from his eyes. He had to tell his father about Krayola and couldn’t wait to do so. He was talented beyond measures, and if Allah willed it to come into fruition, he would most definitely be a man of his word on behalf of the plans they had made. Entertainment was an industry they had never tapped into and Krayola, along with his recording aspirations, would indeed prove to be a lucrative investment.

###

Several Days Later

“McFadden,” an officer stood at their cell door.

“What’s up?” Don responded as he attempted to block the light from his face that the officer shined in their cell from his flash light. It was after 12 am.

“Make sure your things are packed after breakfast. You're being transferred to a different institution,” the officer stated.

“Alright,” Don responded.

“Damn, pimp.” This revelation saddened Krayola, although he wanted to see Don move on. He'd become attached to him.

“I know, man. You really had me oblivious to the fact that I was actually on lock up.” Don had never been served any charge papers.

“They must’ve concluded your investigation. I told you as long as those pigs didn’t see anything they don’t have a case unless they got info from one of their informants. It’s a good thing cats liked you.” Not only had Don confided in him, he had also received a kite from Scramble about him. “I wonder where you’re going?”

“Your guess is as good as mine. But you got my info. Just wait a few days and call my father. He'll keep you posted until we touch bases again, Insha’Allah.”

“True. That’s what’s up.”

“It was good meeting you, man. Just stay focused, stay out of trouble and keep writing those hits! And stay funny!” Don added and laughed.

“You already know, fool. Just remember what I told you.” Krayola looked at Don as he sat on the floor leaned up against the wall across from Don’s bed.

“What’s that?” Don asked quizzically as he looked at Krayola’s dark figure in the dark room. Only a faint light illumed through the dull, steel-meshed window. To the eyes of one another they were nothing more in appearance than silhouettes.

Krayola allowed silence to fall between them briefly before

he spoke, then said: “About that fly that violated me. That shit’ll kill my career as a gangster rapper!”

Simultaneously, they fell over in fits of laughter. After the laughter had simmered they chatted with one another until breakfast, as usual, until it was time for Don to leave.

“But on some real shit, pimp,” Krayola said with a sense of solemnity that Don had never seen. The lights were now on and the officers were at the door waiting to restrain Krayola so Don could exit the cell. “Stay up and stay strong, homie. God is going to see you through because you’re one of the chosen few. One love, homie.” He gave Don a pound and hugged him.

The two officers were pretty cool. They allowed them the moment to say their good-bye's as they looked on. Separations was always tough on the inmates that became close after spending so much time with one another.

“Insha’Allah,” Don replied as Krayola stepped to the cell door to be shackled. He didn’t know why every little gesture of sincerity from others made him emotional. His chest tightened as he departed the cell. He wondered what it was next that lay in his path, on his journey of innocence, as he left this chapter of his life behind to enter another.

Chapter Thirteen

Palmetto Correctional Institution

Orangeburg, South Carolina

July 22, 2014

Instinctively, Canary jumped up out of her bed as if it had been on fire or swarming with venomous snakes. She looked at the little alarm clock that sat on the night stand next to her bed. She panicked at the time! It was 7:51 am. The clock had sounded well over 45 minutes ago. Surely, she would be late for work. She had to be to the institution by 8 o'clock. She lived about 45 minutes away from the facility. But if she pushed, she could narrow it down to 30 minutes.

She high-stepped towards the bathroom to clean herself up hygienically, gave her appearance a once-over in the mirror, shook her head, then high-tailed back into her bedroom to slip into her uniform. She dreaded being late. She had never been late for work before until now so she knew that her supervisor would understand. It was just the fact of the recent promotion she'd been given to lieutenant from sergeant. She had also been moved to a different dorm – this one she ran.

It had been almost a week since her promotion. Other officers was disgruntle about her promotion because they had more time in than her and felt more deserving of the position, but schooling and education played a significant role when dealing with rank, not wages. And the fact that the Warden held her in his favor, secretly, had been an advantage. But to her, the favoritism was a waste of time, she would never entertain him nor any of her colleagues for many reasons. She didn't think herself better than anyone but she knew her worth and would not settle for less when she knew that if she so chose to she could have so much more.

She slipped into the black button down shirt with the polished, gold lieutenant bars on the tips of each collar and tucked the tail of the shirt into her pants. No longer did she wear the tan shirt that all other lower ranking officers wore. The color of the shirts changed from tan to black once the ranking position of lieutenant had been reached.

Leaving everything strewn about inside her room, she plucked her keys from the night stand and high-stepped from her apartment to her car, jumped in and peeled out. She didn't have time to prepare any lunch and snacks; she would order out or eat from the prison's canteen.

Just as she hit the road she remembered that she'd forgotten to lock the door to her apartment. "Shit!" she hissed in resentment of the negligence. She quickly assessed the situation and concluded that she trusted the area she dwelled to at least be safe long enough until she returned. She punched the gas.

She had had a very exciting and, exhausting weekend. She had spent it in Charleston with Danyell and Tay.

Tay was the receptionist from. Danyell's practice. They had

a glorious time on one of Charleston's beaches where they picnicked and feigned as if they were thirteen-year old girls all over again just discovering life.

Danyell and Tay were both originally form Charleston so, for Canary, they were wonderful tour guides. She had seen a major fraction of Charleston's most popular land marks and sites and had also learned some historical facts about slavery and the role that the "Holy City" played in the grand scheme of things. And the new bridge that was recently built was astonishing! It was the tallest bridge in America, towering the Golden Gate in San Francisco by 12 inches. She had never been to Charleston and had really enjoyed seeing the city and its natives. It was beautiful. She had fell in love with it and had even contemplated moving there given the opportunity.

Over the past two months, Danyell's comradery had brought her along just fine. Though impossible, she felt as if she was a virgin that had lost her virginity for the second time. Justin being her first experience of happiness, Danyell and Tay her second.

She fought to discard thoughts of Justin because she knew that the slightest thoughts of him could be catastrophic to the healing she was experiencing. She was fighting hard to let him rest and let go.

After several outings of movies, dinners, and other little activities together, Danyell's receptionist began joining them. They were an amazing trio of strength and joy for one another as they all had issues they were combating to overcome. But none of their problems was like hers. Theirs wasn't psychological issues of depression, but normal issues that women experienced in life pertaining to men and their strive to be independent black women in America – well, Danyell had an issue in dealing with a certain level of insecurity due to her being over-weight but she'd been taking the necessary precautions in bringing it under control.

They had rented a Chevy Suburban for the excursion and had dropped her off home around 12 am last night. She knew that she would be tired because she had to take a shower to wash the remnants of the salty beach water from her skin and sand from her hair. They had left Charleston straight from the beach because she had always wanted to experience the beach at night to listen to the smooth, assuaging sounds of the waves rolling towards the shore under the quietude of the dark blanket of the sky above with its incalculable amount of twinkling stars.

Last night, she had laid beneath that blanket, and amongst the stars, she selected the most brilliant of them, depicted it to be Justin, and silently spoke to it as if it was him, promising it that she would let go and live her life. Then she got up and dove into the water and swam out as far as she dared with the intentions of washing away all the pent up pain and agony that she had carried for so long, leaving it behind to be carried away and sink into the lowest depths of the Atlantic oceans abyss.

WHOOP! WHOOP!

The sound of police sirens interrupted her thoughts. She looked into her rearview mirror. It was a cop. "Damn!" Just her luck, she thought. She pulled over to the side of the road. The area was rural and unpopulated. Trees and foliage lined both sides of the two-lane road.

She watched as the officer exited his vehicle and approached her car as if he had all the time in the world. She wished he would hurry! She glanced at the clock display on her console. It read: 8:11 am. She smacked her hands on her thighs then lowered the window.

"'Morning, ma'am," the officer greeted kindly upon approaching the window.

"Good morning, officer," she returned just as kindly.

"I'm sure you're aware that you were speeding. I clocked you at seventy-eight miles per hour and this is a sixty mile per hour zone." The officer was caucasian and very country in accent.

She thought that he was attractive with his deep set emerald green eyes. But she didn't do white men. "I'm sorry officer. I'm just running a little late for work. I work at Palmetto Correctional Institution."

He peered in at her uniform. "Well, being that both of us are in the same line of work I'm going to allow you passage. Good day, ma'am," he tipped the brim of his hat and left her to her mission.

"Thank you, officer," she yelled out her window to his back because he was already heading back to his cruiser. She had the temerity to tell him that he had a nice ass but she subdued the urge and sighed in relief of dodging a speeding ticket, gave thanks to her uniform and peeled out from the side of the road kicking up dust since she had the green light to do so.

Actually, she was beginning to feel herself.

###

Palmetto Correctional Institution was *wholly* antithetical to where Don came from! He looked around at the old, solid structures of brick and steel that surrounded him. He had arrived at the facility approximately 2 hours ago inside a van. He didn't know why, but for some reason or another, as he trekked across the small yard with his property crammed into a green, army duffle bag that was hefted on his back, his type writer in hand by its handle, slavery crossed his mind. The yard and its old structural design reminded him of a maximum security college campus. But more over, the positioning of the buildings was of the same design around the yard.

This yard in particular consisted of 4 dorms, each containing a single wing and a lobby. Each held 250 inmates. Top tier, bottom tier. Some of the rooms were two-man cells and some held three.

The dorms were named after the four major geographical areas in South Carolina: Columbia, Greenville, Charleston, and Myrtle Beach. He had been classified to Greenville.

It was around lunch time and the yard was in a frenzy of activity. Inmates loosely moved about like ants! He had heard about this facility from his roommate at Ogeechee in how it was considered to be the best yard to be *institutionally* because of its laxness in enforcing police and security. It's corruptness – appalling! Although he couldn't see what the hype was about as he neared the dorm he'd been assigned to, he had long ago came to the realization that in prison, nothing was as it appeared to be on the surface. Penitentiary life was arcane. And by the unwavering traffic of the inmates moving to-and-fro carelessly with no seeming worries in an environment that was suppose to be controlled, all hinted to the fact that Palmetto Correctional Institution was in a class of its own. He didn't even see one security officer on the yard watching the movement of the inmates!

Inmates looked at him as they passed one another but quickly dismissed him as a nobody upon unfamiliarity and kept moving. The ambiance of the prison reminded him of the stark somberness of the ghetto where his father was raised.

He reached the cherry-red brick cube that was the dorm. A small white sign was above the threshold of the entrance; painted in black was the name of the dorm. He walked through the open door of the entrance into the lobby and was greeted by the strong air of marijuana. The wing officer and the dorm's sergeant stood inside the lobby conversing with four other inmates. They all looked at him as he approached and extended the placement slip towards them. The sergeant retrieved it.

The sergeant was a very tall, sinewy, flat-chested guy of Spanish descent. Don wasn't quite sure his ethnicity. His name tag read: Sergeant Granada. His bald head shone beneath the light above as if he had soaked his scalp in olive oil.

"What's shaking, homeboy?" Sergeant Granada addressed Don. "New arrival?"

"Yeah," Don replied. The Sergeant's hipness didn't surprise him at all. Prison was nothing like he had depicted it to be or had seen on television. Not in South Carolina – at least from what he had seen thus far.

"He's next door to my room," one of the inmates said, smacking his lips, that stood near the sergeant. He had glimpsed the slip. "I'll show him. Come on," the inmate offered.

Don looked at the inmate and thought that there was something strange about him, then it dawned on him that the inmate was gay. He looked at the other three inmates and officers, discarded it, hefted the heavy bag over his shoulder once more, and with his type writer in hand, he followed behind the swaying hips of the punk that led him to his cell. He knew that punks were prevalent in prison, but he had never interacted with any of them in any manner. There were gays at Ogeechee, but none resided on the wing in the dorm he had occupied.

As he followed the trail of the punk at a fair distance, he concluded that all three of the other inmates in the lobby were homosexuals. Birds of a feather flocked together, he thought. The officers were probably homosexuals also. Anything had proven itself possible!

The wings was larger than expected! Eight rows of benches

sat in the middle of the wing. Four television sets hung beneath the awning of the upper-tier. Three microwaves sat on stands against one of the walls. There was top and bottom tier day rooms and inmates packed them both as they gambled in games of Poker, Tunk, Spades, and Rummy. Unbeknownst to him, some of the pots topped $10,000!

As he passed the bottom dayroom, he could see inside. The air was thick with weed and cigarette smoke; the rambunctious voices of the inmates inside the dayroom reverberated through the dorm. For a minute he thought all was cool until he remembered that marijuana was still illegal and that tobacco had been banned from the agency years ago.

Some of the inmates around the wing looked at him to see if they knew him. But just as the other inmates had done when he peregrinated across the yard to the dorm, these inmates disregarded him as if there was much more pertinent business at hand.

The punk stopped in front of one of the rooms in the flood zone, which was the lower level of the bottom tier. Don looked at the faded numbers on the door -- it read: 109. A flap covered the window. The punk knocked.

"Y'all have a roommate," the punk said in an overly soft voice that didn't belong to him. "This is a three-man cell," he looked at Don. "You don't look like someone who want to be crowded, so if you got a little money to spend, I advise that you get with the dorm lieutenant's clerk that stay upstairs and pay him to put you in the next two-man that comes open. Some of these dudes will be mad because people have been waiting in line to get them, but everybody already know it's all about money around here, so it is what it is."

The door opened just as the punk finished speaking and Don looked into the crowded room of 5 white guys. They had just finished shooting cocaine.

"What's up, foxy?" One of the white guys said.

"Ain't nothing Jeff. This is their new roommate," Foxy returned and smacked his lips coquettishly.

Don gathered that the punks name was Foxy. He stepped to the side and three of the inmates came out of the room.

"We'll holler when your roommate gets situated, bo," the white guy stated that Foxy had called Jeff.

"No, Jeff. We'll be up to your room. Do you have the tools?" One of Don's roommate's asked.

"I got 'em, bo."

Before entering the cell, Don gave it a once-over and thought that it was fairly clean and tidy for a couple of junkies. "Sorry that you walked into this, man."

"You guys are fine, man. Your business is your business," Don responded as he sat his bag up against the wall by the door until his roommates was finished making room for him to maneuver around. He could tell that the cocaine they'd been shooting had them lit. "Thanks," he said to the punk and began pulling the door close dismissively. He had been uncomfortable in the presence of the punk and was glad to be free of him. But he would surely take his advice in paying his way into a two-man cell. Staying in such cramped confines with two other men – junkies at that – would not work. Whatever the price, he'd pay it ten times over to ensure that his request be taken as a V.I.P.

"They call me Mark Shaw, man. Who are you?" Mark Shaw extended a hand.

Don looked at the small white guy who badly needed a shave. His eyes was bloodshot red and he had large, saggy bags beneath them as if he hadn't slept in days. He shook the hand. The grip wasn't firm. "I'm Don," he said as he looked at the powder blue state issued fitted cap that sat awkwardly on Mark Shaw's noggin. He didn't know why, but for whatever reason aside of his addiction, he thought that the little white guy was an alright fellow.

"I'm Nebraska, from Nebraska," Nebraska said as he fidgeted in his locker for something he probably wasn't even aware of. Just an effect of the drugs. "We ain't nothing but a couple of country junkies so don't pay us no mind. You go ahead and get settled in, bo. Come on Shaw." Nebraska abandoned the search as if he wasn't looking for anything from the start and headed out the room.

Don looked on sagaciously as they departed the room. He figured he could get along fine with both of them but was in opposition of living amongst addicts of hard narcotics. Nebraska had carelessly left the doors of his locker swinging; Don politely closed them. They weren't bad as he expected. But still, 3 bunks, 3 bodies, 3 lockers, 1 sink, 1 toilet, was *way* too much and not enough all in the same breath. But for the mean time, he would make it work.

After wiping out his locker and wiping down his bunk of dust and impurities he began unpacking his things. He came across the wooden stand to his TV as he removed the crammed items from the duffle bag. The stand instigated a quick flash back through his minds eye when he took Kane down. Now he was inside a new environment, one probably more pugnacious than the other; once again a new face. He hoped that he wouldn't be violated again because he "was" going to order another TV. But this time, he wouldn't be so careless.

###

It was routine that the dorm lieutenant from each dorm cover security inside the cafeteria while the dorms ate lunch. The last of the 4 dorms, which was Greenville, was leaving the cafeteria heading back to their dorm – her dorm.

Lieutenant Rose followed behind the herd of inmates; her clerk in tow. She had been a bit late for work and had missed the morning briefing. But after being informed by the shift's captain, all was well and her day had set out to a smooth sail.

The air had cooled a bit from its earlier state of heat and now it appeared as if it would rain. Her mind ran across the unlocked door to her apartment. She wondered if a bunch of lucky teenage delinquents had discovered it and wiped her clean of all her energy drinks and coff –

"We got a new arrival today, L.T.," the Hispanic-American clerk stated as he walked along side the lieutenant.

"From the evaluation center or another institution?" She asked.

"Another institution," the clerk answered.

"Does he appear to be a trouble-maker?" She inquired.

He hated when she asked such questions as if he was a snitch or an ass-kissing inmate. "No. Not that I can tell. He doesn't come off as the typical thuggish type."

Lieutenant Rose knew that it was impossible to have a dorm wholly free of trouble-makers, but she had set her aim to have the best dorm on the compound, and for the past two weeks since she had been lieutenant, she had shipped out many of the trouble-makers and masturbators to other dorms around the yard.

"I already picked up the toilet paper and cleaning supplies from the Commissary. I passed out the toilet paper."

"Okay."

"Only thing that really needs to be done is adding the new arrival to the dorm's roster."

They reached the dorm and all of the inmates headed on the wing. They knew that when she was around, loitering in the lobby wasn't tolerated.

There was two offices inside the lobby. One belonged to the dorms lieutenant and the other belonged to the case worker of the dorm. The sergeant and other officers had access to them but they didn't have codes to access the computers, nor did they possess any keys to the file cabinets.

Lieutenant Rose unlocked the file cabinet inside her office, by the only window it possessed, and the clerk retrieved the necessary things he needed to log in their new arrival.

The office wasn't large. It contained a nice size desk that she kept neat. One of the inmates in the dorm that she knew had a crush on her had had a nameplate made for her through the hobby-craft wood shop. "Lieutenant Rose" was engraved in fancy cursive letters on it. It sat at the front of her desk. Another file cabinet sat in the left corner of the office. A flower pot containing a beautiful plant with shiny leaves sat atop of it. A wooden cabinet containing snack items of her preference sat adjacent to the file cabinet; a clock radio sat atop it. And, another file cabinet sat in the far left corner of the entrance with an identical flower pot and plant as the other, sat atop it. A 3-seater chair sat along the wall across from her desk and a small table sat next to it that held a coffee pot, cream and sugar.

Ricardo, Lieutenant Rose's Hispanic-American clerk, spoke both languages fluently. He was in his early 30's. Very mannerable and well-kept. She had terminated the last clerk when she first got the dorm because he was power struck and demanding as if he was the lieutenant and she the inmate. Ricardo had proven to be a good pick because of his diversity and work ethic. And, she didn't have to worry about him drooling over her like a dog all day. He was serving a 20-year sentence for several thousand pounds of marijuana he'd been caught with about 8 years ago after being snitched out by a white guy he'd befriended from Rock Hill, South Carolina.

"Ricardo, would you please put on a pot of coffee for me?" Lieutenant Rose asked as she sat behind her desk and relaxed. She was still exhausted from her weekend adventure and couldn't wait until 4 o'clock so she could go home and sleep.

"Si, senorita," Ricardo replied loyally.

She reached over and turned on the clock radio and the sounds of a new Kelly Price song filled the small confines of the office just as a slither of lightning struck through the sky as it began to pall over.

###

After his bunk had been made, Don grabbed the duffle bag and headed out the cell to return the bag to the officers. He also needed to find out what he needed to do to have a stolen property report filed so he could order another TV. He approached the desk where the wing officer sat talking to the same group of punks.

"How can I be of service to a brother?" The officer inquired optimistically.

Don looked at him and instantly concluded that he was queer. "I'm trying to turn this bag in. I'm also trying to have a missing property report done so I can order another TV."

"Go in the lobby and holler at the sergeant and lieutenant and they'll help you with those things."

"Alright." Don headed off the wing.

When he got inside the lobby and approached the lieutenants office, Sergeant Granada sat behind the desk. A Spanish looking guy, whom Don assumed to be the clerk, sat drinking a cup of coffee as they engaged one another in Española. They looked at him.

"What's up?" Sergeant Granada asked as he leaned back inside the chair.

Don raised the duffle bag. The office smelled of freshly brewed coffee.

"Give it to Ricardo."

The clerk retrieved it.

"I also want to have a missing property report done on a missing TV from my property. I don't know what happened to it," Don prevaricated. He didn't see the need in getting into what actually occurred. He had his receipt, the TV wasn't inside his property, nor listed on the inventory form of his property so that was enough.

"Alright, but you'll have to wait until the lieutenant return and she may not be back until tomorrow because they needed her assistance at the front gate. Shortage of staff. You just missed her," Sergeant Granada informed. "Until then, just chill out, jack your pecker, and get your bid on."

Don scrunched his face and his eyebrows furrowed in disdainment towards the sergeants statement.

"No pun intended, hombre. It's just prison-jargon. Don't get all bent out of shape," Granada stated upon Don's apparent discomfort by his statement.

"You're the new guy, right?" Ricardo asked Don.

"Yeah."

"Okay. I'll make sure we get you situated as soon as she return," Ricardo assured.

"Thanks." Then, as an after thought, Don told Ricardo to make sure he stopped by his room when he got the opportunity to do so. Then he headed back on the wing with Sergeant Granada's statement careening through his head. Once again, he couldn't help but think what his life had succumbed to.

The phone room was the first room in the flood-zone. He descended the three little steps and headed inside. It was empty when he reached it. Three of the six phones was destroyed. He found one in fair condition, took the phone from its cradle, used the tail of his shirt to wipe the ear piece clean, and called his father.

After a couple of unsuccessful attempts he headed back to his room. His father was busy more than likely. He would see the missed calls from the strange number and know that it was him who'd been trying to call.

He was hungry. His stomach sounded like the thunder that had begun roaring above. He went inside his locker and fetched a cheese soup, a can of tuna, his can opener, and a honey bun and headed to the microwave. He would have to restock on some things because he noticed that many items was missing from his property that he once had. The boxes of cereal, instant mashed potatoes, etc. were all missing. He knew that he had extremely too much canteen to fit inside the duffle bag with all his other belongings. Whatever didn't fit inside the bag had to stay behind.

There was about three inmates in front of him at the microwave. The other two were also occupied. He leaned up against the wall and watched the many inmates around him that moved about as he awaited his turn to heat up his food. Suddenly, the beautiful sounds of the adhan resonated over the many voices as one of the Muslims made the call for the noon prayer. He looked up towards the dayroom where the call came from as devout worshippers of Allah gravitated towards the call to success. Just then, he remembered that it was Ramadan, he was suppose to be fasting! He had got so consumed by the process of moving that he had completely forgot. He picked up the food from where he'd sat it and headed back to his cell to replace them. And, his birthday was tomorrow. This had also slipped his mind! He expelled a breath of dismay.

After replacing the items, he fetched his hand held mirror, brush, electric shaver, and headed to find how he could get his hair cut.

Chapter Fourteen

Orangeburg, South Carolina
Palmetto Correctional Institution
July 23, 2014 - The Following Morning

Lieutenant Rose had conducted her rounds on the wing ensuring that all of the rooms were in compliance. She didn't strive to be a bitch and pester the inmates about small things. She'd been getting along fine with them.

Yesterday after work, after ensuring that no one had invaded her dwelling, she showered and ate a nice hot meal that she had picked up from a soul food restaurant on her way home from work. After she ate, she touched bases with her girls and was fast asleep.

Now, it was Tuesday morning. She was well rested and felt better than ever in spirit. She was even optimistic about life again and had been thinking about her past aspirations of becoming an attorney. "You need to take this flap down, sir," she knocked on one of the cell doors as she was moving along.

"Just got out of the shower," came a faint reply.

Most of the inmates was either at work, school or still in bed. She knew that most of them spent their time partying and getting high all night. It was pathetic. But it was their lives they were wasting; they were free to live it how they deemed.

A few of the morning elders sat around drinking coffee being nosey just as old folks in neighborhoods on their front porch in the free world. They greeted her and she returned formalities. A few other inmates moved about connivingly, plotting and scheming on something or another. It was a world of many minds that never ceased in its schematics.

The wing was quiet. It was around 10 am.

"Good morning, empress," an inmate greeted her.

She looked to the left of her and smiled. "Hello, Mr. Wright. How're you this morning?"

"I'm fine. You know it's always good to see you," he replied as she stopped to speak with him.

"How's the new book coming along?"

"Better than expected. I had to conquer a few hurdles of depression but I'm handling it."

James Wright III, had authored several urban, and commercial fiction novels. He was combating an unlawful drug related murder conviction. She'd done a background check on him. "Wright, why do you call me 'Empress'; what does it imply?"

"To be honest, I call you that because it fits your aura and persona. You have an imperial glow. But an empress is the wife of a ruler, or a woman who's a ruler."

She conversed with him shortly and adroitly slipped from his clutch. She had told herself when she first met him and found out that he was the author of her favorite novels that she had to watch how she dealt with him because out of all the inmates she had encountered, he really did intrigue her with his charm, articulation, and intelligence. She was glad that he didn't make it his business to pursue her as so many other inmates did. The frightening part about it all was that she could see herself falling for him.

But really, she knew the reason for his hesitance in pursuing her as she had seen him too many times in the office of the grievance coordinator. She didn't know with certainty, but she was willing to bet that coordinator Montgomery and him had something going on. He was too finesse.

She left the wing and went back inside her office where the mellifluous tunes of an unfamiliar singer serenaded. "Girl, Carter, I meant to ask you who did your hair? It looks nice," she said as she sat behind her desk.

Carter was the female officer that worked the wing. She was in her mid-twenties, brown skin complexion, petite physique, mildly attractive. She had just completed the training academy for new officers and today was her first day working the wing without a training officer over her. "Girl, one of my cousins hooked me up. He got his little cosmetology thing going on. Thanks for the compliment," she said as she tugged one of the tendrils that dangled down the side of her face. She sat in the three-seater across from Rose's desk.

"He?" Rose asked surprisingly.

"Mmhmm," Carter giggled. "You already know girl. He's one of those men who's real feminine. There's rumors in our family about his sexuality but he's adamant about his straightness. I don't know, though.

"But personally, I think he's gay."

Rose reached inside the cabinet next to her desk and fetched a bag of Cheez-It crackers. "So, how's things been coming along so far with the guys?"

"It's not that bad. They're really too much, though," she blushed.

"Girl, tell me about it! I know it's hard not to be attracted to any of them because it really does seem like this is where all the cute ones are hiding. Just be careful in what you decide to do and think before you act. Try not to lose control of your emotions and think intelligently because you never know what you may be getting yourself into. This is totally different than the streets.

I'm not going to sit here and pretend like some of our colleagues do, feigning as if they don't indulge in improper acts with these fellas when they do, so I'll be the first to say that I don't criticize decisions in the matter. I just advise that you do whatever you deem best for your overall objectives and aspirations in life," Rose explained affably.

"Have you ever dealt with any of them?" Carter asked with childish curiosity.

"No. Never have and never even entertained the thought of doing so. There's guys that I may have dated under different circumstances but this type of life is not for me. The thuggish image isattractive but I don't want a thug who's actually living that lifestyle. And, I'm not motivated by money."

"Good morning, ladies," Ricardo greeted as he entered the office. "I'm not interrupting anything, am I?"

"No, Ricardo, you're fine," Rose answered.

"Do you want me to go ahead and get the guy that need the property report done while things are calm around here?'

"Yeah, go ahead so I can get it out of the way."

Ricardo exited the office and Rose picked back up on the conversation that her and Carter were having before his respectful interruption.

###

Both of Don's roommates worked in maintenance. They had departed for work as soon as the 7 am count had cleared. Don had got up a little after 9 o'clock and hopped inside the shower. He usually got up earlier. But not only did he had to readjust himself from the late-night excursions on lockup with Krayola, his roommates had been geeked up and had loquaciously kept him up throughout a major fraction of the night.

Yesterday, after finding out the dorms best barber, he got a nice low cut with the sides and back of his head lightly faded. Then, he showered and prepared himself a light meal of fish, sausages and rice to break his fast with when the sun went down. He had confined himself to his room an started constructing the business plan surrounding the music business on behalf of the plans he had made with Krayola. He would send Krayola and his father a copy for feedback when he completed it.

He also wanted another smart phone. The internet access was a plus. Although he had yet to see one so far, he knew they were present. He had also chatted with his father last night and had been informed that he'd been dispatched to an important meeting in California with the CEO's of the company that manufactured the products of a snack line he had launched approximately 10 years ago. This was why he couldn't reach him when he first called. His father had also told him that since he was already in California and had an interview with Steve, he was going to spend the night there. He was told to listen out for the show in the morning.

He squeezed some Jergens lotion that was mixed with an oil fragrance he added to it in the palm of his hands and applied the mixture to his arms, face and neck just as a knock sounded at his cell door. "Come in," he called out.

"Que pasa, amigo?" Ricardo entered the cell.

"Que pasa, amigo?" Don returned.

"You sure got it smelling good up in here," Ricardo wriggled his nose at the pleasant scent.

Don smiled.

"I would've came through yesterday like you requested, but man, these cats around here be runnin' me like crazy."

"I understand."

"But what was on your mind, amigo?" Ricardo inquired.

Don examined Ricardo. His top and bottom incisors were capped in sterling silver, and for a brief moment he thought about his deceased mother. It was hard not to every time he saw the metal – or anything silver for that matter – because of her name. "I heard that you were the man for the room changes and I'm trying to get up out this three-man into a two. What will it cost me?"

Ricardo stood around 5 feet, 2 inches, 130 pounds tops. He looked up at Don. "Man, I normally charge twenty bucks. Green Dot or canteen. I used to charge ten, but the demand has gotten loco with cats paying extra just to make sure they get first dibs. I got a couple' people waiting now."

"Well how does a hundred bucks sound?"

"Are you serious? You must really want that two-man. The thing is, I know if I moved you in the next one that comes open, cats will scream all the way to the Warden because you just got here.

"I'll tell you what, though. If you can find someone in a two-man that will swap out with you it'll work better instead of me moving you into a room with an available bunk. There's a lot of dudes that need money around here, so if you got it to spend, that'll be the best route. I'm not a Jew, and I am not in need of money. I do what I do to pass time."

"That's what's up. But the problem is, I don't know anyone around here," Don stated.

"Are you from South Carolina?"

"Yeah."

"Where?"

"Charleston."

"Man, amigo, you have plenty compadres around here! All you got to do is let them know who you are and you'll be plugged into the fucking Matrix!" Ricardo ejaculated.

Apparently, Charleston's infamy was prevalent. "Alright," Don said.

"In fact, I know a few of your homeboys that are real good amigos. I'll tell them about you. What's your name?"

"Don."

"Okay, Don. But for now, lets go see our gorgeous lieutenant so we can get you situated to order another TV."

Don secured his locker and parted the cell behind Ricardo. Just like that, things was beginning to move again.

Don had been all over the world, country to country,

continent to continent, and had the privilege of seeing, meeting, and dating some of the most beautiful women that God had created. But he had not been prepared for the woman that sat behind the desk when he entered the office behind Ricardo.

Although it had only been a brief moment that they looked at one another, Don thought that it was an eternity before she broke the connection. He didn't even notice that the other female officer had been present until she excused herself. He couldn't stop staring at her! Her name tag read: "Lieutenant Rose". She seemed to fidget under the intensity of his gaze. This wasn't a normal way of his upon first contact with women he was attracted to, but he couldn't help himself. He would have never thought to find a woman of such sui generis in an environment of such grief and danger. This made him stare at her harder. He chastised himself inwardly and pulled himself together just as Ricardo turned around from the file cabinet with the property forms he retrieved.

Don felt clumsy in that he didn't greet the lieutenant when he first entered the office and felt that it would make him feel lame and fatuous if he did now so he continued to be cool. He sat his I.D. card on her desk and pushed it towards her with a finesse stroke of his index finger.

Lieutenant Rose looked at the I.D. that was placed before her. She couldn't believe who was standing before her and the name on the identification card solidified what she questioned upon seeing him. He was indeed the son of the wealthy Muslim guy who had caught the life sentence for allegedly murdering Fedora Armanti-Teressa Sanstrom down in Charleston. The last time she checked he had been sent to Ogeechee. She wondered what he was doing at Palmetto in her dorm. Her heart was hammering, but she maintained her composure professionally. She would do a background check and find out his status in what led him to being shipped where he now was.

She cleared her throat as Ricardo sat the forms before her. "You can have a seat, Mr. McFadden."

"Thank you."

She looked at him as he seated himself. The same feelings that had once stirred within her when she had been following his murder trial begun to churn within her once again. She needed to hurry and complete his forms so he could leave. She needed to be relieve of his presence so she could breathe and ruminate these new chain of events that unexpectedly came upon her. "So what is it that you need done, Mr. McFadden?"

"I need a missing property report done so I can order another TV."

"Okay. What happened to the one that's missing?" She watched him as he struggled with himself to refrain from looking from her eyes to her lips. He was trying to be a gentleman. She couldn't help but notice how demanding his presence was. She didn't know his level of experience with women, but if he was experience, she knew that he could sense the energy of her trepidation just as well as she could sense his. The pressure was as if both of them was holding one another at gun point!

"It was stolen while I was in school at Ogeechee," he was reticent.

"Why didn't you have a report done there?" She inquired.

He looked from her to Ricardo and lowered his brows thoughtfully. "Because I was locked up under investigation for an inmate that had been stabbed. Then I was transferred here." It was all he was going to say. If it wasn't enough, then so be it. He'd find another way to order the TV.

Immediately, Rose concluded that he had stabbed the culprit and because there wasn't a witnessing officer he'd been locked up under investigation. And, the only reason he'd been transferred so quickly instead of being dragged by Ogeechee's administration was because of his status and his father's influence. She decided to complete the forms for him anyway.

After completion of both forms, she slid them towards him. "Put your signature by the x on both forms." She handed him her ink pen. He got up to retrieve it.

Don looked at her as he took the pen from her golden hands. He took advantage of the opportunity of being a couple of feet away from her to scan her features. Audaciously, he looked at her lips. They were full; the color of the flesh of a ripe mango. She may've had on chap stick but nothing more. Her delicate hands resting on top of the desk made his chest swell. She aroused him. "I'm sorry," he whispered through his lips and began stroking his signature across the lines of the forms.

Although the music was playing, it played at a discreet interval. She caught the whisper of "sorry" that escaped his caramel toned lips. She wondered if he apologized for the way he had looked at her.

She watched as he signed the last form and noticed that his penmanship was skilled. He stood erect from his bent posture over her desk and handed her the pen. He had nice hands for a man. Strong. But, hands that had never known strenuous labor.

"Is your fragrance a body wash?" he asked with the pen extended between neatly kept fingers.

She didn't respond. She just looked at him and took the pen politely. Ricardo had begun plucking weeds out a flower pot in the corner by the window; his back facing them.

"That scent is called 'Inamorata'," he said as he picked up his I.D. "It's Italian. It means 'A woman whom one's in love'. I came up with it and my father launched it. I know you don't know who I am but it's a body wash off my father's cosmetic line."

"Oh, I know who you are indeed, Mr. Donatello Furqān McFadden," she said to herself as she continued to observe him.

"Well, anyhow, thanks for the help Lieutenant Rose," he smiled a brilliant sparkle of beautiful white teeth.

She nodded her head and he left the office. She leaned back and sighed. She looked out the door of the office into the empty space of the lobby lost in thought. The affect he had on her frightened her and excited her. She wondered if she should have him removed from the dorm before slipping into the inevitable.

Don headed back to his cell to cogitate the last 10 minutes he just spent with the woman who'd instantaneously became the very thing he had designed an intimate fragrance around: Inamorata.

He didn't know what the future held in the plans of Allah, but what he did know was that his stay at Palmetto Correctional Institution would indeed be interesting.

Though he didn't celebrate birthdays or other pagan holidays, today was surely a good day to start his 20th year on Allah's green earth!

Chapter Fifteen

Orangeburg, South Carolina
July 23, 2014

The soft tinkling sounds of dining ware could be heard throughout the restaurant accompanied by discreet tones of voices and laughter.

It was around 8:45 pm, Tuesday night. Canary sat at a table inside Apple Bee's with her friends: Danyell and Tay. After she clocked out from the prison, she drove straight to where Danyell resided in an up-scale trailer park inside a triple-wide trailer where she and Tay awaited her. She had phoned them on her break at work and had told them that she had something shocking to tell them and that they needed to get together. For a variety of different reasons she couldn't get over the fact that Donatello McFadden was inside her dorm! And, he was even more striking in person! She had never been so physically attracted to a strange man.

After sitting inside the living room of Danyell's trailer for a while pouring out the details of her dilemma in rush excitement, they jumped inside Tay's Audi and headed out to eat.

Canary sat before a chef salad, a well-done T-bone steak and a baked potato with cheese and sour cream smothering it. Tay ordered the same. Danyell settled for broiled chicken, broccoli and cheese, a fruit salad, and crackers. They all settled for glasses of water for drink.

"So, what're you going to do; are you going to kick him out?" Tay asked as she used a steak knife and a fork to cut the tender meat into cubes.

"I don't know. It wouldn't really be fair for me to do so. The other dorms are a little more rough and rugged and I don't think he'd like the environment much," Canary responded on behalf of having Don removed from her dorm.

"I mean really, though," Danyell stated between bites of chicken. "Why are you so caught up on him?"

"I don't know. I mean….I followed his case since it started, and when I first saw him, I thought he was attractive as we all think of the attractive men we see that are. I guess since I've been going through so much at the time, he began to intrigue me. I know it probably doesn't make any sense. You guys know that I was in a lost realm of stress and confusion. His situation just kind of grew on me because nothing has been going on in my life. I was in a deep state of boredom confined to my little apartment just like the guys in their cell where I work. And it's a shame that their lives are more exciting than mine. I'm the one that's free," she pouted childishly and poked her fork into her potato shamefully.

The psychologist in Danyell kicked in as she picked up on the mood swing in her friends demeanor. "Girl, don't go beating your self up. It's a good thing that you can feel. This may all be a good thing for you because this is the most I've ever seen you open up. Just breathe and relax. No crime has been committed."

"Here goes my counselor," Canary teased. "And for the crime: it hasn't been committed 'yet'," she said impishly.

"Girl, are you really thinking about screwing him back there?" Tay asked incredulously.

"Honestly, I don't know what I'm thinking. But I do like him and how it feels to be in his presence," Canary responded. She took a sip from her glass of water.

"I got to see this guy," Tay stated and begun eating again.

"I remember him," Danyell said. "He's cute."

"But what if he did murder that girl?" Tay reasoned. "I know you said you don't think he did, but knowing and thinking are two different aspects."

"I know," Canary agreed. "And I didn't say that I was going to deal with him. I just said I like him."

"Just be careful because looks can be deceiving. We don't need you being the next Fedora Armanti-Teressa Sanstrom," Tay said through a mouth full of lettuce.

"Is there anything more I can do for you ladies?" A petite, caucasian female waiter approached and smiled.

"No thanks. We're fine," Danyell smiled up at her.

"Okay. Just give a shout if you guys have a change of heart," the young waitress said enthusiastically.

Canary looked at her admiringly. The girl was excited about life. This was probably her first job. It was summer time and school was out. She looked at the waitress as she went to the next table displaying the same hospitality.

"Back to you, Lieutenant," Tay started. "But on the real girl,

I think you should try getting over this little bug you got for this guy because he is incarcerated with a life sentence. What if you fell in love with him; what would you do then?"

"She has a point," Danyell said, as she began to attack her broccoli and cheese.

"And, what if you get caught?" Tay added.

"You guys are right. But lately, I've been cogitating pursuing old aspirations."

"Being an attorney?" Danyell asked surprisingly.

"Yes," Canary responded as she sat back in her chair. She had had enough of the unfinished food before her.

"That's great!" Danyell said cheerfully.

"Sure is," Tay chimed. "Maybe you should start tomorrow. Quit your job before you end up with a bad resume for getting caught being banged by your prisoner."

"Tay!" Danyell scolded.

"No, she's right," Canary took a breath. "I'm beginning to feel anserine."

"Don't feel anserine, Canary," Tay assuaged sympathetically. "I'm just saying that it's something to think about because no prominent firm would accept you with a background of such. You'd have to start a private practice."

None of them was ever offended by Tay's spontaneous remarks because it was her way. She was outspoken and daring.

"Okay," Canary leaned toward the table and braced herself on her elbows. "Enough about me. What about you and your crazy escapades with John?"

Danyell snickered.

Tay beamed with eyes like a lantern that had just been lit. "Nothing has changed. We're still seeing one another discreetly."

"How could you settle being second, I don't understand?"

"That's where y'all keep getting it misconstrued. I'm not second to anyone. If anything, his wife is second to me because I don't love him. He had a wife when I met him and that's that. Our relationship is strictly sex, gifts, and pillow talk. He's a handsome and brilliant guy and that's what turns me on about him. And," Tay brought her voice to a whisper as she leaned toward the center of the table as if revealing a one-hundred year old secret. "I love the way he eat my pussy."

Canary and Danyell exploded in laughter!

"Girl, you are too much!" Danyell stated.

"And besides, y'all don't need to be worried about me and John. We should be worried about the cob-webs growing inside our friend over here," Tay directed towards Danyell.

"Don't even start, bitch," Danyell shook her head and waved dismissively. "When God bring that special person in my life that's when it'll happen. Until then, I'm not even thinking about a man," she prevaricated. Really, she was longing for a man to love her unconditionally. It had been 3 years since her last relationship and it had only lasted 18 months before she had had enough of the mental abuse that her ex had relentlessly distributed. He had been a handsome street thug that had finessed his way into her heart through deception. She had moved him into her trailer with her, and while she was at work he would have other women in her home having sex in her bed. She had caught him on several occasions before finally coming to her senses and got rid of him. She had been a counselor that had been beginning to need counseling herself. Finally, she mustered the strength to pack his things and give him the boot. Now, she wasn't in any rush to be suckered by another man. She was feeling good about herself. She had loss a considerable amount of weight and was still working towards her goal of 165 pounds.

"Are you guys done?" Canary asked as she leaned back in her chair.

"Damn, you sure are anxious about getting ready to see your prisoner," Tay goofed off.

All of them giggled.

"Nah, seriously though. I have some laundry I have to get done before I hit the sack as well," Canary said.

"I was just teasing," Tay stuck out her tongue. She fetched her wallet from the Louis Vuitton pocketbook she had sat by her chair, took out some cash, and left a generous tip for the waiter.

Danyell respectfully covered her mouth while she yawned and pushed her chair back from the table. "Yep," she quipped. "It's sleepy time almost for me, kiddos." She glanced at her watch and stood.

They gathered their belongings and headed out the restaurant into the warm night air. The air smelled of baked bread and grilled beef.

They climbed in Tay's Audi and headed back to Danyell's house.

"Oh my God!" Tay said as she slowed the car. Police cars, a fire truck, and an ambulance was parked haphazardly in the middle of the road. The brilliant flash from the sirens of the emergency vehicles dancing on the faces of the people standing around made the scene appear surreal as officials from each side pulled a man through the windshield of a crushed vehicle.

"Damn, what the hell happened?" Danyell asked to no one in

particular as they all looked on at the wreckage from the collision of the van and the SUV.

A couple was standing on the side of the road by the wreckage talking to a couple of officers while the others worked to pull the man from the vehicle. Apparently the couple had been lucky. Whether the man was dead or alive, neither of them knew.

They were finally directed around the wreck and they quietly drove on lost in their own thoughts until they made it to Danyell's trailer.

The night air was warm. The trailer park was in quietude. They were the only beings moving about the upscale trailer park with its beautiful, au courant, built-in mobile homes. Danyell paid a pretty penny to reside in this residence. "I'm beat too, girl. And I have to be to the office early in the morning. I got some things I need to catch up on, and I have some house calls to make on several clients," she said as she looked from Canary to Tay who still remained in the driver seat of her car. She had her window down.

"Well, y'all prosaic bitches go find your beds. I'm going to find the one on John's yacht," Tay said with impish promiscuity. She had received a phone call from John while en route back to Danyell's domicile, informing her that he was free to play.

"We already know, whore," Canary ejaculated. "You better hope his wife or the media don't ever catch you connivers."

"Girl, there's already so much scandal in politics another one want hurt. Besides, he may get some cool points along with the support of the black community during next election for bedding a fine black chick," Tay lasciviously ran a hand over her soft breast and laughed.

"Girl, you are off the chain," Danyell shook her head.

"Tell me something I don't already know," Tay said. "And, I'll still see you at work bright and early tomorrow morning. All after my politician suck the life out of me."

"You better before I fire you, trick," Danyell said playfully as Tay backed out of her drive.

Tay shot Danyell the bird. "Night-night," she twiddled her fingers at them and headed to the waterfront where her amorously lecherous politician awaited her.

"Well goodnight, girl," Danyell gave Canary an amiable hug. "I'll talk to you later."

Canary embraced the hug amicably. "I'll call you when I get home to let you know I made it home safe, Doctor Brown," she smiled.

"Okay," Danyell responded. "And girl, stay away from Mr. McFadden as much as possible. When you talk to him I see it all in your eyes. Be careful."

"I will," Canary responded reassuringly, but inwardly, she was ambivalently challenged by this new dilemma.

Danyell watched her friend walk across the plush, green grass of her lawn to her car. It wasn't what she saw in her eyes, it was what she didn't see. It had been a time when her friends eyes had been filled with sorrow, pain and emptiness. But now, there swam a collage of phantasmagorical alacrity, strength, excitement, and adventure. She knew that Canary was responsible and would make the right decision, but the last thing she wanted to see on the news was: "Ex-correctional officer Canary Rose terminated and charged with improper sexual relations with an inmate." And not just any inmate, but Mr. Donatello Furqān McFadden – the celebrity murderer who was recently convicted of murdering –

Honk! Honk! Honk! Canary tapped her horn interrupting Danyell's silent thoughts of her.

Danyell waved good-bye and went inside her home to shower and await Canary's phone call verifying that she had made it home safe before tucking herself into her comfortable bed to spend another night alone.

Chapter Sixteen

Orangeburg, South Carolina
Palmetto Correctional Institution
July 24, 2014 - Wednesday

The following morning Canary sat inside her office with the door closed with a "Do Not Disturb" sign on the door window. She had been listening to Steve's morning show while on her way to work. Just her luck, when she was trying to be oblivious of Donatello McFadden, his father's voice touched the core of her soul as it came from her speakers live and direct from Steve's Studio in California. Her mind was cloudy, her concentration was off, her equilibrium discombobulated. Today had been the first time that she had actually sat in briefing in a daze, oblivious to all that was said. She just wanted to get to the dorm so she could tune back in to the interview.

"So how is he holding up back there?" Steve asked.

"He's fine. He came from strength and have a good support structure, so he'll be fine until things get better, God willing," Caesar answered.

"Man, I know how it is as I've once was incarcerated," Steve revealed. "But as we've discussed over and over on this show during, and after your sons trial, it was unfair how the public condemned him the way they did because of you guys belief system.

"I mean, I'm not Muslim, but I'm aware that the true religion of Islam is not what the media portray it to be."

"Well, you know Steve, with all that's been going on in the Middle East with the West, it's all kind of innuendo and preposterous dogma that the government launder through media to cover the guile and mendacious antics of their capitalistic ideals. And with nine-eleven and all, it really made Americans hate all Muslims in totality when in all actuality the Muslims of the Quran and Sunnah have nothing to do with terrorism period. You know what I'm saying?" Caesar explained.

"It's a lot that Americans don't know and most people believe whatever the government or someone else tell them with an educated tongue without realizing that they are being led astray as if people are infallible.

"I don't blame people for standing with their faction but I do have a problem with people that blindly follow belief systemsand ideologies without even being properly educated of what they embrace before passing judgement on things they have no knowledge of. This is why what happened to my son happened. It's also why we didn't select a trial by jury."

"So what about appeals?" Steve asked.

"There's no appeal. Everything went accordingly. The presiding judge returned a guilty verdict because of the deoxyribonucleic acid found in the victim. Open and shut."

"For our listeners that is unaware of what 'Deoxyribonucleic Acid' is, it's what the letters DNA stand for," Steve informed.

"So, I mean," Steve continued. "What's the plan in helping him regain his freedom if he's dead on the appeal process?"

She heard his father sigh.

"Our only hope is that someone comes forward – which is a very slim chance. It's why I'm relentlessly advocating on his behalf with the hopes of touching the hardened hearts that may be able to help us that may possibly hold the key to his freedom. I've also hired a team of investigators that I have working an angle I won't discuss. And since money moves and motivate people, I'm here today to offer five-million dollars on a solid lead for anyone that comes forward."

Steve whistled and Canary stretched her eyes at the large sum of money being offered!

"And not only that," Caesar continued, "for the individual that actually killed that poor girl, I'm offering you ten million dollars for a confession. Most likely you did what you did for money to support your family or fancies. But whatever the case, I'll give you ten million in cash to take responsibility for your actions and to bring forth the individuals that hired you to frame my son."

She gasped!

"Why do you feel as if he was framed or someone was hired to do such a thing?" Steve inquired.

"I wont go too deep in details but my past life was a little unrighteous I would say and there's a possibility that this was a form of pay back. Why my son and not me? I don't know. It's what I seek to discover."

"Hold that thought man, we have to break for commercial. But America, y'all get it together and start recognizing what's real – fifteen million is on the table! It's not a game, man. Y'all know I keep it real and in this situation, I really do think this young man is innocent. Lets get him home!"

The show broke for commercial just as Warden Atlee Prince and Major Wigfall entered the dorm to make their rounds. Canary stood up to greet them and headed on the wing with them to inspect the environment.

Atlee Prince resided in Charleston. He was a well-kept man that stood approximately 5-feet-7-inches. He dressed in a button down casual shirt, slacks, and a pair of comfortable running shoes. His hair was soft and curly; he wore it in a fade. He was fair, but he wasn't one for bullshit. As long as the inmates wasn't killing each other and escaping, he really didn't care what went on. He was probably the coolest warden in the state by account of the inmates.

The major was also from Charleston but had moved to Colorado, Springs for some time before returning. She was nicely shaped in physique. As the other ranking officials, she wore brown fatigues and a black button-down shirt with gold leaves of her rank on both collars. She wasn't one to compromise, but she was very lenient at times. Although she could be ruthless.

As they made their rounds around the wing, Sulayman Azeez Mustafah and the 15 million dollars he'd just put up paraded through her mind. She thought about his son, whom was present in her dorm. She canvased the wing to see if she saw him. She wondered if he was listening to the program.

When she left home she had departed with the intentions of staying away from him. She didn't even want to see him. She hadn't listened to Steve for a week or so, so she didn't know that his father would be on the show. She knew that the warden and the major usually conducted morning rounds, but she wasn't expecting them to come around this morning.

The warden had stopped in the middle of the wing to speak with a couple of inmates while she and the major conversed as they ascended the stairs. She still hadn't seen Mr. McFadden. The dorm was quiet as usual around this time. But due to the big-wigs, more people moved about and was up out of their beds. More than likely someone had spotted the major and the warden long before they entered the dorm and had alerted their comrades, as was their custom.

About 15 minutes later the three of them left the wing. She went back to her office and the warden and major headed to the next dorm to their rounds and sign the log books. She knew that she had missed a good portion of the show and more than likely the interview was almost over if it wasn't already.

A rap song by Baby and Lil' Wayne was ending as she entered the office. She wondered where Ricardo was. He probably over slept as he sometimes did. He'd pop up within the next twenty minutes or so. He had told her once that he was never a morning person and struggled with the new morning demands of being on time. She started a pot of coffee and seated herself until it fully percolated.

Steve continued. "Well, Mr. Sulayman Azeez Mustafah, it was nice having you man, and I wish you the best.

"And Donatello, if you're listening man, keep your head up son and keep the faith in God and He'll pull you and your father through this madness. You got a good father that loves you."

"Thanks, Steve. It was a pleasure to be here," Caesar said fervently.

"Anytime, man. It was good meeting you and having you on the show, and if you need me, you got my full support."

"Thanks for everything, man," Caesar reiterated.

“America!” Steve shouted into his microphone. “Put your hands together for Sulayman Azeez Mustafah and get over those bias ways man, and don’t further persecute this man and his child just because they’re Muslims. Do your research and educate yourselves before passing judgement and condemning innocent folks...”

“Good morning, Lieutenant Rose.”

Canary looked up from her gaze. It was Officer Raysor. She had been working this particular dorm for the past year on night shift. She had recently been under investigation for allegedly dealing with one of the inmates that was once at Palmetto but had been transferred after she took a polygraph test and passed it with flying colors. Canary didn’t like indulging in conjecture, but she was willing to bet that she was guilty of the accusations. She was just too adroit. One day she’d drive a 2011 Jaguar to the facility then the next she’d pull up inside a tricked out 2012 Cadillac Escalade. There was no way she could afford the luxuries of those vehicles on her salary! And next to her, she was probably the sexiest officer that paraded the compound.

Canary liked her though. She was cool and down to earth. And besides, her business was her business and anyway, the name of the game was “don’t get caught.”

“Hey, girl,” Canary smiled.

Officer Raysor sat down her see-through back-pack containing her belongings. Her hair was trimmed in an old school Toni Braxton style that enhanced her features. “Girl it’s a bitch trying to adjust to this day shift thing. I'm so used to night shift.” She had been moved from night shift to day shift. She figured that the administration felt that they could keep a closer eye on her in the day time. They were waiting on her to slip. “Please tell me you don’t mind if I get a cup of your coffee when it finish percolating?”

"Sure."

"Thanks. I'll be back. Let me go do my rounds and get caught up in the log book," Raysor replied brightly. She had got to work a little late.

Canary looked at her admiringly. She was so full of life. "Okay."

Raysor departed and soon after, Ricardo materialized eating a bowl of cheese grits and corn beef hash. "Bueno dias, Teniente Rose," he smiled.

"Buenos dias, Ricardo," she returned pleasantries. She didn't speak Spanish fluently but she knew enough to get her through Mexico or any other Spanish state if need be.

"Sorry for being late again, senorita," he seated himself and attended breakfast.

"You're fine, Ricardo," she reassured him.

"Where's Sergeant Granada?" he inquired.

"He called in sick."

"Oh."

"When you're finished I need you to get with Harrison and clean out that upstairs storage room. I've been meaning to get y'all to get rid of all those raggedy things and other junk. I've been having reports of mice being seen coming from beneath the door. Just bag up those old blankets and uniforms and we'll carry them to the commissary later."

"Okay."

She tossed him the keys to the closet. Normally she would go on the wing and watch as they cleared the closet to make sure that the blankets and other excess junk didn't end up being passed around to the inmates, but right now she didn't care. She wasn't going back on the wing unless someone got stabbed or severely injured! She was still trying to avoid Donatello McFadden until she figured out if she was going to have him moved or not. For one reason she wanted him to stay, and for another she wanted him moved. She didn't want to be the cause of further discomfort for him. She found her heart going out to him and Steve and his father only made matters worse in her decision making with their heartbreaking interview. She now had two celebrities inside her dorm; both alleged murderers that intrigued her in some form or fashion. And, they were both associated with Islam: the author James Wright III, and the son of the wealthy Muslim tycoon – Donatello Furqān McFadden.

The coffee pot beeped. She got up and poured herself a cup of the steaming brew. She added two spoons of cream and a sweet-n-low, stirred it and reseated herself. One thing was for certain, she'd have to do something about this dilemma with Donatello McFadden because she couldn't continue to allow one man to consume her thoughts and distract her from her work. Since his arrival, all she thought about was him. Although she felt sorry for him she didn't believe in sympathy. She empathizedwith him. But hey, he wasn't the only one in need of help! The world was filled with people in much worse situations than him! Hell, she was just now getting her own shit together!

"Are you okay, senorita? It seems like something heavy is on your mind," Ricardo asked as he swallowed the last spoon of his meal.

"Yes, I'm fine," she smiled weakly.

Ricardo sat his bowl on the table by the coffee machine just as Raysor returned.

"What's up, mi amigo?" Raysor said as she squeezed between Ricardo and the desk to get to the coffee maker, a styrofoam cup in hand.

"Chillin'. I see they got you on day shift now," Ricardo said as he stood.

"Yeahhh," Raysor scrunched her face playfully. She knew that everyone knew about her suspicious activities but she didn't care. It wasn't as if she was the only one with hidden bones inside her closet. To her, everyone in the world was sneaky motherfuckers and would steal stink out of shit if they could. Preachers of churches was robbing their congregations blind openly and no one complained, so she didn't see the big deal in what was so wrong about her hustle!

"Well, I'll see you around. I'm about to go get Chico and attack this closet, teniente."

Canary nodded her head as she sat back with her hands clasped across her abdomen. Chico was Marquise Harrison, her head dorm worker.

Ricardo departed the office and headed on the wing. Raysor fixed her coffee with heavy cream, thanked her and headed back on the wing, leaving her alone to her ambivalent thoughts.

###

Don had been up since 4:30 am stuffing himself with a variety of different foods in preparation for the strenuous fast ahead.

Under the dim glow of the lamp he had quietly moved around so not to disturb his sleeping roommates. It probably didn't matter how much noise he made because they had come to the room sloppy drunk last night.

And Ricardo had yet to introduce him to anyone. He knew that he was a very busy guy. It probably had slipped his mind.

It was now after 10 am, both of his roommates was at work. He didn't see how they maintained their schedules for work living the lives they lived.

He now laid in the quietude of his cell on his bunk listening to his walkman. He hadn't occupied the rock much since his arrival other than to shower and use the microwave. He had just got through listening to the shocking interview his father had on Steve's show. His eyes had sprang open in amazement when he heard his father mention the multi-million dollar reward! His father hadn't mentioned any of this when they last spoke. He wanted to call him now but he knew that he was probably tied up with things, especially after the astonishing announcement he just made. He'd call him later.

He removed the earbuds from his ears, turned the radio off, and sat the walk-man set beside him.

The window was very large, about four-feet in length, two-feet in width. It was on the back wall of the room, which was the wall the bunk was positioned against. So where he lay, he could look directly out the window from atop his bunk. The view sucked but he could see the entrance in front of the dorm.

As he gazed out of the window he saw a casually dressed man accompanied by a female official exiting the dorm. Unbeknownst to him, it was the warden and the major. He had been so engrossed in the interview he didn't even hear when the inmates shouted "fire in the hole," alerting that the officials was in the building. Had he known, he surely would have taken the opportunity to glimpse the gorgeous woman that had begun consumimg his thoughts. He had already made a habit of laying by the window just to have the advantage of seeing her coming back and forth to the dorm. He saw her this morning when she entered the building this morning, and from that very image of her, he couldn't subdue the things that stirred within him just from the way she walked. He wondered if one of the present inmates had already finessed their way into her heart. But for some reason, he doubted this. She had a sui generis aura about herself that stood out from everything and everyone around her. She was a masterpiece of Allah's artwork in design and craftsmanship!

He'd be patient and discreet and find out what he could about her through discreet inquiries. He may even have his father do a background check on her to give him a prototypical view that would assist him in categorizing her. Maybe he'd discover some things that may be able to guide him in how to pursue her effectively. Yeah, that's what he'd do. He'd have his father handle the background on her while he profiled her from a distance for the meantime. He couldn't get over the way they looked at one another when he first entered her office. He knew that he was at a disadvantage due to his position but he could've sworn that he picked up on something from her. He just couldn't put his finger on what it was. This environment was so strange and foreign, and the people so alien, he didn't know if his judgement in things was sound. And, he wasn't out to catch any frivolous charges for soliciting improper relations due to his perception being misconstrued. But he would need to get another cell phone because using the institutional phones was out of the question for what he had planned to discuss with his father.

But little did he know, extra-sensory-perception was in full effect. They were indeed thinking on the same wave link.

It was almost lunch time and he knew that Lieutenant Rose would be headed to the cafeteria. He turned on his side facing the window and patiently waited for the next opportunity to see her.

Chapter Seventeen

Orangeburg, South Carolina
Palmetto Correctional Institution
July 24, 2014 - Wednesday

"What's up, diva?"

Canary looked up from her reverie as the inmate entered her office mellifluously sauntering in all femininity as he seated himself in the chair across from her desk and crossed his legs. She smiled at him. "Hey Foxy, how're you, girl? You've been M.I.A. What's going on with you?"

"Girl, me and my boo been having problems. I had to put this thing on his ass to get his mind right," Foxy smacked his lips.

"Girl, you are a hot-mess!" Canary laughed.

Fernando Brown was one of the punks inside the dorm that attributed himself "Foxy Brown", and was one of the only inmates that she allowed to leisurely sit inside her office to converse. She didn't have to worry about what he wanted because, he was so psychologically discombobulated, he had long forgotten his true gender of masculinity. He had been incarcerated since the age of fifteen and had been raped at the age of seventeen when transferred from Juvenile Hall to the Department of Corrections. Now he was 27 years old and thought that he was just as much of a woman as her. But Canary thought that he was cool. He helped her time pass. He'd been missing-in-action for the past couple of days. But as he stated, he'd been having domestic issues with his lover.

"Oohhh girl, did you see the new guy?" Foxy asked dramatically.

Canary knew who he was talking about but feigned ignorance. "What new guy; is he in this dorm?"

"Hell yeah, girl! Have you been sleeping?" Foxy cocked his head. "He lives next door to me. His name is Donatello McFadden. And girl, you know we are Steve fanatics! Did you listen to the show this morning?"

"Yes. Why?" Canary asked quizzically.

"Because I don't know if he's the same guy they were talking about, but everything seems to match up surrounding him. His name is the same and he's from Charleston. And I think he's fasting so he may be the son of the Muslim they're talking about. I don't know what he's locked up for but maybe you should check into it because if it is him, he's a celebrity and got monay-monay-monayyy!" Foxy rubbed his hands together.

Canary laughed. "I'll see when I get time and let you know."

"But how are you doing, girl?"

"I'm fine. What about you – other than your domestic issues?" Canary asked as she fought to suppress thoughts of Donatello McFadden.

"Girl, I'm really thinking about leaving him." Foxy said

about the inmate he was seeing. “I mean, we’re cool and everything, and I love the way he eats me out, but he be wanting me to fuck him and I’m not with that. I like to be served. I'm not a server. It makes me feel like he’s a bitch. I'm all woman, you feel me,” Foxy laughed.

“So I assume that this is the cause of you guys problems?” Canary asked.

“Part of it,” Foxy answered. “I’m really not into him anymore. He go home in a few months and I know he’s not going to keep it real with me. And he’s too stuck on being a thug. I want to be stimulated mentally and, I do look forward to going home one day so I want to be working towards a future. You know what I’m saying?” Foxy’s mood had become serious.

Canary may not have identify with the twisted psychological thoughts of two men engaging in amatorious relations with one another, but she did identify with the hunger and want in wanting specific things out of life that one aspired to achieve. “Well girl, do what’s best for you. Just be careful because you know how it is when love is involved. And please make your decision when I'm not here because I don’t want to be the one that have to intervene in you guys dispute if it gets violent.”

“I got you diva,” Foxy answered.

“But listen, its almost time for lunch and I need to get ready to go to the cafeteria. Please go on the wing upstairs and tell Ricardo I said bring my keys. He's cleaning out the upstairs closet,” Canary said as she stood.

“Okay.” Foxy stood also. “But don’t forget what I told you about my new neighbor. I may not be able to get him because he may not get down like that. But girl, I think you’re going to like this one when you see him.”

“Whatever, Foxy,” Canary smiled. “Don’t be ridiculous,”

she added.

Foxy departed and she thought about how it seemed as if Donatello McFadden was inescapable. Everywhere she turned something or someone would bring him to her attention. She wondered if it was the God that she didn't believe in really trying to speak to her through these individuals.

Ricardo brought her keys and she gathered her things to head to the cafeteria. As she left the building and walked into the air of the beautiful day, more and more she was beginning to think it best to have Mr. McFadden packed up and removed from her dorm.

Oblivious to the fact that he watched her from one of the windows with increasing desire and hunger, she continued to move along.

###

Los Angeles, California

Once Caesar's jet took off from the airport in Los Angeles and leveled itself en route to South Carolina, he returned Cecelia's missed call. His phone had been ringing relentlessly since his announcement, but he'd been ignoring the calls.

"Hey," Cecelia answered sweetly.

"Salam, beauty. How are you?" he returned as he reclined his seat and kicked off his loafers. Other than him and the two pilots, his flight attendant Husayn was the only person on board.

"Shocked like hell about your announcement," she stated with mild elation. She had sat in her office and listened to his interview.

"I know, I know. Tell me about it. I'm shocked myself," he

admitted. He took in a breath and expelled it through his lips. "I didn't even know that I was going to offer the money, I just did," he explained on behalf of the spontaneous decision he made about an hour ago pertaining to the millions in reward money that he offered for a lead and confession. "What do you think?"

"What do you mean?"

"I mean, what kind of results do you think it'll produce?"

"Pandemonium!" she said precisely. "I think it'll shake the perpetrators but nothing more. Your bravado and temerity was amazing, but everyone and their mother will be trying to stake the claim rather they did it or not. People would check into prison willingly for those kind of numbers and then escape and disappear, Sulayman.

"But whoever the conspirators are, I know that they're panicking because they may have very well left some loose ends untied or may have people amongst them that your offer may provoke betrayal.

"But on another note, put yourself in the shoes of the killer. I don't think the offer would spring a confession because the stakes are too high. The killer knows that he'd be killed in prison in retaliation by some group or another so he won't confess even if he wanted to."

He agreed. He hadn't thought of this. And, he surely would have the killer killed if he cornered him.

"And," she continued. "if it has anything to do with the kind of people you told me about from your past life, the chances of a confession doesn't need to be expected. But although slim, we may receive a lead from a traitor."

"Damn. I hate to admit it, because you just crushed my hopes. But you're right, sweetheart." He was beginning to realize that they needed a miracle from Allah for Don to be legally released.

"And on my end my people keep running into dead ends."

"You can pull the plug on the investigation," he concluded.

"Are you sure?"

"Yes, It's a waste of time and manpower. I'm just going to go into the second phase of my plan."

"What's that?" She inquired.

"Honestly, I would love to tell you. But now isn't the time."

"That's understandable," she responded. By the type of man she had discovered him to be, she knew that anything was possible. They had begun dating and spending time with one another, but they had yet to engage in any sexual activities. Although he had never came on to her he had told her that the only chances in any sexual relations was if she became his wife legally under Islamic law. He had taken his time and explained that he was trying to adhere to what Allah had legislated and she respected his decision. She was also learning a lot about Islam and was coming to respect it more than she ever expected.

"Do you mind if I talk to you later?" he asked politely. " I need to make a call."

"No. Handle your business, babe. I'll talk to you later."

"Okay. See you soon, and take care."

"You too, Sulayman."

He disconnected the call, sat introspectively for a moment, then he phoned Al-Salam.

###

Orangeburg, South Carolina

Palmetto Correctional Institution

Don was on his way back to his room from the microwave. The sun was beginning to set so it was almost time for him to break his fast. He had quickly discovered that the smart thing to do was to use the microwave before the sun went down instead of waiting until after it set because it would be swarming with famished Muslims trying to cook or warm up their food. He had put together chicken and dumplings, fried beef sausage and mushrooms over rice. He wasn't spectacular in his culinary skills as Scramble, but he had learned a few tricks of the trade that got the job done until he stepped up his skills.

Their dorm went to the canteen on Friday's. He couldn't wait to go so he could stock up on the things he needed. He was also going to send an extra $125 bucks to one of his cellmate's account so he'd be able to get some extra things because the spending limit was only $125 per inmate weekly.

As he descended the four steps into the flood zone, he saw Ricardo and two other inmates standing in front of his room: one of them was shirtless.

The noise inside the dorm was moderate. Inmates moved about as they mixed and mingled. The officer that worked inside the dorm had arrived about thirty minutes ago. Shift had changed while he was at the microwave. The little sexy officer that had worked the wing during the day had already departed. He thought that she was super cool. She was that around-the-way-girl. His roommates had told him that her name was Raysor. She was very coquettish! She had allowed some of the guys to masturbate while she teased them through their room doors during the 3 o'clock count. His roommates had told him about the rumors floating around about her having sex for money and bringing contraband, but he didn't care. The lieutenant of the dorm had his undivided attention!

His roommates was upstairs with their buddies, probably drinking or injecting some sort of controlled poison into their veins. He didn't know where they were getting their supply from but figured it came from someone like Scramble. Whatever the case, they kept it to say they didn't have much of anything else.

"Que pasa, amigo?" Ricardo smiled as Don approached. "Thought I forgot about you, huh?" His teeth twinkled.

"Yeah, I sure did. Would you open that door for me?" Don said. His hands were occupied with his bowl of food. He held the bowl with both hands by the edges because it was hot.

Ricardo opened the door.

"Thanks," Don said as he entered the room. He sat the bowl on the table then turned around to face Ricardo and the other two individuals along with him. "What's up?"

"These are two of your compadres."

"What's up, babe?"

"What's happening family?"

Both Charlestonians greeted Don simultaneously.

"I'm cooling, about to break my fast," Don stated. He thought that both of them looked extremely familiar.

"Are you Muslim?" one of them asked.

"Long story," Don informed.

"Well, I've done my part, amigo's. I'll see y'all around," Ricardo stated. "Don, just holler at me when you find a candidate about what we discussed."

"Alright. And thanks, man," Don told Ricardo.

"No problem, hombre." Ricardo shook Don's hand and left the room.

Don seated himself, said Bismillah, excused himself and began eating.

"You're cool, homie. They call me Chess."

Don looked up quizzically at the shirtless fellow before him. "Were you at Ogeechee recently?"

"Yeah," Chess answered. "Why, is that where you came from?"

"Yeah."

"Man, I thought you looked kind of familiar. I think you came the same day that shit jumped off with me and the home team against those Columbia niggas." Chess recollected.

"The day before," Don corrected.

"So you know Scramble?" Chess asked.

"Yeah. That's my big bro," Don brightened by the mention of Scramble.

"I just spoke to him about an hour ago," Chess revealed.

"Yeah? Man, when you speak to him again tell him I said what's up."

"I got you, babe," Chess assured. He was from an area in Charleston called Rose Mount. He stood about five-feet-six and weighed about 169 pounds. He had a high yellow complexion like a stick of butter. He was handsome in an innocent sort of way with soft, thick wavy hair. He stood before Don shirtless in a pair of gray jogging pants that the officer he'd been dealing with at Ogeechee had brought him. His upper body and arms was littered with scattered chess pieces that he had tattooed all over him.

Don looked at the other guy quizzically.

"Most of the homies call me Geez, but I'm attributed Yahseen. I'm Muslim."

"Alhamdulillah!" Don responded. "I guess we'll have to politic about some things in the future."

"Insha'Allah," Yahseen nodded his head up and down in agreement.

"Man, I don't mean to pry, but what's your birth name?" Don asked as if he was on to something. The familiarity of Yahseen and not being able to pin point where he had seen him kept eating at him.

Yahseen and Chess both laughed. Apparently they were used to this with Yahseen.

"James Wright III." Yahseen looked at Don as if his response answered his questions.

"Man, I thought you were familiar. I read a couple of your books," Don laughed. "Man, this is crazy." He shook his head in disbelief." You have some great books, man. Keep up the good work," Don complimented.

"Thanks babe. And Insha'Allah, I will." Yahseen was from North Charleston off of Remount Road. He stood about five-seven and a half, one-hundred-forty-five pounds tops. He wore his hair low and had it freshly taped and groomed; his waves swam with the reflection of the light. He was handsome and stylish. He had a complexion of raw honey. Several tattoo's was on sporadic locations of his body including his neck.

Don thought that the author had a very strong, demanding demeanor. It kind of reminded him of Ali's.

"But shed homie, it's some more of us around here that you could meet later, but right now it's some things Geez and I need to handle that we were dong before Ricardo came and got us," Chess said.

"Alright," Don said as he chewed his food.

"Do you need anything?" Yahseen asked.

"Nah, I'm fine."

Yahseen told Don their room numbers. "Just holler if you need anything."

"Alright."

"What are you about to do?" Chess asked.

"After I call my father, I'll probably go and catch the news and come back and do a little studying before calling it a night."

"If you need a little access," Chess made a phone gesture with his hand insinuating his possession of a cellphone, "Just holler."

"Thanks bro. I'm fine for now."

"Alright babe, we'll holler later. Stay up," Chess said.

They shook Don's hand and went to attend to their affairs.

Don thought that the both of them had good character. Once again, he thanked Allah for placing more suitable brothers along his path.

As he finished his food he thought about the irony in him not only bumping into Scramble's right hand man, but the author of the books he read that Scramble had given him. If the book A Penitentiary Holy Book was indeed a true story, he could tell by Yahseen's aura and persona that he was indeed the legendary individual the novel was based on. This unfortunate journey of his was surely interesting.

He fetched a bottle of Ajax dish detergent from his locker and headed to the sink to wash his bowl. After completing the task, he fetched his walk-man, out the room lights and headed to the phone-room to call his father. Thereafter, he would head on the rock to catch the 10 o'clock news.

Chapter Eighteen

Orangeburg, South Carolina
Palmetto Correctional Institution
July 25, 2014

The morning count was at 7 am. It usually cleared around 7:30. Although it had cleared this morning in a timely fashion, Greenville – the dorm Don was housed in, was still locked down. It was around 8:45 am. Shift had changed at 8:00 o'clock. Although it wasn't unusual for this to happen, it was not a good sign for the inmates. More than likely, they were about to be shook down. Inmates shouted from behind cell doors alerting everyone to get on point and tighten up. Some inmates could see the yard from their rooms, and due to this, they knew that they were the only dorm on the compound still locked down because movement was active on the yard by the inmates that occupied the other three dorms.

Officer Raysor was back and she had made a discreet announcement telling everyone to stash their contraband after inmates inquired about the reason for them still being on locked down. This was something she wasn't supposed to do because it was a breach of security. But she wasn't on the administration's side. She had brother's incarcerated and had grew up in the ghetto. This job was just a hustle for her. "The call came from upfront to keep y'all locked down till further notice," she informed before leaving the wing.

The perplexing thing about the lock down was the fact that the water hadn't been turned off as it usually was when the dorm was about to be shook down in its eternity to prevent inmates from flushing contraband.

"WARDEN, MAJOR AND CAPTAIN COMING UP THE SIDEWALK!" an unidentified inmate shouted thrice from behind his cell door.

Don and his cellmates looked out of their cell window and saw the stated officials entering the building.

"What do you guys think the problem is?" Don asked his roommates. Due to the lockdown they hadn't been able to go to work.

"There's no telling around here, bo," Nebraska said as he stood looking out the window of their cell door. "Around here, anything's possible," he continued. "Someone probably tried to score a package and something went wrong," he guessed.

"FIRE IN THE HOLE!" Someone yelled around the wing. "THEY'RE ROLLIN'!"

The giant keys that the officials carried could be heard jingling as the officials entered the wing.

"THEY'RE ROLLIN' IN THE FLOOD ZONE, THEY'RE ROLLIN' IN THE FLOOD ZONE!" Different inmates informed.

"Sounds like they're nearing our room, ain't it?" Mark Shaw

asked in a state of paranoia. He had a bit of contraband in his possession. He had several syringes, a few grams of cocaine and about an ounce of tobacco. He had it stashed fairly well, though.

From the top bunk, Don watched as Nebraska backed away from the door. He heard the keys enter the lock and the door was pulled open.

"Good morning, fellas," the warden said politely.

Don looked down from the top bunk at the crowd of officials who all appeared to be looking up at him, and although it was a crowd of them, the most distinguishable of them was the lieutenant in whom he had depicted "Golden" because of the golden, silky texture of her hair and skin. She looked away from him. His roommate's returned the warden's greeting.

Along with the warden, stood the major, a captain that Don had never seen until now, Sergeant Granada, Officer Raysor, and Lieutenant Rose.

"Donatello McFadden?" The warden directed towards the top bunk.

"Yes?" Don asked in reply with a quizzical expression.

"We need you to step down and come with us," the warden informed.

"What's the problem?" Don asked as he prepared to step down from his bunk.

Mark Shaw and Nebraska had both got on their bunks to get out of Don's way.

Mark Shaw was relieved that it wasn't a drug test or shake down.

"We'll inform you. It's a security issue." the warden enlightened evasively.

Don climbed down from the bunk and grabbed his uniform pants from where it hung neatly folded from a hook on the wall and slipped them over the short pants he wore. He slipped into his shirt next and then his tennis shoes. As he tucked his shirt into his pants he looked up at the lieutenant who was looking at him with a piercing gaze as if questioning him about something unknown. She looked away from him again. This time it was as if she had just been caught doing something she wasn't suppose to.

After he was completely dressed he stepped from the room as the captain got on his walkie-talkie and ordered that all movement on the yard cease until further notice because they were escorting an inmate involving a security issue across the yard. An affirmative reply came back and moments later a female voice bellowed over the institutional P.A. system stating that all movement should cease and that the yard was closed until further notice.

He didn't know what was going on and all of the unexpected activity was making him nervous. Inmates stood to their cell doors looking on trying to figure out the ordeal.

All of the officials kept looking at him as if seeing him for the first time and he found it strange. Their approach with him hadn't been one of abhorrence but they handled him respectfully. He walked along side the major – who was a black woman – the warden was also black. The rest of the officers was behind them as he was escorted off the wing.

When they got inside the lobby, Lieutenant Rose, Sergeant Granada, and Officer Raysor headed inside the office as the warden, major, and captain escorted Don across the deserted yard to operations.

As Don walked through Operations with the officials, he couldn't help but notice the inquisitive stares from all the other employee's around the area as if he was an exhibit. The officials had yet to say anything to him until they entered the spacious, windowless office of the warden's.

Don looked around the office in admiration. The office didn't look as if it belong inside a prison. The blue carpeting was soft. The desk that sat in the middle of he room was large, polished oak wood. A computer monitor sat on the far side of the desk and it displayed vivid shots of various locations of the institution. Beautiful tree's sat in flower pots in every corner of the room; two soft-seated polished oak chairs sat in front of the desk and a blue leather sofa sat along one of the walls. The major and captain seated themselves on the sofa as the door was closed behind them.

"You can have a seat, Mr. McFadden," the warden directed as he pointed to the chairs in front of his desk as he seated himself in his leather chair behind his desk.

Don knew when he was in the presence of powerful men and, the man that sat before him exuded the aura.

"I know you're curious as to what this is about so I won't hold you in suspense any longer but let me introduced myself and my staff," the warden commenced. "I'm Atlee Prince. I'm the warden of this institution. And over there," he directed towards the sofa. "is my major – Mrs. Wigfall..."

Don looked towards her and she nodded with an expression of austerity.

Warden Prince continued. ".... and that's one of my captains – Captain Holmes."

Don looked toward the couch again, this time, at the tall, muscular, black captain who nodded the same as the Major.

"Mr. McFadden," Warden Prince leaned forward on his desk. His chair strained as it adjusted. "Yesterday your father made a very shocking announcement on Steve's morning show that went viral. Are you aware of the fifteen-million dollar announcement he made?"

"Yes," Don answered as he looked into the eyes of the Warden.

"Does it worry you, son?" Warden Prince asked.

"What do you mean does it worry me?" Don asked respectfully.

"Mr. McFadden, this is a very rare situation and my supervisors in Columbia at Head Quarters are concerned about your safety due to the announcement your father made. We don't know the extent of what you guys are involved in but fifteen million dollars is a lot of money and due to this announcement, it also alert the other inmates around you that you are potential prey. Our concern is your safety against extortion and other various dangers that may befall you because of your status of celebrity," the warden explained. "Does this concern you?"

"No. I'm fine. I can take care of myself fairly well – with all due respect," Don replied as he sat erect, properly articulating himself.

Last night had been truly bizarre! After Don had attempted several unsuccessful attempts at reaching his father, he had called Ali, and Jabbar had spoke with them for an hour or so until the 10 o'clock news began. Jabbar had told him that his father had had a very exhausting day and that things were physically beginning to wear on him. He needed the rest.

Don knew that although his father was a strong man, his incarceration was slowly abrading his strength. Ali and Jabbar, had both informed him that his father had scheduled them for a private meeting at Head Quarters, which was at McFadden and McFadden's man base in downtown Charleston. They didn't know what the meeting pertained to.

After he got off the phone with them he headed on the rock and stood beneath the plasma TV's and watched the news. As soon as the news began it started with a breaking report – a picture of him during his trial flashed across the screen – he gasped and had held his breath. He had looked from side to side and every inmate surrounding him looked from him to the TV's incredulously!

"Damn homie, is that you?" a strange inmate asked that had stood next to him.

So caught off guard by the news break he hadn't responded to the many more questions that came from the surrounding inmates as the report went on about his father's recent announcement on Steve Harvey and the 15 million bucks in reward money that he had put on Steve had went viral, and once again, he knew that he was all over TV and radio around the nation.

Things with the media hype surrounding his case had calmed a bit but now, he was in direct line of the spot light. Now he saw why his father was exhausted. He was surely showing how adamant he was in what he had once said about allowing the hype to simmer surrounding his case and fifteen million in hard cold cash had surely turned a calming storm into a full-fledge hurricane!

"Well, listen," Warden Prince said as he opened a manila folder that lie before him. He removed a form. "This is a form indicating that this agency can not be held accountable in the event something happens to you. The only way I can release you back to the yard is if you sign this stating that you do not want to be placed in protective custody and that this agency is free from any liabilities concerning you."

Don retrieved the form that the Warden pushed towards him and read it carefully. "Can I use your pen?" he asked after reading the form. The warden handed him his pen and he signed the form indicating that he didn't want to be placed in protective custody. He handed the pen and the form back to the warden.

"Okay," Warden Prince said as he accepted the items. "Other than that, how are you doing so far?"

"I'm fine," Don smiled.

"Okay, but should you have any concerns or problems don't hesitate to contact me through your dorm's supervisor. Okay?"

"Yes sir," Don responded.

"Okay. That's it. You're free to go back to the dorm, Mr. McFadden." The warden stood; the major and captain did as well.

"Thank you," Don said as he stood to leave. All eyes were on him. He sauntered to the door and headed into the morning air, the acid bubbles of Lieutenant Rose surfaced from the bottom of his stomach to the top of his cranium. It seemed as if she was telekinetically pulling towards her.

Apparently, the yard had been reopened and their dorm released from lock-down because inmates were beginning to flow from its entrance like lava from an erupting volcano.

###

"Well, I'll be damned!" Sergeant Granada had ejaculated after Don had been escorted from the building. "Did you guys knew that that was that dude the whole time?"

"No." Canary and Raysor had responded simultaneously.

Canary had lied. Her days was already starting off all wrong. She didn't know what the outcome would be with Don and his situation. But she was silently praying that he returned. This only substantiated the fact that she wasn't going to have him removed.

After she had left the institution yesterday and went home, showered and settled in, she had been ignoring Danyell and Tay's phone calls and began reading a novel by Zane that she had picked up about a week ago from Barnes and Nobel. But as she laid in her bed in her bra and panties under the covers, thoughts of Don kept interfering with her concentration. She had closed the book last night, turned out the lights and allowed herself to sink in deep contemplation about the dilemma she had with Donatello McFadden. After a while, she came to the realization that she was only fooling herself. She liked how it felt to be in his presence and knowing he was near. Then all of a sudden her phone had begun to ring non-stop! It was Danyell and Tay calling on 3-way. She could tell by the way the phone rung. She had flicked on the lamp beside her bed and picked up the phone. "What do you whores want?"

"Girl, stop tripping and hurry up and turn your TV to the news!" Danyell had ejaculated in excitement. "You almost had me thinking something was wrong. You didn't even call me today," she sounded disappointed.

"I'm sorry," Canary said sympathetically as she flicked on her TV. She saw that Donatello McFadden was on the news. Danyell and Tay were both shouting into the phone but she couldn't hear nothing neither of them had said as she had given the TV her undivided attention. After watching the segment, she told them goodnight and that she would talk to them tomorrow, then hung up the phone without waiting on a response. She knew that they couldn't wait until she got off work so they could talk to her about these new chain of events. She sighed.

She had turned off the TV and picked back up on her thoughts before the interruption.

After a long moment, she decided that she would not be the aggressor in the matter but would allow destiny to manifest itself without interfering with it. It was inexplicable how he made her adrenaline boil! Her heart had hammered so hard against her breast plate as he looked down upon her from his bunk when she stood in front of his door with the warden and others, she thought that the morsel of flesh would surely explode!

Canary looked from Raysor to Granada, who had both succumbed to their thoughts. She had long ago heard stories about Granada. He was just like Raysor. He was very conniving. Canary knew that she could pretty much guess where both of their minds was, because they were motivated by money. And since Donatello McFadden was the richest person that all of them had ever been around so closely, they were already beginning to scheme on ways to get inside his pockets. Granada was cool but he was schematic and dirty. And Raysor wasn't any different. Canary knew that Mr. McFadden had instantaneously become a target of hers. She knew that most men incarcerated would stick their phallus in just about anything due to their destitute status of women, but Raysor wasn't just any broad nor one of the ugly ducklings that paraded the facility looking for someone to whisper sweet nothings and assuage her insecurities. She was confident and ambitious. Canary knew that she would no doubt pursue Donatello McFadden, even if there was already someone present she was dealing with, which – by Foxy's account – she was.

With these thoughts, suddenly, she began to dislike Raysor and looked at her in a total different light of disgust. She looked away from her before she caught the look of contempt and scorn that had just been born in her eyes. She now had a new dilemma and another decision to make, because she didn't know if Mr. McFadden had doggish ways or would be subjugated by the savageness of his lower desires due to his current position and fall victim to the barbaric ways of the penitentiary as so many of his peers had.

But Raysor wasn't the only potential obstacle in her way, the facility was flooded and swarming with ambitious, hot panty women that would die to meet him regardless if he was guilty of murdering his alleged victim or not. And now, being that the cat was out of the bag on behalf of his identity, he was a commodity.

This troubled her and placed her back inside a semi-state of ambivalence because she would not follow any clichés like a groupie. Because if indeed he fell for the low life individuals of this environment, maybe she had really misjudged him.

She looked at Raysor just as she looked at her. Canary smiled. If it wasn't one thing it was another, she thought.

About 30 minutes later, Canary looked at Donatello McFadden as he entered the lobby where she stood with Raysor, Granada, Foxy, and Ricardo. She noticed that his demeanor was very calm, his body posture proper. He did not avert his attention from hers as he entered the lobby until Granada spoke.

"Did everything go fine, buddy?" Granada asked.

Don noticed the change in Granada's approach and knew it was because of who he was. He wanted to tell him to go fuck himself, because he still felt a little sour about the comment he had once made about him jacking his pecker, but he nodded his head and directed his attention back to the lieutenant once more before heading on the wing back to his cell. He never once looked at Raysor. "Good morning, Lieutenant Rose. What's up

Ricardo?" he greeted as he pulled the door open the wing.

"Aint nothing hombre, just chillin'," Ricardo responded as he looked at Don with new found uncertainty.

Canary noticed that he hadn't paid Raysor the least attention but had only acknowledged and looked at her. This warmed her. After he had disappeared on the wing she headed inside her office to be alone with her thoughts. As soon as she seated herself and glanced inside the lobby, she noticed that Raysor had headed on the wing. "Bitch!" she uttered silently. She couldn't believe that this boy – and she said boy because she was 10 years his senior – had her feeling this way! She needed to get away from the dorm because she was beginning to feel as if she was suffocating!

Just as she grabbed her keys an stood, Foxy entered the office in a state of animated excitement.

"Well girl, there's no need for you to check out my neighbor since we all know who he is now!"

"Yeah, I guess you're right about that," Canary forced a smile.

"So be honest diva, and tell me he aint fine as hell?" Foxy cocked his hip and placed a hand on the hip he had arched.

"He is."

"Ooohh diva, I can see it in your eyes. You either like him or it's something you're not telling me!"

Canary hated this about him. It was weird that men that thought they were women seemed to have the intuitive instincts of one. "There's nothing wrong with me. And no, I don't like him," she responded ridiculously.

"Well, I do," Foxy giggled girlishly.

"Girl, you are too much." Canary laughed at Foxy. "Well, I was just on my way out. We'll have to sit down and chat later."

"Okay. But remember that I'm your girl so don't hold out on me," Foxy said gnostically.

She couldn't front, Foxy was her incarcerated road-dawg. She would talk to him, but first she had to figure out the extent of what she would reveal. "We'll kick it one of these days. Right now I need to go and get some fresh air."

"Ooohh diva, don't tell me that you, out of all people, got hit by cupid?"

Canary blushed.

"Girl, I can't wait to find out who's the man that's responsible for that sparkle in your eyes," Foxy pursed his lips and shook his head knowingly. "Well, I'll talk to you later, diva."

"Okay, Foxy," Canary responded as Foxy left her office and headed back on the wing.

Canary departed the office, told Granada and Ricardo that she'd to back momentarily and departed the building.

Chapter Nineteen

Orangeburg, South Carolina
Palmetto Correctional Institution
July 25, 2014

When Don got to his cell he saw that his roommates had departed for work. He entered the cell to ponder his thoughts.

As he entered the wing headed to his room, the wing had become quiet as each and every inmate on the rock looked at him. He hated this type of attention. He thought about what the warden had said about extortionist and other threats and hoped that no one would be foolish enough to try him again.

Peripherally, from where he sat, he saw someone walk past his window and realized that it was the dorm's lieutenant leaving. He got up and leaned against his roommate's middle bunk and watched her as she floated down the walkway like the angel she was. He looked at the way her uniform pants so perfectly hugged her hips and booty. Her walk was innocent but provocative. Today she had her hair in a style other than the tight bun that she normally wore – this one he couldn't explain, but it was hers because it matched her eyebrows and eyelashes. He had never seen a black woman with original hair of such and it made him wonder if the pubic hairs between her –

Knock – knock – knock...

A knock at the door interrupted his fantasy and he turned from the window. It was Chess and Yahseen. He told them to come in as he reseated himself.

"What's happening? Are you cool, bruh?" Chess asked as Yahseen closed the door behind him.

"Salam, lil' bro," Yahseen greeted.

"Salam," Don returned. "Yeah, I'm cool. But let me guess – y'all now know that I'm the alleged celebrity murder," Don said exasperatingly.

"Man, and last night you pulled my card about who I am when you're the biggest celebrity in the building," Yahseen humored to lighten the moment.

Don just shook his head dismayingly. For some reason he always tended to worry about if people thought he had really killed Fedora. "I didn't do what I was accused of, though." he looked up at them dolefully.

"No one's saying you did, homie," Chess spoke. "And besides, that shit doesn't matter to us anyway.

"I spoke to Scramble again recently, he told me all bout you. He told me about what happened and why you got shipped. He want to talk to you as soon as possible. He said your father should have a message for you from him that he left on his answering machine." Chess continued.

"But shed bruh, Scramble told me to hold you down so that's

what it is. You're family, babe. We're all in a worldwide struggle so don't even trip." Chess was fighting a conviction for two counts of murder.

"Did y'all see the news last night?" Don asked.

"Nah," Yahseen stated. "I saw you and heard your pops announcement on TMZ late last night while I was on the phone with my peoples."

"Are you serious – TMZ?" Don asked amazed. "Wow!"

"Yeah, they got you all over the mix, family," Yahseen informed.

"I found out from Geez and everybody else when the doors popped," Chess said. "Then I called Scramble. He saw the news last night, too."

"Man, I need to call my father." Don explained the situation and why he'd been pulled by the warden.

"Man bruh, you don't have to worry about no violations around here. I'm not saying what anyone will or wont do but motherfuckers know how we're putting on for the murder capitol of the state. Just chill and do you," Chess assured.

"Yeah lil' bro, everything's one-billion and one. And from what Scramble told Chess about you, niggas don't want any problems with you. Trust me. Soon, everybody will know about what you did at Ogeechee. One thing about the pen', your rep follow you wherever you go." Yahseen stated.

"Alright," Don responded. "If it's possible, I need to use one of you guys phone to call my father. I know there's something he want to discuss that he probably don't want to say over the institutional phones. I'll pay you for the favor."

"Money isn't an issue, lil' homie. You're straight, babe.

You're around ghetto legends and hood bosses. I told you, you're family so kill all that paying for favors shit," Chess said defensively.

"Okay." Don rubbed his hands over his face. He felt so out of place. "Man, don't pay me any mind. All of this stuff is just new to me and overwhelming."

Yahseen rubbed Don's shoulder. "Insha'Allah, you'll be alright, babe. Trust in Allah and continue to vie in patience. The brothers here are inquiring about you so they'll be getting at you also.

"And I know once word gets back to the Imam , if it hasn't already, he'll be wanting to meet you. He lives in the Myrtle Beach dorm. We have a real good community of brothers out here. Just take your time and be easy and remember that Allah says that he places no burden too heavy on a soul that it can't bear, so stand in steadfastness and fortitude lil' bro, and remain as a Muslim."

"Insha'Allah," Don replied.

"Go ahead and gather your bearings and come to the room when you're ready," Yahseen stated.

"Alright. Thanks, guys."

"Off top, lil' bruh," Chess replied as him and Yahseen departed.

Don looked at them as they left his cell. He thought that Chess was very hard and straight forward, but cool. He had never been around so many gangsters and killed outside of his father, Jabbar, and Ali. And with them, he had been safe guarded from the grim reality of their past lives. He had only been exposed to fun, education, and people that didn't know what it was like to kill a fly, or a roach for that matter. But now, here he was, not only surrounded by, but affiliated with the individuals that was literally the cause of the execrable murder rate of the city he had been born in.

He gathered his bearings and headed to Yahseen's cell to call his father.

###

Charleston, South Carolina

McFadden & McFadden Enterprises

Caesar drove around to the back of his establishment in downtown, Charleston inside the blue, candy painted Lamborghini Diablo he had bought Don as a graduation gift when he got his high school diploma. The car was Don's favorite. It had so many coats of gloss, it made the car appear as if it was moving in a body of water.

He pulled up and parked next to Ali's Porsche truck. He climbed from the vehicle and saw Jabbar's honey colored Astin Martin. They were all on time for the meeting he had called with them. Other expensive cars littered the parking lot that belonged to his executives. Khalil's Rolls Royce Phantom was also present.

He entered the building through a private door at the back of the towering structure, boarded an elevator, and headed straight to the 13th floor.

The entire 13th floor was considered his office space. It was like a suite in an elegant five-star hotel. When he reached the top floor the elevator door opened and he was greeted by Khalil. He returned the salam as he removed the Roberto Cavalli frames her wore from his face. "Where's the brother's?" he asked. He was prepared for business.

"They're in the conference room waiting on you," Khalil informed.

"How's things been going, akhi?" Caesar asked.

"Smooth sailing, big guy," Khalil responded. "Ever since the meeting with our manufacturer in California with the snack line we've been able to be more competitive with our competition. I've also got us into Asian markets so the snack line is well. Everything else is just as you left it."

Caesar smiled. It was always good to know that business hadn't faltered. His phone rang and he retrieved it from the pocket of the slacks he wore. He started to ignore the call but decided to answer the unfamiliar number knowing the possibilities of it being his son. "Salam," he answered.

"Salam, abu."

He smiled at the sound of his son's voice. "Hey, son! How're you holding up?" he headed to a sofa in the room that he was in and sat down to talk to his son. He looked at Khalil and raised a finger indicating that he needed a moment.

###

Orangeburg, South Carolina

Palmetto Correctional Institution

Don sat inside Yahseen's room on an au courant smart phone that he had never seen before.

Yahseen's room was amazing! He had yet to see a cell like it. Upon first entry he thought he had walked into a palace in Mecca! The blankets on his bunk was crisp and white, meticulously made and folded. Freshly starched tan sheets covered the back wall of his bed. Fresh white towels draped the rails of the bunk so the steel structure was obsolete. Beautiful prayer rugs was draped across the lockers and table and everything around the room was clean and in order of precision. Beautiful pictures that he would later discover him to have drawn was framed in various different color frames, And the room was freshly painted. A TV sat inside a beautifully made stand that was coated in dark gloss with the Basmallah engraved in Arabic in the stands platform. The window was covered with another freshly starched sheet and due to the fact that he had a flap over the window of the door, the only light that lit the room was the lamp and it smoked from the oil that burned on top of the bulb soaked in a ply tissue. Don found the setting relaxing.

Various different skully caps were also dropped over the white towels on the bed rail and several nice watches sat on a stand that Yahseen seemed to have had built for the sole purpose. The room wasn't crowded with unnecessary junk and paraphernalia. Everything it contained seemed as if it was necessary.

"I'm doing okay, abu. I heard your interview with Steve," Don responded after his father had answered his call.

"Yeah, tell me about it," Caesar laughed.

"You didn't mention that you was going to do what you did."

"Hell Furqān, I didn't even know that I was going to do what I did."

"Well one thing's for sure – I know it rattled the cages of the perps."

"Insha'Allah," Caesar replied.

"Your friends at Ogeechee called and left a few messages,"

he told Don about the message Scramble, Jamal and Krayola had left.

“That’s what’s up. Some of the guys here from Charleston know Scramble and have contact with him. I’ll touch bases with him some time today. And, if you talk to Krayola tell him I said be looking for the business plan in the mail that I told him I would put together.”

“Got you,” Caesar assured.

Don also told him that he needed some extra money sent to one of his roommates account. “I’ll text you his info when he get off work.”

“Okay. But listen, I'm at Head Quarters about to have a meeting with Ali and Jabbar. There's been some change of plans. I've pulled the plug on the investigation,” Caesar briefly explained why. “Insha’Allah, I’ll be there with Ali and Jabbar to see you this weekend to talk face to face about our new plans. I've already discussed it with Al-Salam. I'm pretty sure you know what my line of thinking is.”

Don did.

“It’s what the meeting is about today. I'm going to need you to figure out a few things about where you are. And you may need to find out some pertinent information from one of your comrades back there that may be the key to our success.

“I trust that you are a good judge of character. It depends on the success of our plans. So for future references, start affiliating yourself with someone who’s in to the *know* like your man Scramble at Ogeechee. Do you follow my drift?”

“Yes. And in that regard, I think I already have,” Don thought about Yahseen as he looked around the cell he sat in. There was no way he was living the way he was without being connected to the right individual, or individuals back here!

"Alhamdulillah!"

Don explained what took place recently with him being escorted to the warden's office. Then he briefly told him about the lieutenant that had knocked him off his feet at first sight.

"There's no way she's that stunning!"

"I'm serious, abu. You have to see this woman. She's crazy!"

"Okay, okay. I'll have Cecelia pull her up and give me an extensive background on her. I'll have it together for you soon, Insha'Allah. She may very well be the key to our success. Allahu alim," Caesar reasoned.

"Thanks, abu."

"But the brother's are waiting, Furqān. Let me get with them and if you could, call me later. I won't be tied up, Insha'Allah. Call me and we'll talk about your recent adventures in that place."

"Okay, abu. I love you."

"Love you too, son. And hold on, I got you."

Chapter Twenty

Charleston, South Carolina

McFadden & McFadden Enterprises

Caesar disconnected the call with his son and headed to the conference room where Ali and Jabbar patiently awaited him. Khalil had went back on the lower floors to attend to the officers of the Incorporation. "As salamu alaykum. Ramadan Mubarak, ikhwan," he greeted as he entered the room and seated himself at the head of the table that seated 15.

"Ramadan Kareem," Ali and Jabbar returned the blessings of Ramadan simultaneously.

"How are you my brother's?" Caesar asked.

"Alhamdulillah!" came a reply in unison.

Caesar commenced. "I know you brother's are wondering what's up. The last time I called a meeting like this was when I announced that the heroin operation was being shut down forever..."

Ali sat in a very serious state inside a green and gold Gucci outfit, a pair of matching Gucci shoes cladded his feet and a pair of green and gold Gucci eye glasses sat on the bridge of his nose. He knew that the meeting was one of seriousness in all degrees because Caesar didn't call meetings here unless it was.

Jabbar also sat in a state of serious calm while he gave Caesar his undivided attention. He was dressed in casual Burberry from head to the sandals he wore.

"But to get straight to the point… This meeting pertains to the escape of Don," Caesar looked from Ali to Jabbar, whose focus remained attentive. "I've already discussed things with Al-Salam. I have an idea that I think would suffice and I want feed back from both you in what you think of it. Or, if y'all have any ideas or suggestions, feel free to voice them.

"Ali," he looked at Ali. "You've been back there before so your opinion means a lot."

Jabbar was also incarcerated before but not to the extent of Ali in South Carolina.

"What's your plans so far?" Ali inquired.

"I've been thinking about an escape not from the inside out, but from the outside in. I've been thinking that if we had a tunnel dug starting about half-mile away from the facility in the middle of the woods towards his exact location in the dorm he's in by using laser sighting, we can have him removed beneath them straight from his cell. The facility is surrounded by woods so we'll have all the time in the world to properly have a tunnel constructed."

Ali and Jabbar both looked at Caesar enthralled. They saw that it could very well work.

"I think that's a brilliant idea, akhi!" Ali stated. "And it's less hostile. But for the sake of discussion and ideas, I remember when I used to be back there and thought about escaping – transportation runs...

“When an inmate is being taken to see a private doctor or dentist, is one of the best ways because he’ll only be escorted by two officers in a mini van. And these officers are regular joes from trailer parks and ghetto’s that lack adequate training to handle a full blown hi-jack. It may be a young broad in her mid-twenties and an out of shape fat man with breathing problems who’s thinking that that day won’t be the day.

“We can pull up on the van at a Stop sign on one of those country roads, jump out with machine guns and extract him from the van, and/ or hi-jack the entire van and leave the officers dead or stripped naked,” Ali offered.

Caesar really gave thought to this.

“He’s right, akhi,” Jabbar agreed. “I remember when I had to go see a doctor about my back. Along the ride I thought about how easy it was for someone to come and get me. Those idiots stopped to get gas, cigarettes and sodas. Some of them even stop to restaurants and leave you in the van with one officer listening to country music or hip hop and R&B.”

“Are you guys serious?” Caesar asked surprisingly. He had never been incarcerated.

“As a heart attack,” Ali confirmed. “There’s various other ways, but I think this way and your tunnel idea is the best.”

“I think hi-jacking – and/or extracting him from the vehicle on a transportation run is more easier, because it’s not only less strenuous, but the less people involved the better the chances of a successful attempt.

“With us having a tunnel constructed we have to hire a team of qualified diggers who we’ll have to have watched throughout the entire project. We don't need any slip-ups so I advise that we go with the plan with the highest percentages in confidentiality," Jabbar voiced his perspective.

Caesar and Ali both agreed.

"What if we could have the officers down with the plot that drives the van?" Caesar inquired. "I'm really trying to pull this off without leaving any casualties. But if not, then so be it."

"That's the tricky part akhi, because there's no telling who'll do the runs. The officers fluctuate and they don't know that they'll be doing specific runs until around four-thirty a.m. when the major or captain call them at home. Sometimes they won't know until they actually get to the institution for security purposes as what we're planning," Ali further explained. "The good thing though, is that even though the inmates are informed late as well, they have those cell phones back there so a signal of heads-up could still be sent."

Caesar strummed his beard in cogitation as he took all of this into account.

"Money move mountains akhi, so I'm pretty sure we could persuade any one of those broke bastards to get down with the gamble as long as the price is right," Jabbar said. "Especially if it's numbers that would set them straight for life."

"The thing is, how will we go about finding the necessary individuals to proposition?" Caesar asked quizzically.

"The only ways is through, Don," Ali stated. "He'll have to step his game up and play the field to gather the necessary intel we need. We can also have him start collecting names of the officials that normally conduct these runs. We'll do backgrounds on them. Then, we could proposition some of them with a million or two and if they decline, I'm in favor of killing them to ensure that the plot is kept silent."

Caesar had already been thinking along the lines of having Don gather the names of the potential officials that conducted the runs.

"Worst case scenarios, we run with the tunnel. Overall, I think it's the most discreet way. And he'll be long gone before anyone even knows he's missing. The prison he's at is so lax he could have a dummy in the bed and be gone for forty-eight to seventy-two hours before anyone even discovers that he's missing." Ali sat up and leaned on the conference table.

"About two years ago," Ali continued, "they had a murder down there when this white cat killed and mutilated his cellmate and had him in the room with him for two days before deciding to throw the body in front of the showers. Imagine if he had kept the body in the cell. They wouldn't have known until the stench of the body became unbearable."

"I remember that incident," Caesar stated.

"Yeah, me too," Jabbar added. "That situation was wild, man." He sat up also.

Things got quiet around the table for a moment as they cogitated their choices. The humming from a near-by refrigerator could be heard over the quietude.

"There's no imminent rush in the matter," Caesar broke the silence. "I just wanted you brothers to know where I'm at with Don and the situation.

"But on behalf of the escape routes, I like both of the ideas and I think we should go ahead and put them both in motion. Whichever's completed first is the route we take. This weekend we'll go see Don and explain the details of all this to him in person and let him know the position he has to play, Insha'Allah."

"We get him out and to the air strip where one of Al-Salam's jets will be waiting on him, and off to the Middle-East he goes."

"We got your back, akhi," Jabbar assured.

"Alhamdulillah!" Caesar stood and shook Ali's hand.

"I love y'all brothers for the sake of Allah," Caesar told them. It felt damn good to have the kind of brothers he had on his team. "Alhamdulillah!" he thanked Allah inwardly.

"Just be easy, akhi," Jabbar shook Caesar's hand and hugged him. "We'll get him home, Azeez. Insha'Allah."

"As salamu alaykum. Ramadan Mubarak," Khalil entered the room with profound sincerity and a smile.

They returned the greeting.

"Are you done, akhi?" Khalil directed toward Caesar.

"Nam," Caesar answered in Arabic confirming that they were.

"Ms. Wilson is on the phone," Khalil informed.

"Okay. But tell her I'll call her in five minutes." It was Cecelia. He needed to talk to her anyway about what Don wanted him to do on behalf of Lieutenant Rose.

Caesar knew that Cecelia was falling in love with him because she was overly interested in any and all things involving him. even the Deen of Al-Islam. A day had yet to go by that he didn't talk to her. But right now, he couldn't give her what she wanted in attention, love, and affection with all he had on the table with Don. He loved the fact that she was attentive when it came to him and his way of life. She was very studious and had the gift of discernment and understanding. It was a possibility that she would very well become a Muslimah rather they married or not, Insha'Allah. He knew that she was worried about him and

Don. This also touched him.

"Well, I appreciate you brothers coming through along with the support. We can get together Saturday night and catch the Sunday visit if that's fine with y'all," Caesar said as they all prepared to exit the room.

"That's fine, akh," Jabbar agreed.

"Insha'Allah," Ali said. To him, it didn't matter if they drove a tank through the fence of the institution and extracted Don mafia style! He thought about offering this as an option then discarded it knowing Caesar would be oppose to the extremity of it.

"What's up, akh?" Caesar asked Ali as they entered the main office area where the elevator was located.

"Nothing. Just some wild thoughts of the shaytan I had to seek refuge with Allah from just now. I'm cool. You know how I get."

All too well, Caesar said to himself as he headed for a glass of water before retrieving the phone to call Cecelia. He exchanged salutations with Ali and Jabbar and they loaded the elevator to attend to the private affairs of their lives until they met again.

Chapter Twenty-One

Orangeburg, South Carolina
Palmetto Correctional Institution
July 25, 2014

Don had just gotten off the phone with his father. Yahseen had been absent for the past 30 minutes or so. He guessed to give him privacy with his father. He didn't know Yahseen's roommate's whereabouts, nor did he know his identity.

Don knew that things wasn't copacetic with his situation. He had also came to the conclusion that the only way out would be if he escaped. God! It felt as if he was living inside a movie! Things was so surreal it made him want to look around and see if Spike Lee, Tyler Perry or some other famous film director was shooting footage of this madness!

Honestly, inside, he felt as if he would crumble into a heap of misery and defeat any moment. But some inner sense of power and strength kept him pushing. If his escape was indeed successful, he'd be a fugitive on the run all over the news, and America's Most Wanted. Dang! He found all of this hard to believe. It seemed like yesterday he was traveling the world with his father, having fun with his brothers and friends, bedding promiscuous women, a bright future ahead, and just as quick as light moved at the flick of a switch, it all had morphed into something he had never known.

He sat in a chair inside Yahseen's room on the far side of one of the wall lockers that blocked the view of the door. If an officer pulled it open while using the phone, it would appear as if one was watching TV. He twisted the phone in his hands contemplatively. His stomach had begun to feel queasy. For some reason the idea of what lie ahead frightened him. He began to weep. The tears had fell over the bridge of his eyes on its own and he had no control over the flow as sobs began to rumble inside his chest cavity like an earthquake.

He sat the phone on the table beside him and lowered his head, allowing himself to lie on the mighty shoulders of Allah, submitting to the fact that he was no more than a weak child in need of His help.

###

Canary had just returned to the dorm. She didn't know what compelled her to go on the wing even before stopping by her office where Ricardo and Granada sat chit-chatting in a frenzy of Español about God knows what. But during her leisure rounds around the facility in attempt to escape what she knew she could no longer run from, she wanted to see Mr. McFadden.

She normally conducted rounds by herself anyhow and it was time for her to quit tripping as if she was not a grown ass woman.

It was almost 11 o'clock and she needed to be getting on her way to the cafeteria, in which she was already 30 minutes behind. She stepped on the wing and several calls of "fire in the hole!"

instantly reverberated around the wing.

Around the door of the wing was crowded with inmates as they awaited the call for chow as a great many of them didn't get any financial support from the outside.

"Hello, L.T.," an inmate greeted her.

She nodded politely and kept moving. She noticed that several inmates rushed inside the upstairs and downstairs showers feigning as if they were about to wash. Most of the shower curtains had holes poked inside of them so she knew that they just wanted to masturbate off her to relieve themselves of the tension she knew she caused them by her sex appeal. Still, it made her feel dirty! But as long as she didn't see them she didn't care. Hell, it wasn't just the showers, some of them stood behind room doors perversely taking sneak peeks as she walked around the wing. She didn't mean for her uniform pants to hug her hips and booty the way they did but she couldn't help the way she was built. "Sorry, fellas," she said inwardly due to the fact that she knew the depth of their desire. Her sensuality didn't make it any easier on them.

She flashed Raysor a counterfeit smile as she walked pass the officers desk where she sat talking to Chico. This only solidified what Foxy had told her about Chico carrying the torch for his home boy from Greenville that had been administratively transferred behind Raysor. Foxy had told her that he didn't know the extent of their relationship, but he did know that Raysor was bringing contraband for Chico and his Greenville affiliates.

Raysor returned the smile.

"Hey, L.T.," Chico greeted.

"Hey, Mr. Harrison," Canary returned the greeting as she headed towards the stairs to begin her rounds as if oblivious to Chico and Raysor's relations.

As she rounded the top tier looking inside cells, she removed some of the flaps that covered some of the windows on the cell doors.

"What's up, beautiful?" an old school convict greeted who sat inside his room along with his roommate eating a bag of popcorn as they watched TV.

"How're you today, Mr. Bradly?" she returned with a smile of gratitude.

"I'm hanging in there," he grumbled with a smile of perfect white teeth containing a twinkling golden crown on one of his upper incisors.

"Well, continue to take care." She continued on her way.

After touring the top tier under the penetrating stares of the many teenagers and other youngsters of their early twenties with raging hormones, she headed down stairs.

"L.T. COMING DOWN LOW!" someone alerted.

As she descended the stairs in the flood-zone and neared Mr. McFadden's cell she noticed that it was empty. She did not see him around the wing. She wondered where he could be. When she got to the end of the row of rooms in the flood-zone she saw that a flap was covering the window of the door. It was James Wright's room. Normally, she would've just knocked and made and announcement to take the flap down since his room was in a blind spot at the end of the row, but she had just seen him on the yard headed to Grievance Coordinator Montgomery's office as she was coming back to the dorm, so she knew that he was absent His cellmate worked the morning shift in the cafeteria so she knew that he was absent also.

Although she knew that the author and most of his comrades was highly respected amongst their peers, she knew that nothing could be put past expert klepto's of the penitentiary.

She pulled open the door to the cell...

Don stood up as the door to the cell was pulled open. Subsequently, he heard someone yell "fire in the hole!" but it was too late. The woman whom he couldn't get out of his mind stood before him in the threshold of the doorway. She took a step forward and flicked on the lights to the cell and her eyes immediately lowered in concern at the sight of the tears streaming down his face. So caught in the fact that she, out of all people, had caught him doing the last thing he wanted her to see, he forgot that Yahseen's phone was sitting on the table behind him. But from where they both stood, she couldn't see the device. "Damn!" he cursed inwardly and clenched his jaw muscles in self-disgust. She had caught him sitting in a dimly lit cell all by himself crying like a baby in a place where he was surrounded by the most harden of men. He wondered what she thought of him because of this as he continued to look at her in his broken state.

Out of all the things she had stumbled across, from usage of cell phones, usage of drugs, men performing lascivious acts on one another, she had not expected for him to be on the other side of this door crying. Out of all the times she had seen him he had exuded a profound aura of strength and confidence. But now, as he stood before her exposed at his lowest, she saw that he was broken. And alhough she had caught him in thid state, he didn't cower nor show any signs of shame. He reminded her of a cute lion cub.

As they looked at one another, to her, it seemed as if they were in the world all alone and she wanted to go to him and take his fine face in her hands and kiss his tears before pulling him into her bosom assuring him that it would all be okay. She cleared her throat. "Are you okay?"

He nodded. "I just got some disturbing news from home and came over here for a little seclusion to gather my thoughts. I'm fine."

"Do you need someone to talk to? We have two chaplains here that's from your home town that are really caring individuals," she offered. "Or, you could talk to me if you like."

He just stared at her.

The glare and glossiness of his eyes made her stomach tighten and for some reason, she could swear that water was welling up in her eyes as if she was about to cry. It seemed as if they were one and she felt whatever pain he was feeling.

"Excuse me, empress –"

Startled by the intrusion from behind her, she looked over her shoulder. It was James Wright III. She stepped to the side and allowed him to enter his room. God, she was glad he materialized, because she was sure that in the next few seconds or so, tears would surely have slipped from her eyes. "Hey, Wright."

"What's up?" Yahseen smiled as he quickly browsed the features of the woman that stood inside the threshold of his door. For the life of him he couldn't shake her beauty. He was confident that if he pursued her vigorously he had a good chance at winning her heart. But he was already caught in the web with one of her colleagues and one never knew the extent of ties in whom knew who. It wasn't worth being a player.

Yahseen looked from the lieutenant to Don who appeared as if he'd been crying. "What's up Don, are you okay?" He looked from Don to the lieutenant inquisitively.

"Yeah, I'm fine," Don took in a deep breath.

"Well, I'm going to leave y'all to speak with one another," she took the opportunity to escape before adding. "Remember what I told you if you need anyone to talk to."

Don just looked at her yearningly but didn't respond.

"Take care of him, Mr. Wright," she directed towards Yahseen.

"I got him, empress. Trust me," Yahseen responded as she closed the door behind her and left.

Don re-seated himself as Chess knocked on the door before allowing himself in.

"What's up lil' bro?" Yahseen asked with concern.

Don explained bits of the conversation with his father, minus the escape. "I just got a little overwhelmed, man. I'm still trying to get used to this prison thing, you know what I'm saying?"

"Just take it one day at a time babe, and stay strong and don't even think you'll get used to this shit because it aint shit to get used to," Chess schooled wisely. "And never think that there's something wrong with crying because it doesn't make you no less of a man. The best of us cry, bruh. I've had my days. Trust me."

"Pardon self, lil'bro," Yahseen said as he went beneath his shirt as he maneuvered toward the table where Don sat. "I dipped out the dorm to take care of a little business, that's why I didn't know ole girl was in the mix," he referred to the lieutenant as he pulled several packages wrapped in duct tape from beneath his shirt that he had picked up from the Grievance Coordinator. "She's good people, though," he said as he began sitting the packages on the table that he extracted from around his waist line.

"I was upstairs taking a shit when she came on the wing." Chess said as he handed Don some tissue to clean his face. He looked at Yahseen. "Everything' good, babe?" he asked.

"Yeah. Everything's toashus," Yahseen smiled as he seated himself and began unwrapping the packages. He handed two of the packages to Chess to unwrap then handed one to Don "Help us with this since you're here."

"What is all this?" Don asked quizzically as he looked at the large, flattened package Yahseen handed him.

"A pound of weed, a couple pounds of tobacco, and ten smart phones and chargers," Yahseen responded as if this was all routine.

Don looked from Yahseen to Chess in astonishment!

"When you unwrap those, pick whichever one of those phones you want. You may want something else later but one of those'll keep you tight for the mean time, Insha'Allah," Yahseen told Don.

"What do you sell these for?" Don inquired in amazement.

"A grand," Yahseen answered.

Don stretched his eyes in amazement. At Ogeechee he had gotten his iPhone free through Scramble, but the phones Scramble sold went for half of what Yahseen had just stated! "Man, I have to give you something for this –"

"Bruh," Chess interjected. "Not only are you from the Port City, you are my main man's lil' protégé. He said fuck with you and make sure you're tight. That's law!"

"And you're the son of a Muslim so be easy, lil' bro,"

Yahseen added as he pulled the remnants of the duct tape from the weed, causing the intoxicating aroma of the grass to fill the room with its pungent odor.

Chapter Twenty-Two

Orangeburg, South Carolina
Palmetto Correctional Institution
July 25, 2014

Don had just gotten off the phone with Scramble and some of the others he had met while at Ogeechee. All was well with them. He had also discovered that Yahseen and Sinso was cousins.

Yahseen and Chess had departed to stash majority of the contraband they had just received after breaking it down to their standards. The dorm had just been called for lunch by Officer Raysor so they took advantage of the opportunity to surreptitiously do what needed to be done while the dorm was partly deserted.

Don had spoken with Scramble for about 30 minutes, mostly about what had happened behind his TV. They enjoyed a bit of laughter and promised to keep in touch with one another as much as possible. He had asked Scramble why he never made mention of Yahseen and Sinso's kinship and that he knew him.

"I don't know, lil' bruh. It just never crossed my mind," Scramble had answered.

After speaking with his buddies he had called his father to give him the information to activate the phone Yahseen had given him. It was nice and would work for the mean time, but he would get another iPhone.

Yahseen returned by himself and sat down on his bunk. Don handed him his phone. "Are you straight?" Yahseen asked as he accepted the device and sat it beside him on his bed.

"Yeah, I'm cool. Thanks, man. And I didn't know that you and Sinso was related," Don stated.

"Yeah, that's my lil cousin," Yahseen replied. He pressed the power button on the Sony walk-man he had attached to his bed rail and hip hop tunes filled the air.

Don looked around amused, in search of where the tunes wasvcoming from because he didn't see any speakers. By the way the music resonated, it sounded as if it was coming from various locations. He knew there was no way a little cheap FM/AM walk-man could put out so loud – at least that's what he thought.

Yahseen smiled at his inquisitive glances. "I got a little three-inch speaker that came out one of the old TV's inside a coffee creamer container facing the corner of the wall under the bed. And the reason it's so loud." he showed Don another walk-man connected to the bottom rail of the bunk, "is because I use this one as an amp. They're all connected."

Don now saw the hidden wires as they ran to and fro.

"There's some very talented cats back here," Yahseen stated as he picked up his phone and began browsing through it.

"Tell me about it," Don agreed as he sat back and observed

the author in all his poised coolness. Don liked him. "But yeah man, Sinso can rap his ass off, too!" he picked up where they had left off about Sino.

"I know. I hope when he go home he stay focus and purse that shit. On some real shit, sometimes I wish I had come from that side of the family," Yahseen stated ruefully. "My side of the family doesn't know what it is to be loyal. A bunch of selfish bastards that think they got life all figured out."

Don didn't respond. He sensed that this was a personal issue that somehow came to the surface because he saw the ill glare of resentment that lingered in Yahseen's eyes.

"But that's another story, lil' bro. You got to pardon me. I admit that sometimes I tick-tock-boom!" Yahseen laughed.

Don laughed also, but as he did, he realized that the individual that sat in front of him was crazy – crazy but cool. And so far, by what Yahseen had been displaying in ways and actions, "A Penitentiary Holy Book", one of the books by him he had read – the protagonist inside the book depicted "Geez" was indeed him.

"Insha'Allah," Don replied. "Where's Chess?"

"He shot on the yard to take care of a little business with one of the homies in the Colombia dorm, "Yahseen informed. "But shed, Ricardo told me you were looking for a two-man?"

"Hell, yeah!" Don ejaculated. "Do you have any ideas of a candidate?"

"Yeah. Just chill. I got you. I might can get you in here with me. My roommate is about to go home in a couple of months so I know he'll probably swap out until then. Especially if we gave him a hundred-and-fifty or so. He's cool people. A white cat from North Carolina name High-C. I fucks with him," Yahseen informed. "I'll holler at him when he get off from work. He should be here within the next thirty-minutes or so. I'm surprised he ain't back already. He probably shot in one of those other dorms to sell whatever he stole or cooked inside the café. That's one thing about him, he gets his hustle on."

"That's what's up." This was music to Don's ears. He sure hope that things went in his favor in this regard because he didn't mind being roommates with Yahseen. He was very cool, intelligent, disciplined, he was Muslim – and his room was cool and relaxing.

"But man, what's good with you and the Deen? I see that you don't pray. What's good?" Yahseen inquired seriously.

Don sighed. "I don't know. I guess I was never really ready to accept all the responsibilities because of personal ambition and aspirations. I Know this doesn't justify my actions but it's the only explanation I have," he answered earnestly.

"You know that Allah tell us in the Quran in surah forty-seven: seventeen: that those who accept His guidance, He strengthens them in guidance through deeper knowledge and submission, and gives them piety and protection from sinning," Yahseen relayed. "A lot of times lil' bro, people obstinately oppose religious duties because of worldly ambition and this causes them to fear death because they're so caught up on trying to achieve futile goals before they die. And this, in turn, causes the death of the heart which is spiritual intellect, the blindness of the eye of the heart, and the deafness of the ear of the heart," he explained with profound wisdom. "For whatever reason you're experiencing what you are now is only by Allah's leave, and He know best.

But keep in mind that a believer, and one who believes, are two different aspects. A believer just acknowledge that something exists. But one who believes follows that belief and act upon the principles it propagates. Being a mere believer isn't enough, lil' bro," he further explained.

Don listened attentively. He thought that Yahseen took the place of Jamal at Ogeechee on behalf of keeping him in remembrance of the Deen.

"I know you got what it takes because I see it in you, and I know if I do, Allah in His infinite knowledge, wisdom, and sight does also. He has plans for you. I know you may've grew up around Muslims, but sometimes it's hard for us to relate to specific things a person may explain due to the way they explain it. I tend to have a good way with words and brining forth understanding by use of prototypical views. So, Insha'Allah, we'll work on getting you on the Straight Path, because right now you're slipping, lil'bro," Yahseen sat his phone back beside him.

"I won't drop too much on you now because we have nothing but time, Insha'Allah. But I will leave you with this to ponder, because I see the same fire in your eyes that's in mine, and it's the fire of ambition.

"Beware of ambition because just as well as it can be a gift, it can be a curse. Scramble said you're a beast with words, 'Dictionary Don', so I know that you know that ambition is a deep desire to achieve something…"

Don nodded agreement and smiled at the familiar nickname.

"Ambition is dangerous to the growth of Muslims if we can't control it. It's detrimental to spiritual growth, social growth, etcetera, etcetera, because it'll breed all types of unwanted evil and cause destruction if you can't contain it. I compare ambition to the acid in a bottle of soda. If you shake it and disturb it without being mindful of its inner contents the bottle will explode from its pressure. But if you remain aware that this ambition/acid exist, you know that you must keep it tamed in order to keep the body/bottle calm.

"Ambition absent patience is disastrous. It needs to be accompanied by patience because without it, aggravated ambition will cause conniption. Control your desire of ambition and it'll keep you humble to be able to compartmentalize and properly discern between right and wrong, truth and falsehood."

This made Don think about the meaning of the attribute "Furqān" that Al-Salam had given him. Yahseen was on point.

"The proper knowledge is to know not to shake your bottle recklessly because of the reaction it'll cause. Ambition is like fuel to a car. Without it the car can't move. So ambition is a necessary factor that's essential to achieving goals. But don't allow it to control you. This is when it becomes a curse. The material things of this world is nothing to the believers ultimate strive of the hereafter. The Prophet of Allah said that we aquire three things in this world: wealth, children, and deeds, but only one goes with you to your grave: your deeds.

"Cogitate this and be patient, because our plans in life may be contrary to the plans of Allah. Do you understand this jewel?"

"Alhamdulillah," Don confirmed.

Tap-Tap-Tap, came a sound at the door.

"Come in! "Yahseen shouted. The flap still covered the window. He had a habit of leaving it up even when he wasn't occupied with official business.

"What's up, what's up?" Yahseen returned as he stood.

"You already know. Got to get fresh to death. You know what I'm saying, big homie?" High-C bounced his shoulders gleefully as he looked at Don.

"That's my lil peeps: Don," Yahseen introduced." This is who I was telling you about," he stated to Don.

"What's good, homie?" High-C extended a hand.

"Just chilling." Don shook his hand.

"Let's let him get fresh, lil' bro," Yahseen said in reference of letting High-C get his things together to shower and settle.

"I want be long," High-C stated as he headed to his locker.

"You straight, bruh. Take your time," Yahseen assured. He knew that High-C knew he handled a lot of business and probably thought him to be handling something esoteric." I got a little something for you, too," he told High-C and sat aside 7 grams of weed he had for him to smoke.

"True, true. That's what it is, big homie," High-C smiled. He already knew what it was: The fruits of having a resourceful roommate!

"Come on, lil' bro. I want to introduce you to one of my favorite companions. He should already be in from work. He work in the Commissary. He handles all the laundry for the brothers and keep our uniform pressed. His name is Sulayman," Yahseen stated as he closed the cell door behind him.

"Sulayman? That's my father's attribute," Don informed.

"Trust me, the whole nation knows. But this brother here is sharp in the Deen and he's good people. Insha'Allah, you will like him. He's from Sumter County. Let's roll."

Don followed Yahseen as he led the way to Sulayman's cell upstairs.

As they headed across the rock towards the stairs, inmates was returning from the cafeteria. Officer Raysor was out in the lobby with Sergeant Granada. Lieutenant Rose crossed his mind and for some reason he wondered if she was thinking about him. He saw it in her eyes as she stood in the threshold of Yahseen's room door when she had caught him crying. He had taken advantage of the opportunity to read whatever he could in her façade of expressions. He didn't know if it was empathy, sympathy, or interest. But whatever it was, he knew that it was something unspoken brewing between them.

Yahseen knocked on the door when they got to Sulayman's room. Don heard a faint, "Come in."

"As salamu alaykum. Ramadan Mubarak, akhi," Yahseen stated as he entered the brightly lit cell.

"Wa alaykum as salam warahmatullah. Ramadan Kareem," Sulayman returned as he closed his locker to entertain his fellow brothers. He looked at Don.

Don looked up at Sulayman. He was a very large young fellow; about six-seven or so.

"What's up?" Sulayman smiled toward Don and extended a large hand of welcome for him to shake.

Don shook the hand. It was strong.

Yahseen took a seat in the chair at the table. Don looked around. The room was the same as every other, but the décor here was of a very studios person. History books on the Deen was stacked everywhere: locker, floor, table, etc.

"Have a seat, akh," Sulayman offered as he directed Don towards the bottom bunk. A purple prayer rug was draped across the foot of the bunk.

Don sat down.

"So, how's it going, akh?" Sulayman initiated as Don seated himself. "I've heard a lot about you...."

And just like that, Don had found another gracious companion that Allah had placed in his path along his journey of paradoxes.

Chapter Twenty-Three

Houston, Texas
July 25, 2014

Marcellus Rothenstein went into his study inside his mansion and closed the door behind him. He made sure to lock it so his nosey, nagging wife wouldn't intrude as she often did while he was attending to important affairs that he didn't want her to know about for her own safety.

He went into his safe and retrieved a pre-paid disposable cell phone and dialed the number that appeared on the screen umpteen times as missed calls.

At 53, physically fit and handsome, he thought that he was getting too old for the shit he was tied into. He put the phone to his ear and waited for the disreputable, Italian lawyer to answer the phone. The prick had been disbarred for unethical performances of gambling and shiesting his drug dealing clients.

"Is it you?" came a rushed question.

"Yes, it's me. And calm down!" They stayed away from

names over telephones. “What’s the problem?” Marcellus Rothenstein inquired annoyingly, in which he already knew what Edward’s concern was.

“Man, did you see the fucking news?” Edward asked hysterically.

“What part of the news?” Marcellus intentionally irritated him.

“Don’t fucking bullshit me, man! You know ex – ”

“Calm down, calm down. Yes, I saw the news. The entire goddamn nation saw the news! So what’s the problem?”

“Man, fifteen-fucking million! I hope you ass-holes didn’t tell anyone about me. And I hope you assholes didn’t leave any loose ends!” Edward said in a frenetic state of conniption.

“Calm the fuck down and watch your mouth you despicable prick! You’re the one that better hope you didn’t leave any loose ends! You better remember who the fuck I am and don’t ever forget that. I’ll have your ass wearing cement shoes if you ever disrespect me again!” Marcellus promised.

“I apologize, man. Damn! That stunt that bastard pulled just fucking shook me, man. I’m just saying,” Edward rationalized.

“Just be cool and get on with your life. No one’s even thinking about you, nor us, for that matter. I’m destroying this phone after tonight. Don’t contact me again. Get on with your life!” Marcellus ended the call just as his wife knocked on the door.

“Are you okay in there, honey?”

“Yes. I’m fine, Trish,” he responded. “Now go do what you do best and spend some goddamn money,” he stated to himself. He got up, slipped the phone inside his pocket and headed to dispose of it, forever ending contact between him and the low-life attorney he'd just spoken to.

Reno, Nevada

Edward Butler disdained the fact that he had ever gotten himself in debt with those bastards! He didn't know what the hell was going on, but something just didn't feel kosher. He had been dirty long enough to know the intuitive feeling of a problem at hand.

As he had laid inside a ranky-dank motel last night beside a cheap whore, he caught the segment of the news and it froze him to the core! He had kicked the whore out and been ringing Marcellus ever since. The fucking Muslim bastard had offered 5 million for a lead, and 10 million dollars for a confession! Had he given any thought to this angle before he carried out the hit for those assholes, he would have found another way to cover the quarter-million-dollar debt he owed them and their casinos.

Right now, he would surely flee the country, but all he had was about 15 thousand bucks left to his name – all after the hundred-grand he'd been given along with the settlement of the debt to carry out the hit on Fedora Armanti-Teressa Sanstrom to frame the son of the Muslim prick for whatever sick reason Marcellus and his cronies had. His career was shot. He didn't know what to do. He had thought about going into private investigative work but he couldn't control his gambling habit long enough to make the necessary decision before going down in winnings. Greed had been the cause of his destruction. Money had turned him into a monster.

His Lexus was parked on the side of a road in a town on a street lined with bodega's and strip joints. A casino was up ahead. He thought about trying his luck to relieve some stress as it normally assuaged his worries until it was all over and he realized that he was 10 thousand dollars or more in the hole. But it was always the chances of winning that got the best of him. He even gave thought to confessing to the murder that he still couldn't believe he had committed, but quickly realized that it would be suicidal. The Muslims in prison would kill him without a shadow of a doubt. But what if someone sold him out for the 5-million-dollar reward? Nah, this was unlikely because the cock suckers was too organized. And to their circle, 5 million bucks was peanuts. And, if they sold him out, they knew that he would sell them out in return: eye for an eye, tooth for a tooth!

This made him feel better. He opened the door to his car and dropped the phone inside a drain he was parked over. It clattered like the disk in the game Planko on the Prize Is Right game show as it fell between the steel grill of the manhole.

He put the car in gear, said Fuck Marcellus Rothenstein and his faggot ass organization and headed to the casino to continue screwing up his life.

###

Orangeburg, South Carolina

It was almost 9 O'clock. Canary meandered through the streets of her neighborhood, careful not to hit any of the kids that rode bikes and played Double-Dutch, as she piloted her vehicle to her apartment. Physically, she didn't know where the new found source of energy came from that surged through her body, but she wasn't even tired. Normally, she couldn't wait until it was time to leave the facility. But now, she found that she wanted to prolong her hours. She anticipated the return!

Was this absurd? She looked into her rearview mirror and questioned the quick glimpse of herself that she caught before turning on the street that led to her home.

She began upping the windows as she neared her refuge. The night air felt marvelous so she had rode in silence and allowed the air to mingle with her thoughts. All she could see in her minds-eye was Don's eyes as she replayed their last encounter over and over in her head. He knew that she liked him. She was sure. But she was sure that this wasn't a one-sided dilemma because, in that moment they had shared in a realm of their own, she had sensed something so intense in the way he stared at her, she knew that he wanted her all the same. She had seen a similar look in Justin's eyes when they compassionately shared one another in bed as the moon light allowed her to catch the penetrating glare of his eyes as he slid in and out of her love. Don had this same glare. But she found it profound because they were strangers to one another. She could only imagine how that look would be if –

"What the hell!?" She sat up on the steering wheel as she pulled in her driveway. Danyell and Tay was siting on the steps of her apartment chatting away. Both of their cars was parked behind one another on the side of the road infront of her apartment. She parked and stepped from the car.

"Come on, whore. Let's get moving," Tay stood with an impish grin. Danyell stood also as she giggled.

"What are you guys doing sitting on my steps?" Canary smiled as she shook her head. They were ludicrous, she thought. She had loosen her hair and it swam over her shoulders and back in a stream of golden locks.

Danyell placed her hands on her hips as Canary approached.

"Girl you know damn well you were going to ignore us and try to keep us in the blind."

"Don't forget that we are originally from the hood, bitch," Tay laughed. "You can't fake us out."

Canary shook her head. "I was going to call you guys," she lied.

"Lier," Danyell giggled. "Girl, what's really up with you and this Mr. McFadden guy? You know you got to give us the four-one-one."

"Well come on. Let's go inside so I can tell you gossip queens all about my prisoner and what happened today," Canary expelled a breath as she stuck the house key in the lock on the door and entered her domain; Danyell and Tay in tow.

"Do tell all," Tay chimed as she entered the apartment. Slipped out of her stiletto's and left them at the door.

"Well for starters," Canary said as she sat her keys on the table in the living room before heading to the largest sofa. "I don't know if I'll stoop as low as sexing him back there, but what I do know is that something is going to happen between he and I. I can feel it," she confessed.

"Girrlll, are you serious?" Danyell asked, somewhat appalled by Canary's confession.

"Well it's about time someone besides me took a walk on the wild side," Tay clapped animatedly as she seated herself with her legs folded beneath her in anticipation of hearing the rest of the details.

"Tay!" Danyell scolded. "Don't encourage her in this."

"I'm just playing, dang," Tay pouted childishly.

"Before y'all go jumping down my throat let me explain..."

Canary took a breath and precisely broke everything down to her girls on behalf of where she stood and why. "You know – all my life I've been lost and living inside a box. And not only that, I'm tired of it! I just really think that all of this is happening for a reason. I think it's meant to be for various reasons. I think about Justin's death in how it led me to accepting employment in a place that I would thought to never have worked in a million years – to seeing this guy on TV month after month and feeling strange things by just watching him on a screen," she looked at the 52 inch plasma TV on her living room wall where it all started. "to him being inside a dorm that I run. All the way up to what I just told y'all about me walking in on him crying today. I'm willing to take the chance to see what comes from it all."

"But what about you falling in love with him and he never gets out?" Danyell asked. She was deeply concerned.

"I know that it would be good to have the physical pleasures of being able to have a man beside you daily, but life isn't about material things and sex," she reasoned.

"Okay. But what if you get fired for messing with him and have no more physical contact with him?" Tay asked.

"I don't know. I've thought about all of this, trust me. I'm just really willing to throw the dice on this one. I can't even begin to explain how this is all making me feel," Canary further explained.

Tay and Danyell became serious as they saw that what their friend was experiencing with Donatello McFadden was not a game. They had never seen her so consumed or serious about something, or someone, other than her deceased fiancé.

Canary sat up and faced her girls solemnly. "Please," she began. "You guys are my girls and I love y'all for being there for me over these past months through my screwed-up life. But please support me on this one," she said pleadingly.

"Girl, you are really fucking serious, aren't you?" Danyell asked upon realizing that she was.

"Yes. I don't know what the future is going to bring with me and him but I'm ready to find out. I feel so alive and nothing has really even happened yet," Canary looked off into space of the unknown as she hugged herself.

Tay got up and sat beside her and placed an arm around her. "If this is what you feel and want then go for it, Canary. I got you, girl. Besides, you only live once," she felicitated.

Canary smiled. Her life had been bovine long enough. "Thanks, Tay."

Danyell got up and sat on the other side of Canary and lapped her arm over Tay's. "Girl if this guy got this kind of magnetism you need to find out if he got a brother because I damn sure need what he's doing to you!" Danyell shook her head felicitously.

"I will."

They all melted in a fit of congenial laughter.

Chapter Twenty-Four

Orangeburg, South Carolina
Palmetto Correctional Institution
July 26, 2014

After the sun had set yesterday, leaving a beautiful display of red plastered across the sky, Don had broke his fast with Yahseen and Sulayman. Yahseen had prepared the meal. His culinary skills rivaled Scramble's. He would surely give Scramble a run for his money! He had whipped up fried rice mixed with fried noodles, eggs, diced fried sausages, fried oysters, corn, sauteed onions and jalapeno peppers with a side of spicy chicken wings. It had been the best dish Don had eaten thus far. He had ate the entire meal in one sitting!

After congregating with Yahseen and Sulayman and making the acquaintance of a few more Muslims and Charlestonians, he had confined himself to his cell to utilize the phone Yahseen had given him. He had spoken with Al-Salam over in Saudi Arabia. They had a beautiful conversation of profound magnitude. Al-Salam had told him about things over there and informed him that he sent him some pictures that he should be receiving soon. His daughter Fatimah had also asked about him. He thought that he had a very gorgeous daughter, as he had seen her on several occasions without her coverings as permitted by the religion due to her obstinate ways.

Then, he had called his father. They spoke about the Enterprise and Don was informed that all was well and that Kalil was doing a superb job in handling things. They spoke about Cecelia and where he was with her. His father had also told him about the hundreds of lunatics that had called in so far trying to stake the claim on the reward he had offered. Anybody couldn't stake the claim because the whereabouts of the murder weapon was one of the top factors needed to authenticate the claim.

He also told his father about Yahseen and the conversation they had about the Deen. He told him him about Sulayman, Chess – and of course they spoke about Lieutenant Rose. His father had told him that Cecelia was compiling the information on her. His father had never seen him so taken-aback by a woman! Then he told him about his cocaine shooting roommates and the punk that lived next door, in which they shared hefty laughs before the phone started alerting that the battery cells was low.

Now, it was Friday morning. He had just returned from the canteen with 3 mesh bags bulging with food items, a couple loaves of bread and two cases of sodas, that Mark Shaw had helped him tote back to the dorm. The money he had his father send to Mark Shaw's account didn't go through on time because it had been sent a little too late, so he would have to wait until their next canteen day unless the dorm's lieutenant got him in Monday. It was all good, though. He had more than enough to carry him through. If he needed anything, he was sure that the individuals he was surrounded by would see that he got it.

After Mark Shaw had helped him get the bags back to the room he shot back out the dorm to work.

After Don had unloaded his groceries and properly organized everything, he shaved and gathered his things for a shower in preparation of attending the Jummah service held inside the visitation room.

That afternoon Don entered the visitation hall to attend the Jummah service with Yahseen and Sulayman.

It was exceptionally quiet inside the visiting hall as Muslims prayed, sporadically around the hall, as it was an obligatory act to offer two units upon entry of the mosque's before the service commenced.

About 60 Muslims was cattered about and more was still arriving. A line of beautiful prayer rugs was diagonally stretched across the middle of the floor facing the East. Muslims sat on some of them reading Quran's or quietly conversing with the brother that sat next to him.

As Don entered the door, a Muslim that stood security swiped his hand with a roll-on oil fragrance. Salutations of peace were given and returned as they signed the sign-in sheet at the table by the entrance door.

"Come on lil' bro, let's introduce you to the Imam." Yahseen led Don towards the podium that sat in the middle of the hall where the Imam stood browsing his notes for the khutbar he was preparing to give.

"As salamu alaykum warahmatullahi wabarakatuhu. Ramadan Mubarak,akhi," Yahseen greeted as he approached the Imam from behind.

The Imam turned around and smiled at the sight of Yahseen and returned the greeting. "Yahseen, how's my brother?" He hugged Yahseen warmly.

"Alhamdulillah! I'm well, akh. This is the brother Don. His attribute is Furqān."

The Imam greeted Don and he returned the greeting.

"I'm Qaseeb, Furqan. I've heard a lot about you, akhi. Insha' Allah, after the khutbar we'll sit down and talk for a while," Qaseeb stated.

"Insha Allah," Don replied.

Qaseeb eas the Imam at the institution over the body of Muslims that was responsible for the affairs of the community and coordinating their activities. He was originally from New York, but resided in the upstate area of Greenville, South Carolina. He stood around five-six or seven and weighed about one-ninety. His head was cleanly shaved. A pair of expensive, rimless specs sat on the bridge of his nose intelligently.

Don figured Qaseeb was fiftyish. They were the same incomplexion. He was well mannered and properly groomed. They allowed him to get back to his notes and Yahseen introduced him to more of the Muslims inside the Community.

There were about 30-40 inmate visitors present that sat in several rows of chairs behind the Muslims that came to listen to the khutbar that had some form of interest or another inside the Deen.

Some just came as a means to get out their dorms, or to meet affiliates from other dorms. Sulayman had headed to offer his prayers upon entry.

After Yahseen had introduced Don to Jabaree, who was second in command next to Qaseeb, he went to offer his prayers.

Jabaree was also from Greenville. He was very short and stocky with a meat head. Very endowed in knowledge of the Deen along with a wide range of other things. He was also incarcerated for murder. Don didn't know if it was just him, but it seemed as if everyone he met was incarcerated for murder. He didn't know if they were guilty of their crimes, but he hoped that they didn't think him guilty of his. He was not a killer.

Don took off his shoes, placed them behind the row of rugs in the middle of the floor, and sat by Jabaree. They conversed about Don's situation until the adhan was called by one of the brothers. The service was about to begin. All fell silent as the adhan resonated through the quietude of the hall.

A male caucasian officer sat at the officers desk in the distance, looking on as if intrigued by how the Muslims interacted with one another so fervently and performed their duties so meticulously with such precision.

Qaseeb opened and delved into the khutbar after recitation of other Sunnah acts. Throughout the khutbar, Don noticed how he had voiced things surrounding gang activity and figured that they'd been having problems with brother's trying to be gang-bangers and Muslims when this was strictly prohibited by Allah and His Messenger.

"Brother's!" Qaseeb stated emphatically, as he looked around the body of believers that sat before him. His demeanor stern. "There is no such thing as Penitentiary Islam! There's only one Islam and that's Al-Islam! There is no such thing as a Mushm-Crip or a Muslim-Blood or a Muslim-folk, etcetera, etcetera. I hear it all the time from non-Muslims and Muslims alike who even try justifying this as it's right because what goes on in bigger cities as if it over-rides the Book of Allah and His Messenger. Sallallahu alayhi wa salam.

"Al-Islam is not about cities and states! It's about the Quran and the Sunnah of our Prophet. Sallallahu alayhi wa salam. Allah tells us time and time again to worship Him alone and to not associate partners wth Him, which is the only unforgivable sin." Allah tells us in surah forty-five and eighteen, that in this conclusive Revelation, He has set us on a way of life which is the Shari'ah based on the Religion. Not Tookie, Hoover, Big Meech, Scar Face, nor ghetto-hood legends! So follow it and do not follow the fancies of those who do not follow Divine Guidance.

"Is this not as clear as day?" He held up his Quran as he looked over the rim of his glasses at the brothers before him who listened attentively. "And don't just think that when Allah talks about the Shari'ah that it just consist in the assembly of the Islamic social, economical, and political laws. These laws were laid down in Madinah. This surah was revealed in Mecca. So the Shariah is the practical aspect of the Religion of Islam and also includes words of worship..." Qaseeb continued.

Don would later discover that before he came, a professed Muslim had gotten tied up in gang activity that led to him being stabbed behind a robbery he committed. The Muslims felt some kind of way towards the individual that had stabbed him and wanted to retaliate for the bloodshed of their brother, but Qaseeb had ordered them to stand down. Because by the Quran and Sunnah, it was forbidden to retaliate in unjust causes. The brother was gang banging. This had caused some of the brothers to loathe Qaseeb. But as always, Allah and His Messenger prevailed and they came to understand what they knew not and all was understood and reconciled.

Don thought that he was an awesome leader.

###

Charleston, South Carolina

A beautiful Friday it was. Alhamdulillah! Having too much of anything else to do other than plot and strategize the escape of his son, after attending the Jummah service at the mosque he had built in NorthvCharleston about 10 years ago, Caesar sat on the 13th floor of his building in seclusion on the internet researching the construction of tunnels. Then he would find prospective Muslims that specialized in such work, background check them thoroughly, then have them begin the escape route of his son.

As he sipped coffee from a thermos, a signal came across his laptop notifying him that he had a call coming from Wilson's Intuitive Firm. It was Cecelia. He activated the webcam and Cecelia's beautiful face graced the monitor. He smiled. “Salam, Investigator.”

“I just faxed all of the paper work on Canary Rose to you. It should be coming through your facsimile as we speak,” she said with a bit of an attitude.

“My, you work fast, don't you?” He picked up on the unusual attitude but didn't inquire into it.

“It's why I'm the best,” she boasted. “But who is she Sulayman and why does she interest you?” She asked with a bit of jealous attitude.

So this was what the strange attitude was about. He lowered his eyes and studied her. Then he laughed at the childish expression of being treated unfair plastered across her face. “Are you Jealous?”

“Don't play with me, Sulayman! I would punch you if I were near you. Now stop playing and answer my question,” she demanded. “Okay, okay, okay,” he forced himself to subdue his laughter. “I told you she work at the institution where my son is. For some reason he has a thing for her. I don't even know that woman. Never heard of her. I need to see her though, so I can see what's causing so much raucous from you and Don.”

“Whatever, Sulayman. But anyway, there's pictures of her. One is the picture from her drivers license and the other is what I had one of my investigators take when she was leaving the institution yesterday after work.”

“Wow you are effective,” he complimented. “I bet not get on your bad side.”

“Thank you,” she cut her eyes at him playfully. “I'm glad you know that,” she added impishly.

“If I come and get you and take you out to lunch would it make you feel better, dear?” he asked as he looked at her as if she was the only woman he adored and desired.

“Maybe,” she responded seductively. “I’ll be waiting, Sulayman.”

“I'll be there in thirty-minutes,” he blew her a kiss and the screen to his lap top went back to the web page it was on after she ended the call.

He got up anxiously and headed to the fax machine to retrieve the papers. When he looked at the pictures of Canary Rose, he whistled! He was awestricken by the pulchritude of her! He looked at her for a long moment in captivation and saw why his son was so engrossed with her. If her inner characteristics was any where near her outter characteristics like Don had said it was, she was very well worth being pursued. She was a trophy. He didn't think that she looked like Beyonce, though. They favored in features and style, but the picture of the woman he was looking at seemed unreal. She wasn't cosmetically enhanced. There was no doubt in his mind that his son couldn't get her because he was a real ladies man. But the down-side of the matter would be the fact that he wouldn't be able to enjoy the fruits of possessing her because of his escape, unless she ended up being his Bonnie to Clyde.

"Damn, son!" he said ruefully, as he sat the pictures back on top of the packet of papers. He paged Khalil as he rose from the desk and notified him that he was leaving the building.

After tidying up a few minor things around the office, he got on the elevator and made way through the building to the parking lot. He headed to the Lamborghini, got in and cranked it. When it rumbled to life, he dashed West Ashley to Cecelia's firm.

Chapter Twenty-Five

Orangeburg, South Carolina
Palmetto Correctional Institution
July 21, 2014

Don couldn't wait until the arrival of Monday so he could see Lieutenant Rose. Ater coming from the Friday Jummah service, he had discovered that she wasn't working inside the dorm because they needed her for shake-down at the front gate. It seemed as if he had begun living for her and found himself slightly depressed when she wasn't around, so he had confined himself to his room. Yahseen, Chess, Sulayman, and others came through to check up on him from time-to-time. Other than that, he was finishing his business plan for Krayola and surfing the web. Only thing about the penitentiary that interested him was Lieutenant Rose.

Yesterday – Saturday – after the morning visit, Nebraska came rushing back to the room. He needed the room immediately. With this, Don discovered that Nebraska was a mule that smuggled packages through his rectum on visits for one or his Charlestonian homeboys in the Columbia dorm because Chess had come to the room and stood outside the door with him while Nebraska pushed the package out his anus. Chess made sure that everything went accordingly. Now Don saw why they kept so much cocaine to abuse!

But for Don, time had been moving by expeditiously. He had gotten locked up when he was 18 and had turned 19 and 20 in jail. It had been a little over a year now since he had been confined.

It was Sunday morning, a little after 9 o'clock am. After he'd been shaken-down by the officer in the entrance area before entrance of the visitation hall, he headed through the double doors and headed to the table where his father sat along with Ali and Jabbar, who looked like the millions of dollars they were. They were decked down in designer suits and gators with diamond encrusted wrist watches that sparkled brilliantly. A broad smile stretched across his face at the sight of them. They stood to greet him as he approached.

He didn't know if it was just him, because although the voices of the visitors was already at a discreet volume, it seemed as if all talking had ceased. All eyes was on him and his visitors as he greeted them. He hugged them warmly, then seated himself. He guessed they were the topic of discussion at every table because every where he turned he looked into the eyes of other visitors. They smiled at him politely. "I guess it's the effect of a fifteen-million dollar reward and having a father worth over a quarter-billion," he rationalized as he seated himself before the sodas, burgers and chicken wings his visitors had bought him from the vending machines.

"Tell me about it," Jabbar laughed.

"So, how're you holding up back this bitch, Bruce Lee?" Ali teased. "Yeah, your man Scramble said you did some serious ass kicking at Ogeechee!"

They all laughed.

"I'm maintaining," Don snickered as he attacked the food before him.

They had four hours to enjoy with one another so they reminisced about some of everything before Caesar brought his voice to a whisper and explained the details of where they were with his escape and what they needed him to do.

"You follow me, Don?" Caesar asked seriously.

"Yeah, I got you, abu," Don answered as he looked at his father. "All of this stuff just seem so surreal."

"Tell me about it," Caesar agreed. "Don't be in any rush and make any rash decisions. Yahseen may be the only person you need for info, Insha Allah. So just wait until you get in the cell with him and get to know him better.

"And from where you said his room was located it may be perfect to line up with the tunnel, Insha Allah."

Don had told them about him preparing to move in the room with Yahseen. High-C had accepted the $150 offer for the swap out. They were just waiting on the return of the lieutenant so Ricardo could make the move.

"Make sure you get the names of these officials too, so we can start background checking them," Ali said.

"Okay, big bro."

Afer things had been in perspective with updating Don on his future escape, Caesar, Ali, and Jabbar took the remnant of time to inquire about the lieutenant. Caesar had showed them her pictures.

Don brightened at the mention of her.

"Man son, she is tough!" Caesar whistled. "I thought you was over exaggerating because you were horny or something. But word up, she's a winner!"

"Word up, lil'bro," Jabbar agreed. "Just try not to get too caught up on her on the strength of what's ahead," he warned with sagacity because of their plans for his escape.

Don nodded. He had taken all of this into account. But for some reason he had allowed himself to get caught in a twisted fantasy of him and her on some foreign island all alone as he evaded captivity.

But really, he knew that he needed to disregard her and not allow her to consume his thoughts with dreams because they would never be. Soon he would be an escapee on the run wanted by the United States of America.

"Are you alright, lil' bro?" Jabbar asked. They were all concerned about him.

"Yeah. Just kind of zoned out." Don sat back in his chair and looked around at all his fans. He nodded and smiled at an elderly caucasian woman a few tables over.

"Insha Allah, It'll be alright, son." Caesar could tell that the lieutenant had grown on him. "Who knows what Allah has in store, Don? As I once told you, she may very well be the key to our success so continue in your pursuit until it's all said and done. Allah is the best of planners. He knows best so don't forget that!" he told his son amatively.

This made him feel a bit better. It gave him something to hold on to.

"But on the real, D. It's about time for you to get right on your Deen," Ali stated. "Things are too serious for any loose links. Remember what Allah stated in surah Al-Ankubut, ayat forty-one?"

Al-Ankubut was translated "The Spider". Don remembered.

"What does it states, D?" Ali asked. He knew that he knew, he just wanted him to speak the words of Allah from his tongue.

"'The parable of those who take to them other than Allah for guidance to entrust their affairs to is like a spider: it has made for itself a house, and surely the frailest of houses is the spiders house. If only they knew this!'" Don recited the verse in arabic as he spoke it fluently.

"Get in the ranks back there with those brothers, and quit playing!"Ali encouraged.

"He's right, Furqān. We're about to put a lot on the line and we need the full support of Allah. So think about this," Caesar added.

"Alhamdulillah!" came simultaneous declarations from Caesar, Jabbar, and Ali.

Don knew that they were right. They didn't need any weak links for the devil to attack. But he didn't want to do it for a successful escape. He wanted to do it solely because it was what lie in his heart.

An announcement was made that visit would be over in 15 minutes. All of the visitors began wrapping things up and after hugs and salutations, Don joined the long line of home-sick inmates that was a bit stressed because they couldn't depart with their loved ones.

After he'd been stripped searched in assurance that he wasn't smuggling any contraband, he headed back to where darkness resided.

- Part Two -

In The Name of God, Most Gracious, Most Merciful

Imam Muhammad Al-Baqir (R.A.) quotes Prophet Muhammad (S.A.W) as follows: “Allah says that,' whenever I intend to gather the good of this world and the Hereafter for a Muslim, I give him heart which is humble (to Me), a tongue which (praises to Me), a body which can bear (worldly) affliction and a believing wife who is a cause of his pleasure whenever he looks toward her and who protects herself and his property when he is absent’."

Chapter Twenty-Six

Orangeburg, South Carolina
September 8, 2014

It was around 9 o'clock pm. The raging storm had finally began to simmer. The day had been boring and uneventful for her. She had stayed in and got caught up on laundry and other house chores while pondering Donatello McFadden as she normally did. She also pondered an anonymous letter she had received about a week ago. She found it in a beautiful golden envelope that was placed beneath one of the arms of her windshield wiper's one morning on her way to work. She had the slightest clue as to how it got there. It was signed: Scrooge McDuck. Wasn't that the damn duck off the cartoon Duck Tales that was obsess with his gold treasure in the 90's?

Yesterday – Saturday – she had spent the day with Danyell and Tay in Charleston. She had been introduced to both of their families, then they had rendezvoused at the Carolina Ice Palace in North Charleston where she made a continuous ass out of herself on the ice trying to skate. But she had a great time. And of course, they talked about Mr.McFadden and the intriguing letter she had received from whoever the hell Scrooge McDuck was!

Over the past month and a half or so, she had been in high spirit and her golden complexion had seemed to brighten a notch. Mr. McFadden had moved inside the room with the author and she thought that it was a good move for him because of the author's discreetness and maturity. She had also begun taking Foxy into her confidence. She knew that this was risky but she really didn't care for the job any more. Even if things didn't go right with her and Mr. McFadden, she was giving thought to resigning. There was so much more to life.

Foxy had become her in-house spy on Mr. McFadden. She wanted to know how he interacted with everyone. Because although she liked him and was willing to put it all on the line for him, she wasn't going to be stupid and get tied up with a young idiot who enjoyed the hype of the attention he got and kept everyone in his business. But Foxy kept telling her that he was such a recluse. He also told her that he didn't even socialize with the other female officers although she had seen Raysor in his face on several occasions. But he never appeared to be pressed. Foxy said that sometimes people forgot that him and the author was even in the dorm because they seldomly showed their faces on the rock.They were in their room in their own world majority of the time.They didn't interact much with the other inmates.

To a degree she was beginning to become frustrated with things because she didn't know how to proceed in the matter with him. When she worked she seldomly saw him unless she went on the wing to conduct her rounds. He acknowledged her, but other than that he never made any passes at her nor attempted to engage her in any conversations. She thought about being the aggressor but decided against it because it would make her feel cheap and make her appear as if she was desperate. The only thing she could do was continue to be kind and hope that what she had once saw inside his eyes compelled him to come to her. Foxy, Danyell, and Tay had all encouraged her to pull him inside the office and go for it, but it was something she could not do. Such performance, in her book, was unlady-like. And to add insult to injury, she had a letter from some unknown jerk that probably resided in her neighborhood that had a crush on her playing mind games. But she had to admit that the letter was sweet and suspenseful.

She twirled the golden envelope in her hands. The name "Golden" was scrawled in fancy cursive across the front of the envelope. She laid in her bed beneath the sheets. The TV was off. She had the music playing softly. Melanie Fione's "4 am" played in the background of her thoughts. She removed the letter from the envelope and read it for the hundredth time, as if it would expose something it already hadn't. It read:

Golden,

Long ago someone explained Paradoxes to me. For many reasons, I hope I get the chance to explain to you in the near future why I think I discovered you for a reason. I've been trying to approach you for some time now, but due to my peculiar circumstances, along with your pulchritude, I was lost in how I should proceed in with a proper apapproach. Because not only do you mesmerize me – and although I can handle a constructive rejection – I seek not to fuck up an opportunity of a life time!

I don't know if you are aware of what a "Siren" is, but she is a seductive woman that men yearn to possess regardless of the dangers that surround her. You've grown on me so and have begun to consume my thoughts to the point I pray and ask God to bring you to me and I trust that He will if it's meant for me to have you. I know as you read this you're wondering who I am, but in due time Golden, I'll make myself known. And no, I'm not some deranged, sadistic stalker so you can rest assured that I'm not lurking in the bushes near your home. (smile) I just wanted to take the initiative in letting you know that there exist someone that feel this way about you. And that just as in time, seconds forecast the coming of the minute, the minute predicts the coming of the hour, and the hour anticipates the coming of the day, I anticipate the very next time I'll be blessed with a chance to steal a glimpse of You...

Scrooge McDuck

She refolded the letter and placed it back inside the shiny golden envelope. It reflected a blurry image of her as she stared into it pondering who Scrooge McDuck could possibly be.

###

Palmetto Correctional Institution

Earlier That Evening

Lightning cracked through the dark evening skies in conniption as if electrical gods was at war, relentlessly throwing bolts of lightning at one another. Thunder roared roarously and shook the earth in ambition as the raging thunder storm manifested the might of the Creator of creation as every creature in its midst did everything in its power to escape its belligerence as they took shelter in every nook and cranny.

All the power had been knocked out around the facility. The backup generators had yet to kick in for the past several hours. The dorms around the compound were locked down for security purposes. The storm raged on and the pressure from the down pour of the rain washed away pools of blood into the grass that had stained the concrete walk-ways around the compound from the inmates that had been stabbed and rushed out the dorms for help.

It had been 6 peaceful weeks since Don had moved into Yahseen's room. Around the yard things was appallingly chaotic. Especially inside the Charleston and Columbia dorms. Execrable gang activity and youngsters that sought reputations was the cause of several riots and perennial stabbings. Yahseen and Chess constantly sent weaponry to affiliates in those dorms because it was necessary. Several officers had been caught engaging in lascivious acts with inmates, and others had been caught smuggling after being snitched out for envious, or other retaliatory reasons by inmates, and even staff.

Luckily, the dorm Don had been confined to was the second most peaceful dorm on the compound next to the Myrtle Beach dorm where the Imam resided. It was the faith based/ honor dorm. And even in this it had its fair share of corruption. It just possessed a more sensibly, mature crowed of inmates so things were a bit more low-key.

About 2 weeks ago, after being in the room with Yahseen for about a month or so, he had taken the chance of exposing his plans of escape. In this, he discovered that Yahseen held the key to the people he needed to accomplish this feat. He had found out that Sergeant Granada, Captain Holmes, and a female on the institutions contraband team named Sergeant Smith that Yahseen knew from the streets, all did transportation runs frequently and would be the ones that would most likely take the bait. He had also been informed that the coordinator he dealt with was first cousins with Captain Holmes, who appointed security teams to make the runs – and he was about making a dollar. Especially if the price was right.

They had spoke about so much on profound levels. And although they came from wholly different backgrounds and upbringings, both of them spoke intelligence, ambition, and Islam. They became tight.

Don had given his father the names Yahseen had given him for background purposes. Then his father had Yahseen propose hypothetical questions to all of them. He had Coordinator Montgomery on Captain Holmes but she hadn't had the opportunity to get with him because he'd been busy. His father had told Yahseen to have her offer him 50 grand just to put Granada and Sergeant Smith as the escorting officials. Yahseen had already propositioned them both hypothetically asking if they were given a million cash apiece would they play as if their prisoner was hi-jacked. Granada sad yes without thought and Smith asked when she could be paid! Yahseen had her phone number. He spoke with her frequently.

And in regards of the tunnel route, his father had already found prospects so the construction had been underway for the past 2 weeks. Now, it was just a matter of time and patience to see whichever came into frution first. His father had offered Yahseen the opportunity to come along through the tunnel or the setup of a transportation with full backing for his support in handling the odds and ends for Don, but Yahseen had told him that he'd get back with him by the time they were ready to move because he had a promising case and wanted to see how it played itself out. His father had assured Yahseen that even if he didn't break with Don, if things didn't work in his favor in the courts, they'd regroup and come back for him also.

Don had also sent out the business plan he had finished to his father and Krayola. Both of them approved of it and Krayola had sent him a letter through his father which revealed that he eagerly anticipated the future. Alhough Don's fate would strain the position he wanted to play in launching their entertainment enterprise, he would make sure that it was done through his father.

The August issue of Jet magazine contained an article about him and his father and the 15 million in reward money. The magazine didn't surprise him, he was now accustomed to the hype and surrounding elements that continued to unfold with his case situation. The only thing that had yet to happen was some idiot asking him for his autograph.

He'd received a packet of pictures from Al-Salam in the mail and live footage on his phone of the beautiful exterior and interior of the masjid he bad built. It was stunning! He had also received pictures from his father, Ali, Jabbar and surprisingly, he'd received some from a good many females from around the country that he thought had long forgotten him. But he knew they had. For some reason or another he knew that they just wanted to be apart of the hype his falter had inflamed with the reward on Steve. He wouldn't respond. He showed the pictures to Yahseen, Chess, Sulayman, and Chess's roommate Success.

Success was Yahseen's protégé. He came through frequently for wisdom. He was from Sumter County – the same as Sulayman. Don thought that he was a bit hard-headed, though. He stayed in fights. He had just knocked some dude out on the basketball court yesterday that almost resulted in a knife fight!

A month or so ago his father had reviewed the packet of information on Lieutenant Canary Rose with him and he had discovered almost everything about her since birth. It saddened him that her mother and father was listed unknown and that she had been an orphan. She had a degree in Criminal Justice and was licensed through the Bar of Association to be an attorney. This made him wonder about her change of course in life to something as abject as a female correctional officer.

She had a deceased fiancé and had been seeing a

psychologist for the past several years. He had stopped his father from any further details and asked him to destroy the documents because he had begun to feel as if he was intruding and violating her rights of privacy. Most importantly, she was single and had been a loner up until befriending her ex-counselor Danyell Brown and her receptionist.

After weeks of ruminating Canary Rose and seeing her as she walked through, and ignorant as to how he should proceed with the matter because of his novice in such foreign environment, he had confided in Yahseen on behalf of how he could approach her. Yahseen had smiled; this was up his alley.

Don began telling him everything, starting with the first time he saw her. Yahseen had advised him to construct an intelligent letter and let her know how he felt about her. "But how would I give it to her without being certain she wouldn't flip the hell out?" Don had asked, perplexed and concerned about the idea.

"You wont. It's what makes the pursuit even more interesting. But I do have a few tricks of the trade." Yahseen had begun coaching him on the science of how to not only approach her without her reacting in asperity or charging him with solicitation, but how to also move successfully around the many jealous, and envious snakes they were surrounded by, by use of a theory he had developed called "Intellectual Strategy".

"Listen, lil' bro... I really do dig you as a person. But the only reason I'm being so open with you, exposing my most intimate affairs to you, is not because you've exposed yours to me," he began after he'd explained his theory to Don. "I'm a very reticent dude. I don't sit up and talk about CO's with dudes period because you never know an individuals aspirations. I'm only kicking it with you the way I am because I know for a fact that you won't betray me in the long run because you are free from succumbing to potential savagery because of your status.

"It's axiomatic that when a man is hungry he's dangerous. Everything isn't to be discussed back here and ninety-nine percent of these dudes back here fail to realize that. Your loyalty is due to the individual back here that gives you the opportunity to feed your family and potentially help you regain your freedom and these simple-minded niggas neglect this and handle positions like I'm in so negligently it's pathetic. I don't see why a man would sit up and expose something so crucial as the officer he deals with, or seek to deal with just to have something to talk about anyway. I be that nigga the whole time everywhere I go lil' bro, and no one's the wiser because I learn from my mistakes and constantly strategize and do the knowledge to master not only my environment, but myself. Instead of looking for fault in others, I look for fault in me," he had pointed to himself as Don listened.

"I don't even tell Chess nor my closest Muslim brother what I tell you because this prison shit breeds the lowest in cut-throating, slimeballing, double and triple-crossing, because of the dire need to survive. And to a degree, I don't blame niggas for their ways and actions. Everybody get into polemics of who's snitching, who's a homosexual and vex themselves about these things when it's a part of the ignorant life we live. Everything in life has an opposite just as death is the opposite of life. But little do we reflect.

"Theres no such things as friends or homeboys when money and pussy is involved with people of material ambition and aspirations. It's why I fucks with Sulayman the way I do. He doesn't desire material things. He's a true Muslim. It's so rare to find true comrades that would starve themselves to death before they cross you to eat I don't take any chances.

"How could you ever be infiltrated if no one knows that you are worth being infiltrated? Never teach the tricks of the trade to anyone that could end up being a potential opponent or enemy to you, lil' bro.You feel me?"

Yahseen had left him to ruminate this one night as they laid in their bunks during lock-down. He was very philosophical and pragmatic and had a very unusual way of thinking and seeing things. After a few weeks of being around him, he had inspired him to submit wholly to the decree of Allah. Ramadan was over and he was now Muslim in all aspects of the Quran and Sunnah.

Although Yahseen did the same thing as Scramble at Ogeechee, no one knew what he was up to because how he handled his business. He had select distributors and an elder Muslim brother named Fahtah that acted as a relay-man between him and Coordinator Montgomery. Yahseen only retrieved the packages when he was unable to. No one knew that he was responsible for a major fraction of the contraband around the compound.

Chess had also learned a valuable lesson from his mistakes at Ogeechee in openly putting himself out there and had begun following Yahseen's footsteps in how he handled his affairs, so their affiliation didn't cause the exposure of either of them. He didn't have a route of his own. He'd been getting stuff through Yahseen.Yahseen was the only Charlestonian inside the dorm with immediate routes. He looked out for some of them from time to time but he wasn't too fond of them because too many of them had betrayed his trust over the years so he kept them out of his business. Charlestonians was the most treacherously, conniving people he had ever met in his life! And although it was the city he represented, he was hyper vigilant when it came to the way they machinated!

Chess hadn't been at Palmetto much longer than Don, but Yahseen had been at the facility since March of 2012 and had positioned himself quite well in this time frame into what he called The Matrix. He was also careful how he dealt with their

Muslim brothers because some of the things he indulged in was illegal in regards of the Deen and didn't want to be the cause of their deviation. One of their brothers attributed Shabahah was his main distributor. He resided in the Columbia dorm. He came over to see Yahseen from time to time but mainly, Yahseen strove to handle all business over the phone to alleviate unnecessary conjecture.

Then, approximately a week ago, Yahseen had helped him construct a letter for Lieutenant Rose and had it smuggled out by Coordinator Montgomery to his father. And by suggestion of Yahseen, he had a courier deliver the letter to her home. The letter was placed under the windshield wiper of her car like a parking ticket. The way it had been scripted, she wouldn't know if it came from an inmate or civilian. She had already received the letter but the times he had seen her since then he couldn't tell if she had been affected by it.

Now, they were about to pull off his next move before he approached her. Insha Allah, it would surely knock her off her feet. He was romancing her from a distance!

The thunder, lightning, and rain continued on perniciously. As the storm pressed on, Don sat in the chair at the table in their room reading a neatly typed poem that Yahseen had written.

Yahseen wasn't asleep. He laid in a deep, meditative state of cogitation and relaxation as the dorm shook from the thunderous roars in the heavens. The storm had commenced after their dorm had left the cafeteria for dinner.

As Don read the poem, he had to admit that Yahseen was prodigy. The poem was called "Insha Allah".

“Man, I don't mean to interrupt your thoughts akhi. But man, what made you write this? And did you really experience and did all that stuff in A Penitentiary Holy Book?” Don asked as he continued to look at the words on the paper as if they were moving vibrantly.

“Yeah,” Yahseen answered as he opened his eyes and took a breath and began the tale of how the poem came into fruition. “You read the book so I don't have to go in-depth of things. And I already explained that situation and my overall strive to you.

“But man akhi, when I first got here, I had a similar situation like yours at Ogeechee. But this clown stole my headphones. Long story short – one weekend, I just rolled in his room and stabbed him twelve times. Head shots, face shots, etcetera.

“While I sat on lock up, all type of things was flashing before me. But I was cool. I prayed, wrote, studied, and plotted. Sitting in that cell day in and day out at a stand-still had me thinking about things I didn’t want to be thinking about or wasting thoughts on. Especially that broad in general that I wrote about in that book. I'm a real vengeful individual, akhi. I hate when an adversary get the best of me. I don’mind taking a loss and keep on moving, but when people pledge oaths and betray them, I think they should be killed by all means. Gorilla warfare,biological warfare, chemical warfare, whatever...”

Don listened, but thought that Yahseen in all his poised standoffishness, was cold.

“That situation fucked up my case. Got me on a roller coaster ride with the courts, my mom’s stressed beyond demension. That situation affected me on so broad a level it's inexplicable! It was the the ultimate test, akhi. One that I failed. A chess game that I loss. I slipped to the point I could no longer think straight being emotionally involved over intelligence, forgetting that ninety-nine percent of these broads back here are immoral sluts. Instead of remaining about my business, I slipped into her lies and deception and it cost me. It happens to the best of us, though.

"Even with who I'm dealing with now, I keep a vest over my heart and a leash on my emotions, and constantly stay in the remembrance of Allah and my strive for freedom and success. My peoples are cool, but for me lil' bro, that love shit is out the window. Only female that would ever have a chance at capturing my heart is one who's Muslim. Period bout blank!" Yahseen spoke calmly, but emphatically about a past situation he'd been caught up in with a couple of officers he'd been separated from at the last facility he resided due to a couple of evil plots concocted against him. He closed his eyes and allowed the somberness of what he felt to pass. Bent on revenge, he couldn't help the perennial effects that mere thoughts incited.

"I had to learn the hard way Don. The biggest mistake I made was thinking that the next man would battle fair. Thinking that, these dudes will always keep you behind or get you killed. And, the crookedness of these administrations are even more sinister."

Don remembered that all the chaos that had started in the book was due to a very promiscuous female employee's deception, evil inmate plots for supremacy, on top of a gung-ho investigator that did everything he could possibly do to bring the operation down even if it took him forging documentation to accomplish this feat no matter who he slandered in the process. And it all came down on Yahseen extraordinarily. He still found the story hard to believe.

"But I've reset my chess board, lil' bro. Insha'Allah, I won't lose this game I'm playing now. Bitch placed me in a real critical position. But alhamdulillah! Something better came out of it all. The experience in itself just took a toll on me and my overall situation. These crackers pounded me out at trial, PCR, Writ oCertiorari.... Now I'm on my Habeas Corpus, but can't move forward in regards of it because the Attorney General sabotaged my litigation. And the crazy thing about all this shit is that these motherfuckers aren't playing fair. They're breaking all the rules! They can't beat me without their guile and deceptive tactics. That's why I'm going so hard with this book shit to ensure that I stay caked up enough to play in their arena."

Yahseen opened his eyes. Don remained reticent. He enjoyed listening to him talk. He looked on as Yahseen lowered his eyes malignantly.

"Akhi... a promise that I've made to myself that I will stand on no matter how long it takes, is to avenge those wrongs. I won't allow it go unpunished. One day all involved will wake up thinking that day won't be the day....

"They say revenge is best served as a cod dish, lil'bro. And trust me - I'm one of the most creative and vicious butlers and chefs when it comes to preparing and serving them."

An eerie chill ran through Don as Yahseen spoke. For whatever reason it was, he knew that whoever the individuals were that was responsible for the perfidy against him, had a very somber day ahead.

"But all of this built up shit incited that poem," Yahseen sat up. "I'm going to go ahead and put this food together real quick because we might be dead for the night. That storm doesn't seem like it's going to relent any time soon."

"Alright. Let me get out your way." Don handed him the poem back and jumped up on his bunk while he prepared tuna, sliced pickles, and cheese sandwiches that they would eat with sides of potato chips.

Yahseen was just like him when it came to the room. Both of them confined themselves to the room majority of the time so they spent a lot of time together. Don also spent a lot of time with

Sulayman studying Islamic literature.

They both possessed personal type writers. Yahseen had several extra's that he had issued to individuals with broad typing skills. Hr used them as his typists' for his manuscripts and other business correspondences because the in-house labor was cheaper than the companies he dealt with.

Don had also thought about getting another job in education but had decided against it because he had too much going on with his escape and interest in Lieutenant Rose. He had already received his new TV and other shoes.

He watched Yahseen as he moved around preparing the food. He intrigued him.

"But for me lil' bro, everyday has been a search for a way out. A lot of these cats amongst us are lost and not even aware that they are. They think I'm crazy and delusional, lil' bro. But inside I laugh. They don't understand intelligence Don, because it's foreign to them. Intelligence, to most of them, is like dropping a Mexican in Japan. It's about growth and maturity.

"I tell Chess and Success all the time to not get caught up in the illusions of this life and to stay away from stagnating adages like DMX told Nas in the movie Belly about his kids not being able to eat books. What type of shit was that?" Yahseen looked up at Don as he opened the cans of tuna fish.

"Holding the position that one can't eat books is preposterous and stagnating to the growth of people and further subjects them to loss and ruin. This is why drug dealers acquire large amounts of cash and never become millionaires, but continue to push it until they're indicted due to the ignorance of the adequate knowledge that books possess to take them to higher-heights.

"Just as you can't eat money but can obtain things to eat by usage of money, surely you can't eat books but by obtaining the knowledge that a book may contain, you utilize that knowledge to 'know how' to do 'whatever' in order to obtain the 'money' to obtain, and maintain, your desires and survive. The smartest criminals accumulate their savvy from books. This is why the crime arena of white-collar domain is so profound.

"But I'm not going to waste air on these idiots when there's more promising things to talk about," he smiled, knowing that he got carried away when caught in the moment. "But anyhow akhi. On behalf of our lieutenant, I really think she's a jewel that's out of place. Go for it, lil' bro," he encouraged. "I think she deserves a brother like you since I'm unavailable," he teased.

Don laughed. "Insha Allah, big bro."

"Shit, by the time I'm done putting this together it'll be time for Maghrib," Yahseen stated in reference of their prayer when the sun set. Since the sky was cloudy and dark, due to the weather, he timed the prayer by one of his watches.

Don had the iPhone that he had gotten through Yahseen laying beneath his pillow. He had returned the other touch screen back toYahseen after he had his service switched over. He thought about Canary Rose. From where he now dwell he could still see the walk-way in front of the dorm. The room was on the same row as his old room. He anticipated her return.

"But Insha'Allah, this storm passes over and Monday be beautiful because we can handle the next step with Rose first quarter," Yahseen stated as he mixed the tuna with hefty scoops of mayonnaise.

Don couldn't wait! There wasn't too many things that he eagerly anticipated in his life. The Lamborghini that his father had bought him was the only thing he could remember ever being overly eager about at the moment. But what he and Yahseen had planned, he eagerly anticipated! He wondered what she would do when she got what he would send her this time. The thought alone intrigued him and made him nervous at the same time.

The lightning and thunder had subsided to distant flashes and roars, but the down pour had continued to fall from the heavens as if being poured from buckets. They had removed the sheet from the window and allowed the gloomy light to illuminate the cell. They had also cracked the window to allow the smell of the rain to full the room with its fragrance of nature.

What Yahseen had prepared didn't take no more than 10-15 minutes or so. He fetched a loaf of honey wheat bread from atop his locker, fetched a pack of sliced cheese from Don's cooler and began eating voraciously. He was famished. He hadn't eaten anything throughout the day other than two honey buns. "Dinners served, Donatello," he chimed through a mouth full of masticated tuna and bread.

"I'm sure glad I watched you prepare that, Mr. Jim Jones," Don humored as he sat up to jump down from his bunk to join the feast. All too often he'd listen to Yahseen speak about poisons and other forms of things to inflict death.

Yahseen caught the inside joke as he remembered the infamous poisoner. The both of them shared the laughter.

Chapter Twenty-Seven

Orangeburg, South Carolina

Palmetto Correctional Institution

September 9, 2014

The next morning when she had awaken for work, before she had even brushed her teeth, she headed outside to inspect the wind-shield of her car to see if another letter was present from Scrooge McDuck.There wasn't.

The day was so beautiful it was as if the contentious thunder storm had never existed the previous day.

It was exactly 10:21 am, Monday morning and she sat inside her office listening to Steve make a clown of himself while she drank a strong cup of creamy coffee with heavy sugar while she spoke with Foxy. She was so energetic and joyful she thought she could very well do a backward flip if she chose to. She had just asked Foxy about Don.

“Oohh diva, I still don’t believe you are serious about him with his fine self,” Foxy shook his head as he smiled. He really didn't think she was serious about Don because of what he was used to in dealing with her since he'd known her. The sudden change was strange. But he was sure that her interest was play so he did as she asked because it passed time for both of them. To him it was all an innocuous game that he figured both of them found interesting. But little did he know, the same way he had grown to feel about the handsome, intelligent, debonair, Donatello McFadden, so did she. And with his lover, alhough he was no longer interested in him, to alleviate the dispute that would surely ensue if he told him how he felt, he would just allow him to continue to please him until he departed the first of November.

"LIEUTENANT ROSE, PLEASE REPORT TO THE FRONT GATE," came an announcement over the PA system.

"Did they just paged me?" Canary asked as she turned the radio down.

"That's what it sounded like," Foxy replied.

Canary picked up the phone and called the front gate as Chico entered the office. He waited until she was done.

"Front gate," Sergeant Sloan answered the phone.

"Sloan, this is Rose. Did you just page me?"

"Yes indeed, girl. I have a little surprise for you that just arrived first class," Sloan said hintingly.

"Okay. I'll be up in a sec," Canary replied and hung up the phone. She looked up at Chico. "What's up?"

"Aint shit. I came through because I need some more wax so I can buff the floor in the lobby," chico stated.

"Don't worry about it because there's no more around the entire yard.They're waiting on a supply in the commissary now," she smiled.

"A'ight. Where are you headed?" Chico inquired.

"To the front gate," she responded as she stood.

"Can I walk with you?" he lowered an eye flirtatiously.

She blushed. "Good-bye, Mr. Harrison," she smiled him off.

Foxy giggled.

"I swear that you're going to cause me or somebody around here to have the 'Big One' like Fred Sanford one of these days," Chico humored.

They all laughed as he turned in departure.

Canary thought that Chico was cool in his brown skin tone, chubby, but muscular stature. But she wasn't interested.

She looked at Foxy after Chico departed. "I'll get back with you later, bitch," she laughed.

Foxy laughed also as he stood up to his five-seven height. His hair was cut low. His hair line stayed razor taped. His eyebrows was finely arched and he wore a bit of mascara and lip gloss that one officer or another had brought him. He even had several pairs of thongs! "Okay diva, your crazy ass. Let me find out you've been around here frontin' knowing your ass was hot the whole time."

Canary giggled as she grabbed her keys and headed out the office. Granada was on a transportation run. Raysor was working the wing.

Foxy went back on the wing and Canary departed the dorm and headed across the yard through Operations to the front gate.

"Hey, girl!" Sergeant Sloan greeted with a very bright smile. She was pecan complexion, fortyish. A pair of prescription designers glasses gave her an appearance of sophistication. She was very cool, warm, and down to earth.

"Hey," Canary responded as she approached with a like smile. "What's the urgency?"

Sloan fetched a large golden box from beneath the counter of the booth she sat behind. She placed it on the counter top with an impish grin. "So who's the special man?" she inquired.

Canary's heart lurched at the sight of the golden box. "Your guess is just as good as mine," she said as she looked at the beautiful box. It had a satin red ribbon wrapped around it.

"It just arrived," Sloan said. "Are you going to open it or stare at it?" she teased in anticipation of the boxed surprise.

Canary grabbed the box. It was weighty. She started to shake it for hints of its contents but decided against it because a puppy or cat could be inside.

As she untied the ribbon, Sloan locked on eagerly. She removed the lid and inside the box sat a beautifully crafted glass bowl filled to the rim with the most beautiful, luscious strawberries she had ever seen! So big, red, and plump they were with fresh green leaves they seemed fake! They were flawless! Someone had sent her flawless strawberries! Another golden card was lodged in the middle of the fruits.

No one had ever sent her flowers or fruits before!

Although she found the gesture of whomever her admirer was, sweet and flattering, she would surely dump it all in the trash! She was beginning to be aggravated by it all! It wasn't that she didn't like surprises or the suspense of a secret-admirer, but her mind was elsewhere. So whoever it was sending her these things needed to stop and she couldn't wait until he exposed himself so she could kindly tell him that she wasn't interested. She was beginning to think that it was one of her "wanna be a player" colleagues. The thought made her cringe and she began to abhor the gift.

"What's wrong, girl?" Sloan asked with concern upon the look of derision that seemed to have crept into Canarys facade.

Canary expelled a breath of warm air. "You don't know the halfs," she said as she removed the card from the envelope and read its contents. The card read:

Golden, When I think of you, I think of them. The lusciousness of them reminds me of your lips...

For now, forever... INAMORATA ...

Scrooge Mc Duck

She started to rip the card up and trash everything until her eyes fell on the word "Inamorata". Other than the TV commercials that advertised the body wash she used, only one person had ever made mention of this term in her presence....

She gasped!

Canary sat inside the stuffy cafeteria at a table in one of the unoccupied sections of the cafeteria as inmates ate and watched her. But her mind was far away from any institutional matters, as she was supposed to be standing guard with the other dorm lieutenants. Donatello McFadden had literally knocked her off her feet! She had bit into one of the sumptuous fruits along with Sloan and had slipped the card into the side pocket of her uniform pants before departing the front gate. She could still taste the savory flavor of the berry in her mouth. Scrooge had made a couple of smooth moves on her! She beamed inwardly and tried to keep the smile suppressed so it wouldn't manifest through her facial expressions.

So he did like her and wanted her. She had left the box of berries upfront with Sloan until it was time for her to clock out. Now that the moment of truth had come, she was running from it. She didn't want to go back to the dorm now. He had made her feel like a little girl. Not that it was a bad feeling. But God, she didn't know what to do! She didn't know if she should let him know she got it, thank him, or act as if she didn't know anything about it. Yeah, that's what she'd do. She'd play dumb as if she hadn't received a thing. She really found that he thought to do this hard to believe! She couldn't wait to talk to her girls! She would call them when she got through with her duty and tell them to meet her at the Apple Bee's they frequented when she got off. Right now her equilibrium was like a river of white water! Thrashing, slushing, and –

"Are you okay, Rose?"

She looked up from her dreamery. It was Lieutenant Royce. He was the dorm lieutenant of the Columbia dorm. She smiled up at him. "Yes, I'm fine. How about yourself?" Her heart was roiling like drum beats. He had been one of the individuals that had crossed her mind as the suspect of the gifts because she knew he liked her. He was cool and humorous but she just wasn't into her colleagues or men in such profession for that matter. For some reason, hard men didn't attract her. She liked the smooth, business oriented office types.

She spoke with him as they supervised the rambunctious flow of inmates and, after all of the dorms had been fed, she would not return back to her dorm. She would help out on lock up. She was eluding her revealed admirer.

###

Don and Yahseen both had heard the announcement for Lieutenant Rose to report to the front gate so they knew that she had received the delivery. But she had yet to return back tothe dorm and Don was extremely nervous. "What do you think happened? Do you think she got in trouble or something?" He was worried.

Yahseen laughed.

Don frowned.

"Nah, just be cool, akh. Trust me. All is well. I don't know why she haven't returned to the dorm. Maybe they needed her elsewhere. Be cool and let destiny manifest itself," Yahseen coaxed his brother. He was a veteran at these things and had done such things many times before.

It was around 2 o'clock in the afternoon. They had made their prayers and was just parlaying around. Yahseen was working on a new novel called "Revenge From The Casket," He was at the table and Don sat on his bunk with the Introduction of the book in his hands that Yahseen had allow him to read.

"Read the Introduction akhi, and chill," Yahseen smiled and shook his head at Don's novice.

Don laughed. He knew his anxiousness and nervousness was absurd. "Alright, akhi," he snickered. "She just got me drove!"

"Insha'Allah, you got her lil'bro and everything's all good. Just maintain your grown man and lay like an actual don'. You feel me?"

Don pulled himself together and read the short passage. It read:

The Penitentiary Is A Cemetery…

The Dorms Are It's Lots…

The Cells are its Graves….

And My Bunk Is My Casket.

Don read the passage several times and looked up at Yahseen as his ink pen glided back and forth across the paper he wrote on."Man akhi, this is deep. Where do you come up with these things? Don asked but already had realized that Allah had granted Yahseen aptitude.

"I don't know, lil' bro. Alhamdulilah, though," Yahseen answered without breaking the stride of his pen flow as Success knocked on the door.

Don waved him in.

"What's up, big bruh?" Success sauntered in the room. He was agile and sinewy at 165 pounds, five-eleven. "What's up, Don?"

"What's good, bro?" Don returned.

"Sit down and let me holler at you real quick. You know you got me hot with you," Yahseen stated as he continued his pen strokes.

Success seated himself next to Don. He knew that school was in. He knew that Yahseen was upset with him. He was his mentor. He'd been slipping on everything that Yahseen had been teaching him in how he should strive and conduct himself and it hurt him that he was disappointing him because he had given him a chance when everyone else had turned their backs on him. He knew that when Chess told him Yahseen wanted him it pertained to the fight he had started over the weekend on the basketball court becauseYahseen had been ignoring him since then and wouldn't speak with him until now.

"What did I once tell you that was the three steps to accomplishing dreams?" Yahseen never looked behind him.

Don sat the Introduction on the table next to the other papers and excused himself to allow Yahseen and Success to have a private one-on-one. He knew that Yahseen was mentoring him and trying to make sure he kept a level head and stayed focus on the goal he had attributed himself – which was Success. He headed to Sulayman's room.

“Waking up, interpreting it, then acting upon the interpretation, putting the dream into effect making it a physical reality," Success answered.

"Well, why aren't you waking up? I'm going end up pushing back from you lil' bruh because you are still asleep and dreaming. Word! Tough love is a bitch. When you see me switch up don't wonder why. Read this passage," Yahseen handed him the Introduction that Don had just read.

Success read the Passage.

"Wake up lil' bruh! That's for niggas like us with a thousand fucking years! If not, your bunk is where you'll die!" Yahseen laid down his pen and looked at him.

A tear escaped Success' eye.

Yahseen got up and left the room to give him time to gather is thoughts.

###

Downtown, Charleston, SC

Cecila's dress flowed around her ankles as her and Caesar

walked hand-in-hand around the historical Battery in the cool night air where his mansion was located. It was around 9 o'clock pm.They were the only beings out. The only noise came from the currents that pushed the waves up against the wall that fortified the water. The smell of the sea was thick in the air.

Caesar's phone began ringing and he answered it. "As salamu alaykum."

The greeting was returned.

"Hold on for a minute, akhi," he turned to Cecelia. "Excuse me dear. I need to take this call."

She smiled meekly. He walked away. She was used to him doing this to her. She felt like he didn't trust her.

"Whats good, bro? How's everything going out there?" he askedAli.

"Everything's fine. I'm just letting you know that we got everything under control but had to change spots again because we ran into plumbing pipes. We found a prime spot though. Alhamdulillah," Ali informed.

"Alhamdulillah," Caesar replied. He had found everything he needed to properly have the tunnel constructed and had meticulously picked 4 Muslims that he'd found on Facebook for the job. They had begun digging the tunnel in a heavily wooded area about a half-mile away from the facility. The operation would take between 4-6 months before the tunnel was completed. They only worked when night fell. He had paid them handsomely with a sincere promise of future benefits. "Just keep me informed, akh. I'll try to get out there some time this week, Insha Allah. Tell the brothers I send my salutations."

"Got you bro," Ali replied.

"But listen, bro. I'm out here with Cecelia on the Battery so we'll talk later. I know she feels as if I'm leaving her hanging."

"Go do you, bro. Salam."

"Salam." Caesar slipped the phone back into his pocket and headed back toward where Cecelia leaned up on on the guard rail over looking the dark sea.

"Hey, there," he smiled as he approached and leaned upon the rail beside her.

"You're plotting the escape of your son, aren't you?" She asked without blinking or looking at him.

She had caught him by surprise! He looked at her studiously but remained reticent.

"I'm not green, Sulayman," she spoke with quiet fervor. "I had a father that was once a major drug dealer and although I'm a girl – the only child at that, I was taught about that life. You remind me of my father." Her father had passed from aids. "It's why I became an investigator. I've always been curious about things and I named my firm its name because I really do have hellafied intuition." She leaned up off the rail and turned to face him. "I'm for you, Sulayman. Not against you. And, I love you," she told him for the first time and began crying.

"I respect how things have been going between us with you being Muslim, but I want you to know that I feel what you feel for your son and I'm here to support you one-hundred percent. Don't shut me out."

Thas had all touched him in his abeyant state. He lifted the chin that lowered and kissed her for the first time.

She cried harder.

He pulled her into his broad bosom and held her as he calmly began conveying everything he had underway, beginning with the dream he had of his deceased grandmother. In this moment, he knew that they had entered that special realm of their relationship. And now, there was no turning back.

Chapter Twenty-Eight

Orangeburg, South Carolina
Palmetto Correctional Institution
September 10, 2014 - Tuesday

The following morning Coordinator Montgomery strutted across the yard to the education building where her office was located as inmates that traversed throughout the yard gawked at her in the civilian attire she wore. With the stack of papers she carried, she ignored them and continued on. She was used to the unwavering attention after 15 years of working inside the facility from officer, ranking official, to her current position. She'd seen it all. Out of all the women that the institution employed, at 43, she was on the top 3 in beauty and sex appeal. She wore her hair cut short in an urban-chic style. She was the complexion of a Werther's Original piece of candy with elegant facial features, beautiful teeth, intoxicating eyes. She stayed properly groomed at all times. Very high maintenance – even before meeting Mr. James Wright III, who had her living like a queen in a quarter-million dollar house in Columbia, South Carolina. Her body rivaled the younger girls at 155 pounds, five-six in height. She wore a two piece cream in color Fendi suit that accentuated her curvaceous thighs and other assets, and a pair of cream Marc Jacobs pointed toe heels donned her feet.

When she entered the education building she saw that Captain Holmes was present in the hallway speaking with the black security officer. He was awaiting her.

"Good morning, show girl," he smiled as she approached after excusing himself from the officer.

"Hey, Rick," she acknowledged him by the name their family called him.

"Sorry for not getting with you sooner but the warden been working a brother to death!" he said as he walked beside her headed to her office.

They moved along through the throng of ambulanting inmates as they headed to class, the law library, computer lab, or through the back exit that led to auto mechanics, carpentry, etc.

They reached her office. “So what’s on your mind, big Cuz?" he asked as he seated himself in the chair in front of her small desk after closing the door behind him. She headed to the Xerox machine and began photo copying the grievances she carried to send back to the inmates that the warden had responded to. “This is some unusual stuff so listen...

“Let’s just say someone offered you fifty-k to make sure that two specific officers transported a specific inmate on a medical run that was going to assist in his escape. Would you do it?" She looked at him. She was careful not to disclose the parties involved.

"Fifty thousand! Girl, are you serious?" he laughed as if she was pulling his leg.

"Hell, yeah I'm serious. When did you ever know me to play

games?" Her expression austere.

He pondered this. She was right. She had always been serious. Even when they were kids. "Putting them together would be my only duty for fifty thousand bucks?" he found the offer hard to believe. He would have done it for a thousand bucks!

"Ummhmm," she said as she stacked the papers that came out of the machine.

"Damn right I would! But what made you ask that?" his eyes followed her as she headed to sit behind her desk and began slipping the forms she copied into cofidential envelopes

"I'm not telling you yet so don't ask," she told him as she wrote the inmates name and location on the envelopes they were for. "If it's official, I'll make sure you get the money," she remained evasive.

"Alright," he acquiesced. "I've been knowing you long enough not to pry so I won't. I trust your judgement. You've been saving me since we were kids.

"But anyway, I got a meeting with the warden and the major so I need to run," he looked at his watch then stood.

She smiled at him and winked connivingly.

"You are a mess," he laughed as he headed out the door.

When he departed she picked up the phone on her desk and called the officer working James Wright's dorm. She needed him to report to her office. She wondered if they would have time for a quicky because she didn't have any panties on. Her suit jacket hung a bit below her booty so no one could tell. Without it, the soft, thin fabric would certainly reveal this fact!

For some reason she was teenage-horny! Mr. Wright hadn't

been inside her in over a week. She needed him to assuage her yearn. She prayed that the lawyer they had hired got him home. If not, they most definitely would emulate the actions of his roommate!

She expelled a breath of frustration his salacious love caused her. She kicked off her heels as Officer Carter answered the phone. "Would you have Inmate James Wright report to the Grievance Office, please...."

###

"What's up, empress?" Yahseen greeted Lieutenant Rose as they passed one another on the walkway as he headed to the Grievance Office.

Canary smiled at him as she headed towards the dorm. "Hello, Mr. Wright," she returned as the both of them continued along. She knew where he was headed. She didn't know if she was tripping, but it seemed as if he'd had a knowing look in his eyes when they passed one another. But what should she expect? She had read enough of his books to know that he'd probably been the one that was coaching his roommate in his pursuit of her. If so, she thought that it was kind because most guys would probably be envious toward the other. She looked over her shoulders at him as he entered the education building. "Smooth you are, Mr. James Wright III," she said to herself.

Moments later she entered the dorm and found that the lobby was swarming with activity. The case workers presence had caused a bit of an uproar with her flowing hair and tantalizing street wear that all non-officers had the privilege of wearing. She was inside her office doing reviews and assisting inmates with questions. A line of about 8 inmates was in the lobby lined up against the wall outside her office. Some of them didn't have anything to speak about. They just wanted to smell her scent like animals and flirt with her beauty.

The barbershop was also located in the lobby. There was two barbers, but one was only allowed to cut at a time. Two inmates were allowed in the shop other than the barber: the one getting his hair cut and the one waiting. The one waiting was Mr. McFadden and he looked at her with a penetrating stare that made her temperature rise!

Ricardo and Granada stood in the lobby also. Officer Carter was on the wing. And something that struck her as odd was Sergeant Smith of Contraband was standing next to Mr. McFadden in her little tight, provocative uniform chatting away. A streak of jealousy swam through her heart but she still forced a smile and greeted everyone as she canvassed the lobby making sure that no one was leisurely lingering around before entering her office.

Ricardo had a pot of fresh coffee waiting on her. She poured herself a cup with no cream nor sugar. She needed the recharge, because for some reason, she suddenly felt down and sluggish. Just before entry of the dorm she had been exuberant. She knew that the sudden change of mood either confirmed that she was indeed bipolar as Danyell had once diagnosed her, or seeing Mr. McFadden and Sergeant Smith in conversation had touched her dolorously. Just this morning, and last night after she had left the facility with her strawberries enroute to Apple Bees, the jubilation that Mr. McFadden's actions had inspired, there was no way she should be feeling the way she felt now.

She looked out the door to the lobby from behind her desk as she sipped from her mug. As she looked over the rim of her mug, she saw that he was watching her as Sergeant Smith chatted on. In this instance she knew that Sergeant Smith being in his face was the cause of her mood change. She thought about how hard she had loved Justin and realized right then that she was a woman that was possessive of anything her heart was contiguous to.

He looked away as Sergeant Smith turned her body in the direction he was looking, as her back was to Canary. Apparently, he didn't want to give her the indication that he was watching her.

She could no longer sit in his line of sight, so along with her cup of coffee, she got up and headed on the wing to leisurely walk around and chat with a few of the guys for a while. There wasn't anything else to do. And, when he came back on the wing and saw her engaging one of his fellow peers in conversation he'd know how he had made her feel.

But dang! She didn't want to play head games with him, because she knew he didn't mean it. She was acting like a little girl. She would not do anything to intentionally cause him anymore distress. She would just make her rounds, and by the time she was done, he would no longer be standing in the lobby.

It seemed as if every time Don saw her she was becoming finer like wine. He didn't know how much longer he could wait before approaching her and probably would have a moment ago when they looked at one another. But Yahseen had told him to be patient. Timing was everything. And besides, too many people was around. Although they didn't know what he intended to discuss, Yahseen had precisely broke down the dangers in conjecture in his theory of Intellectual Strategy. So he'd be patient and continue to manifest the qualities and characteristics of the lion and crocodile.

Sergeant Smith stood next to him talking about the article she'd seen in the Jet magazine and wished him the best. She had told Yahseen last night that she was coming to the dorm today because she wanted to see him and meet Don.

Don thought that she was a very cool, cute broad. He saw why Yahseen dealt with her. Yahseen had told him that he had never bedded her because of rumors that had surfaced around about her that scared him due to her lascivious, promiscuous ways. But they weren't true. And when it was all said and done, she was one of the last individuals that never abandoned him; always there when he called. She was his best friend.

But it had been a while since the last time he and Canary had seen one another close up in person. He wanted to see her reaction after the recent delivery. She hadn't communicated any signs whatsoever that said she'd received any of them, or knew that it was him that sent them to her unless he had missed something.

The barber signaled that he was ready for him and he bidded Sergeant Smith farewell.

"Well you stay strong and hang in there, Mr. McFadden," she said as the few gold crowns on her incisors twinkled, her Charlestonian accent sexy and thick.

“Insha' Allah,” he smiled and headed in the barbershop as she headed on the wing.

“What's up with you?" Will smiled as he popped the cape to rid it of debris in preparation to drape it around Don.

"Alhamdulillah!" Don replied as he sat in the chair. “What's good with you?"

"Man, I can't call it. I'm just out here enjoying the view of the females. Ive been to a few other spots locked up. But man, I aint never seen so much beautiful woman working in a prison in my life. These chicks are wifey material,” Will slipped the cape around Don.

“Tell me about it," Don agreed.

Will was from Greenville, South Carolina. He was one of two barbers the dorm possessed. The other barber didn't cut too well so majority of the guys opted for Will's expertise. Don had found him to be stand-up in character, as they spoke from time to time.

Too many good brothers was confined, Don thought as he looked in the mirror on the wall at his reflection. He wasn't narcissistic like Yahseen, but he did approve of his image and kept himself properly maintenanced.

"But boy, I saw you and your pops in the recent Jet," Will initiated an amiable conversation.

"Yeah, tell me about it," Don replied. "The media's having a field day with it."

"I aint bullshitin'," Will agreed, "My peoples on the street just asked me about you when I called home wanting to know if you're back here with me."

"It's all good, man. Tell them I said what's up and that I'm not guilty!" Don stated and they both laughed. "Do y'all have some bleach upstairs for sale?" he asked. He tried to keep bleach on hand because of the filthy environment.

"I think Chico got some up there." He and Chico was roommates. "Just holler at him when you go back on the wing. And tell Chess to come on because he's next. After I cut his hair that's a wrap for today,"

"Me and Chico got a nice lil' batch of wine coming down and I'm about to get on it early!" Will said. "Shit, that's Chess right there. He just came out the case workers office. Hold up, Don... Chess!" He stepped to the door of the small room to catch Chess before he went on the wing. "You might as well post out here until I'm done with your homie. You're next."

Chess stepped inside the room "What's happening, lil' bruh?" He greeted Don.

"Chilling." Don returned as he looked at Chess' reflection in the large mirror on the wall.

Little did everyone know, Chess had just gave the case worker his phone number to call him. He had been discreetly pursuing her since the first time he met her when she had conducted his Initial Review when he first got to the facility. She'd been out on sick leave for a while due to a car accident and had just returned.

"What's up with you?" Don inquired as Will began giving him a line-up.

"Check Mate, " Chess grinned impishly.

Neither Don, nor Will, knew that he was insinuating that he had just captured a queen.

After passing a few words with Ricardo and Sergeant Granada, Don headed on the wing to his room to prepare for a shower just as Lieutenant Rose and Sergeant Smith was headed towards the wing door. He looked from lieutenant to sergeant, sergeant to lieutenant. He still couldn't get pass the fact that such beauty peregrinated through such ugliness and darkness. But boy, did it give a man in all his agony and anguish a purpose.

Canary looked at him with an expression of beautiful austerity. How She did it was beyond him. Smith smiled and he could tell that she eagerly anticipated the million in cold cash that she would be given for assisting in his escape.

Don saluted Smith with a suave wave of two fingers and a slight smile, then gave the last few steps of his attention to Canary before they passed one another. "Hello, Lieutenant Rose," he dropped the smile he'd given Smith and looked at

Canary with the same austere expression she had given him. What was going on between them was too intense for smiles.

She nodded and moved along as if he didn't interest her. Don headed to his room. He didn't like the way she was responding to him. He couldn't read her for the life of him. One minute he thought the feelings were mutual, then he thought otherwise. He was becoming a bit discouraged. He sat down and forgot all about the shower as he'd been distracted by her evasive behavior.

Maybe he should just forget her and focus on his future life in the Middle East, which was approaching expeditiously.

Yahseen entered the dorm just as Canary and Smith was leaving. "Hello, ladies," he greeted.

"Hello, Mr. Wright," came simultaneous responses.

He and Smith kept it moving as if there was no propinquity between them. He headed on the wing with the scent of Montgomery's sex in his nose. The inside of his thighs was sticky from the semen that continued to drain from his penis.

"What's good, bruh?" Success greeted as he descended the stairs shirtless.

"Traversing throughout this barren land. What are you up to?"

"You already know," he smiled as he hinted towards the officer's desk.

Yahseen laughed. He was already aware that he was chasing behind Carter. She seemed to like him, though. "That's what's up But remember not to linger too long. Stick and move because the evil eye' always watching, ya'dig?"

"A'ight."

“I’m about to go holler at Don real quick about some issues. We’ll link up later, Insha’ Allah," Yahseen stated.

"That’s peace,” Success replied.

They gave one another pounds and parted ways.

Yahseen headed in the flood-zone to his room. When he entered the cell he saw that Don was sitting in the chair with his head down adrift. He forwned. "As salamu alaykum, akhi. What's the matter?"

Don returned the salutation. "Just ruminating that damn broad. I hate being in this position!" Don conveyed in frustration. “I think I'm just going to wash my hands with futile dreams and ‘wake up’ like you told Success.”

“What happened to make you feel this way?”

Don explained.

"First and foremost akhi, you're tripping. You know we have a very veritable relationship so I'm going to always be raw. You’re acting like a baby in a mans world. Tighten up, lil’ bro. You know that mature women are unpredictable. Don't fret. If she didn't throw you to the wolves for that move, trust that you're straight. It's time to take charge. Fuck it. May Allah forgive me, but you're all in."

“You're right," Don agreed. “I started to approach her today but too many people was around. Tomorrow, Insha'Allah, I’m going all the way in!”

"That's what I'm talking about! Get motivated, lil' bro. We're Muslims! The best of mankind!

“Now dig it… I spoke with my peeps and she said that the captain agreed to the fifty grand so holler at your pops and let him know that everything is everything on our end back here.

Now, all you got to do is go to medical and complain about your back, or teeth, and within the next month or so they'll pull you."

Don couldn't believe how fast things was moving! The tunnel was already under construction, the officials were on stand-by, waiting to receive their money to assist in his escape. It looked like the construction of the tunnel could cease because the transportation route was locked and loaded. He'd notify his father of everything tonight. "Alright. And thanks for everything, Yahseen," he said humbly. "May Allah reward you with Paradise for all you've assisted me with thus far."

"Alhamdulillah! Now just chill out and relax and make your move tomorrow. You don't have time to be playing. Maybe she'll be on one of those islands chilling with you on some Bonnie and Clyde type shit," Yahseen laughed. "Now let me go purify myself from the sexual impurities I'm drenched in."

Don shook his head. His big brother was amazing. He was going to really miss this dude. "Yeah, I need to shower also."

###

Later That Night

"You are one confused bitch," Tay teased congenially. "Scary-cat!"

"Girl, this is one time that I truly agree with you," Canary acquiesced. "I don't know what the hell is wrong with me. Back there is antithetical of the free world. That environment fucks up your equilibrium!" she sighed. She had explained what happened when she saw Don earlier today and had not responded to his kind greeting. She was upset with herself, as she laid in the comforts of her bed on the phone with her girls.

"If you are serious about him Canary you need to stop doing what you're doing because you're only going to discourage him," Danyell stated. "Keep in mind the circumstances that you guys are under."

Canary knew that they were right. After talking with them for a moment longer, they ended the call with pleasantries as they all had to be up in the morning for work. She looked at the clock on her nightstand. It read: 10:59 pm. She turned over on her side and placed one of her pillows between her bare thighs and thought about Donatello McFadden until she knew consciousness no more.

###

Charleston, South Carolina

Caesar and Cecelia both laid in their beds at home as they spoke with one another via Face Time on their iPhones.

"I just spoke with Don. He told me that the officials I had you background was down with the play," Caesar informed.

"Thats terrific," she responded as she looked at him attentively on the screen of her phone.

"Yeah. I was considering having the plug pulled on construction of the tunnel. Then I thought about letting it continue out of spite just to free a bunch of people from back there. B8ut I don't know.

"The real reason I want it completed though, is because of Don's roommate. He's not ready for an escape because of the potential of his appeal. Do you think I should let them complete it?"

“I don't know Sulayman. That'll have to be a decision you make on your own.”

"Well, I think I'll let them finish it. But I won’t burden Ali and Jabbar with supervising it since the other route is officially ready. It may be of benefit to some of Don and Yahseen’s comrades one day, Insha' Allah. Only thing that'll be left to do is crack the floor of the cell. I'll have the top of the hole in the woods covered and preserved."

She just watched him in amazement as she laid on her side with the phone propped up on her pillow. "But what I do think you should do is contact Steve and make another announcement. But this time, I think you should double the reward. I just got a hunch that one out of two things will come out of it."

"Yeah, and what are those two things, dear?” he looked at her interestingly.

"One: it will not only be the largest reward in history, but it may very well entice someone that knows something that the standing five-million was peanuts to and not worth the hassle.

“Two: while we work towards the escape, everyone will be so focused on the money, we’ll slip him right out of their hands. You can bet your bottom dollar that people are anticipating a prison break, Sulayman. You are a wealthy black man, and you're Muslim at that with strong Middle East connections. If I knew that you were plotting this, everyone else does also.

“But you have the benefit of the doubt, because for the mean time, every one's thinking that you're trying to use your money to spring a confession. But when this proves futile and it loses momentum, they’ll be expecting the reaction of a caged animal and may even relocate Don to a more secure location because of his status."

"You truly have a beautiful mind. I love the way you think. If I had you in my life ten years ago we'd probably be billionaires."

"It's not too late, sweety," she smiled.

He kissed the screen of his phone and she did like-wise.

In the morning he would contact Steve and set up the interview. He would broadcast over the telephone. This time he would put 20 million on a solid lead or confession!

After conversing with Cecelia, he called his son in hopes that he was still up. He didn't want him to be caught by surprise this time.

###

Palmetto Correctional Institution

Orangburg, South Carolina

"Twenty-million!" Yahseen ejaculated incredulusly.

"Twenty-million, akhi," Don reiterated. He had just got off the phone with his father and had been told what to expect and why.

It was after 12 o'clock am. They were locked down. The dorm was quiet. An older black officer in his late fifties worked the wing. He was currently asleep at the desk, snoring away his time on the clock.

Don had explained to Yahseen what his father intended.

"Shit akh, it makes a helleva lot of sense," Yahscen agreed with his father and Cecelia's theory.

The both of them laid on their bunks, both TV's playing. Yahseen's TV was hooked up to the speaker set so the sounds of the TV filled the room. Prior to his father's phone call, he'd been talking to Scramble at Ogeechee. Scramble had told him that the red-bone amazon that had been bringing him the packages for Chess had been busted this morning at the front gate.

"Good things don't last that long, lil' bruh," Scramble had told him.

But Don had a different opinion and had told him that good things could very well last forever. Being around Yahseen and seeing how he conducted his affairs, he knew that with the right level of intellect and maturity, one could very well he successful forever. "Just because some guys get in boss positions doesn't mean that they are built for those positions," Yahseen had once told him.

Scramble had also told him that Ms. Bratton had asked about him. He told him to tell her that he said hello and that if God willed, he'd see her again one day.

Scramble was also about to take his GED. He wished him the best and told him as long as he studied he'd pass. Then his father had called and he ended the call with Scramble.

Yahseen had been on the phone with Sergeant Smith just before Don shocked him with the stunning news. He had told her that he'd call her back.

"Yeah, it does make a lot of sense," Don said as he looked into the ceiling as he laid on his back. He didn't know why, or where it came from, but he began telling Yahseen about the night of the party.

“Man akh, we were having fun out of this world! Fedora was only about five-four, one-hundred-twenty pounds. One of the finest white girls I've ever seen. Everyone loved her because she was fun to be with. She was bi-sexual and so coquettesh and promiscuous it was crazy. But it was her prerogative, you know what I'm saying...

"It was probably a hundred of us at this beach house, Yahseen. Word! Ecstacy was everywhere! Cocaine, weed, mushrooms, acid, beer, wine, liquor – psshh, I was probably the only sober person in there!

"After it was all over, I swear by Allah, I left with her and we went to her condo. Once we physically drained one another, I departed because I had some later business to attend to with my father and needed to rest. I don't know what the hell happened when I left. And even though she was sluttish and high-natured, there was no way she had it in her to take any more sexual rounds. Someone machinated this, and when they saw me depart they raped her with protection, killed her, and framed me. Why? I don’t know til this day."

Yahseen was reticent. He allowed Don to release. He had never suspected that he was guilty. He just had the kind of nature that said he was kind, intelligent, and harmless. He must’ve been overwhelmed by all that lie ahead because seconds later, he heard a light snore coming from above him.

Yahseen got up, made ablution, offered a superorgatory prayer, and made a special supplication for Don and his father before climbing back in his casket.

Chapter Twenty-Nine

Orangeburg, South Carolina
Palmetto Correctional Institutions
September 11, 2014 - Wednesday

The following morning after the count had cleared, Chess sauntered down to Yahseen's room where they was still asleep. He knocked on the door. When Yahseen looked up, he entered. "Get y'all ass' up," he laughed. "Rise and shine."

"What's good, family?" Yahseen said as he pulled the blanket down to his chest.

Don awaken and greeted him also. "Man, Ive been meaning to ask you how you got your name? Im curious about nick-names," he yawned and stretched as he sat up.

Yahseen and Chess laughed. Duue to the fact that he just awaken and asked such a question, they found it bromidic.

"It came from my robbing and murdering game in our city, lil' bruh," Chess answered honestly. "I'm a legend for check-mating adversaries since I was fourteen. That's when I caught my first bid. I come from a family of notorious robbers. Not petty robbers, but professional bank robbers and any caper exceeding a hundred grand. A powerful attorney got me five years juvey time. And when I came home, I turned it all the way up to the max for almost ten years straight. If I told you how many people I've killed lil' bruh you'll probably think I'm lying.

"But the name also grew on me from how I perceive the game of life. Every move has to be a calculated step because just when you think you're on the board of life by yourself on the road to success, potential opponents that seek what you seek will catch you slipping and sink your battleship. Chess is a very profound game," he explained.

"Don't only master the usage of self, which is king, but master all the pieces on the board of life no matter what type of piece it is: snitches, homosexuals, robbers, murderers, drug pushers, government, bums, so on and so forth. And never underestimate the mind of the most insignificant pieces because they'll be the ones that slay you. I don't Just talk a good game Don, I live this shit. That's why I only fuck with cats like Geez and Scramble." He never called Yahseen by his attribute.

Chess made Don think about the enigma of his situation. Although he was blind to the cause of his plight, he was intelligent enough to realize that he had a faceless adversary.

"Okay. So what did you mean yesterday when you said 'check mate' when you came inside the barbershop? It means you've conquered adversary. So what did you conquer?" Don was very inquisitive and perceptive. He picked up on things and learned fast.

Chess looked at Yahseen and smiled. Since Yahseen was also a model for Chess' intellectual strive, and Don was harmless, he enlightened him about the case worker.

"Oh," Don's brows furrowed as if he should've known. Although he had seen that anything was possible, it still surprised him at times to see how corrupted and out of control things was in prison. He had thought to be guarded by robotic personas in a windowless, concrete and steel structure, but had discovered it all to be like living inside a fenced in project in the toughest ghetto. It was a wonder he couldn't just saunter through the front gate like he was going to the store to grab a pack of chewing gum!

Chess seated himself. He looked at Yahseen. "Man, bruh, I got to kick out five grand to bond that bitch out."

"What bitch?" Yahseen asked quizzically.

"Scramble didn't tell you what happened? He told me he spoke with y'all last night," Chess asked.

"Nah, he spoke with Don. He didn't say anything about Scramble."

"Man, after my father had called and told me his plans it threw me for a loop," Don stated.

"The chick I left down there with him got knocked off with a pound of Purple Haze, an ounce of cocaine, and an ounce of crack," Chess informed.

Yahseen whistled. "Damn!"

"She got a fifty thousand dollar bond. Scramble said he'd put up half, but I told him I got it. He kept shit so real with the business it's the least I can do," Chess said amiably of Scramble. "I got her, though. Even though I never truly loved her, I won't turn my back on her because she's a real bitch. I'll hold her down until she get back on her feet. She's not a dumb broad who just splurged her money so she got all lil'cake. I hate that it happened to her but it was a game we played. Mistakes was made in the past that cost us today. So it is what it is. We live and we learn. Life goes on."

Ricardo knocked on the door. Don waved him in.

"Que pasa, mi amigos?"

"What's up, babe?" Yahseen returned.

"Another day in this hell hole," Ricardo said cooly.

They all agreed.

"The case worker want to see you for your review, Don," Ricardo looked at Don. You got about three people ahead of you so you got time to get prepared."

"Okay, thanks." Don yawned and scratched his scalp.

Ricardo disappeared.

"Well, I'm going to let y'all get situated. I'll holler later. I'm going to holler at the lil' homie, Curtis. Y'all know he stay in his own little world."

"He ever finished that last package you gave him?" Yahseen inquired about their younger homeboy who Chess used as a distributor.

"Yeah, I'm just waiting on you G," Chess told Yahseen.

"A'ight. We'll go back to the drawing board later today. I need to get at my lil' cousin anyway." Yahseen said. His little cousin Omar handled his street affairs with Montgomery.

"Bet." Chess stood to leave. "Peace."

"Peace," Yahseen and Don returned simultaneously.

Don got down from his bunk after Chess departed and cleaned himself up to attend his over due review.

As he prepared to leave, Fahtah – the elder brother that Yahseen used as an relay-man between him and Montgomery, appeared at the door. He came to bring Yahseen a tray of lobster tails that he had picked up from Montgomery for him. Greetings was exchanged as he entered the room with a warm smile. His eyes bright behind the lens of the glasses he wore. He stood around five-six, muscular physique wrapped in about 160 pounds of flesh.

"What's good, shaykh?" Yahseen asked Fahtah after he seated himself.

Don didn't know what business they had to attend to but there was no telling what Yahseen was ever up to. He told them he'd see them in a few and headed to the case workers office. He had over-slept through shift change, missing the opportunity of seeing his dream walking up the walkway, so he didn't know if she was in the building. But if she was, she would either extinguish his fire, or he would melt her ice.

"What's good, Don?" Success acknowledged Don as he headed past the officers desk where he stood conversing with Carter.

Don acknowledged them both as he headed off the wing into the deserted lobby.

Perfect.

Don had just got through speaking with the case worker who notified him of his custody level, institutional procedures that no one followed, and asked if he was interested in a job. He wasnt.

He had seen Lieutenant Rose inside her office speaking with abomination itself! Foxy. He hated the little group of punks! He knew that they sat up talking about him in all their twisted thoughts. But he swore by Allah that he would kill anyone of them at the slightest sign of disrespect! But Alhamdulillah, since he'd been at the facility everyone stayed clear of him.

But as he had spoke with the case worker, he thought that Chess had got himself a good catch this time. They shared a few laughs, as she wasn't pompous and sadity, then he departed her presence and headed straight to Lieutenant Roses office. He didn't know Sergeant Granada's whereabouts, but figured he was on a transportation run as usual.

As he approached the door to the office he didn't feel a pinch of anxiety. He felt like his true self in all his debonair.

He stepped in front of the door...

Canary and Foxy sat inside her office talking about various shoes Foxy had seen on the internet of his phone. Steve's morning show played in the background. Suddenly, in the middle of the show, the program went quiet. Moments passed, then Steve spoke in a very serious, but calm tone as he made a special announcement to his listeners throughout America. Sulayman Azeez Mustafah was back once again. But this time he had doubled the reward to a whopping 20 miillion for a solid lead *or* confession!

Canary and Foxy's eyes stretched in disbelief as they looked at one another, mouths agape in stunned silence! And not a second later after the announcement had been made, his son appeared at the door. The both of them looked at him as if he wasva figment of their imagination....

"Goodmorning, Lieutenant Rose," Don greeted, unaware that his father had just made the announcement. He furrowed his brows in question as he looked from Foxy to Canary who both appeared as if they'd seen a ghost.

Canary fought for control of the anxiety that began to consume her. She Smiled. She would not push him away. "Good morning. What can I help you with?"

He did not return her smile but remained aloof. "I have an issue I need to discuss with you. Do you have a moment?"

She cleared her throat and looked at Foxy as she placed her trembling hands beneath the desk and twiddled them. "Would you excuse us so I can talk to him for a minute." Her heart hammered. For some reason she knew that "that" moment had arrived. It was as if they were wild animals. She could sense his heat.

"Sure. Hey, Don," Foxy acknowledged kindly as he departed.

Don started to be rude. It wasn't in his nature so he chucked up a peace sign. "Can I close this?" he referred to the door when Foxy left.

She nodded that he could and watched him intently. She could hardly breathe! He sat down where Foxy had been seated across from her desk.

"Listen," he begun. "Im sure that you are aware of my situation..." he paused and looked at the radio as Steve mentioned his father's name. But this time he wasn't surprised so he remained calm, never taking his eyes off her. "The last time that announcement was unexpected," he maintained eye contact with her. So deeply he looked into her eyes he thought he saw the vibration of her soul "But I was informed this time," a slight smile cracked his lips.

"But as I was saying," he continued. "You know my

situation, so I don't have to explain. Although there's things pertaining to me that nobody knows that's esoteric.

"But before I get into what I came in here for, I want to know if you got the things I sent you?"

She began looking around the office. She was nervous. He wasn't Justin, and this sure wasn't no damn college campus. This was the son of Muslim tycoon, Sulayman Azeez Mustafah! And, they was inside the penitentiary where he was serving a natural life sentence for murder!

Come on girl, don't blow this, she encouraged herself. "Yes. I got them. That was sweet of you. Thank you."

His heart rate accelerated by her responsiveness. He thought that she would repel him in some form or fashion. This only compelled his temerity to move in for the kill. "I know that this is crazy and that we're in an alien predicament, but I like you. I need you. Ever since the first time that I saw you I thought that I found the treasure that the world had been looking for since the commencement of its creation. You remind me of Scrooge's treasure of gold in Duck Tales," he smiled.

Her heart melted from the fire of his charm and articulation. She remembered how obsessed the duck had been with his treasure and how miserable he was without it.

"That's why I call you 'Golden'," he continued. "The only thing I fear in all of this is my situation and how it may effect me in possessing you."

She just listened as she watched him. He was making her moist in places she had long forgotten existed. Her legs twitched beneath her involuntarily.

"Do you like me, Lieutenant Rose?"

She slowly nodded her head "yes" as she bit down on her

bottom lip. All of these actions were involuntary reactions that she couldn't control. She felt as if she would burst!

"Well, now that we know for certain where each other stand, I don't want to stay here too long to avoid unnecessary conjecture. So, if I gave you a number to contact me so we could talk, would you call me?" It seemed as if sound had went abeyant, movement to a crawl, breathing intensified in the solidarity between them as he awaited her response.

"Yes. What is it?" she breathed a faint breath as she fetched a pen and a slip of paper.

Sound was reinstateed, motion recalibrated and breathing allayed. He gave her his number and silently took in the sight of her eyes and lips, mentally kissing them before he departed.

He departed the office leaving her sitting in a state of stupor. She looked at the numbers she had scrawled on the slip of paper that was a means for her to contact Donatello McFadden. She pinched herself to make sure that she wasn't dreaming. "Ouch!" she winced from the pain of the pinch and shook her head at her fatuity.

She slipped the number into her pocket just as Foxy re-entered the office. He had to be near in anticipation of finding out what her and Don had discussed because of his hasty return. Something intuitive told her to keep these chain of events from him.

"Girl diva, what happened?"

"Oh, he just wanted someone to talk to about all the pressure from everything he's combating. I told him that I'll refer him to the Chaplain," Canary prevaricated.

"Oh. I thought he was trying to holler at a bitch," Foxy

smacked his lips perfunctorily and crossed his legs. “But anyway girl, twenty- fucking-million...”

As Foxy ran his mouth loquaciously, she thought about what had been initiated between her and Mr. McFadden. This was what she wanted so she wouldn't play head games with him. He had enough going on that he was burdened by and didn't need to be distracted by balderdash. She would call him tonight – after Danyell and Tay. She knew that this, along with the amazing announcement his father had just made, would TKO them both!

###

Yahseen was on the phone speaking with his cousin Omar when Don entered the room with a smile that rivaled the Kool-aid mascots! He could hear an infant yammering. The phone was on speaker. Fahtah had departed.

"Why is he crying?" Yahseen inquired on behalf of the baby Omar had just been left to watch that belonged to his sister. She had departed to the studio as she pursued a career as a rapper.

“Man, he’s crying for his mama, kid. Then she had the nerve to act like she didn't know why he’s crying. I told her ass if I had been sucking her titties all this time and she was leaving me I’d be crying, too. Know what I'm saying, kid?” Omar spoke with an up-North twist from his time spent in the Big Apple.

All of them erupted in a frenzy of laughter, including Don.

“Boy, you’re shot the hell out,” Yahseen chuckled. “But dig it, babe. I'm going to holler at you later and let you know what I need you to do.”

“A’ight, kid. Omerta,” Omar saluted.

“Vice-versa,” Yahseen returned. “Salam.” He ended the call and looked up at his beaming Muslim brother.” As salamu alaykum, akhi. What's up?"

"Wa alaykum as salam warahmatullah," Don smiled. "I approached our lieutenant," he said proudly.

"What happened?"

Don explained the details of his footsteps. "She accepted the number."

"Word?"

"Word!" Don confirmed.

Yahseen got up and hugged him in congratulation. "Alhamdulillah!"

"Alhamdulillah!" Don agreed.

"Now, just be easy, lay back and drive safe. Who knows what Allah has in store for you in the future."

Don took a breath of fresh air. He felt good. "I'm about to call my father. He just made that announcement. He did it via telephone so he shouldn't be too tied up." He retrieved his phone and called his father to talk to him about the announcement, and to share the news of his accomplishments with Lieutenant Canary Rose.

Chapter Thirty

Orangeburg, South Carolina
September 11, 2014
Later That Nlight

Canary sat up in her bed with the pillows propped up against the headboard. Tunes of Avant and Keke Wyatt mellifluously resonated throughout the dimly lit room. She had just ended a call with Danyell and Tay telling them about Don's sizzling approach earlier today! She twiddled the slip of paper in her hands as she looked at the number he had given her.

After she clocked out from work she headed directly home and showered, wrapped her hair, and slipped a T-shirt over her nudity. As had become a routine of hers, she had stopped by a restaurant on her way home from work. She had sat down and slowly ate the soft-shell tacos she had gotten from Taco Bell as she thought about Donatello McFadden.

Now, it was around 10 o'clock. She'd been off since 4:30. She knew that he was probably laying next to his phone in his cell waiting on her call, probably thinking she had stood him up.

She crinkled the slip and sat it on the night stand next to her bed. She no longer needed it. The numbers was embedded in her brain.

She picked up the phone from the crevice of her thighs, dialed his number, and stared at them for a moment before pressing SEND. Her heart-rate accelerated and her palms became moist from trepidation. As if preparing for a duel, she rotated her head, took in several deep breaths, said, "Come on Canary, lets do this," then pressed the button...

###

Palmetto Correctional Institution

Yahseen was absent conducting business in Chess' room but had left his phone, which was connected to the speakers in the cell. It was playing a slew of everything from old school Kenny G to new school rhythm & blues. At the moment, J-Holiday's *Suffocate* absorbed most of the oxygen inside the cell. Don felt breathless as he paced the floor of the cell in its ambiance of red light. Lock down time was at 11 o'clock. It was after 10 o'clock.

As time ticked away, he began to feel as if she had backed out. Yahseen had told him to be cool as always, but this time he couldn't. She had him on fire and he was burning in an infernal of anticipation and anxiety. His phone was in his hand and every few minutes he looked at it to see if he had somehow missed her call, knowing that he wouldn't have because the ring setting was on vibrate. He had even checked it to make sure it was functioning adequately! If she stood him up tonight, he would forget her and move on with his life. For the past hour, he'd been walking back and forth across the cell pondering what he would say to her when she called – if she did.

Tired of the fiendish pacing, he jumped up on his bunk, sat the phone beside him and looked around the room adrift as his legs dangled from the bed. The affect she had on him was insane! He had shared the news with his father, Ali, Jabbar, and even Scramble and Jamal, who were all jubilant for him. And just when he thought he had literally struck gold – she had backed out on him.

He expelled a breath of defeat and took off his T-shirt. He folded it and draped it across the railing at the foot of his bed and laid back with his hands clasped behind his head looking into the space of the room while the music played. He closed his eyelids and began replaying all the times he had seen her. And suddenly, the device laying next to him sent vibrations through the bunk and his eyes sprang open! He fumbled for the device and saw that the call was from a private caller. He stared at the face of the phone as it vibrated. Quickly, he regrouped and pulled himself together before he missed the call that could possibly be her.

He touched the sensitive TALK button on the phone and placed the device to his ear....

###

Orangeburg, South CarolinCarolina

Just as Canary was about to end the call thinking that he was probably asleep or busy, the call connected and she heard a smooth, "Hello".

“Hey”, she beamed a smile of such brilliance it may have very well lit the room if the lamp hadn’t been on.

“Is this who I think it is?" Don asked in a state of disbelief; a look of skeptism on his face.

“And who do you think it could be?” she toyed with him playfully.

They were finding a a groove.

"Ahh, I don't know. But I know who I want it to be," he returned just as playfully.

“And who could that be, Mr. Scrooge McDuck?” she inquired with sexy seduction.

"My treasure of gold," he responded like the casanova he was.

"And what would you do with such treasure of riches, Mr. McDuck?" She bit her lower lip intriguingly.

He pondered her question momentarily then responded, "Swin inside of it... Protect it with my life. ... And even though it’s against my belief system, I'd be stingy with it and keep it to myself.

“Why? Are you my treasure of gold?” he grinned.

“It’s a possibility that I could be your treasure of gold, Mr. McDuck. But only time will tell," She replied. "So, what are you up to, Mr. McFadden?"

“Nothing really. I've been pacing about anticipating your call. I thought you caught cold feet at the last minute and had a change of heart. Now, I'm just laying here in the confines of my cell with the music playing listening to you. And I'm smiling.”

"Why are you smiling?"

“Because you make me happy. There's so much going on with me in my world it seems unreal. And since the commencement of all this mess in my life, you're the only person that I've encountered that made me smile and feel as if I have something to live for. You drive me."

"That's sweet," she was warmed.

"Let me ask you something before we move any further into this. It's something that troubles me in all that pertains to you and I."

"I'm listening."

"As I told you earlier inside your office, you are aware of my situation. There aren't any appeals in my case. I have a natural life sentence without parole. The only chance I have at freedom is if someone comes forward or if I break out of here. So why is it that you're taking a chance with me; I'm curious?"

She sighed."Trust me. I thought of all of this before I even made the decision to allow you to stay in my dorm. I knew that this would happen between us because ever since the first time I saw you on TV over a year ago, there were things about you that intrigued me. I always thought that you was innocent. I never thought that I would really meet you. Then you popped up in my office about your TV.bI thought I was dreaming," she explained. "Then as days moved along, I knew that something would inevitably happen between us and I made the decision to accept it.

"I know your situation. All I can say as of right now is that I'm willing to be there for you through it all. Because if we really find true love in one another, the material things of this world that stand between us are obsolete. I won't depict myself a gangster chick, but I am loyal and will ride to the end of the universe for you if I fall in love with you. Which I can be women enough to tell you I'm not far from, as I've caught a bit of feelings for you from a distance."

She blew him away. His chest swelled in humbled greatfulness. "Wow. So where do we go from here? This is such a peculiar predicament."

"I guess we just take the time to get to know all we can about one another and let destiny take its course."

"What about the dangers that comes with dealing with me on behalf of your job?" he asked.

"That's far from my concern. I was thinking about resigning lately anyway, to pursue old aspirations. And besides, I think that you are mature and intelligent enough not to expose our relations to any of those idiots back there."

"Well, I can see that you took the time to think all of this through thoroughly. And, I'm sure as hell glad that I met you before you resigned, which I'm all for. I don't think that this is an environment for women – especially one that belong to me. So we'll have to talk about this in the future, Insha'Allah."

"Then if I'm not back there with you, how would I be able to see you?"

He thought about his escape but said nothing about it. "I don't know, Golden. Let's just take it one day at a time for now," he said.

"Okay," she responded. She turned off the lamp and spoke with hm in the dark recesses of her bedroom as she cuddled under her covers.

"And call me Don, or Furqān, or whatever little sweet name you decide to give me."

"Okay, sweety."

"Are you ever going to give me your number, or do I have to always anticipate your phone call?" he smiled.

She giggled. "No, I'll give it to you," she gave him the number.

"I may not remember it off the top of my head so you may have to give it to me again," he stated as Yahseen entered the room.

"Who's that?" she inquired. She could hear the environmental change as the noise from the wing swam into the quietude of the cell.

"My roommate," he answered.

"What's up akh, are you cool?" She heard James Wright ask him.

"Yeah, I'm cool," Don smiled and winked.

Yahseen smiled. He knew that Lieutenant Rose had finally called. "It's lock down time, babe. You might want to tighten up until they lock these doors." he warned.

"Okay. Listen, boo. It's lock down time. Is it okay if I called you back after the doors are locked?" Don asked as he sat up.

"Yes. Do you remember the number?"

"No."

She repeated them.

"Okay. I'll call you back in about thirty minutes, Insha' Allah."

"Okay." She ended the call and pulled the phone into her bosom as if it was him and patiently waited on him to call her back.There was no turning back now. Her breast filled with an inexplicable joy and she knew without a shadow of doubt that she was going to fall into a solar system of love that consisted of planets, and stars, and moons that were all attributes of Donatello

Furqān McFadden;

###

Palmetto Correctional Institution

The lazy, old black man, that normally worked their dorm on night shift that spent most of his time sleeping at the desk, had began locking the doors on the top tier as inmates scurried about trying to do this and that at the last minute before going into their cells to conclude another day successfully served in no-mans-land, which was a blessing in itself.

Yahseen cleaned up behind himself. He'd just finished urinating.

"You're straight, akh. I'm done," he notified Don, who had faced the opposite direction to allow him privacy. "Well, I see all is good with you now lil' bro, so you can stop stressing that aspect."

"Yeah," Don agreed. "But the crazy thing about it all is that with this, it makes things a bit harder because now I'm caught in a dilemma between her and my escape. You don't think it'll be crazy of me to get emotionally tied to her and then have to leave her behind in the next month or so?"

"Yeah," Yahseen agreed. "That is a tough lil' dilemma, lil' bro," he stated as he stood in the center of the room looking at Don.

"I know everyone keeps saying that she may be some sort of blessing but really akhi, what kind of blessing could she really be with me and a planned escape right around the corner?" Don asked in befuddlement. "It wouldn't be fair for me to lead her on then vamouse!

“I even asked her why was she chancing me knowing my circumstances and she said she had already given thought to it all and that she was prepared to ride or die." He looked at Yahseen questioningly.

“That's deep,” Yahseen replied as the lazy, old officer locked their door. "Have a goodnight, Mr. Scott," he told the officer.

He grumbled something unintelligáble and continued on.

"Maybe she'll go with you," Yahseen reasoned. "Trust me, akhi. Speaking from experience, love makes people do some of the most strangest shit," he shook his head in astoundment. "So don’t count her out. Just let everything play itself out and if she's oppose to it all when you break it to her, just keep it moving and do you. Life goes on.”

“I guess it can't be put any simpler than that," Don said acquiescingly. “But right now, I can't even front Yahseen. I feel good about myself," he smiled.

"Alhamdulillah! You got the baddest chick on the compound. No doubt in the Department of Corrections. I don't know what the future holds for neither of us. Allahu alim. Just continue to strive in Allah's cause and be the best Muslim you can be. And for the mean time," Yahseen smiled, "enjoy the time that you do have with her and keep it raw and uncut so she'll always know what's at stake.”

“Insha'Allah,” Don replied.

“But go ahead and call her back because I know she's wasting,” Yahseen stated as he headed to his bunk. “Besides, mine is waitng as well," he winked.

The both of them got comfortable, picked up their phones, and called the women that awaited them.

Chapter Thirty-One

Orangeburg, South Carolina

Palmetto Correctional Institution

September 27, 2014 - Two Weeks Later

It was the 27th of September; Friday. The 3 o'clock count had just commenced at the facility. An inmate's face had just been slashed with a razor by his roommate on lock up and First Responders had been dispatched. Sergeant Granada had just ran out the dorm in response to the call. Canary had decided to go and be nosey but decided against it while en route due to a dire urge to pee.

The weather was changing into Autumn and a light chill sat in the air. The leaves on the surrounding trees, and grass, was beginning to change colors and die out.

She had left Raysor in her office and Ricardo had retired to his cell early due to a stomach ache from spoiled chicken he'd consumed

Over the past couple of weeks, her relationship with Don

had blossomed like a field of sunflowers. The harmony and chemistry between them was that of the heavens and earth. She had shared so much with him, and had learned so much about him. But she could tell that there was something that he wanted to tell her but was holding back. She didn't push. She was allowing him the time to come to terms with whatever it was. She trusted him, as he had a heart and mind of pulchritude like none she had ever seen, or had the privilege of acquainting. He was such a well mannered gentleman. He had been by her office a couple of times to speak with her in person over the past couple of weeks, but kept his appearances to a minimum to avoid unwanted speculation.

Then, there was Foxy, who she had tailing her in his suspicion. He had began watching them closely as if there was something she wasn't telling him. She had really begun to be leery of him. She didn't know if it was intuition or paranoia, but she opted not to discuss Don with him anymore and had told him so. He'd been coming around less than usual.

But her and Don had been having some of the most stimulating conversations she had ever had. His intellect and education was so broad, profound, and sexy, it made her wet. His voice tone was so controlled. He never became overly excited. His tongue intrigued her and made her wonder if it was experience in more adult things. She knew that he wanted her. Many times during the wee-hours of the night, and over the weekends, their conversations had become so intense, he groaned out in agony, fighting his lower desires to remain civilized.

As the days passed, she thought about how she could somehow give herself to him to show him how much she loved him, alhough she had never told him so.

She headed up the walkway to her dorm and glanced over at

his window to see if she saw him, as he told her how he used to watch her walk to and fro everyday. She didn't see him, though.

She picked up her step because her bladder felt as if it would burst. She entered the lobby and headed straight to the restroom. Raysor was nowhere in sight. Probably on the wing.

She opened the door to the bathroom and gasped as her eyes stretched in disbelief! "OH MY GOD!" She pulled the door close quickly and headed to her office, momentarily oblivious to the fact that she had to pee!

"Girl, I am so sorry you caught that!" Officer Raysor entered the office with a hand over her mouth in embarrassed shock. She seated herself as Chico scurried on the wing.

Canary waved a hand to silence the apologies. "I'm going to pretend as if I didn't just walk in on you and him having sex, Raysor. I won't be the cause of your demise. But you should be more careful."

Relieved, Raysor expelled a breath and thanked her lieutenant. She looked up from the floor at Canary.

"You're welcome," Canary shook her head and smiled to lighten the moment. "But excuse me, I need to use the restroom," She got up and headed to the bathroom where she had saw Raysor in all her naked glory, bent over the sink being drilled from the rear in a state of perpetual bliss. She couldn't pass judgement though, because she wished that it was her and Don – but not in such position. She wanted to straddle him while he held her tight.

She shook her head and closed the door to the bathroom behind her.

###

Although all was in perspective with Don's escape, he had postponed things to see what was building between him and Canary. Only remaining thing to be done was for him to go to sick call and for the money to be turned over to the officials. But he had told his father to hold off and his wishes had been respected. He wanted to see if she would come with him. He was falling in love with her. It was a ludicrous thing to think or say, but he never thought that a man could be so happy in prison!

His father had borrowed the 2 million-50 thousand bucks from Al-Salam to pay Captain Holmes, Granada, and Sergeant Smith. They knew that after his escape the Feds would surely check his accounts to see if any large amounts of money was transacted with no logical explanation for potential pay offs. So Al-Salam's cash would be used to counter this.

Over the past couple of weeks things had been chaotic with the media on behalf of the 20 million his father had offered as it ran through talk shows, radio, and every social media outlet in existence. The administration hadn't bothered him this time, but Warden Prince had came to his cell to speak with him when he conducted his rounds.

It had been an eventful Friday thus far. The khutbar during Jummah had been profound. It had been given by an Arab brother by the name of Umar Shaykh from the Islamic Society of Augusta in Georgia. He was originally from the Middle East. He knew his father, and Al-Salam very well. He was a sixtyish man with skin of burnt bronze with a plush beard. He wore simple clothing and worn Penny Loafer's as if he wasn't a millionare. He assisted the incarcerated brothers around the state in inside, and outside affairs.

In his Khutbar, he spoke on how most people wanted this and that to believe in God when the creation was a miracle in itself. He spoke on how most people prayed and asked God for insignificant things when they splurged their wealth on useless things as jewelry and designer shoes and clothes when they were already in poverty. They got on their knees and asked God to bless them with houses and cars when they spent money on foolish things within a year alone that could have bought them those things.

"You don't pray for expensive shoes because some of you got the ignorance to sell crack, but you pray for millions and mansions because you don't have the patience to take time to intelligently learn how to acquire these things," Umar Shaykh had said in his decisive, but humorously thick, Arabian tongue.

"You want this to believe. You want that to believe. You want miracles," he educed with his hands. "Some of us are such stupid people to say we are the most comprehensive beings. We ask for material wealth and success without realizing that it was already given to us. The world possess everything for our every need and desire. Some of us just don't apply ourselves to go after them out of laziness then you curse God for being poor. You want riches – invent things to become rich. You have talents you don't use and pursue," he said as he fondled the little toboggan he had rolled up on his head.

"You want all sorts of things but won't organize. You won't work. You won't exercise your ability to learn. You won't excereise your independence. You always want hand outs when Allah has already given us the world on a platter of gold, platinum, and diamonds. Pray for Paradise. Pray for the less fortunate; the poverty-stricken due to oppression. The world is already at our disposal. Most of us do not reflect..."

Don had found this deep and had called Jamal at Ogeechee to share this with him earlier in the day. It was now around 7 o'clock in the evening. His lieutenant had long departed. She had called him when she departed the facility and had told him that her and her girls were getting together for an in-house seafood fest of crabs and shrimps at her apartment, in which they would spend the weekend.

And Oh! When she had told him about walking in on Chico and Raysor earlier, he laughed lightly and shook his head in amazement. There was no use in telling Yahseen because he was already aware of Raysor and Chico's relations.

Canary and her girls was at her apartment now and he could hear them in all their rambunctiousness over the loud music in the background as they got tipsy off bottles of wine coolers while they cooked the seafood they had bought to feast on and gossip over. "HEY.DON!" He heard them scream in the background

"Do you hear your supporters, sweety?" Canary giggled.

"Yeah, I hear them Golden," he laughed. "Tell them I sad what's up and don'tget too wasted."

She yelled the message over the music and noise.

He could tell that she was happy. She radiated it and he could see it in her when she was at work. He hated to dampen her happiness with his escape, but he had to tell her. He was just waiting for what he felt would be the perfect opportunity.

"I love you, Scrooge," she told him for the first time.

His brows furrowed at the unexpected comment. "You do?" He asked piquantly.

"Yes. Do you love me?"

"I loved you from the very first time I saw you, Golden. It's just deeper now, and it gets deeper as time progresses," he told her.

"Ummhmm," She said with playful doubt.

“I’m serious,” he assured.

"I know you are Furqān, I'm just teasing.”

He loved the way she said his name.

"Dang, Don! Could you please let us have her for a while!? We're becoming jealous!” Tay yammered near the phone.

Don snickered as he heard Canary struggle with Tay.

"Don't pay them any mind, baby. Call John, bitch!" Canary yelled over her shoulder as Danyell laughed over the boiling pot of crabs and shrimps.

"Nah baby, go entertain your girls. I'll be right here thinking about you, us, and our future. Send me some pictures.” She always sent pictures to his phone and he'd delete them after studying them so intensely, a catalog of them could be seen forever in his mind’s-eye.

She whined.

He laughed.

"Okay. I love you."

“I love you, too.”

“And don't go to sleep on me FFurqā. I'm serious!" she said deliberately.

"I'm not. Trust me. You got me too intoxicated." He blew her a kiss and disconnected the call.

“Salam, akhi,” Sulayman said at the door.

Don got up and opened the door for him as he had returned with the food he had prepared for them to eat.

###

Orangeburg, South Carolina

“Enough about me and Furqān you heffers!” Canary beamed as she sucked the juice from a succulent crab leg. They sat on the floor of her living room on top of plastic and newspapers eating the deliciously boiled, spicy creatures. “What's been up with you and John lately? You've been spending more time with him than usual.”

“Spill the beans, Tay,” Danyell said knowingly, as if she already knew what Canary didn't.

Tay smiled. "Well, I think things has gotten a bit serious between us. Well, with him. He told me that he loved me yesterday and wanted to leave his wife for me.”

"Wouldn't that be disastrous to his career?” Canary asked. "Yes. But he doesn't seem to care. He's actually talking about giving it all up. He seemed to be hinting at something. Something's been bothering him lately.

“I asked him what was bothering him but all I get is evasive answers. It may be matters with his wife, but I doubt it because he's always been so open with me in dealing with their affairs,” Tay said as she sipped from her bottle of wine.

"Well, what do you think it could be? "Canary asked.

"I don't know, Canary.” Tay answered honestly.

"So what did you say when he told you he loved you and wanted to leave his wife for you?" Canary asked.

"I told him that he was confused and needed to think things through. He told me he already had. We'd been seeing one another for almost two years now and he knows what he wants.

That's what he told me."

"Do you love him?" Canary again.

"Damn bitch! Am I on the stand being crossed-examined?"

Danyell exploded in a fit of laughter and so did Canary at Tay's temerity.

"I'm not going to front Canary, it did sound like you was on some Johnny Chockran shit," Danyell admitted.

"Whatever," Canary said as she playfully threw a shrimp at Danyell's leg.

Tay struggled opening the body of a crab. "Honestly, I think I do," she answered Canary's question.

"Oohh, girl. I just knew you was going to end up falling for him," Canary teased.

"I told him to give me some time to think things through. I also told him he had to be open with me and tell me what's eating at him so.

"Y'all don't understand when I say something's eating at him. I mean it's like he's guilt ridden or something," Tay gestured with her hands educibly. "We're getting together Sunday. Everything will come to the light then.

"But I do love him, though," she confessed as she dipped a shrimp in butter and a special sauce they had made after saying to heck with the crab she struggled to open.

The music continued to play in the background as they reminisced with one another. Canary's thoughts had drifted back on Don and she wondered if he was thinking about her.

She told Danyell and Tay how she had walked in on Raysor and Chico and they fell in a frenzy of laughter after she performed a little reenactment of Raysor's frightened expression of a deer caught in headlights!

After the enjoyment of the seafood, they cleaned up everything and showered.

Tay had retired to Canarys extra room to talk to John.

Under dim lights and mellow music, Canary continued to sit inside her living room chatting with Danyell about where she was at with Don.

It was getting late. Danyell had noticed that Canary kept looking at the clock. She knew that she wanted to talk to Don so she told her good night and headed to her room to sleep in her bed.

After Danyell had retired to her chambers, Canary retrieved her phone after the retrieval of a blanket. She turned off the lights, turned the music down a few decimals, climbed on her sofa, and called Furqān.

Chapter Thirty-Two

Columbia, South Carolina
September 29, 2014

Sunday morning, Tay departed Canary's apartment to Columbia where John was staying at the Sheraton hotel. When she arrived, valet intercepted her car and she headed to the 5th floor where her lover was shacked up. She knocked on the door and he opened it with a smile. Neither of them moved nor spoke as they took in the sight of one another. She looked at him in all his disheveled handsomeness. He needed to shave. About 2 days of stubbled growth peppered his face giving him the harden edge of a cowboy on the Western frontier. She stood on her tippy toes and kissed him as she backed him in to the suite. His mouth tasted of sweet liquor. She kicked the door closed behind her with a foot and slipped out of the Air Max Nike tennis she wore sockless as she began fondling his erection through the boxers he wore. He was thick and warm in the grip of her small hands. A word had yet to be spoken as was a usual custom for them at first sight. Such fierce fire seemed to always ignite and burn between them.

She led him backward all the way to the bedroom of the suite and began slipping out of her jogging pants and tight T-shirt as he plopped on the bed groping at her goodies. "Miss me?" she asked as she removed her garments.

In John's inebriated state, he looked at her hungrily, but did not answer. He just removed his boxers and began massaging his hardened phallus.

She dropped to her knees and took him into her mouth. He moaned out in ecstasy as she pleasured him until he climaxed. “Miss me?" she licked her lips seductively as she stood to face him. Her perky tities stood erect and firm with hardened nipples that protruded about half an inch from the tips of her areola. She pinched one of them and massaged her clitorist with her free hand as she stepped up on the bed to straddle him. She inserted him into her galaxy of pleasure. “Uhhmmm...” she breathed breathlessly as he stretched her walls. She placed the fingers she had massaged herself with inside his mouth. He savored her flavors greedily as he held her by her petite waist as she gyrated atop his lap. “I asked you if you missed.... me?" she whispered in his ear as she nibbled on them. Her body spasmed.

“Yes,” he uttered incoherently as she undulated her hips. His hands firmly gripped her buttocks.

“Then come inside of me... Ahh, baa-by,” she moaned as she dug her nails into the toned muscles of his back. "Johnn....ohh..oohhh...." she heightened. "I'm coming, John!" she yammered!

As both of their moans and perspiration intermingled with one another, she repeatedly orgasmed on his thick shaft. He built up his second climax and flipped her over on her back. He kissed and sucked her tongue savagely as if his life depended on it. She wrapped her legs around his waist and he relentlessly drove into her as he grunted and she screamed out in ecstasy.

“Tell me you love this pussy, John! Tell me....”

"I love.. this… pussy.” Droplets of sweat dripped from his chin. “I'm... I'm coming, Tay! I'm coming!" he told her as he released a gush of his milky fluid inside her vaginal cavity, his face buried in the crook of her neck. His body convulsed violently as he spent himself – then he collapsed.

He fell asleep immediately. She laid beneath him until her heart rate decreased then slipped from under him and headed to the shower.

She had showered and had returned to the bed where he had slipped into a very relaxing slumber. She woke him. "John," she called sweetly as she laid next to him with a towel wrapped around her body.

He opened his eyes and smiled. “Do you love me?" he desperately wanted – well needed to know. He'd been drowning himself in Scotch to evade his conscience.

“Yes, I do love you, John. But first we need to talk about what's troubling you. This is so not like you to be moping around, drowning yourself in liquor. You won't even go home to your wife anymore.”

"I left her, I told you." He got up. "Let me shower real quick and we'll talk,”

While he showered she changed the dressing on the bed then relaxed in her thoughts of a possible future with him, until he returned with a towel wrapped around his damp body 15 minutes later.

He climbed back into the bed and laid next to her. He pulled her into his arms and began the tale that had been troubling him so....

"Twenty years ago, baby. I was propositioned a position by an organization that call themselves The Seven. They're a body of senators from various locations around the country...

"Before I delve any further, just know that I am not, and never was, an immediate part of their organization. I was an extra leg. Something similar to the adopted child," he explained. "And this was only because they ran into a dilemma. What the dilemma was, I never knew nothing about. I never got into the details because it didn't concern me.

"But they needed my assistance because the individual that played a major part in their drug enterprise resided in South Carrolina. They needed me to 'quote unquote' give him a *key to the* state to be able to move freely. The figures they offered was impressive."

"What were the figures?" she asked.

"A million to accept the offer and a million annually for me to turn the other cheek while they smuggled tons of pure heroin through the port in Charleston and move it throughout the country."

"Who was the undisclosed individual?"

"Sulayman Azeez Mustafah."

She gasped and her heart skipped a beat! She remained reticent and allowed him to continue.

"I really don't know the intricacies to the why's and how's of the matter. All I know is that the senator of Texas called me up then and told me that he needed to see me. I flew out to Houston and met the actual body of The Seven and they proposed that offer to me. "

"Marcellus Rothenstein is corrupted?" she was aghast.

“Yes. He and so many others beyond The Seven itself," he sighed.

"But what troubles you about all of this; are you still involved?"

“No. Around May of last year, Sulayman announced that he and Al-Salam – who's an Arab from Saudi Arabia that had been supplying the drugs – shut down the operation forever due to their religious strive. Marcellus and the others was infuriated about the decision. They hated Muslims anyway. Some of them are even racist. I don’t know the indvidual personally that they used. It was an ex-attorney by the name of Edward Butler from Reno, Nevada. He’d been disbarred for various reasons. He had owed The Seven a quarter-million in gambling debt. So with a hundred-thousand-dollar incentive along with the quashing of the debt, they had Sulayman’s son set-up and framed as a vindictive act of retaliation and the only reason I was notified of this much was because they knew that Sulayman and I had established quite a rapport over the years as his son grew up playing with my son. They knew I would have helped them."

"Donatella McFadden?” Tay sat up in stunned disbelief! "OH MY GOD!”

"Believe me Tay, I wanted to help them. The hardest thing I had to do was deny them assistance and watch them go through all that they've been going through and it's been eating me from the inside out. I don't know what to do because of my affiliation with them. They had been running a very clandestine crime ring for decades, Tay. I fear for the lives of my wife and son, and even you. They know everything. The call on behalf of framing Don was beyond my control. And to make matters worse, Fedora’s grandfather is my mentor! I have her blood on my hands and Don's life, Tay," he said ruefully. "And every where I turn there’s Sulayman's reward. I'm ridden in guilt.”

Tay was so shocked by what he had just told her she couldn't even move to console him. "Just be easy, baby. We'll figure this all out somehow. As you stated, you didn't have any immediate affiliation. If you gave them up you may be able to get out any conspiracy charges by the Feds. Especially if you assisted them. But your career will be shot most definitely.

"I don't know, John," she sighed in defeat.

Senator Johnathan Ethan Brody had indeed found himself caught between a rock. "Coming forward could be dangerous, Tay. Once I do, The Seven would no doubt do all they can to bring people down with them – even Sulayman."

"Well John, it's only fair that he be locked up instead of his son if it happens that way. It's all his fault anyhow; not his son." She never exposed the fact that she was affiliated with a friend that had begun dating Donatello McFadden.

Now, she didn't know who she should remain loyal to. Canary was her girl, but her heart was with John. Somehow she had to figure out a way where everything would work in everyone's favor. For the mean time she'd remain reticent until she found some type of reciprocity. She was still finding this hard to believe. They were all connected in a complicated circle of paradoxes and destiny. "John," she called out to him.

"Yes, Tay?" he looked up at her with sparkling hazel eyes.

"I love you," she kissed him

###

Palmetto Correctional Institution

Orangeburg, South Carolina

Don Jogged around the rec-field in the early morning air by himself listening to hip-hop tunes by recording artist Young Jeezy on his phone. He wore headphones that was attached to the hand-set. The device was concealed in an inside pocket of his pants that he had made for such purpose.

He cogitated his relations with the woman he had depicted "Golden".

Things had became so serious between them in such short period of time. He wanted to say that it was all meant to be, but in light of what lie directly ahead with his escape, he couldn't see through the complexity of the ordeal no matter how hard he tried and prayed, asking Allah for guidance and insight.

It was Sunday morning and just a few hours ago he had gotten off the phone with her after she had fell asleep on him from the strenuous hours they spent talking to one another through the day and wee hours of the night. He was inlove with her and had almost broke the news to her of his escape last night, but hadn't.

He hadn't slept no more than 2 hours or so before the doors was unlocked this morning by the queer officer that had been working the dorm the first day he got to the facility from Ogeechee.This was his first time seeing him since then.

Sleep had really became something unfamiliar to him since her inauguration in his life unless his body shut down on its own. She had him wired! He had become so worried about losing her he had found himself stuck between abeyance and flight. But today he would have to make a decision because other people lives were being held up for his cause. His father and Cecelia's, Ali, Jabbar – even Canary's, and all concerned. He couldn't keep them subjugated by way of his selfish desires when much greater issues was at hand.

He jogged at a steady pace around the rectangular shaped field, introspectively. He was the only inmate outside. A security truck slowly circled the perimeter. He had already jogged 15 laps. He would jogb10 more and call it quits. He was in great shape. He exercised intensely three times a week with Chess. Yahseen joined them at least once a week, maybe twice. He was too cool for his own good.

As he finished up his laps he concluded that their was no need to prolong revealing his plans to her. Besides, things had been getting deeper than he ever imagined could happen over a phone. And, for many reasons, he trusted that she would not snitch him out even if she was in opposition of him wanting her to join him over seas. After she caught up on her beauty rest and they reconnected, he would see where she really stood with him and his situation. For now though, he would shower, prepare himself a hefty breakfast of sardines, corn beef hash, and cheese grits. Then he'd take a little nap.

He rounded the field on his last lap as a song Young Jeezy collaborated with T. I. on drove him to completion. Drenched in sweat, he headed back inside the dorm.

###

Orangeburg, South Carolina

Sunday Evening

Canary stood beneath the soft, warm flow of the water inside her shower thinking about Don as she massaged her swollen clitoris for the first time since her sex escapades with Justin. Don had built up such desire of profound magnitude within her she could no longer contain it. It was like a pot of boiling water atop a stove with the pilot turned on high beneath it and the only way to stop it from boiling over was to lower the fire or the pot would boil over. Thing was, she didn't want the fire to be distinguished, so her only other option was to allow her fluids to spill.

Her body convulsed and shuddered as she braced herself with one hand on the wall and the other between her legs as she massaged the miniature ball in circles while slipping a finger in and out of her tightness. She tilted her head back in ecstasy as she climaxed and screamed out Don's name as the orgasm in all its power racked through her body. Her knees buckled and she collapsed on the floor of the shower and began crying in want and need of him.

Danyell had departed about an hour ago and Tay had left before sunrise to join John in the state's capitol.

She laid on the floor of the shower as the water intermingled with her tears and orgasm and knew that she was deeply in love with Donatello Furqān McFadden and never even kissed him!

It was around 6 o'clock in the evening. Canary had slept like a baby and had dream after dream of Don touching her. In the dream's he'd been with her in her bed, living room, shower–everywhere!

About 10 minutes later, composure regained, she rewashed and headed to her bedroom with a towel wrapped around both body and hair. She fetched the blood red bottle of Inamorata lotion from her dresser and stared at the label before applying the cream to her skin. After she finished massaging her body down from head to toe she looked at her caller I.D. to to see if there was any missed calls from him. There wasn't. She pouted at the fact that he hadn't called her. And just as she got up to eat and start a pot of coffee, her phone rang. It was probably Danyell.

She turned around to fetch the cordless phone from its cradle. “Hello,” he answered without viewing the I.D.

“I've been missing you, Golden,” he said yearningly. The soft sound of his voice made her heart melt and she stopped in her tracks to the kitchen and sat on the carpeted floor of her bedroom. Things was so deep and tense between them he made ber lose her bearings! She forgot that she was hungry! He brought her so much joy! She had never experienced this type of feeling – not even with Justin. Don had even made her realize that there existed a God. He made her understand the Grand Scheme of things on behalf of the ills of the world. “Furqān," She called out to him.

"What's wrong, Golden?”

“Why do what I feel for you hurt?” She sat in the quietude of her room, anxiety prevalent in her chest.

“I won’t ask what you mean because I'm experiencing the same thing. I think part of the problem is a physical yearn. It's the only realm of our existence we haven't explored. I don’t know. It may only add fuel to the fire.

“But what I do know is that I don’t want to ever loose you nor this feeling.”

“What are you dong?” she asked him.

“Laying on my bunk on my side facing the wall. What are you doing?"

"Sitting on my room floor.”

“Your room floor?"

“Yes. I had just got through showering when you called and was about to fix me something to eat.”

"Well don't let me –“

“No!” She interjected emphatically. “You're fine. I want to be right here talking to you,” she said as she got up and got in the bed. Her heart pounded. Her harmones in a state of conniption. “Wheres your roommate?"

"Below me resting. Why?"

"Because I'm inexplicably hot and wanted you to listen to me come for you.” She didn't know where the temerity came from that made her say what she said because she was not sexually aggressive nor experienced in such things. “I don't know what has gotten into me but I've been contemplating how I could give myself to you to show you how much I love you.”

“Trust me, I can feel every bit of your love.”

“Do you think it would be a good idea if I had Raysor watch out for us one day?" she asked.

“No. Because the same way you told me about her and Chico, she would tell him and rumors will start to float because there’s no telling who he would tell,” he responded sagaciously. "Be patient, love.”

His response made her love him even more. It was good to know that he wasn't selfish. She opened the towel around her. An involuntary moan escaped her lips and she found her fingers parting the delicate flesh of her sex. She gasped as she pushed two fingers inside of her pool of bliss. "Furqān,” she moaned.

"Yes. I'm here, boo. Does it feel good?"

"Yes," she shuddered.

"God, I wish I was next to you,” he breathed in frustration as his man-hood strained against his shorts as it hardened from her moans. He spoke to her salaciously with a lubricious tongue as she masturbated herself into a powerful climax that cramped her stomach!

“I love you, Furqān,” she breathed after she came.

“I love you more, Canary.”

Silence fell between them momentarily as he listened to her breathe. He thought that there couldn't be a more better time than now to fold the cards he held. Here goes nothing he thought. “Golden, I need to speak to with you about something of extreme importance”

"I'm listening,” she said as she laid on her back with her legs open as clumps of her juices flowed from her into the sheets she would have to change. She was relaxed.

"Golden...." he paused briefly, “I’m about to escape and head to the Middle ea East.”

Her eyes sprung open! “What?” she asked incredulously.

He sighed. "It's going to happen within the next month or so.

"Are you seriousl?” she sat up.

“Yes. We've been planning it for some time now. This was why you caught me crying when you did. He broke everything down from beginning to end leaving nothing to the imaginaton.

She listened as he explained all that they had done and all that they were doing and couldn't believe that an actual tunnel was under construction from the outside into the facility. She was about to lose him! She began to weep.

“Whats wrong?" he asked her. "Just when I thought I wouldn't lose you, I am.”

“Listen, Golden- the reason I exposed all of this to you is because I vwanted to know if you’d come with me. I don't want to leave without you.”

"Of course I'll come with you, Furqān,” she answered

without hesitation.

Her response made his heart soar like an eagle. “Alhamdulillah! We can move forward then.”

“When will you go?”

“I’ll go to sick call this week and have everything set-up. And Insha’Allah, by Halloween I'll be in Saudi Arabia waiting on you.”

Silenec fell between them. The magnitude of the situation began hitting her slowly.

"Are you there?" he asked.

"Yes, I'm here. I'm just taking this all in.”

“If you have a change of heart between now and then just let me know. I'll understand.”

“Listen, Furqān,” she stated. "I told you from the start that I’m here for you and have long made my decision in regards of you. I'm not changing my mind. The only thing that can separate us is death. And from what I've been learning from an Islamic perspective, we’d still be together even through that in the Hereafter.”

“Only if you become a believer,” he warned.

"You know what I mean. And who knows what the future holds?

“But anyhow sweety, I'm going with you and that's final. Handle your business,” she told him.

“Allahu Akbar!” he asseverated inwardly

“I love you, sweety,” she added.

“I love you, too. Let me contact my father and tell him where we're all at."

"Okay."

"And besides, I want you to meet him."

"When?" she asked with a bit of trepidation.

"As soon as possible. Don't fret, he's cool."

"Okay. Go ahead and call him." She blew him a kiss and ended the call.

She sat up in bed as the day light outside that illumed through her bedroom window began to darken, casting shadows throughout the room. She ruminated all that Don had told her and for some reason, although the thought of the escape made her fear for him, it made her happy and gave her hope in the possibility that they'd be able to live life together freely. It didn't matter where they was in the world as long as she was with him.

But what she couldn't, and would not do, was reveal any of this to anyone whatsoever. Not even to Danyell and Tay!

She got up to shower again and change her soiled bed sheets. Then finally, she prepared something to satisfy the pangs of hunger rumbling in her stomach.

###

Palmetto Correctional Institution

Don stared at the wall thinking about how everything had been playing itself out since the commencement of his unfortunate, but seemingly fortunate predicament. Although he wouldn't be able to live the life that he had aspired to live in the land of the Beast, Home of The Slaves – as Al-Salam had depicted America – the most precious things he could ever find in life had been discovered and gained gained in the most unusual of circumstances. He was now officially Muslim, and he had found the most beautiful woman in the world in mind, heart, and spirit. The paradoxes that Allah spoke about in the Quran had indeed manifested itself to be true. What he had found was priceless! And truthfully, it was entirely too early to pass judgement on the outcome of his future because of the escape ahead. But he had enough faith in Allah that he would be victorious.

He wanted to wake Yahseen and tell him the good news but he'd inform him later when he got up. For now, he would offer his prayers and call his father.

Chapter Thirty-Three

Orangeburg, South Carolina
October 2, 2014 - Wednesday

Tay sat behind her desk at work. She was waiting on Danyell to conclude the session she was having with a client so she could speak to her. For the past couple of days, she had felt like a traitor in concealing the information. She didn't feel such perfidy in light of her friendship with Canary, although that was her girl, but her and Danyell had been friends since kids. She loved John, but all of what he'd been involved in was too deep for her to keep to herself. She needed to confide in someone to help her figure out what she should do.

It was around lunch time. The practice hadn't been busy thus far. They had a few scheduled appointments. Danyell was the only doctor in today; the other two were out conducting house calls.

She heard laughter coming from Danyell's office as the door opened and out walked her clients: husband and wife. She smiled up at them as Danyell showed them out. They were experiencing martial problems and was trying to save the marriage for the sake of their children.

"Okay, so what's on your mind, Tay?" Danyell asked as she sat in one of the chairs by Tay's desk in the reception area after her clients departed.

"Girl, you are not going to believe what I am about to tell you I found out Sunday when I went to see John," Tay commenced almost at a whisper as if there were others present that could hear their conversation.

"I'm listening," Danyell said.

"Listen to this..." Tay began the tale that John had revealed to her…

Danyell sat in her chair in disbelief of what Tay had just told her about Don and everything surrounding his case and his. "Girl, I know how you feel about John and all. And not only is Canary our friend, but I think helping that boy get his freedom back is the right thing to do. I don't know what you have planned in all of this, but I wish you hadn't told me this if you don't intend to tell Canary to help Don. This shit is going to drive me crazy and eat at my conscience."

"I know, Danyell," Tay sighed." That's why I told you so we could come up with a remedy for all involved."

"Girl, all of this will cause a lot of past things to come out in the open and John will be in trouble one way or the other. If not for immediate involvement in the murder of that girl, for his involvement with that organization," Danyell said. "He'll have to come forward and maybe things will be lighter on him. Especially if he aided the government in bringing them down.

"You and John need to figure something out fast. This shit makes me don't even want to see Canary until you do," she sighed. “Tay, you know that I’m a loyal friend and I’m not good at pretending.” She looked at her as if telling her not to keep her burden with this revelation.

“I know, Danyell. I’ll talk to John and we’ll figure something out.”

“Please do, because I’m going to duck Canary until you do,” Danyell stated.

“Okay. I’ll get with him tonight.”

Danyell got up and headed back to her office with a new burden.

###

Orangeburg, South Carolina

Red Lobsters - Wednesday Evening

Caesar pulled into the parking lot of Red Lobsters in his powder blue Bentley coupe and parked. It was five o'clock.

“Well sweetie, I'm here. I'll call you when I'm about to get back on the road, Insha’Allah.”

“Ok, Sulayman,” Cecelia responded. Her soft voice filled the confines of his coupe, as the call was connected to the car's audio system.

He climbed from the car after ending the call with Cecelia and stepped into the cool autumn air.

Things had been coming along magnificently with him and Cecelia. He had already told himself that he would marry her once he got Don safely squared away out East. He loved her and had slipped into his lower desires one night when they had been together. One thing led to another and he ended up taking her to his bed.

Now, here he was in Orangeburg, South Carolina entering Red lobsters where the love of his son's life awaited him. He saw her as soon as he entered the establishment. She was an amazing woman. Very hard to miss amongst a throng of people. Stunning she was, even in the uniform she wore!

He headed to the table where she sat. She stood to meet him as he approached.

"Hello, Sulayman," she beamed up at him. Don had sent her pictures of him and she had seen him on TV countless times, so she knew who he was – as did some of the looker-ons present around the establishment. "It's a pleasure to meet you."

He smiled and shook his head as he shook her delicate hands. "No Canary, it's a pleasure to meet you."

She was taken aback by his grace and aura of power. They seated themselves.

"What's wrong? Are you ok?" he asked as he picked up his menu.

"Yes, I'm fine. Your presence is just enthralling!" she laughed as she looked into his steel grey eyes.

He laughed. "I've been told." He hadn't over dressed, but had dressed casually in a pair of Sean John jeans, a button-down Sean John shirt and a pair of black-on-black Timberland boots.

"Mr. Sulayman Azeez Mustafah?" A caucasian man approached hospitably. He was dressed in a blue button-down shirt with khaki Dockers.

"Yes," Caesar looked up at him questioningly.

Canary looked at him curiously. A caucasian female approached with the same hospitable energy and stood beside him.

"I'm the manager here. One of our employee's noticed you. We just came to ensure you quality treatment and to thank you personally for dining at our establishment."

Caesar was used to this formality.

"If there's anything we can do to accommodate you and your company let one of my staff know. My name is Christopher." He extended a hand.

Caesar shook it firmly. "Thanks for the hospitality. But we're fine."

"As you were," the manager smiled and departed with the female that accompanied him.

"Happens all the time," he smiled towards Canary.

She shook her head. "Celebrities," she stated as she picked up her menu. "Must be nice," she added.

"Trust me, it gets annoying after a while."

"I can imagine."

"So, Ms. Rose. Tell me some things about yourself…" he commenced and they became acquainted with one another over a mini feast of steaks and lobsters. He liked his new daughter-in-law very much and thought that his son had surely found himself an indelible treasure of gold.

###

Columbia. South Carolina

Tay and John stood outside on the palisade of his suite over looking the river and the city beyond it, as they sipped from glasses of Chardonnay. The sleeves of the button-down dress shirt he wore was rolled up to his elbows. She looked at him in all his Kevin Costner handsomeness. He brushed his fingers through his hair and licked the dry wine from his lips after taking a pull from his glass. She had been with him for about 45 minutes. This was one of the first times that they hadn't sexually savaged one another on sight. “John,” she commenced. “I love you. But I can't be with you with all of this hanging over your head. I'll stick by you through it all if you come forward. I promise,” she said as she looked at the lights that peppered the surface of the river.

“I've been giving it a lot of thought, Tay. Trust me. I was once a lawyer, so I know the game that potentially lie ahead. Once all of this hits the fan, the President and the government will want to handle as much of this mess under the table as possible. Too many prominent politicians are involved.

“I don't know what I was thinking back then,” he said rediculously. “Greed, I guess. I was also thinking that we could cash in on the twenty-million, disappear and say fuck the world.” His hazel eyes sparkled like the wine he held as he looked at her and crushed her with his award-winning smile.

She turned to him and looked up at him as she placed her free hand on his chest. “John I'm not concerned with pelf, although I like nice things. I just want you to get this from over your head. If the twenty-million comes with it, that's fine. But clear your conscience, baby.

“I also think that you should call Sulayman first and speak with him. Maybe the both of you can put your heads together and come up with a solution to straighten all this mess out,” she connoted. "You know your career is shot to pieces. You are a secured party with diplomatic immunity so all will be well in the end."

"Sulayman would probably rip my head off." He snorted.

"I don't think he will. This is the break they've been looking for at the price of 20 million dollars, John. It's a blessing for him and his son. I think you owe them that much. You said it yourself that you guys was once friends. And you owe as much to Elfane."

"You're right, honey," he acquiesced. He brushed the tips of his fingers down her face. She shuddered at his touch. He kissed her. "I'll contact Sulayman in the morning and set up a meeting with him for this weekend. There's no need in prolonging our future.

"And I'm filing for divorce. Fuck it. Might as well put it all on the line. They thought that Bill getting his cock sucked in the Oval Office and the election of a black president sent the country in an uproar – well America, wait until you get a load of this!" Senator Jonathan Ethan Brody said somberly as he looked at the twinkling lights of the city.

Later that night, after her and John had sexed each other crazy and he had fallen asleep, she picked up the phone. She headed outside the living room of the suite and called Canary so she could relieve her conscious of the 20 million dollar secret it possessed since John had came to terms with what he was going to do.

Chapter Thirty- Four

Orangeburg, South Carolina
Palmetto Correctional Institution
October 3, 2014

It was Thursday morning. Canary had yet to sleep due to the elation of the electrifying news Tay had told her last night! At first, she thought that Tay had been playing a diableric game, but when she swore in all honesty about what John had told her about Don and his father, she knew that it was all horribly, but satisfyingly true.

She had started to call Don back and tell him last night, but had decided to tell him face to face. She was so excited for him, for them, it took everything in the make-up of her anatomy to restrain herself against the urge of running on the wing to his room and jumping in his arms, planting moist kisses all over his face! This could very well be his ticket to getting his life back legitimately.

But there was a downside to it all like Tay had told her. It was the possible danger of his father being indicted for conspiracy, which would cause all of his assets to be frozen, and his property would be seized. This was the horrifying part of it all.

Her and Don had spoken until around 10 pm. He needed the sleep. She was killing him, he had told her. She smiled inwardly.

She had also told him about the glorious evening she enjoyed with his charismatic father and saw where he got his qualities and charm. Then, Tay had called with 20 million dollars worth of information! She had connoted that they could cash in on the lead! And although the idea would be tempting to most, Tay had been only playing in her humor.

Now, it was a little after 9 am. Majority of the dorm had departed out on movement to designated locations. Chico was wiping down the walls in the lobby with bleach. They had spoken briefly about him and Raysor, which she had told him not to let her catch them again. He just smiled bashfully. She didn't blame him though. If she was a man incarcerated, she'd be doing the same thing before playing Russian Roulette with your life with men like Foxy. And if she did catch them again, she'd do no more than she had done the first time.

It was Officer Carter's shift, and since she was out sick, Granada was working the wing.

Canary had sent Ricardo to fetch Don. The jubilation that permeated through her body had her feeling spontaneous and reckless as she sat inside her chair waiting on the love of her life. But regardless of how she felt, she knew that she had to remain mature and professional. At least until all the wrinkles in the matter was ironed out.

She sipped from a steamy cup of coffee, sugar, and cream.

Don had been reading a book called the Sealed Nectar, which was one of many biographies on the Prophet Muhammad's life, when Ricardo had stopped by the room to inform him that their lieutenant wanted to see him.

Yahseen had departed the dorm to Coordinator Montgomery's office. Chess and Success was knocked unconscious from all the wine they'd consumed last night. The Dallas Cowboys had polarized the San Francisco 49ers and it had sent many drunken sports fanatics in an uproar, and a few fights had broken out.

Monday, he had made a sick-call and complained of lower back pains. He had been examined by a very gorgeous nurse practitioner that he'd been unaware that even worked at the facility. So soft and beautiful she was it seemed as if she was carved out of a block of cocoa butter. She had charted him for an X-ray at the main medical facility in Columbia, South Carolina. With that out the way, the wait was on.

He headed down the stairs across the wing. Sergeant Granada sat on top of the officer's desk talking to Foxy, Ricardo, and few other inmates. Some of them greeted him and he returned the greetings with a smile and peace sign and headed off the wing to the vault that possessed his treasure.

Foxy watched Don as he headed off the wing to Rose's office. He knew that something was up between them, but Rose had begun to close him out for whatever reason, which he found fucked up of her to do when they supposed to have been cool.

And he'd been exposing all of his business to her, which was unfair! He began to loath her. He had refrained from going to her office as much, but still went by every once in a while to make it appear as if all was well between them. He could see it all in her face. She was in love. She was in love with Donatello McFadden. He knew it! Even though he was homosexual, he was loyal to his friends, and Rose made him feel as if she'd betrayed what they had as friends.

And being honest with himself, he didn't like the fact that she had won Don. "Walking around like her shit don't stink and the whole time bitch you're just as dirty and sneaky as everybody else!" He said inwardly in derision and contempt as he watched the wing door close behind Don.

"Are you fucking serious?" Don asked incredulously after Canary had finished conveying what Tay had conveyed to her.

"Yes, I'm serious, Don!" she answered a bit defensively.

"I believe you boo, but damn! This is so hard to believe!" He hadn't been expecting this out of all things. He was speechless. So much he wanted to say but he couldn't find the words he was so superb at articulating. He just stared at her as if he was waiting on her to scream out "April Fools!" and it wasn't even April!

And although it was music to his ears, the burden still existed. It just would shift to his father. He couldn't believe that John had allowed him to take such hit after he'd looked up to him like an uncle and played with his son Daniel. He needed some time to ruminate everything.

"Don!" she called for the second time.

"Yes, G?" he answered calmly. He'd been looking at her the entire time lost in thought. All sound around him had went silent.

"Listen... You can inform your father, but tell him not to say anything to John yet. We got to give him a chance to do as he said. Just find out if he contacted your father and arranged a meeting with him this weekend. We don't want him to feel as if

Tay betrayed his trust," she said sagaciously.

"Okay," he replied solemnly.

"Are you okay? I mean, this is good news regardless of what," she told him.

"Trust me Golden, I know. I'm just on a spiritual trip right now. As I told you… All that I've been going through seems to be some sort of paradox and test by Allah.

"From the commencement of all this, one inexplicable thing keeps happening after another, and now this.

"Remember the dream I told you about that I had in the lion's den like Daniel?" he asked her.

"Yes."

"John's son name is Daniel. It all makes me wonder if it was a parable the entire time. Everything seems to be braided through a chain of events and individuals. If you had never went through what you went through in life that led you to seek counseling, you would have never met Danyell, which led you to meeting Tay, and I would have never met you. This would all never be. My father even would have never met Cecelia.

"Do you see the complexity in how Allah has woven this all tother? It really makes you wonder about life and the people you walk past every day. Everything and everyone has a divine purpose."

She hadn't thought of this. This was what she loved most about him. His level of intellectual discernment. She nodded.

"For this reason, I think everything will pan out fine, Insha'Allah. But you should know that if my father need me to go through with the escape to safeguard our empire, I'm all in," he continued to look at her.

"A lot is at stake. He may come up with a different remedy besides having John come forward. But whatever his decision, I trust his judgement. So don't get your hopes up too high. Just as I didn't know it would hit close to home, I know that he's not going to expect it to hit so close either."

This dampened her bliss, but she still tried to remain optimistic. "Okay."

"Don't get sad, boo," he saw the light dim in her eyes. He wanted to kiss her. "Let's just see what happens and remember that Allah is in control first and foremost.

"But I need to go think for a moment and see if John contacted him yet. This is a situation that has to be dealt with assiduously baby. So maintain your fortitude and be patient," he smiled.

"Okay, Furqān. I love you."

"Always and forever. My Inamorata. Remember?"

"Yes."

"Call me," he stood to leave.

"Okay." She watched him as he departed, thinking that there was nothing like being in the presence of the on you loved. Her heart sunk to her stomach in dismay. She didn't think that it would be so complicated. She wanted to cry. And just as she was about to after forgetting where she was, she heard Foxy's voice and it brought her back to reality! She forced a smile up at him.

Oblivious to his wicked game due to her doleful state of emotions, feeling defeated and uncaring, she told Foxy a vague story about how they just talked from time to time. Nothing more.

Foxy knew that she was lying and that it was deeper than

what she had revealed. The sickness of love wa plastered all over her face But if she wanted to continue to play him when he knew she had fallen in love with his fantasy, he'd show her how dirty the game could be played!

Oblivious to his twisted way of thinking, she lied and told him that she was feeling under the weather.

Lying bitch! Foxy smiled as he prepared to leave, in which he had never taken a seat.

Don got to his room and fetched his phone and call his father repeatedly until he reached him.

"As salamu alaykum, Furqān. What's the urgency, son?" Caesar asked from his office. He had been on the lower floors entertaining Inter Departmental Affairs the first few times Don had called.

Don returned the salutation. "Did you hear from John this morning?"

"Yeah,":Caesar's brows furrowed quizzically at the inquiry. "What made you ask that?"

"What did he want, abu?" Don evaded his father's inquiry momentarily.

"He just said that he and I needed to get together Saturday. Now, what made you ask that?"

"I found it hard to believe so I know you will also. But here's something Canary told me John's girlfriend told her. They're friends, abu. This is going to rock your world!" Don told him what Canary had told him from beginning to end.

"Marcellus!" Caesar growled. He was enraged! Although execrable, it all made sense. "By Allah, I will kill each and every one of those punk motherfuckers!" he vowed. The hoodlum in him had surfaced and he began to dhiker in remembrance of Allah. His blood was boiling! He was trying to remain calm and subdue his rage.

"But, abu. They ask that we keep this to ourselves until John has the opportunity to come to you first so it doesn't make Tay appear to have betrayed his trust."

"Insha'Allah," Caesar replied with controlled fortitude after the dhiker. "But Allahu'Akbar, son!" he asseverated in gratitude of the blessing.

"Allahu'Akbar!" Don agreed gratefully. "So what now, abu?" he inquired.

"Insha'Allah, Furqān. But for now, we call off the escape and hold on to the payments. After I get with John we'll go from there. This is a very serious situation that has to be handled with efficiency. Just make du'a for us all, and Insha'Allah, we're properly guided in what to do."

"Insha'Allah."

"Tell Canary I said thanks to her and her friends, and tell her to call me as soon as she can. I told you that she may very well be a blessing from Allah, Furqān.

"But for now, let me gather my thoughts. I can't really think straight right now. Be cool for the moment and chill. I'll call you."

"Okay, abu. I love you."

"You already know what it is, lil' man."

They exchanged salutations and ended the call. Don

continued to sit where he sat at the table. He looked around the room. A collage of scenarios parading through his head.

About 15 minutes later Yahseen materialized. He enlightened him about the chain of events and it stunned him in disbelief as it had done everyone else.

###

Charleston, South Carolina

Caesar stood at the large window in his office as he watched the tiny cars move across the glorious bridge over the distance between it and his office. The distance made the cars appear like the micro machine toys cars he had bought Don as a child.

He knew that there had been something strange about John when they had met on his yacht at the beginning of Don's case. But he was relieved to know that he had a conscience and that history between them stood for something.

But this revelation came with another problem. This one pertained to the exposure of him and Al-Salam, and their past. John coming forward would indeed free Don, but in this, not only would Marcellus and the rest of his squad be brought down, him and Al-Salam would take a hit as well. He could very well have John remain silent, break Don out, assassinate The Seven for their transgressions, and move on with life. But he didn't want his son on the run in hiding like a terrorist. He wanted him to be able to freely enjoy the bounties of Allah in its entirety. Even if he took a hit, which he'd probably lose everything in a conspiracy to the Feds. Al-Salam wouldn't be touched due to his non-citizenship, but he didn't need such infamous exposure.

There was only one option that would free Don, save John as

much as possible after he came forward, protect Al-Salam's honor and integrity, and protect him from incarceration and total ruin. The ex-attorney could be brought to justice. He knew The Seven well enough to know that the lawyer was just a pawn in their wicked game. But other than this, his only resort would be to assassinate all members of The Seven.

His eyes lowered in disdain at the dirty work ahead. To a degree, his actions would be justifiable under Islamic law under the laws of retaliation, as The Seven initiated the war. He had thought that a life of murder was far behind him. Now here he was once again. He had no choice in the matter. After his meeting with John, he'd call Al-Salam, bring him to date, and assemble his executioners.

He left the window and called Cecelia, the woman that had become a part of his mind, body, and soul through all of this turmoil. He knew what he was about to tell her – minus his machinations of murder, in which he would keep away from her forever – would shock her as if she had licked a finger and stuck it inside a socket!

Chapter Thirty-Five

Columbia, South Carolina
October 5, 2014 - Saturday Afternoon

As Caesar stood to the door of Johnathan Ethan Brody's suite at the Sheraton in downtown Columbia, he wondered what the hell he was doing staying inside a hotel. Just as his neurotransmitter began computing it all, a beautiful brown skin complexioned woman opened the door and smiled up at him.

"Hello, Mr. McFadden. Come on in, John's awaiting you."

"Thank you," he smiled at her warmly as he stepped into the warm confines of the suite. "And how are you?" he asked.

"I'm fine. You can have a seat or help yourself to a drink at the bar if you like. John will be out in a minute. He's in the restroom," she said.

"Thanks. But Muslims aren't supposed to consume intoxicants. I'll take a seat, though."

She smiled and headed back to their room. Caesar knew that

John liked to dib and dab with the ladies, but by the looks of things, it appeared as if he'd been staying in this place for some time. Personal items of his was present around the suite and a picture of him and the woman he'd just seen sat on the table in front of him. He realized that she was Canary's friend. And just that quickly, he had figured out that John had fallen in love with her and was probably having marital problems because of it.

He thought about John's wife Valarie. He had liked Valarie. She was a gorgeous, intelligent red head with cute freckles. But Caesar guessed she had nothing on whom he'd just seen. He approved.

"Hey! Hello, big guy," John said brightly as he entered the living room.

Caesar looked to the left of him and smiled at the sight of his old comrade, as he stood. He wasn't mad at John. He understood the game and was willing to reconcile things as long as John was talking along his lines. But for the meantime, until John exposed the cause of the meeting, he'd play along. "What's up, player?" he extended a hand. "What's the cause of this spontaneous meeting?"

John shook Caesar's hand and headed to the wet bar to pour himself a stiff drink.

Caesar thought he looked a bit stressed as bags were under his eyes as if he hadn't been getting much sleep. And he needed to shave. He wore a pair of beige, cotton, cargo shorts. He was shirtless.

John was a bit trepidated. He knew that Caesar could be baleful. He slammed a shot of liquor, poured another and went to sit down on the sofa across from him. "Well, for starters, we have a little catching up to do, Sulayman. But before I proceed, how're you and Don?" Caesar feigned resentment with a look of contempt that said enough.

"I know, I know," John waved a hand ruefully. "I fucked up big time, big guy. I want to set some things straight. It's why I called you."

Caesar's brow furrowed in interest.

"But there's no need to beat around the bush, you've been waiting long enough. I can't imagine what Don has been going through, so let me tell you the story about me, myself," he pointed at himself, "and The sevSevenen…." he paused and sipped his drink, "and you, Caesar."

Calm and collected, Caesar looked at him. John never called him Caesar, so he knew that the story he was about to tell pertained to his past life. "To be frank, Sulayman – I was glad when you guys announced that you were shutting down the heroin business last year. But Marcellus and them was really enraged that you guys had wholly pulled the plug. I don't even know why I got caught up in all of this when they came to me back then. The decision is haunting me now," John explained as he rolled the crystal glass between his two palms thoughtfully.

"About a month after you guys had shut down, I was invited to a banquet at Senator Marshall's mansion in Louisiana – which ended up being nothing but a meeting arrangement consisting of the seven senators."

Caesar listened intently. Jacob Marshall III, was the senator of Louisiana. He was second in command of their organization after Marcellus Rothenstein of Texas. The body of The Seven was once Caesar's secret weapon in his reign of success in the heroin trade, in which they ran a very intelligent, clandestine enterprise of corrupted politicians, judges, lawyers, and cops around the country.

"I was informed of an ex-attorney from Reno, Nevada by the

name of Edward Butler. He owed them a quarter-million in gambling debt. I was told that he was going to execute your son to compensate the debt. I was appalled by the idea, but my hands was tied in the matter. I feared for Valarie and the kids."

It burned him deeply to know that a murderous plot had not been concocted for him, but his son.

"Anyhow," John continued somberly after throwing the remnants of the liquor down his throat. "Things didn't go as planned because the prick attorney was not an expert in this field and couldn't get near Don, and when he did have the opportunity to kill him, he somehow fucked it up by letting him slip away. And in the moment of his screw-up and fear of The Seven, he called himself improvising in the heat of the moment and killed Fedora. She hadn't been raped. It just appeared as such. I guess her and Don had had a mighty aggressive bout of sex before Edward whacked her.

"So, they framed Don for the murder and demanded that I not interfere with the case. I 'm sorry, big guy," he said remorsefully.

Quiet fell between them for a long moment.

"So where do you want to go from here, big guy?" John asked. "It's all your call."

"And you said you know this lawyer guy?" Caesar asked quizzically. His mind was racing with murderous thoughts that he would not expose to John.

"Yes. I Googled him. He's a washed up nobody with a gambling addiction out in Reno."

Quiet fell between them for a long moment again. Caesar was cogitating how he could kill Marcellus and the other 6 senators. He took his phone from his pocket and pulled up the calendar.

"Let's give the situation about two weeks before we make any moves. That'll give you enough time to handle your private affairs before coming forward, as I'm suspecting you're willing tdo..." He looked at John for confirmation.

John nodded.

"We'll break the story on the twenty-first," Caesar said. Unbeknownst to John, he had postponed everything for two weeks to give him time to orchestrate the hits on The Seven. John and the attorney was all they needed alive for information purposes. With The Seven dead, his past would die with them.

"Aren't you concerned about your exposure in all this?" John asked.

"No," Caesar prevaricated. "Don's more important. He's my first concern in the matter. What happened to him was because of me so I'll deal with everything else when the time comes." He thought about the dream he had with his grandmother. It had proven to be true.

John looked into his empty glass as he thumbed the rim. Although Caesar didn't say it himself, he knew that he was probably thinking along the lines of having The Seven assassinated. But he didn't care, and he was glad that if this was indeed his thoughts, that he wasn't burdened with anymore dark and wicked machinations.

"Well, I know that Don is going to be exhilarated," John smiled as he got up to refill his glass. Caesar cracked a smile.

"Yeah, he sure is." He thought about the escape and the money he was just about to turn over to officers.

"So, do you forgive me, big guy?" John asked as he returned and seated himself.

"Of course I do. Alhamdulillah! If God can forgive, who am

I not to?" Caesar smiled. "You need to lighten up on that stuff, man," he referred to the liquor.

"I will when all of this stuff is over with if I haven't killed myself by then."

"I see the new lady. What's up with you and Valeria?"

"It's over. My heart's not in it nor politics anymore. I'm giving them both up," he grinned.

Caesar chuckled warmly. "But hey man, I'm a man of my word so the reward still stands, John," he said seriously.

"The twenty-million?"

Caesar nodded.

"Nah, I can't take it, Sulayman. I'm well enough."

"Not after divorcing Valarie, you won't be," Caesar raised a brow.

John frowned. So lost in thought he hadn't taken this into consideration. "You're right. I may very well need it."

"I insist," Caesar told him. "So how's Daniel…" he inquired about his son, then John introduced him to his fiancé.

Before Caesar's departure an arrangement had been made of John contacting the President October 21st. The agreement had been sealed with a firm, masculine hug, and pats on the back.

Now, enroute to Charleston where Cecelia awaited him, he called Al-Salam and informed him of all the recent events up to the present moment. "It's time for you to come to America, shaykh. I need you," Caesar told him as he got on Interstate-26.

He had awakened Al-Salam from his slumbering as the time

differentiated out East. After listing to the shocking events, Al-Salam told Caesar that he would be on his way first quarter and that he would contact hm when he arrived at the airport in Charleston. He was in furiated! This was the second time Marcellus had crossed him in his avariciousness, and it would be his last!

Caesar allowed him to get back to rest and called Ali and Jabbar: his executioners. It was time to put in a bit of necessary blood work.

Chapter Thirty-Six

Orangeburg, South Carolina
Palmetto Correctional Institution
October 7, 2014 - Monday

Close the door and have a seat Lieutenant Rose," Major Wigfall said from where she sat behind her desk, which was clustered with paperwork, miscellaneous paraphernalia, and numerous "snitch kites" from the inmates on lock up and general population.

Canary closed the door behind her and sat in one of the two chairs in front of the major's desk in operations. The office was twice the size of hers. Pictures of the major's kids and grandkids sat atop various pieces of furniture around the office. Plants and flowers in various size flowerflower was everywhere. It always made Canary wonder if the major needed the extra oxygen to breathe inside the concrete and steel structure. The office smelled of burnt cinnamon.

It was Monday morning and she had just gotten to work and had been through briefing where she was told to report to the

Major's office before heading to her post. She didn't know what the summons pertained to. Throughout the years she'd been employed at the facility her and the major had established quite a rapport. She smiled at the major and the smile was returned as the she leaned on her desk braced on her elbows with both hands clasped beneath her chin.

"How are you this morning?" Major Wigfall asked kindly, her eyes soft and relaxed as always.

"I'm getting along fine. How're you?" Canary returned.

"Ready to retire," Major Wigfall chuckled lightly.

"I know that's right," Canary agreed.

"Well, let's get to business. I don't want to hold you from your duties. I hate to be the bearer of what I'm about to ask you but it's my duty. You'll understand, I'm sure. I think it's a bunch of garbage anyway." Canary looked at her quizzically. The statement perplexed her.

"Is there anything going on between you and Donatello McFadden?"

Canary eyelids stretched open so widely she was sure her eyeballs would fall out and hang on her checks by their veins! She didn't know if she should laugh the question off as an absurdity or frown. "No," she answered preposterously.

"Just as I figured." The major continued to look at her with the same relaxed gaze of trust.

"Why would you ask me such a thing? I don't understand," Canary inquired.

"You know how these inmates are, Rose. I'm not supposed to reveal where it came from but I'm sure you know inmate Fernando Brown, as I've seen him loitering around your office."

Canary nodded in confirmation.

"I'm not sure of his motive, or what compelled him to concoct such a story, but I advise you to be careful and stay away from him," Major Wigfall expressed wisely.

Canary scrunched her brows bemusingly. She couldn't believe Foxy's nerve! What in the hell had she done to him to make him perform so treacherously? He was trying to get her fired!

"And for the sake of my position, please don't say anything to him. Just continue your duties professionally," Major Wigfall told her.

Canary shook her head and laughed dismayingly. She was fed up and tired of the malignant truculence of the environment. And anyway, it wouldn't be long before Don came home. His father had already spoke with John and came to mutual terms. She didn't know the exact extent of the details, but what she did know was that John was going to contact the president for Don's immediate release on the 21st of the current month.

Inside, she was so happy she couldn't wait! Surely, she wouldn't allow something and someone as simple as her job and Foxy to dampen her joy. She took a breath. "With all due respect, Major Wigfall, I quit. I'm resigning."

The major sat up in shock. "No, Rose! Don't take it that way. You're one of our best."

Canary shook her head in disagreement. "I can't take it anymore. It's over. I've been long thinking about picking up on my career as an attorney. This is not for me. It was a hellafied experience, but I can no longer do this," she smiled kindly.

The major relaxed. She understood. She had felt the same way many times over the years, but some how still ended up continuing on. She smiled warmly, “Ok, and good luck.”

“Thanks. I’ll go to the dorm and gather my things,” Canary stood.

“I’ll be back in about twenty minutes.”

The major nodded.

Canary departed Operations feeling as if the weight of the world had been removed from her shoulders. She smiled as she inhaled the cool morning air and headed to the dorm. For some reason, giving up her job made her feel as if she was actually getting out of prison. She knew Don would be ecstatic about her decision.

She headed across the yard, as inmates poured from different doors on movement, thinking how Foxy had snaked her.

The morning movement had just been called for her dorm when she entered the lobby. Inmates flowed around her as she maneuvered through the throng of murderers, rapists, child molesters, robbers, and every other criminal under the sun.

Sergeant Granada and officer Carter was standing in the lobby observing the traffic quietly. They greeted her and she returned the greeting with a very bright smile.

Usually, Foxy would be one of the first inmates she saw, but he was missing in action. Guilty conscience, she conceded. “I’ll be back in a minute,” she told Granada and Carter as she headed on the wing without breaking her stride. She hadn’t even stopped by her office to put down her see-through bag. There wasn’t anything in the office that she really needed to gather. She just wanted to see Don before she left.

As she headed across the wing and descended the steps in the flood-zone she unfastened the clamp that held her hair in a tight bun and allowed it to bounce over her shoulders and cascade down her back in a shimmering stream of gold.

The murmurs of the inmates around the dorm became silent as they stopped and looked at her with inquisitive awe as they had never seen her in such bright and care-free mood. She paid them no mind. Her focal point was Don.

She got to the room and knocked on the door. The flap was up as usual.

"Come in!" a voice yelled.

She opened the door and saw that it was Mr. Wright. He was sitting on his bunk eating a bowl of cereal, reading Think & Grow Rich, by Napoleon Hill. He looked up at her and stopped chewing. She saw is admiration. "Good morning," she smiled impishly. "Can I come in?"

Yahseen nodded, suspicious of her strange actions and appearance.

She entered the cozy confines of the room and closed the door behind her and helped herself to a seat.

Yahseen continued to look at her incredulously! He couldn't believe that he was inside his cell with her behind closed doors with the flap covering the window. He thought that she had lost her fucking mind, and he asked her! "Have you lost your fucking mind?" He looked at her, to the closed door.

"Yes!" she giggled. "I just quit. Where's Furqān?"

"In the shower." God she was so beautiful! Don was one lucky brother!

"Do you mind if I sit here with you until he gets out of the shower?"

"Nah, you're straight, empress. "Yahseen looked at her and shook his head. So much he had seen throughout his bid he thought that nothing could, or would amaze him anymore. But Lieutenant Rose had proved him wrong with this move.

As they awaited Don, she enlightened Yahseen of Foxy's perfidy.

Don had already finished washing. He was just under the shower-head allowing the steaming hot water to relax his muscles, as he thought about the fortunate things that had been happening to him.

The meeting with his father and John had went well. If Allah allowed him to see the 21st, he'd be free again. His father hadn't gotten into the details of what his plans were on behalf of the backlash that would come when John opened his can of worms, but his father had told him to be cool and leave it in the hands of Allah.

He knew his father was up to something, but he really didn't know what it was since he didn't know the intricacies of the situation. But he was informed that it had to do with his father's past life. It wasn't that his father didn't want to enlighten him, he just didn't trust the phones to such extent. There wasn't time for any visits because time was of the essence. And, Al-Salam was on his way over to the States, so he knew that whatever his father had planned was of profound magnitude.

He was a bit worried about what this could all cost his father, but he felt assured in that his father was a man of prodigy and sui generis courage.

He thought about how close he was to being able to go home and begin a new life with Canary Rose. A smile stretched across his face beneath the flow of the water.

Yahseen had told him that Granada and Smith was disappointed at the fact that their lottery ticket had disappeared in thin air. But his father told Yahseen to assure them that he'd still give them 50k each for the thought and inconvenience, at the conclusion of things. Captain Holmes would receive $2, 500.

Scramble and Jamal had been updated on his status and events surrounding him. They were all ecstatic that things was working in his favor.

And since this was potential civil litigation on behalf of the unlawful conviction, defamation of character, pain and suffering and many other damages, he could sue the state, but he had a plan to see if he could have a group of his comrades pardoned with their records expunged in return of him not pursing the suit. He hadn't told anyone of his plans. Not even Yahseen. He didn't want to get their hopes up high. He'd continue to let things play itself out.

He felt his fingers begin to wrinkle so he ended the shower and began toweling himself dry. He wrapped the towel around his abdomen and slipped on his boxers and shorts, gathered his shower gear, and headed out the stall to his cell.

Unaware of the surrounding eyes that watched him and his room, as the lieutenant of the dorm had been inside the cell with the door closed with the flap covering the window for the past 10 minutes, he pulled the door open and gasped at the sight before him!

Canary beamed at the sight of his honey colored, chiseled chest, as he stood in the threshold of the door dumbfounded. She laughed freely. "Mr. Wright, would you please let me have a moment with him?" she asked as she stood.

Yahseen got up as Don entered the room looking at him as if

they had schemed this on him. He looked at Don, shrugged his shoulders and closed the door behind him.

Canary quicky closed the gap between them and threw her arms around Don's neck as she parted his lips with her hungry tongue. He dropped the gear he held and rubbed his fingers through her glorious hair – something he longed to do. So much force their kiss possessed they had to pull away from one another for air!

"What are you doing?" Don asked as he looked into her sparkling eyes. His chest heaved as if he'd just ran a marathon.

"I quit," she said simply.

"You what?"

"I quit," she briefly explained what Foxy had done. "It's what you wanted right?"

"Yeah," he responded as he continued to hold her by her petite waist. Her arms was still wrapped around his neck. He thought they fit together perfectly. "But it's not much longer and I want to be able to see you until then. Can't you tell them you had a change of heart?" he kissed her again.

"Ummhmm," she answered inside the kiss. Her juices was flowing. She was ready to let him take her on one of their bunks.

She released herself from the sweetness of the kiss and breathed. The breathing was labored. "I would give you some, but this is just a taste of what awaits you when you come home. Besides, I should get going I've been in here long enough waiting on you."

"Woman, you are crazy." He kissed her again and massaged the incredibly, soft flesh of her booty for the first time.

She moaned at the caress and her hands glided down his chest into his shorts to his harden manhood. She felt it throb and pulsate as she squeezed it.

He moaned. “Crazy about you.”

It took every ounce of strength in her not to pleasure him orally. “Let me get going so I can call the major,” she released him. So hot she was, beads of perspiration prickled her nose. She fetched her bag. “See you around, Mr. McFadden.” She kissed him once more before departing.

As Canary headed up the flood zone, everybody including Granada and Carter, watched her. They thought she had lost her mind! She smiled at them brightly and twiddled her fingers. She didn’t care. She had what she wanted. She still hadn’t seen Foxy’s connivingly gay ass!

Don continued to stand in the middle of the room in hilarious astonishment! He started laughing. His life was so hard to believe, but yet it was all a very interesting reality!

“Salam, akhi,” Yahseen entered the room and joined in the insane laughter. “Man, what the fuck? You got that woman gone! I thought I had some crazy situations. She fucked me up when she rolled up in here. I didn’t even finish my cereal.” The both of them looked at the unfinished bowl of Captain Crunch that sat on the table.

“Well, just know that you have a life of *golden* hell on your hands. May Allah grant the both of you success in both worlds,” Yahseen chuckled as he moved by Don in the cramped confines of the cell to finish off the soggy cereal.

Don continued to chuckle as he picked up his gear and squared himself away while ruminatingvthe past five minutes.

"Man akh, that fucking punk Foxy on some real ill shit," Yahseen said disdainfully.

"Yeah, I know. But just chill, big bro. We'll just feign as if we don't know what he did. It's almost over anyhow, Insha'Allah."

Yahseen didn't respond. He despised things like what Foxy had done. And as always, in his intolerance of violations, he thought that Foxy should die. He would chill on the strength of Don though, and wouldn't plot his death. But he was sure – due to his wisdom and experience – that Foxy wouldn't relent until he had accomplished whatever sick objective he had. Just as he had told Canary – for whatever reason of Foxy's – he was trying to get her fired or get Don shipped. And when he saw that his attempt was unsuccessful, he was going to take a step farther. It was a good thing that the both of them was on their way out the door.

Yahseen got up and pushed the door open. The both of them got their things in order and began cleaning the room. "What a way to start the day," he thought.

Chapter Thirty-Seven

Charleston, South Carolina

October 7, 2014 - Monday Night

Caesar, accompanied by Ali and Jabbar, waited on Al-Salam by baggage claim. His fight had landed moments ago. The airport wasn't very active as the many other airports around the country, as much of nothing transpired in South Carolina on profound levels outside of its savage street life. It was a place for tourism and retirement seekers. Other than the folks departing the flight and a few other lay overs, they were the only body's occupying the airport. It was 2:30 am.

Caesar finally spotted his mentor/confident and a broad smile formed on his face at the grand sight of the man. Over the distance, the smile had been returned by Al-Salam with the same electrifying broadness. The sight of this man never ceased to amaze Caesar. He was a bear of a man at six-four, three-hundred-twenty pounds. He was casually dressed in soft green, loose fitting garments with a matching turban wrapped around his head looking like all the Muslim he professed to be. His beard seemed to have grown a couple of inches longer. So distinguishing and powerful he was, made Caesar appear to be nothing more than a shadow. As he approached, his grand appearance reminded Caesar of James Earl Jones when he came to America in the movie.

"There goes the brother," Jabbar pointed.

"Yeah, I see'em," Caesar said as they began to approach the man, that by way of Allah, had changed their lives forever.

"As Salamu alaykum, ikhwan!" Al-Salam smiled as he sat down his carry-on bag to properly greet and hug his fellow brothers. The greeting had been returned with hugs, hefty handshakes, pats on the backs, and kisses on cheeks. It had been over a year since they had seen him in person. So much had happened in this short period of time and space, it seemed like a lifetime!

"I hate to be meeting you brothers under such circumstances, but Mash'Allah," Al-Salam said as Ali grabbed his bag. They headed to the luggage line where Caesar fetched Al-Salam's duffle and suitcase.

"They already checked them for explosives, akhi… THOROUGHLY!" Al-Salam humored.

They all laughed as they headed out the airport chatting congenially as they made way through the deep chill of the night air to where Ali's truck awaited them.

###

October 8, 2014 - Tuesday

The following afternoon they all sat at the table in the dining room of Caesar's beach house on the Isles of Palm in Mount Pleasant. They were eating a late breakfast that Cecelia had prepared them with coffee, milk, and orange juice. Caesar had introduced her to Al-Salam then she retired to their bedroom as Al-Salam was deeply rooted in Islamic tradition on behalf of being amongst women. It was one of the reasons he despised being in the States. The Americans and their untamed and immoral traditions brought conflict with the Deen. It was unlawful to be amongst uncovered women. It made him think of his intractable daughter and he swallowed the sour taste the thought brought him. "I think she's a good woman for you Sulayman, Insha'Allah," Al-Salam told Caesar.

"Alhamdulillah," Caesar replied. They had all headed to his house after departure from the airport last night and had all crashed one of the beds inside the large, spacious home of 6 bedrooms and 3 and a half baths. Cecelia had taken a vacation to dedicate her full support to him and Don throughout their ordeal.

"So, what's the status on the tunnel thing, Sulayman? Is it still under construction?" Al-Salam inquired then shoveled a hefty scoop of scrambled eggs into his mouth. His accent was thick, but his English was good. He strummed his beard as he chewed.

"Nam," Caesar confirmed. "I said to hell with it. Once it's completed, I don't care who use it. I see it as a form of charity to the struggle of oppression, Insha'Allah. Most of those guys back there have been wrongfully convicted anyhow. So to heck with it."

Al-Salam nodded thoughtfully. Quiet fell around the table for a moment. The only sounds was that of silverware scraping plates.

"Tell me about you and John's meeting again, akhi," Al-Salam told Caesar as he sipped his coffee and stroked his beard.

Ali and Jabbar sat quietly as they listened.

Caesar reiterated the details of the meeting he had with John

Saturday morning.

Al-Salam wasn't a man of wasteful words, so he didn't talk very much.. Al-Salam picked up one of the napkins in the middle of the table and wiped his mouth before speaking. "I never made mention of this because it was irrelevant at the time, Sulayman. But do you remember when we first met?"

Caesar nodded as he chewed the fried turkey sausage he had just bit into. He remembered every detail of the year 1992 when he was deployed to Saudi Arabia during his time as a United States Marine. It was the year he had almost lost his life.

"Well, when I found you on the road along the way – as you know – I was returning from a business meeting in Afghanistan. I never told you what that meeting was about," Al-Salam strummed his beard with his thick fingers. His skin tone a burnt bronze. "The Seven and I have a long history akhi, that dates back to the late seventies when I was first introduced to Marcellus and Jacob. They weren't senators then.

"There was once a man by the name of Thadeus Crenshaw aka Nasir Rahman. He was an educated imposter that Marcellus and Jacob used to get near me through the Deen They knew that I only entrust in Muslims. They needed a connection with me to launch the drug enterprise they aspired to run. Thadeus had taken theology in college and was well-versed in religious matters. He manipulated the knowledge over a period of time to gain my trust. He was the mayor of Texas.

"After a slew of trips over to Arabia, as he had taken me as his sahabah, he took his Shahadah and became Muslim. Later, he expressed his ambitions with Marcellus and Jacob, as he was an original member of The Seven. Randolf Carenstead of Maryland came on board after I killed him."

They all looked at him in amazement because he had just told them he had killed a Muslim. One of the most gravest sin for a Muslim! "Killed him?" Caesar asked incredulously.

Al-Salam raised a large hand assuagingly. He explained. "He was not Muslim, ikhwans. He was a munafiq. I had begun receiving reports from my sources over here in America that he was a fraud and was only Muslim in my presence, and that it was all an act for me to supply the heroin. I properly investigated. It was true. I was infuriated. I summoned him over to Arabia and beheaded him myself in the name of Allah."

All these years, Caesar knew that the man before him in all his gentleness was cold. Ali looked at him in admiration, and Jabbar thought that a book could never be judged by its cover, although he knew that Al-Salam had to be ruthless for a man in his position.

For a fleeting moment, Caesar wondered what other dark secrets the man held.

"This was the meeting I was coming from when I discovered you. Marcellus and Jacob made it seem as if it was a meeting of war and peace, as if they were thinking along the lines of retaliation. But they didn't want a war with me, they just wanted me to continue supplying them. In which I wouldn't. Caucasian Americans are such treacherously, disloyal people with ulterior motives. I just told them I'd think about it, in which I did to brush them off. Then I found you."

Caesar hadn't known any of this.

"So, this makes the second time that those infidels transgressed the bounds and it's their last, ikhwan," Al-Salam looked around the table. His dark, soft eyes hardened.

Sad as it was, Caesar couldn't help but be in awe of Marcellus' ambition. So, this was the other part of the story. It explained the Seven's savagery. They were still harboring old feelings from the past. Al-Salam had murdered one of theirs, and they had tried to murder one of his. Caesar thanked Allah for the mercy of sparing he and his son's life.

"So, do you have any creative ideas how you want to proceed in the matter?" Al-Salam asked Caesar as he finished the remnants of his food.

Ali and Jabbar continued to listen as Al-Salam and Caesar connected the past 30 years with the present-day.

"Yeah, I was thinking that it would be best if we called a meeting at the ranch out in Montana as if we've had a change of heart on behalf of the operation. With you being in the states I think they'll go for it. They don't have any reason to suspect foul play. I think their arrogance and greed will kill them. Literally, shaykh," Caesar replied.

"That sounds like a good plan. But what if it doesn't work?"

Caesars eyes lowered malignantly. "Then we'll have no choice but to pick them off in the field.

Al-Salam figured that this would be his answer.

"I think we should contact Marcellus today. You speak with him, set up the meeting arrangement, and we'll fly out to the ranch in the morning. All in favor?" Caesar asked around the table.

Everyone agreed.

After all the food had been devoured, Caesar cleared the table and they all headed to the prayer room in the house where Al-Salam led them in congregation of their afternoon prayer.

###

Houston, Texas

Later That Evening

"Darling, the phones for you!" Trisha called out from the kitchen to her husband that had locked himself in his home-study as usual.

"I got it!" Marcellus yelled after picking up the phone on his clustered desk. "Hey, who's this?"

"An old associate," came the reply.

Marcellous thought for a moment, then recognition of the foreign accent dawned on him. "Al-Salam?"

"The one and only."

"Where are you?"

"I'm in the States. I came back for round three in the field of our old enterprise."

Marcellus pondered this. "What about Sulayman?"

"He's in agreement. Things haven't been going well with business for him since the unfortunate situation with his son. The accusation was bad for business. You know how it is. Especially in American industries. Nobody want to be involved with alleged Muslim murderers."

"Yeah, you're right, big man. So, how's things with him? He has the country on fire with the twenty million in reward money. Is it producing any luck?"

"No, Marcellus, it isn't," Al-Salam feigned dismay.

"I'm sorry to hear that. But when would you like to get together?"

"Whenever you're free."

"Let me check my calendar real quick to see a time we could possibly get together with the other members," Marcellus flipped through his book of pl6an and dates. "How does the eleventh sounds?"

The 11th fell on a Friday. "Insha'Allah. It'll be at our usual rendezvous out in Montana."

"Okay. I'll call up the others and see if they can make the arrangement. I know they'll be glad to hear this. Welcome back on board."

"Alhamdulilah," Al-Salam replied, his deceit concealed.

"See you then, big man," Marcellus ended the call and sat back in his chair. He kind of figured that they would have a change of heart somewhere down the line. It was unfortunate that they had to experience such tragedy just to get them to realize this. They were wasting their time with the reward because there was no one to come forward. The desert monkey and the niggers were such dumb people. The white man deserved supremacy over the world! He picked up the phone again and began contacting his associates.

Charleston, South Carolina

"Friday. October eleventh," Al-Salam conveyed after he got off the phone with Marcellus.

"Perfect," Caesar stated.

It was around 6 o'clock. They all sat inside the living room going over the details of how they'd execute The s Seven.

"Well, we know that all of them will be accompanied by at least two bodyguards each, so we're looking at approximately twenty-one men," Ali stated. "Since you two are the primary focus," Ali referred to Al-Salam and Caesar, "once everyone enter the living room, and you two depart to the den to speak with The Seven, I'll enter from the front, Jabbar from the back. We'll disarm the security detail and sound off a signal for you and Al-Salam to draw down on the senators. Escort them back out front, one of you collect the weapons, and we begin the execution."

An extremely vivid vision of this idea appeared in Caesar's mind as he thought about the magnitude of the spilled blood of 21 men. The interior of his living room was going to be destroyed with blood and brain fragments. He had killed a few men in the past, but it wasn't in comparison of gunning down 21 men down execution style at point blank range.

"And listen, Ali. I know how you think. Just remember that we are not gangsters, we're Muslims. This is not a movie," Al-Salam grinned. "No more feeding victims to animals."

"Okay, shaykh," Ali replied respectfully. He was just thinking along the lines. There had been a time about 15 years ago when Ali had used crocodiles as a means of terror and murder on a group of 4 low-level thugs that had attempted to extort him. He had duct taped and tied each of them up and recklessly drove all the way from Myrtle Beach, South Carolina across the country to Montana just to accomplish this feat!

"We mustn't exceed the bounds of retaliation that Allah has set forth in his Kitab. We'll execute them as quick as possible and be done with it.

"Sulayman, do you still have the old log grinder?" Al-Salam inquired.

“Nam,” Caesar confirmed.

“Good. It’s how we’ll dispose of the bodies, Insha’Allah.”

Jabbar’s phone rang. He looked at the display then silenced the call. It was no one important.

They machinated the execution. Refining it, making sure their plan was tight in precision. And after the plotting, they conversed about Don and the inner lives of one another until it was time for them to fly out to the ranch the following morning.

Chapter Thirty-Eight

Orangeburg, South Carolina
Palmetto Correctional Institution
October 9, 2014 - Wednesday

Don headed up the walkway with Captain Holmes en route to the warden's office. He didn't know the reason but figured it was behind the reward and potential threat to him because of his celebrity. The captain had said he didn't know what the warden wanted with him. Don believed him because he knew if he had an idea, he would have told him. The captain was still oblivious to the fact that he was behind the 50 thousand-dollar offer. But Don had seen how down to earth he was through his interaction with the inmates.

It was mid-afternoon. They got to Operations where the warden and major awaited him in the wardens office. The warden told the captain to excuse himself. Captain Holmes closed the door respectful and left.

"Good morning, Mr. McFadden," Warden Prince spoke from behind his desk. "Have a seat."

Don returned formalities and seated himself.

"Mr. McFadden, I know you're thinking this pertains to your status, but it doesn't this time. Someone's been calling Head Quarters in Columbia making reports about you and one of my officers and this is not the first time. I'm not saying it's true, but I must follow protocol. Your status is a very serious factor because I think it'll be easy for you to persuade anyone of my employee's you chose to, because through you, they won't need this job. Hell, I wouldn't need mine if there was something you and I could work out. But that's neither here nor there," Warden Prince looked at Don with a bit of a smile as he rocked his chair back and forth. "Now, the question at hand is, are there any relations between you and Lieutenant Rose?"

Don didn't flinch, his expression austere. "No, there isn't."

"So, she wasn't inside your cell Monday morning?"

"No, she wasn't. I wouldn't mind, though. She's a beautiful woman. But unfortunately, she wasn't." Damn! Someone was hating hard! Foxy again?

For some reason, Major Wigfall had begun to think otherwise of Canary's dealing with Don. Not only had someone called Head Quarters, Foxy had also reported this along with other reliable informants. She didn't really care though, because she knew that if Canary was indeed dealing with him, it wasn't to the extent of smuggling drugs. She didn't need to indulge in such things. She didn't blame either of them. He was very much so worth the gamble. But they still had a job to do. Everybody wasn't fortunate to be rich.

Warden Prince gazed at Don trying to read his expression as he stroked his chin with his index finger and thumb. A sliver of jealousy swam through him because Canary never gave him the time of the day. "Well, Mr. McFadden, I hate to do this but to alleviate any further accusations against you and my officer, I'm going to put you on an emergency transfer in the next few hours to a different institution. It was nice meeting you, Mr. McFadden. Good Luck." Warden Prince concluded the meeting and the major stood to intercept Don.

"Come along, Mr. McFadden," Major Wigfall said.

Don couldn't believe what had just happened! They were shipping him. "Where am I headed?"

"To the holding cell," Major Wigfall replied. "We'll call the dorm to have your property packed while the warden find placement for you." Major Wigfall escorted him to one of the holding cells and locked him inside.

Don sat inside the holding cell in disbelief. He knew that Foxy was the cause of this and it made him wish he had broken his face! He never had the urge to kill anyone. But at the moment, he wanted to murder that dick sucking faggot! He paced about the holding cell trying to calm his nerves. He hadn't even had a chance to say goodbye to Yahseen or his other comrades. The crazy thing about it all was if he had never been blessed with Canary, by way of Tay that led to John's secret, Foxy would have thrown a monkey wrench in the plot of his escape.

He sat down and began to dhiker. There was no need to blow a vessel. He had no control over the situation. He thought about Canary and lowered his head. She would be dismayed when she found out. He laid back on the wooden bench and relaxed his eyes. The only thing that assuaged his trepidation was the thought of October 21st. It was right around the corner.

Insha'Allah, he thought inwardly and waited on them to come get him to take him where he would begin another chapter of his life. Insha'Allah his last: The epilogue.

"What the fuck?" Canary's eyes asked Yahseen questioningly as she stood outside their room door with Raysor and Granada while Ricardo packed Don's property.

The call had come from the major to have his things packed and brought to Operations. Although she couldn't put her finger on it, she knew that Foxy was the cause. So bad she wanted to find him and go whip his ass! But she maintained her fortitude. Her and Yahseen continued to glance at one another skeptically. They'd talk later.

She saw Foxy earlier. He had looked at her audaciously as if he was challenging her. Neither of them spoke. It was cool though, because after she got Don's property together and talked to Yahseen, she was heading straight upfront and resigning on the spot. "Fuck Foxy and this fucking piece of shit job!" she fumed inwardly.

Yahseen and Chess couldn't believe what had happened. "Man bruh, I bet any money that punk was behind this shit!" Yahseen told Chess. "What makes it so bad is if things hadn't turned over in Don's favor with his case it would have fucked up their plans." Yahseen briefly explained what Chess never knew about Don, Lieutenant Rose, and the escape plot.

"Damn, that's deep," Chess said. He was shocked. He didn't know the little homie had all those big things going on.

"Yeah. But I'll get back with you. Let me go holler at Rose real quick. You already know what time it is when we get in touch with lil' bro and get confirmation that that fucking punk orchestrated this shit."

"That ain't even a question, G. You already know."

Yahseen departed Chess' room and headed to the lieutenants

office.

"What's up, empress?" he said as he closed the door behind him. Canary had told Granada to step out. "I think Foxy did something else, but I'm not sure." Canary looked at Yahseen with doleful eyes of a doe.

"Yeah, I've been thinking the same thing."

"I'm about to go up front and quit," she said. "I'm tired of all this stuff anyway. I'll contact his father and let him know what happened. And if I find out what actually happened before you, I'll contact you and let you know what's what. Give me your number."

Yahseen gave her the number. He understood her position. She was in love with his little brother and didn't see the need in hanging around anymore since he was no longer around. "Okay, empress," he responded somberly. "You take care of yourself. You'll be alright, Insha'Allah."

"You, too. It was nice meeting you, James Wright III. Stay focus and keep up the good work and never stop trying. There's bright things ahead of you," she told him.

"Insha'Allah. Just call me." He stood to leave.

She stood also. It was all over for her. "Okay."

Yahseen departed the office and headed back on the wing. He saw Foxy but feigned as if he wasn't even studying him. But little did he know, he had one foot inside his coffin.

###

Greenville, South Carolina

Carolina Wren Correctional Institution

Don found himself all the way in the upstate region of Greenville county in some hick town of woods and farm animals. So, country the area, the air smelled of the pungent order of cattle manure. The facility was named after the states bird: The Carolina Wren.

He had heard about the facility through the grapevine. It had a disreputable reputation for its racism as it was ran predominantly by confederate white folks with Jim Crow ways. The facility was an abomination as it was flooded with snitches and homosexual thugs of all kinds. It was reported to be very minute illegal activity going on at the facility. The red-neck administration made sure to keep it that way.

The institution possessed small, vault like dorms that housed 96 inmates on each wing. Two gun towers was at the North and South points of the facility with trigger-happy white boys itching to pop a cap in an intractable negro. The facility was of the old – the first built in the state.

As Don had headed to the dorm across the deserted yard, he couldn't help but notice the difference in it and the other places he'd been. Everything was in order and freshly painted. And the inmates he did see was properly shaved, shirts tucked in pants, ID's properly worn on shirt collars.... Whatever strategy the beholders was employing at Carolina Wren was surely effective because by the looks of things, they had it down! This was the facility no prisoner wanted to be. But it was all cool with him. It was under two weeks before he'd be free of all the misery and confusion.

The officers had tried engaging him and his celebrity, but he remained aloof and headed to his cell with his property. When he got to the cell, he saw that it was clean. Not Yahseen clean – but clean, nevertheless. Islamic literature laid about the extremely small cell. The cell was almost half the size of Palmetto's. A Quran sat on the pillow of the top bunk. The bottom bunk was empty. A prayer rug was also folded across the bed rail and Don concluded that a Muslim occupied the cell. This pleased him.

He began unpacking his things as a caucasian inmate with red hair entered the room. He appeared to be about the same height as him, about 180-190 in weight. Don glimpsed a tattoo on his right forearm that read "IRISH PRIDE" and concluded that he was Irish. Then he glimpsed a bit of Arabic on his left arm.

"As salamu alaykum, akhi. I'm Baseer."

Don returned the greeting with a smile. He didn't ask how the brother knew he was Muslim because the entire nation knew him.

"I'm Furqān."

"Well, I'm going to give you time to get your things in order. I just came by to greet you and let you know that I was your roommate," Baseer replied.

"Alhamdulilah," Don smiled and shook his hand.

By the time Don had finished unpacking his things, it was count time and Baseer had returned. They conversed throughout the count while Don stored away his things in the little footlocker. He had placed most of his things under the bunk because the locker was too small.

Baseer was 23 years old. He grew up around an area called Cherrydale in Greenville. His conversation was intelligent, and he was quite knowledgeable in the Deen for his age with only a few years as a Muslim. He didn't have much time left in prison.

Don briefly explained how he ended up where he now was,

and when the count cleared, he left Baseer inside the cell hooking up his TV for him while he headed to the phones to call his father.

“Canary already informed me, Furqān,” Caesar replied after Don told him he’d been transferred a few hours ago. “She’s setting up her phone now so you can call her. Her and Yahseen is waiting to hear from you.”

“Well, you know the process takes a minute to become active so tell her that someone called Head Quarters and told them that she and I had relations and that she had been in my room Monday. I think that punk Foxy did it. I know the fatawah on conjecture, but in this instance, he’s the prime suspect.”

“Oh yeah, she quit after you left,” Caesar told him.

“Seriously?”

“Seriously. She loves you boy.”

“Okay, that’s what’s up. Tell her I said I love her when you contact her. And tell Yahseen I said hold it down and stay up.”

“I’m tayyib, abu. Alhamdulillah. I have a decent roommate. He’s loquacious, but he’s cool. He’s Muslim.”

“Alhamdulilah. Just be patient, lil’ man. It’s almost over. But the brothers wanna talk to you.”

“Okay.” Don spoke with Al-Salam for the remainder of the call, then called again after the call had ended to speak with Ali and Jabbar.

After conversing with them, he allowed them to get back to whatever esoteric business they were up to. He looked around the boxed in unit, and everywhere he looked, he looked into the eyes of an observing inmate. He laughed inwardly and headed back to this cell, thinking about Canary and how she had quit after they shipped him. He had really found an undiscovered gold deposit. She was loyal. The thought alone brought him tranquility.

###

Orangeburg, South Carolina

Later That Night

It was around 8' o'clock and Canary had just gotten off the phone with Danyell and Tay, informing them of all that had transpired. They couldn't believe that she had quit. Hell, she couldn't believe that she had the courage to quit! Now, she was jobless. She sat in the quietude of her living room lost in thought, wondering if she had been making sound decision lately. She found herself wondering if Don would even entertain her when he was released. Now, she wondered if he just had an incarcerated fantasy now that she was no longer a part of that world. The disconnection seemed to make her feel as if meeting him had only been a dream. And, he was no longer even at the facility, but farther up state. She had already contacted the phone company to receive collect calls but it wouldn't be active for another 24 hours so she wouldn't be able to hear from him until tomorrow evening. His father had called her back and conveyed his message. It didn't surprise her that his transfer was behind their involvement.

She heard the joyful chatter of women somewhere outside her apartment, then the sound of car doors slamming simultaneously. The vehicle was cranked and its headlights casted a bright glare through the cracks of her blinds as the car backed away, stopped, and moved forward into the night as the light was carried away with it.

Danyell had asked her what she would do about bills, but she didn't know. She needed to go grocery shopping and restock personal cosmetics. She didn't have nothing but a few hundred bucks in the bank, as the little checks she got twice a month only made ends meet from month to month. She stared at the phone wondering if she had just fucked up her life.

Well, if she had, it was too late to turn back now. She might as well ride the wave.

She called Yahseen...

Palmetto Correctional Institution

Yahseen was inside his cell on the phone with one of his homeboys off Remount road in North Charleston discussing exotic weed prices when a beep came though that interrupted the conversation. Normally, he would have ignored the call, but he was expecting Canary's call and it could be her. "Family, let me call you back. I think I'm receiving a call I've been waiting on. He clicked over. "Hello."

"This is Canary, Yahseen."

"Salam, empress. What's up?"

"Furqān's at Carolina Wren. His father contacted me and said that Furqān told him that the warden stated that someone called Head Quarters on us and told them about me being in you guys room," Canary explained. "I told you the last time that the maor told me Foxy was trying to get me thrown, so I know he was behind this, or at least the initial cause of it. And the look he gave me today – I just know he did it, Yahseen."

"Alright, empress. That's what it is. I'll handle it from here."

"What are you going to do?" she asked. "Don't get yourself in trouble. You have to much at stake."

"Just ease your mind and relax. If you need any money for the meantime, I'm sure that the lil' bro got you. But don't be no stranger. Call me, sis'. You're family now," he assured her.

This made her spirit soar for some reason even though she would never ask him nor Don for anything. She didn't want to give off any impression that she was attracted to any of their financial position. She would lean on Danyell or Tay first. "Okay," she responded for the sake of gratitude.

"But let me go. Insha'Allah, we'll keep in touch. Salam." Yahseen ended the call and told Sulayman, Chess, and Success – who was present around the room on phones – what Canary had just told him. Rumor had already began spreading just that quick around the facility about Don and Canary's relations. He knew that it was only one way that it had, because no one knew anything outside of their circle save Foxy. Canary had made an amateur mistake in confiding in him.

"Man big bruh, let me slay that motherfucker!" Success fumed. Officer Carter was on the other end of the phone. She had surprised him by calling for the first time.

"Just lay and be easy lil' bro until we think this through. There's no time for slip ups. And there's no need to rush. It'll get handled, Insha'Allah. Now talk to lil' mama and be cool." In Yahseen's mind a plan had already began formulating. He went back to business.

Chapter Thirty-Nine

Greenville, South Carolina
Carolina Wren Correctional Institution
October 10, 2014 - Thursday

"Why do you sound so blue when you're golden, baby?" Don asked Canary.

She smiled at his charm as she cuddled beneath quilt on the sofa in her Livingroom.

It was after 5 pm and Don had been calling her repeatedly in a fiendish yearn to hear her voice. The only problem he really had with the new facility was the phones was located on an open wall in front of the dorm where everyone looked directly in his mouth. He found this irritating. And, the phones adjacent to the right and left of him was always occupied. He had never seen anyone on an institutional phone at Palmetto nor Ogeechee! Everyone had smart phones!

"I'm scared," she told him. Don seated himself on the cold concrete floor beneath the phone he used and looked at the floor in attempt of blocking out his surroundings. Instinctively, he knew what her fears was. "You're worried about how you're going to maintain and stay afloat, aren't you?"

She sighed, "Yes."

"I should be offended but I'm not. I understand. We did meet under some unusual circumstances. But however, you need not worry about the small things. I'm going to take care of you and us for the rest of our lives. You don't have to work anymore if you don't want to. Insha'Allah I got you, boo. I promise."

This warmed her and she cried silently. But she would work. She wanted to be a lawyer, and she would. She'd tell him later.

Unaware of her silent cries of joy, he continued. "Last night I was thinking that you could move to Charleston and stay in the beach house I grew up in if you like. Cecelia's there. And she's been wanting to meet you. I think you'll like her. The both of you have a lot in common. She's vacationing now until all of whatever my father have going on is over with. The house is huge. I know she's lonely. Y'all can keep each other company and do girly things. And I have a Black card inside a safe in the house you can have."

A black card! Wasn't those things unlimited? She couldn't believe what her life was transforming into. "What about my apartment?"

"Abandon it," he laughed, but was serious.

"Abandon it?"

"Sure. Take your most prized possessions and leave. You can donate everything else to charity. You don't need it."

"Are you serious?"

"Yes, Golden, I'm serious. So, are you accepting my offer?"

"Yes,"

"And would you marry me under Islamic law when I come home?"

"Yes," her cries became audible.

"I wanted to wait to propose to you, but I sensed your trepidation and just wanted to let you know that this is all real. You are my Inamorata, Golden."

"Okay. So when do you think I should leave?" she asked.

"Now if you want. Get your things together. I'll call Cecelia and let her know what's what. Get something to write down her number. You'll need it so she can direct you to the house along the way."

"Okay," she got up to retrieve pen and paper.

He could tell that this excited her. He heard the euphoria in her voice. This made him happy. "I love you, mommy," he smiled.

"I love you too, daddy," she returned.

His heart ached and swelled so great, he thought it would burst!

She retrieved the utensils, and he gave her the number.

"I'm going to call her when this call ends, so go ahead and start gather your things. We'll send your landlord a check until you figure out what you want to do with the rest of your things."

They spoke about her relocation until the phone hung up and Don stood and stretched just as Baseer called the adhan. He headed to the cell to perform ablution, fetched his prayer rug, and headed upstairs to pray with Baseer and the other 3 brothers on their wing. Outside of them, he wasn't pressed to meet any new friends. Baseer would be his last, newfound comrade until it was time for him to leave, Insha'Allah. He'd call Cecelia after his prayers.

###

Orangeburg, South Carolina

"Clam down girl, dang!" Tay told Canary. "You're rambling We can't understand nothing you're saying."

Canary had called Tay and Danyell after she got off the phone with Don. She could barely contain her excitement. "I'm sorry, I'm just so happy. I'm moving to Charleston," she said after calming a bit.

"Are you serious!?"

"When?"

All were simultaneous replies from Danyell and Tay.

"As soon as I get through packing what I'm going to take tonight."

"Where will you stay?" Danyell inquired.

Canary explained the details of the situation to them. "Isn't this great?"

"It sure the hell is bitch. And you need to hurry and get the Black card because I want this twelve-thousand-dollar mink coat I saw online!" Tay stated.

They laughed.

"Oooh, I'm so happy for you, girl," Danyell said congenially. "You deserve this and so much more!"

"Thank you guys for supporting me through all of this. I love y'all!"

"We love you too, girl," Tay returned warmly.

"I've been thinking about relocating my practice back home," Danyell stated.

"Oohh, that'll be great," Canary replied.

They chatted for about 30 minutes longer about Don, John, and all that possibly lie ahead in their lives.

It was now 10:30 pm. She had packed all she intended to keep and loaded them in the back seat and trunk of her car. After speaking with Don once more before he was locked down for the night since he didn't have a cellphone, she kissed her apartment and her neighborhood good-bye, called Cecelia, and headed to Charleston where her new life awaited her.

Charleston, South Carolina

An hour and a half later, Canary had finally found the two-story beach house in all its beauty amongst the other beautiful homes that lined the shore. She knew that the shore-front houses was the most expensive. She knew that his father had spent a pretty penny for this bad boy. The house sat so high off the ground she could have driven her car beneath it to the sand of the beach behind it.

It was a little after 12 am when she stepped from her car after parking next to some foreign looking sports car. She realized after a moment that it was the Lamborghini Don had told her about. She eyed the sleek machine in awe as the wet appearance of it shone beneath the moon and street lights.

Cecelia stepped onto the porch and greeted her with a very warm, late night welcome.

Canary grabbed her bag from the passenger seat after deciding to fetch the rest tomorrow. She inhaled the cool, salty air of the beach.

"You finally made it, huh?" Cecelia's smile lit the night. "Girl, I thought I would never find this place, "Canary replied as she headed towards the steps and climbed them to the entrance high above where Cecelia awaited her.

When she got to the top of the porch, she sat down her bag and hugged Cecelia warmly. They were two women that had found two men through the divine scheme of God's paradoxes. Indeed, they had much in common.

"Come on… Grab your bag and let me show you around."

The start of a new beginning.

Chapter Forty

Fort Lauderdale, Florida

October 11, 2014 - Frriday

The senators meandered up the long dirt road to Caesars ranch in a convoy of three rented Suburbans that had been rented by men of their security detail with fraudulent ID's. They didn't need their unofficial excursions documented to be traced back to them. They had slipped away from inquiring minds surreptitiously. Each of their security men knew of the corruption they were involved in and was paid handsomely for their roles.

It was around 7:30 pm. The sun had already set, the Fall air cool in the high mountain range.

Marcellus ended the call on his cell phone after notifying Caesar of their arrival. As they ascended the dilapidated dirt road, the trucks wobbled on their suspensions. Marcellus' truck led the convoy. When they neared the open field where the house sat in all its sexiness of logwood and glass, Marcellus couldn't help but notice how good the nigger Muslim had done for himself. He watched him and Al-Salam from behind the tinted windows. They stood outside the house with their usual intense expressions of men of business.

The trucks were parked one behind the other and the senators, along with their men, poured from both sides of the vehicles.

"How was the trip?" Caesar asked as the body of men approached them.

"The same as all of them, Sulayman. Boring!" Marcellus answered.

They all laughed.

The group approached, and fake smiles and handshakes was delivered from both sides.

"One day at a time Marcellus. You know me," Al-Salam replied.

"This place never seems to disappoint me," Senator Lindsay MacArthur of New York stated. "I need to buy one of these things, huh?" he stated to anyone willing to take on the answer, his accent thick. He was a stone-cold Yankee. One of his men entertained him.

They all entered the living room of the house. Caesar pointed out the refreshments they had sat out for the security detail while they held the meeting inside the den with the senators.

"You guys stay out here while we go talk to these guys," Jacob Marshall told the detail. "If we scream, come with guns blazing," he humored.

Again, fake laughter.

They left the detail behind in the living room in all their muscled brolicness with their concealed. 45's, and headed to the den. Only five of the senators was present. Caesar wondered about the whereabouts of Timothy Bronze of Florida and Randolf Carenstead of Maryland. Present was Johnathan Titus Aiken of California, Jacob Marshall of Louisiana, Michael John Breen of Illinois, Lindsay McArthur of New York, and Marcellus Rothenstein of Texas.

When they reached the den, they seated themselves on a custom-made couch that lined the wall in an L-shape. Caesar and Al-Salam sat in separate recliners in the middle of the room after facing the chairs in the direction of the senators. He wondered if the two missing senators was a strategic move of war. "Where's Timothy and Randolf?" he inquired as he sat down.

Senator Jacob Marshall of Louisiana answered the question. "Timothy's sick with the flu, and Randolph is tied up in Washington. He'll be back tonight. The both of them send their greetings and sentiments to you and Don."

Caesar nodded.

"Well, to get down to business..." Marcellus commenced.

"I'm moving now, akhi. You read me?" Ali whispered through the head-set he wore.

"Allahu Akbar," Jabbar confirmed.

Ali, armed with an AK-47 assault rifle and two Glock. 40's in shoulder holsters beneath his arms, slipped inside the house through the front door like a phantom as the group of lax security men enjoyed the refreshments.

One of them spotted Ali and reached for his weapon–

CRACK!

Ali squeezed the trigger of the assault rifle and blew the

brains of the man that spotted him all over the man next to him.

The deafening crack startled everyone and before they could react, Jabbar materialized from the rear with his rifle drawn. Him and Ali overwhelmed the detail with the deadly weapons they drew down on them.

Ali ordered them to slowly raise their hands and ordered them to line up against the wall side by side and remove their weapons one by one.

They complied.

When the loud crack of the rifle reverberated through the confines of the house, the senators jumped up in bewilderment! But both Caesar and Al-Salam drew. 45 semi-automatic handguns.

“Remain calm,” Caesar replied with calm lethalness. “Each of you assholes line up and place both of your hands on the shoulders of the man in front of you and head back out front. All of you know what this pertains to.”

“Come on, Su-“

The pistol recoiled in Al-Salam’s hand and dejected a spent shell casing as he blew out the brains of Jacob Marshall, second in command of The Seven.

As Caesar noticed the swift ease of the kill, he noticed that brain and bone fragments had spewn from the opposite side of Jacobs head on his couch. “Not another word. Now move!”

There was no more attempts at bargaining. The remaining four senators headed to the living room trembling in fear of an unknown fate as they left the body of their slain fellow man on the couch in the den.

When they reached the living room, Caesar and Al-Salam saw that Ali and Jabbar had everything under control. They lined the senators next to their security men and Caesar collected the discarded guns.

Al-Salam stood next to Ali and Jabbar covering the group of kafirs. They had sat down the powerful rifles and removed the Glocks they carried from their holsters. Caesar joined them after moving the seized weapons of the enemy far from reach. Side by side, they looked at the remaining 13 men lined along the wall, guns at the ready.

Al-Salam spoke to the pathetic kafirs before them. Some of them had went pallid, whimpering in the face of death. And others looked on pleadingly for mercy as the body of one of the security men lay between them. His head had exploded like a melon form the powerful round of the rife. "There's nothing to explain. You know your transgressions. ALLAHU'AKBAR!" Al-Salam asseverated, and the bloody execution began over screams that was muffled by the deafening blasts of the weapons.

Some of the victims attempted futile escape at the last minute to no avail. Head shots to the back of their skulls caused them to know life no more; Hell, their final abode.

After each man had been executed, the firing ceased. The air was filled with the acrid stench of gun powder and smoke from the blazing hot barrels. Caesar looked around at all the bodies, blood, and gore. "Alhamdulillah!" he breathed. He would have to have the entire living room remodeled. It was ruined! "You brother's cool?" He looked from the bodies to his brothers who looked around at the carnage as he did, weapons dangling at their sides.

"Nam," they all confirmed simultaneously.

"Allahu'Akbar!" Ali breathed, his adrenaline a raging sea

from the kills.

"Okay," Al-Salam started. "Let's get rid of these bodies and clean up this mess. There's still more work to be done. There's two remaining. They have to be hit immediately. Any suggestions?" The massacre had not caused him to lose focus.

"I have an idea, shaykh," Jabbar offered.

"Good," Al-Salam stated, "We'll discuss it after we handle this. And get rid of those vehicles."

They began removing the bodies from the house and loaded them in the SUV's. They drove them to a deep wooded location where the gritty work began of feeding the cadavers through the log grinder. Caesars hogs would eat the shredded carnage. All traces of the senators and their detail would be obliterated and returned to the essence of the earth as if they had never existed.

Fort Lauderdale, Florida

October 13, 2014 -Sunday Night

Jabbar came from beneath the murky water of the immense lake behind Senator Timothy Breen's lake house cladded in a wet suit, snorkel gear, and flippers. In a waterproof pouch strapped around his abdomen, was the necessary tools to accomplish his mission.

It was after 12 am and all was silent. He had swam approximately a mile and a half across the distance of the lake to the senators house. It was the only way he could get on the premises undetected. He had been a star swimmer in high school, but the skill had been useless until now. He climbed up on the landing and quickly removed the flippers. He canvassed the property. A beautiful speed boat was docked near-by. The house sat 40 yards away from the lake. The immense shadow it casted made it easy for him to close the distance covertly. He slithered toward the back deck of the house on his belly.

An owl hooted in the distance.

About 5 minutes later he found himself at the back door of the house. He knew an alarm was installed. This didn't matter, though. He would be in and out in no time. The way he arrived, people only saw in movies and read in books. They wouldn't expect anyone to come as he had. Well – this wasn't a movie nor book – it was real life.

He opened the pouch and extracted the glass cutter and cut a circle hole in the glass near the lock. The suction cup on the cutter kept the piece he had cut out from falling to the floor and shattering. He unlocked the sliding door and entered the dark den of the house.

After replacing the cutter back in the pouch, he removed a revolver with a silencer attached and darted through the house on tip toes, familiar with its inner details from past visits. He knew that if he made the tiniest mistake, he would trip the silent alarm. He moved quickly but silently.

He got to the bedroom where the senator slept with his wife soundly. Soft snores drifted through the large space of the room.

Stealthily, he approached the bed and shot both of them in their head twice at point blank range and fled the house the same way he came.

He slipped back into his flippers and slipped back into the murky water to make his escape on the other side of the lake where Ali awaited him.

Chapter Forty-One

Greenville, South Carolina

Monday morning was pandemonium! Washington, and every media outlet around the nation was in an uproar about the missing srnators and their security detail. Their whereabouts unknown. And on top of this, they were talking about a double murder at the lake house of Senator Timothy Breen and his wife in Fort Lauderdale, Florida that happened sometime last night. He and his wife had been shot dead in their sleep by an unknown assailant. How he got on the property, unknown at the moment and an enigma to investigators because one had reported seeing or hearing any boats.

Don and Baseer sat in their room watching the shocking news news break. He wondered if his father was the man behind it all.

"Damn akh, that's some real life, cold, gangster shit, isn't it?" Baseer said as he looked at the TV from the top bunk.

It was a little after 8 am. They were still relaxing. Don was too stunned to respond so he nodded and got up. He needed to make a few calls.

"Salam, Furqān. What's up?" Caesar answered in high spirit.

Don shook his head in amazement. "Are you okay, abu?"

"Yes, I'm fine," Caesar chuckled warmly. "Why'd you ask?"

"I saw the – "

"Yeah, yeah," Caesar interjected because their call was being monitored. "Just be easy Furqān until you come home, and trust in Allah. I'm tied up with some things so be easy, lil' man."

"Okay, abu." Now Don knew what his father was up to. He was assassinating The Seven. A chill ran through him at the thought.

"I see you got Canary at the house."

"Yeah," Don smiled.

"Listen, Furqān – Canary will let you know when I'm back at the house. For now, let me and the brothers get things right and Insha'Allah, we'll do some catching up in the near future."

"Okay, abu. I love you."

"You already know how we rock, boy. Salam."

"Salam." Don ended the call and stood to the phone with the receiver still in his hand as he looked towards the TVs on the rock. A crowd of inmates – along with the wing officer – stood watching the news break. He started to call Canary but decided against it. He knew that she was very inquisitive as she had the discernment of one of the best lawyers in existence and wouldn't talk reckless over the phone, but he didn't want to chance it. Everyone was liable to slip in the heat of the moment just as he almost had. She would know that the politicians at hand was The

Seven. Right now though, he needed time to register the potential body count. Out 7 Senators, 6 had been taken out of rotation. This meant that there was one more remaining and if he popped up missing or dead, Don would know for sure that his father and brothers had went on a killing spree.

17 was possibly dead in total, so far, with one more to go. "Subhan'allah!" Don said inwardly as he headed back to the room Baseer had depicted "The Bat Cave".

"Akh, this shit is crazy. It's on every damn channel I flip through," Baseer said as he stood in front of the TV.

Baltimore, Maryland

12 o'clock That Afternoon

Senator Randolph Carenstead had just departed a restaurant in downtown, Baltimore where he lunched with his wife before he departed with his two security men back to his call of duty. He was a bit shaken by the news reports of his missing comrades along with the sudden assassination of Timothy and his wife. He knew that Sulayman was behind the hits because they had just met with him and the desert monkey. He was in limbo about what he should do, as exposing this would expose his involvement. He watched the continuing news reports on CNN from the back seat of his bulletproof Suburban as they pulled to a stop light. Leisurely, he looked out the darkly tinted windows of the truck just as a motorbike with a rider in all black leather gear from boots to helmet pulled up beside the truck. He paid the rider no mind until a another like rider pulled up on the driver's side and looked towards the vehicle. It all dawned on him just as the riders reached in their leather jackets and aimed machine guns harnessed to their shoulders at the truck.

Before the security men could react, a hail of armor piercing projectiles ripped through the windows of the truck killing all three occupants of the vehicle instantly.

The engines of the bikes screamed out in defiance as the riders fled the scene taking different routes.

Greenville, South Carolina

Carolina Wren correctional institution

Another breaking report flashed across Don's TV hours later as another senator had just been gunned down in the middle of the city of Baltimore in broad day light, along with two of his security men. Two mask riders pulled up on both sides of the SUV at a stop light and discharged machine gun fire containing armor piercing projectiles into the vehicle killing the three occupants instantly.

Don looked at the TV in astonishment!

Baseer jumped up as if the news had set his ass on fire and giving him an inexplicable burst of energy!

A card had been left at the scene of the crime inscripted: "ALLAHU'AKBAR!" the reporter had said and had quickly attributed the assassination to Muslims and terrorism.

Baseer was so excited, Don had to tell him to relax. With this report, his suspicions was confirmed. His father had effectively eliminative The Seven.

Red Top, South Carolina

Ogeechee Correctional Institution

Scramble and Cam sat inside their cell watching the shocking news break. Scramble had already been informed by Chess on behalf of what had happened to Don.

Don had told him about the crooked senators that had framed him. Scramble didn't know for a fact if Don's pop's was behind all of the sudden drama around the country. But if he had to bet, he'd bet that he was. "Boy, lil' bruh, your pops is one ruthless motherfucker!" Scramble whispered to himself as he nodded his head in approval of all the loyalty and love involved. He grinned wickedly.

Orangeburg, South Carolina

Palmetto Correctional Institution

The entire country was probably holding its breath in panic expecting planes to crash into buildings with suicide bombers running inside major establishments asseverating "Allahu Akbar!"

The news was ubiquitous, indeed. Nothing had happened on a level like this since 9/11!

Yahseen sat back inside his empty cell by himself as he watched the president speak on the sadness of the situation asking all citizens of the United States to support the cause of their senators and help bring forth the criminals responsible. He went on to say that he wished the media hadn't leaked the cards the assailants left behind because it could have very well been done to make it appear as if the Muslims was responsible. He apologized to the Muslim community across the nation and abroad.

Yahseen looked at the TV with profile respect for Don's father and brothers. They had rode for him like none other. He wished that he had a father like Caesar in his corner.

But it didn't take a rocket scientist to figure out that Caesar was responsible because he knew the intricate details of the situation that most didn't know. He said "Allahu'Akbar!" and offered two supererogatory units of salat asking Allah to protect them.

Charleston, South Carolina

"Girl, can you believe all this mess?" Canary asked Cecelia. She sat on the couch in the living room of the beach house watching the news on a 63-inch plasma TV. She had her theory as to what was occurring but said nothing.

Cecelia just shook her head at the bravado of the man she had fallen in love with. What a man she had found! She knew that just as she knew what was going on, Canary knew also. The silent looks from the TV to one another spoke volumes.

Since Canary had been at the house, her and Cecelia had been having a marvelous time together as they shared some of the same hobbies. Both of them enjoyed reading and the house possessed a library with numerous titles from Lisa Scottoline, James Patterson, John Ghrisam, Zane, Sister Souljah, Nora Roberts, and a slew of other popular novelists. She had even told Cecelia about James Wright III.

They had also been shopping over the weekend when Tay and Danyell came to visit. They liked Cecelia and she liked them.

Canary wondered why Don hadn't called yet. But she wasn't tripping now that she was closer to him. But as she listened to the president speak about the missing senators, their detail's, the double and triple murders, she couldn't help but feel as if she was about to marry into the mob. In a strange way, it all gave her a reassuring feeling of protection and made her feel safe. She looked at Cecilia and smile

Reno, Nevada

Edward Butler had been back home with his parents for the past few weeks after hitting rock bottom. He was trying to get his life back in order and had been getting counseling for his gambling addiction.

He sat on the bed of his childhood room eating a bag of plain potato chips in disbelief of what he was seeing on the news pertaining to the senators. "Good for you fucking prick's!" he spat toward the TV set. I knew that someone would get you bastards sooner or later." This had all relieved him until he heard the report of the cards left behind by the killers. It made him wonder if Sulayman Azeez Mustafah had somehow found out about the frame of the murder.

He set down the bag of chips. He lost the taste for them at the discouraging thought. It was possible that him and his family was next. In a state of paranoia, he got up and peeked out his window.

"Edward, are you talking to yourself, son?"

Edward looked over his shoulder. It was his father. He was aging at 72. So brittle and frail he looked. "No, dad. I was speaking out loud about the news. Have you seen it?"

"Yeah," his father strained. "What a tragedy. Well, I was just looking in on you, kid. See you later."

"Alright dad." Edward continued to look out his window for any signs of strange activity. He didn't even own a gun. Was he overreacting? He didn't think so this time. Something didn't feel right. He was scared. He wanted to go somewhere and hide but he didn't have anywhere to go. If he got his mom and dad killed he would never forgive himself–

Well, after he thought about it, there would be no need for forgiveness because he'd be dead also.

###

Charleston, South Carolina

October 19, 2014 - Friday Night

Several days had passed since the execution of The Seven and victim's of circumstances. Caesar was now back in Charleston with his brothers at his mansion on the Battery. He wasn't ready to see the ladies yet because he needed to compartmentalize things and simmer down. He and Cecelia had been texting one another, so she was assured that he was fine.

They had successfully got things in order at the ranch. He had called a crew to remodel the interior after stripping it down of the gore of blood stained walls, carpeting, and furnishings.

They had arrived in the Carolina's a few hours ago. John had also called him Monday in a frenzied state of panic by what he had witnessed on the news. "Be easy, John. I saw the news. I guess God work in mysterious ways. That's why I worship Him and Him alone. Someone did us a major favor," he had told John. He knew that John didn't believe him, but it didn't matter, he couldn't prove otherwise. There was no way he could be so many places at one time by his lonesome in the eyes of the masses, so screw'em!

Now, he would relax until the big day of the 21st.

Chapter Forty-Two

Columbia, South Carolina
October 21, 2014

Hello, Sulayman," John greeted Caesar as he stepped inside the suite. He had called in sick to live up to his words.

"Good morning, John. you look great." Caesar looked him over. "Your security people are very tight I see. I thought I would have had to strip just to see you," Caesar smiled.

"You know how it is with everything going on. No one's trying to be next," John replied. "And thanks for noticing the difference in my appearance. I guess it's because I laid off the booze." John closed the door. "Do you think now is a good time to contact the president with all that's happening around the country with the senators?"

"Why not?" Caesar asked optimistically.

"I just thought it would look strange."

"Why would it?" Caesar feigned ignorance and innocence.

"It's only your conscious, John. Now couldn't be a better time," he smiled. "I'm just a concerned father concerned about the welfare of my son."

John looked at him quizzically and thought that the man standing before him was good! "Well then, let's do it." he smiled as they headed to the dining table and took seats. He picked up the phone off the table and dispatched the president straight through. The right-of-way of a senator. He would miss this privilege.

Washington, DC

The White House was in a *frenzied* state. Everyone was tense from the recent events thet screamed all the signs of terrorism. They just didn't say so publicly to keep the citizens from resulting to a state of panic.

President O'sella took the call of Senator Brody. "Can't this wait, Senator?" he asked.

"I'm afraid not, Mr. President," John responded. "Some of this pertain to the recent events with our fellow men."

"Ok, I'm listening," President O'sella was African American. He sat back in his chair in the Oval office and listened intently to what the senator was telling him on the other end of the phone. He sat up and furrowed his brows. His eyes sharpened as he listened to the appalling story of corruption. "My God Senator! I think you need to come out to Washington now! We need to discuss this matter personally. I don't think now is a good time for the public to hear about this so let's try to keep a lid on it and handle as much of it as we can discreetly. Especially since these individuals are missing and dead.

"This wouldn't look good for our government. How could the people entrust us when their leaders are affiliated in such things?" he asked, but wasn't looking for an answer. It was more of a statement. "Do you think Mr. Mustafah had anything to do with the disappearance of these officials?"

"I'll be lying if I told you, I did," John answered truthfully. His suspicion was only conjecture. Besides, he didn't give a damn about the status of the government anymore. All of them were crooked. Even the president!

"And this lawyer you said, is from Reno?"

"Yes sir, Mr. President."

"Get out here pronto, Senator. Let me speak to Mr. Mustafah."

Caesar was surprised that the President of the United states wanted to talk to him personally. "Mr. President, how are you, Sir?"

"I'm fine, Mr. Mustafah. I apologize for the unlawful incarceration of your son. I wanted you to hear it from me personally on behalf of our country. When this calls end, I will contact the proper officials in South Carolina and order the immediate release of your son."

Caesar's heart soared! "Alhamdulillah!" He maintained his composure. "Thank you, Mr. President." He handed the phone back to John after the president disconnected the call. The biggest smile in the world plastered his face. "Thanks, John!" He extended a hand.

"Hey, that's what friends are for," John said. He stood and shook Caesar's hand. "Well, now that the cat's out the bag, I need to get some things together and hop on a jet out to the White House. I've been summoned. When I see you again, I'll be in normal, broke citizen," John bounced his brows and smiled.

"When you see a me again John, I'll have twenty-million bucks for you to do whatever you please," Caesar emulated, bouncing his brows with a smile. "You know where to find me when you return pal."

Caesar departed the suite and headed back to his hometown to pick up everyone so they could all drive out to Carolina Wren in Greenville to pick up his son. By the time they got to the facility the president would have already given the order.

Greenville, South Carolina

Carolina Wren Correctional Institution

Don had headed out to the cafeteria to eat lunch with his dorm. Things was so drab and boring around the facility he found himself going to the cafe just for the hell of it.

I was the 21st of October. The day that John was supposed to contact the president. He hadn't even slept last night in his excitement. Last night his father had told him that he was attending a meeting with John this morning to ensure that things got taken care of.

Canary and everyone else was excited for him. He had even spoken to Yahseen, Scramble, and Jamal. Canary had connected them on three-way.

Now, he wanted to call his father and find out what happened, but he was afraid. His hopes was so high he didn't want to risk calling just to receive disappointing news. No one amongst him knew of what he anticipated.

"Are you okay, akhi?" Baseer asked as he walked beside Don

headed to the dorm.

“Yeah. I’m cool, akhi. I’m just ruminating some things, that’s all. I’m fine.”

Baseer didn't believe him. he didn't know what it was, but he could tell that something was on Don's mind. Good or bad, he didn't know. “Akhi, let me share something with you that I find deep. Insha’Allah, it assuages whatever it is that’s troubling you. It’s a very short hadith, but it’s deep.

“Imam Bukhari or Ibn Abbas – may Allah be pleased with them – narrated that the Prophet – Sallallahu alayhi wa salam – said: 'The believer is most like the Date Palm tree,” Baseer said, then explained the hadith to Don from his perspective.

“Akhi, the Date Palm tree is deep to me because if you look at the tree, it stands tall and upright. Strong! When a hurricane or tropical storm hit, it bends with the wind and submits itself in prostration, thereby never breaking; and it stands out in the hottest desert, the driest weather and does not wilt and die but stands out as an oasis amongst barren wastelands producing fruit. What little water it does get, it stores and survives and sustains of the gifts of Allah. While in hurricanes, tall and proud buildings crumble and are broken apart, man-made dreams and fantasies are rolled and bowled over. And the desert, no other tree can survive, they choke and die; they are not thankful for the small bit of water made available; they must have more and more to survive and thrive.

“The storms are the trials and despairs of our life akhi that makes us fall down before our Lord and ask for help, thus when it's all said and done, we snap right back in place unlike the ones who depend on their man-made conveniences to make it through life or refuse to bend and would rather stand defiant against the storms in pride and thus are snapped and carried away with the wind.

"The desert is the time when life is stagnant like there is no progress and we are drying out and there is no sustenance or help in sight.

"Be like the Date Palm. Absorb the help of Allah and use His guidance to produce fruits to strive and thrive and grow while all else choke and die with the harshness and heat of life," he stated as they entered the dorm.

Don was familiar with the hadith but had never looked at it from this perspective. "Shakrun, jazakallah, akh."

"Alhamdulillah. It's short but deep."

They headed on the wing. Don headed to the cell and Baseer headed elsewhere.

Once inside the room, Don tediously flipped through the boring stations as he cogitated the depth of the hadith.

About 30 minutes passed and the door to the cell was pulled open. Don looked to the left of him. A group of officials stood at the door. "Here we go again," he sighed inwardly. What now? There was so many of them they made him feel as if they had come to walk him down the Green Mile to electrocute him! He looked at the band of white folks quizzically.

"Donatello McFadden?"

Don nodded "yes" to the woman in civilian clothing that asdressed him.

"I'm Warden London."

So, this was the woman everybody commended for her warmth amongst all the cold bastards surrounding her. She looked at him with the brightest, beautiful eyes carried by a fervent smile. He calculated her to be around 5'6 or 7. She had beautiful black hair that hung almost as long as Canary's. Her skin was a smooth, creamy complexion that glowed. He found her gorgeous. He forced himself to look away from the strong aura of her eyes. She had the most sexiest sideburns.

The other officials stood around like kids in an amusement park with suspicious smiles and grins. He didn't get it.

"Well, today is your lucky day. The president of the United States just order your immediate release! You are free to walk out of this place right this minute. You're no longer in the custody of the state," Warden London told him.

Don stared at her as if it was a joke. They all began clapping and laughing, cheering felicitously!

"It's real, Mr. McFadden! Get your things and let's go! You have a beautiful family up front waiting on you," she told him through a warm smile of beautiful teeth.

This brought him back to reality. The thought of his loved ones – Canary – "Come on, let's go! I don't need any of these things," he stated as he walked out of the cell with only the clothes on his back!

Every inmate on the wing looked on as they cheered for him, happy to see one of them resurrected from the dead.

"Hold on, let me holler at my roommate."

Baseer was nearby watching. At first, he didn't know if it was a bust or shake-down, so he stayed clear of the room until he overheard what Warden London had told his roommate. So, this was what he anticipated to the point of worriation. "Salam, akhi," he approached.

"I'm going home, akhi. Everything in the room is yours."

Baseer thanked him and wished him blessings of Paradise.

"You got my information so call me and I'll explain the details. I'm going to hold you down so don't worry about nothing, Insha'Allah. And stop stressing behind that girl and remember what you told me about the Date Palm." Don hugged him and departed the dorm with the officials after telling everyone behind to stay strong and keep fighting.

As he headed across the yard surrounded by the officials, he looked around at it and thought about all the anguish and misery he was leaving behind. And for some reason, Yahseen's poem crossed his mind. He began to shed tears of pain, and tears of joy as it pained him to leave so many good brothers behind.

"Are you okay?" Warden London asked him as they escorted him towards the front gate.

"Yes, ma'am," he replied cooly. He thanked Allah for the lessons and mercy, as he headed out the front gate where everyone awaited him with smiles and opened arms.

Although he was happy to see them all, he locked eyes with the woman he'd depicted *Golden*. Her hair was pressed and swam several inches below the middle of her back. She wore a blood red Gucci suit that accentuated her curvaceous body. Matching Gucci leather boots with 3-inch heels cladded her feet; blood red Gucci shades concealed her eyes – a touch of Mac lip gloss enhanced the aura of her lips. They had arrived in a 3-car convoy. She leaned up against the hood of his Lamborghini un-smiling. Her expression that of a true diva. Her appearance made him think of the sexy, blood red bottles of the cosmetic line he had designed. She was his vision of Inamorata in the flesh! She made him feel as if he had a blood lust and wanted to bite into her delicate flesh like a vampire. He wondered if she'd be in favor of modeling for their line of cosmetics. She'd be the perfect embodiment of the body wash and fragrance of Inamorata.

All of this flashed through his mind while they stared at one another as if they were the only beings that existed in the universe. No longer able to resist the urge under the intensity of the energy between them, she ran towards him as he opened his arms to intercept her.

They kissed passionately. He lifted her off her feet and spun her in circles as the officials, his father, Al-Salam, Ali, Jabbar, Cecelia, Danyell, and Tay cheered them on! He was now with the woman he had fallen in love with. His treasure of gold.... His Inamorata.

Epilogue

Manhattan, New York

April 12, 2016

A Year and6 A Half Later

Don sat inside a commercial production studio in Manhattan watching Canary pose in all her beauty while photographers snapped off a barrage of shots for advertisement purposes of the Inamorata body wash and fragrance line. Commercials had already been shot months ago. Due to the captivating beauty and panache she possessed, she had aggrandized the market surrounding the line beyond dimension.

As he watched her model and change in and out of the many blood-red robes and towels with the cosmetics in different settings of elegant bathrooms and bedrooms, he thought about his acquisitions as he traveled down memory lane…

The day he'd had been released, the Secret Service had raided the home of Edward Butler's parents out in Reno. He'd been charged with the crime of murdering Fedora. He attempted innocence but after his parents notified him that two masked men had paid them a visit in the middle of the night telling them their lives depended on his confession, he confessed. He now had the life sentence Don once had.

John had loss everything, but was free to do as he pleased. The president had broad-casted live from the Oval office notifying the nation of Don's innocence and his immediate release. And once again – he was all over the news. Everyone suspected that his father was behind the disappearance and murders of the officials that had never been found, but no one could prove it. And since it was a sensitive topic, the president allowed it to die with the senators and their corrupted infedilities. And around the country, President O'sella had informed the nation that everything was under control. Vaguely, he spoke about the corrupt body of The se Seven.

After Don had left Carolina Wren, he and Canary had flown back to Charleston in his Lamborghini to the beach house where they began devouring one another as soon as the door had been closed behind them. The details of their love making–CLASSIC!

And on Thanksgiving of that year, Fernando Brown aka Foxy had been found hanging from the light fixture in his cell by his cellmate when they returned back from chow. A suicide note had been found in his pocket. Yahseen, Success, and Chess had killed him.

Soon after Foxy's murder, Don had his father, along with lawyers, meet with the Attorney General and negotiated the release of Yahseen, Scramble, Sulayman, Jamal, and Krayola in return of them not pursing civil litigation for his unlawful conviction. They attempted to have more released, but the A. G. was only willing to bargain 5. It was all good though, because the tunnel route had long been finished. Yahseen was currently machinating Chess and Success' prison break. They now resided in his old cell.

And after umpteen interviews through tabloids, radio, and talk shows, he found himself on a commercial flight with his father, Al-Salam – who had stayed around until things had simmered – Canary, Cecelia, John, Jabbar, Ali, Danyell, and Tay. They all headed to Saudi Arabia for a two week stay where he and Canary, and his father and Cecelia, had been married under Islamic law. And after visiting the masjid Al-Salam had built and sight-seeing, they departed his lovely palace and returned back to America to resume their lives.

He and Canary had moved to Manhattan to start a new life. His father had set her up with her own private firm along with a trio of talented lawyers that specialized in civil and criminal law. She also modeled for their line. They were happily settled.

Divorced and remarried, John now cruised the Caribbean Islands with Tay on his yacht with the 20 million his father had given him.

Now, Don was 22 years old. It was April 12, 2016. Today was Yahseen's niece, Sodeja's birthday down in Charleston. He had been incarcerated since she was 3. Now she was 17! They had some big things planned for her when they were done with the photo shoot. Yahseen's novels had also broke barriers and won awards.

Don had a position in business for all his brothers and comrades. He had went back to Ogeechee for Ms. Bratton and offered her an executive position – she accepted it.

He had also launched the entertainment company that he and Krayola aspired to. He currently had him in the studio working with a team of talented producers. They were about to release the first single. It was a collaboration with two of the hottest rap stars in the industry.

Captain Holmes, Sergeant Granada, and Sergeant Smith had been paid. And since Coordinator Montgomery had kept it so real with Yahseen throughout the hard times, as most wouldn't have an hadn't, he married her. Loyalty was foremost. Don had also assisted him in launching an Imperial collection consisting of a perfume and cologne fragrance called Emperor and Empress. Canary also did modeling for his campaign.

"Damn lil' bruh, I can't get over how breath taking your wife is," Scramble said, watching Canary pose as he sat next to Don. "You got a winner, akhi. Alhamdulilah!"

Don nodded as he watched her. He was accompanied by Scramble, Yahseen, and Sulayman. Scramble had ended up becoming Muslim! It was a beautiful thing! Jamal was at the studio with Krayola putting in work as Krayola refused to go anywhere. He was dedicated. All he did was eat, sleep, and record!

Don thought about the hadith that Baseer had broken down to him about the Date Palm. It seemed so long ago. He still kept in touch with him and supported him. He only had a couple more years remaining. He had a position for him when he came home.

Life should never be second guessed when unfortunate things happen because God's plan surpasses ours. He thought about how his misfortune brought everyone together around him fortune. And due to his steadfastness and sincere belief, he had been brought greater fortune. Had he never been framed, his father would have never met Cecelia. Allah was so wise and profound! All of this had been preordained before he even came into existence. Because if it wasn't for Mayor Thadeus Crenshaw's deception, Al-Salam would have never killed him, thus – his father would have never met Al-Salam because there would have never been a meeting with The Seven in Afghanistan and Don would not exist because his father would have been left undiscovered on the side of the road and died. All of the events and people surrounding his life would never be without these chain of events. Everything happened for reasons indeed, he thought as the lights went out casting the studio in total darkness. A spotlight did miraculous things to the image of his wife, who was wrapped in a large, blood-red towel as she sat atop a bed on the set, massaging lotion on her legs and feet from the bottle laying beside her. She appeared to be lost in the moment with the lotion. Don thought that she was made for show business. Fleetingly, he wondered if she would be interested in acting. This would be a later discussion.

But as he watched her through the depth of the darkness, he thought that, ultimately – he would have never discovered the treasure before him. Everyone, and everything in existence was interrelated in some form or fashion for divine purposes. No one save God was omnipotent with an independent existence.

In this instance – this thought deepened his faith. If this didn't make a man with discernment a believer, it was because he was arrogant and lost in his own worldly ambitions!

"OKAY! That's a wrap!" The photographer snapped and the lights were turned back on.

About The Author

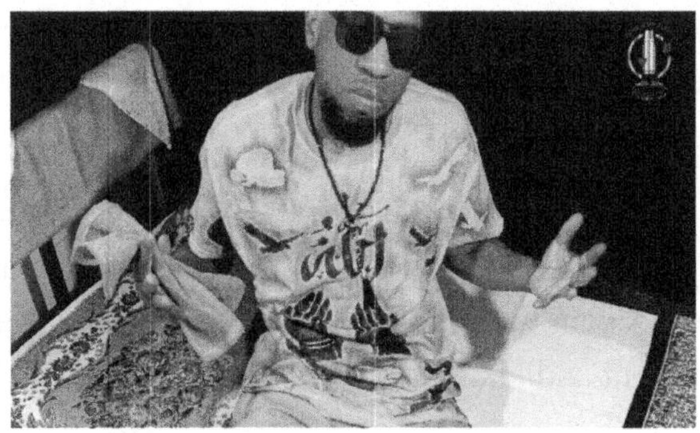

James Wright III is the Founder/ CEO of Final Round United Publishing, LLC. Born and raised in North Charleston, South Carolina, he found himself unlawfully convicted in 2005 of a drug-related murder that resulted in a natural life sentence without the possibility of parole. Along his incarceration, he discovered the jewel he had for writing. An independent thinker, he began devising blueprints that would bring his dream into existence by way of the pen. Talented and gifted in various areas from music to art, he has authored several novels in various genres since taking on his endeavor as a novelist in

2008. Now Muslim and always at work, he's still in the fight for his freedom in – what he depicted – the South Carolina Department of Corruption.

For further details and updates, follow him at the below addresses:

Facebook: James Wright Tha 3rd

Instagram: James Wright Tha 3rd

Facebook: FRU Publishing LLC

Instagram: FRU Publishing LLC

www.frupublushing.com

Thanks For Supporting The Movement!

Future Works To Come by James Wright Tha 3rd:

Blood On Remount Road

Never Surrender

Onion (Sequel to Never Surrender!)

Revenge From The Casket

Silent Whispers

A Penitentiary Holy Book (Based on a true story)

Silent Whispers

Made in the USA
Monee, IL
25 January 2023

26291173R00262